PRAISE FOR D B JACKSON

"A fast-paced tale whose fascinating magic system twists and turns the story in unexpected directions. Now I'm waiting for book two!"

Kate Elliott, author of Cold Magic *and* Black Wolves

"A very intricate tale with some excellent characterizations. It has many strengths and pure readability. I really enjoyed it."

Anne McCaffrey

P9-BZS-680

"War and politics, love and magic, all drawn in detail against a vividly imagined feudal background. A complex and excellent book."

David Drake

"*The Outlanders* is a well worked out story of magic and politics that doesn't sugarcoat either; both are brutally realistic."

Piers Anthony

"A natural born storyteller. Sit back and enjoy the journey!"

Sherwood Smith

"As usual, Jackson's intimately detailed historical backdrop is a major advantage… A thoroughly engrossing and involving entry that no series fan will want to miss."

Kirkus Reviews

"This is a technically accomplished novel; polished, elegantly conceived, tightly plotted without sacrificing characterization. His writing reveals the artistry of an accomplished storyteller at his craft."

Strange Horizons

BY THE SAME AUTHOR

D B JACKSON

TIME'S CHILDREN

BOOK I OF THE ISLEVALE CYCLE

**ANGRY
ROBOT**

ANGRY ROBOT
An imprint of Watkins Media Ltd

20 Fletcher Gate,
Nottingham,
NG1 2FZ • UK

angryrobotbooks.com
twitter.com/angryrobotbooks
Judgment day

An Angry Robot paperback original 2018

Copyright © D B Jackson 2018

Cover by Jan Weßbecher
Map by Argh! Nottingham
Set in Meridien by Argh! Nottingham

Distributed in the United States by Penguin Random House, Inc., New York.

All rights reserved. D B Jackson asserts the moral right to be identified as the author of this work. A catalogue record for this book is available from the British Library.

This novel is entirely a work of fiction. Names, characters, places, and incidents are the products of the author's imagination or are used fictitiously. Any resemblance to actual events, locales, organizations or persons, living or dead, is entirely coincidental.

Sales of this book without a front cover may be unauthorized. If this book is coverless, it may have been reported to the publisher as "unsold and destroyed" and neither the author nor the publisher may have received payment for it.

Angry Robot and the Angry Robot icon are registered trademarks of Watkins Media Ltd.

ISBN 978 0 85766 791 5
Ebook ISBN 978 0 85766 792 2

Printed in the United States of America

9 8 7 6 5 4 3 2 1

For Nancy,
Every bell, every day, every turn

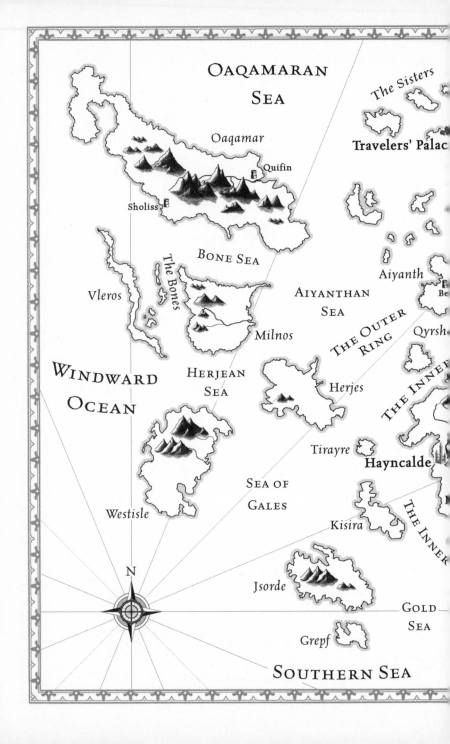

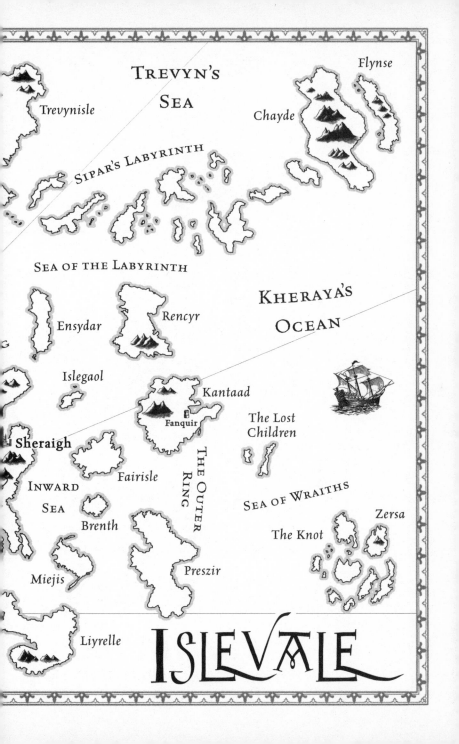

CHAPTER 1

21st Day of Sipar's Settling, Year 633

The between spat him out like chewed gristle.

Naked in the cold and dark, he dropped to his knees, shivering, sucking at precious air. Another Walk, more years added to a body already abused by too many trials and too many journeys through time.

He clutched his chronofor in stiff, frigid fingers and braced his other hand on the courtyard stone. Fear lifted his gaze, despite the droop of his shoulders, the leaden fatigue in his legs. Torches flickered in nearby sconces. Stars gleamed in a moonless sky. He saw no soldiers, no assassins. He heard not a sound.

Had he arrived too early? Too late?

He fought to his feet and turned an unsteady circle to get his bearings before heading to the next courtyard and the castle arsenal. No soldiers here, either. Panic rose within him like a spring tide. Within the armory he found a stained uniform in Hayncalde red, as well as a musket and ammunition. He didn't see any boots that would fit.

He pulled on the uniform and loaded the weapon. He took extra powder, paper, and bullets – habit born of years on the run. But he knew he wouldn't have a chance to use them. This night would end in one of two ways. In neither scenario would he get off a second shot.

As he left the armory, he noticed what he had missed

earlier. A body lay in the grass a few paces off the stone path. A woman with a gaping wound across her neck, and a bib of blood glistening on her uniform. A few paces on, he spotted a second dead guard on the other side of the path. Both from Hayncalde, both killed with stealth. Not too early then, perhaps in the very teeth of time.

He hurried on to the hall, bare feet slapping on stone. Nearing the archway that led into the back corridor, he heard the first explosion rock the west gate. Voices rose in alarm and anger. Bells pealed from the castle towers. Moments now. He stole through shadow and candlelit passages, only pausing when he reached the door.

Another explosion, not so distant, but also not the one he awaited. Inside the hall, men shouted. A baby cried, and his heart folded in upon itself.

He gripped the musket, readied himself. One last explosion made the stone beneath him shudder and buck. His cue.

He kicked the door open, stepped through.

Bedlam. A haze of smoke. And the one he sought. He shouted the man's name and raised his weapon to fire.

CHAPTER 2

26th Day of Kheraya's Waking, Year 647

The summons came the day before Tobias's fifteenth birthday.

His instructors had prepared him, telling him they thought it unlikely he would have to wait the full sixteen years. Yet, for word from the chancellor to come so soon – this exceeded even his expectations.

The herald found him in the lower courtyard, practicing his blade work before an appreciative audience of junior novitiates. He and a few of the other older boys and girls had long since graduated to training with steel blades. Sometimes the younger ones paused in their training to goggle at the blur of gleaming weapons, flinching with delight at the clang of steel on steel.

"Tobias Doljan," the herald called, halting their parries, drawing their gazes, silencing them all.

The arrival of heralds in the novitiates' world presaged either tragedy or opportunity: dark tidings from home, or advancement into the unknown. Rarely did they bring word of anything in between.

Before facing the messenger, Tobias bowed low to Mara, with whom he had been fencing. He knew the others watched him, but didn't spare them a glance. They thought him young still. Too young. He was the least experienced of those who had taken up honed blades. News from home then. That was what they would assume. He sensed their pity, their fear, and he wanted to laugh, confident they were wrong.

"You will come with me," the herald said. "The Lord Chancellor is waiting."

Sweat ran in rivulets down Tobias's face and neck, and darkened the tunic he wore beneath his mail. But one responded without delay to a summons from the chancellor; better he should arrive sweating and filthy than make the man wait. He handed his sword to Delvin, cast a quick grin Mara's way, and followed the herald out of the courtyard.

The chancellor's man said not a word as they walked, so Tobias held his tongue as well. They climbed the broad, open stairway to cross from the lower courtyard to the middle, passing ivy-covered walls of golden stone. Bowmen and guards with muskets patrolled the battlements of the palace's outer defenses, bare-headed and clad in uniforms of purple and black. It had been more than a century since this palace had been attacked by would-be conquerors, but other threats, some unique to a palace filled with Travelers, kept soldiers atop the ramparts.

Tobias and the herald made their way through the middle courtyard, entered the North Keep, and ascended the ancient, twisting stairway to the third level and the chancellor's quarters. The herald knocked once on the oaken door, and let himself into the chamber, leaving Tobias to wait in the corridor. Only a breath or two later, the man reemerged and told him to enter. Tobias stepped into the room, heard the door close behind him.

The chancellor sat behind a large desk, which was piled high with leather-bound volumes and sheaves of curled parchment. Portraits of past chancellors adorned the walls, and a woven rug, rich with browns and blues and golds, covered a portion of the stone floor. Half a dozen messenger pigeons, brown and white and gray, cooed in a wooden cage beside the open window. Otherwise the chamber again struck Tobias as sparse, as less impressive than the chancellor's quarters ought to be.

He had been in the chamber twice before: once the day he

arrived on Trevynisle, uninitiated, confused, homesick; and a second time, three years ago, when he learned of his sister's death. The first instance, he barely remembered. The other haunted him still, not because he grieved for his lost sister, but rather because he couldn't call to mind an image of Yolli. She had been a squalling infant when he left Redcove, his village on Onyi; he recalled the sound of her more than anything else. He tried to mourn her, but it seemed her death had come from too great a distance to affect him as it should.

"Mister Doljan," Chancellor Shaan said, not bothering to look up from the yellowed parchment he held with thick fingers. "It seems I interrupted your sword play."

The man's trim beard sharpened features that might otherwise have been open and friendly. Silver blended with bronze to lighten what little hair remained on his head.

"Yes, Lord Chancellor," Tobias said.

"Do you know why I had you summoned?"

"I assume it's because I've been called to a court."

The chancellor glanced his way, then laid the parchment atop one of the many piles and straightened. "You assume this? A lad your age?"

He held the man's gaze. "Yes, Lord Chancellor."

The chancellor eyed him, his expression resolving at last into a scowl. "You're brash. Royals don't like that, particularly in green Travelers new to their courts."

Tobias wished to ask if confidence was not a desirable trait in a court Traveler, but he sensed that challenging the chancellor on this point would be a mistake.

"I meant no offense," he said instead.

The chancellor stared at him still. Tobias wondered if he ought to drop his gaze, at least give the impression of feeling abashed. He did neither.

The chancellor reached for the parchment again. "You would not have been my first choice. You're young, and you have much yet to learn. Your teachers speak well of you; they see potential. Promise, though, is..." He waved his hand, a vague gesture. "Had the petition been for any sort of Traveler, I would have chosen another. They want a Walker, however, and you're the only one I have."

Tobias stifled a smile; the chancellor already thought him arrogant. He wouldn't add gloating to his transgressions. But behind his calm demeanor, he rejoiced. *They want a Walker. They want me.*

"May I ask where I'll be going?"

"The petition comes from Mearlan IV, sovereign of Daerjen."

He had hoped for such a posting – all of them did. Not necessarily to Daerjen itself, but to a court of prestige and might, for only the most influential courts could afford Travelers, much less a Walker. This time, he couldn't quite mask his joy. He could barely stand still.

"Yes," the chancellor said. "You're fortunate. And so are we. The sovereign has paid handsomely for your services. You won't keep him waiting. You're to sail from Windhome tomorrow, with first light. I trust you can have your affairs in order by then."

"Yes, Lord Chancellor. I'll be ready." As soon as he spoke the words, though, he faltered.

"What is it?"

Tobias sensed impatience in the question, and didn't know how to answer. Even as his initial excitement lingered, fears and misgivings crowded in. Daerjen was at war with Oaqamar, the single greatest power between the oceans. In addition to his grand army and navy, Oaqamar's autarch was said to possess his own company of Walkers, Spanners, and Crossers, all of them schooled in the art of assassination. According to some, Oaqamar's Travelers had found a way to overcome the limitations that forced them to make their journeys naked and weaponless. Tobias sensed that Windhome's masters and mistresses had heard these rumors as well, but they refused to speak of them.

Whatever the truth, Tobias didn't doubt that the moment he reached Hayncalde – and perhaps before – his life would be in danger.

Yet this mortal fear paled next to concerns far less threatening, but still burdensome: he had lived in Windhome Palace for nearly his entire life, rarely venturing beyond these walls. He would know no one in Daerjen. Everything about the place would be unfamiliar.

The chancellor watched him, waiting, an eyebrow arched.

Tobias couldn't bring himself to give voice to his mounting apprehension. Instead, he seized on a trifle.

"I... I have no chronofor. Shouldn't I have one before I sail?"

Another frown creased the man's forehead. "That expense will be borne by the sovereign. He has a Binder in his employ who is crafting one for you even now. I'm sure that soon after your arrival in Hayncalde, you'll be given a device." The chancellor held out a roll of parchment, tied with gold satin. The sealing wax, also gold, had been imprinted with the open hand symbol of the Travelers' palace. "Your letter of introduction," he said. "You'll present this to Sovereign Hayncalde upon your arrival in Daerjen. Naturally, our contract with the sovereign is explicit with regard to the protocols and limitations of Time Walking. Should he ask of you more than he should, you are to refuse him and send a message here with dispatch. Do you understand?"

Master Ojeyd had explained these restraints to him in anticipation of this day. He was not to be sent back more than a year – although even a Walk of that length sounded impossibly long. And he was not to be sent on Walks in excess of thirty days more than a few times in any given turn. Tobias needed to consult his notes again for the exact number. Such strictures were intended to protect Walkers like him, and also to mitigate the effect his kind might have on the course of history.

"Of course, Lord Chancellor. Master Ojeyd has prepared me well."

"Very good."

Again Tobias hesitated. Ought he to say something, to thank the chancellor? They hardly knew each other. Tobias was no more to the man than a single face among dozens. To him, the chancellor had always seemed as remote as starlight. In the end, he sketched a bow and crossed back to the door.

"Mister Doljan."

Tobias halted.

"From this day forward, the world will see in you a reflection of this place: of the palace, of your fellow students, of your teachers, even of me. Your duty is to Daerjen, but you will always be a child of Trevynisle. Do you understand?"

"Yes, Lord Chancellor. I won't disappoint you."

"Good. Go with His glory and Her grace."

"Thank you, my lord. Blessings of the Two upon you and this palace."

The chancellor replied with a nod and a thin smile, but already he had set aside the petition from Daerjen and reached for another curled missive. Tobias let himself out of the chamber. Finding the corridor empty, he hurried back to the lower courtyard.

Long before he reached his fellow novitiates, he heard the sharp echoes of pistol fire. Apparently Mara, Delvin, and the others had set aside their blades and were now practicing marksmanship. Reaching the stairway to the courtyard, he saw that they did so under the critical eye of old Saffern, the palace weapons master, whose white hair shone like a beacon in the sunlight.

Seeing Tobias step into the ward, Saffern waved him over and held out a pistol to him, butt first.

"You are two rounds behind," the master said, his accent

rounding the Os and rolling the Rs.

"I know but I haven't–"

"You will shoot. One in the center and you can skip a second round." Saffern's dark eyes danced. "Three in the center, and you may go."

"Three out of how many?" Tobias asked, approaching the man and reaching for the pistol.

"Three in the center. Surely you don't need more than three shots to do this. You, who are in such a rush to leave us."

Tobias considered him. Did Saffern know?

"All right." He walked to the white line from which Delvin had been shooting.

"Back here, I think."

The master dug his heel into the ground five paces back from the line, and scraped a new line in the grass.

Tobias couldn't help but grin. As good as he was with a sword, he was better still with firearms. Saffern knew this as well.

He loaded the weapon: white powder from Aiyanth, a wad of firepaper, and a lead ball, also Aiyanthan, pushed down the barrel with the ramrod. After priming the pan with a touch more powder, he set his stance, full-cocked the pistol, aimed, and fired. The report echoed across the courtyard like thunder, and white smoke rode the wind up and over the east wall.

"Dead center," Mara said. Was that pride in her voice?

"Luck, I believe." Saffern walked three more paces from the target. "There is less luck back here."

Tobias smirked. Several of the older boys laughed, no doubt hoping Tobias would miss.

He reloaded, toed Saffern's new line, and squeezed the trigger.

The others quieted. Mara clapped, long hair aglow with sunlight.

"Center again," she said, her eyes finding Tobias's.

"Clearly we're still too close." Saffern walked off ten more paces. This time, none of the novitiates so much as snickered.

"That's too far," Mara said, adding belatedly, "master. I'm not even sure you could make that shot."

"I'm not the one who has to. Mister Doljan?"

Tobias joined Saffern at this newest line and squinted back toward the target. For all his skill with firearms, he had little confidence that he could make this shot. He loaded, took his stance, and fired. He didn't need to hear Mara say "Second ring," her voice flat, to know he had missed.

"Ah," Saffern said beside him. "A pity. I fear you'll be training with us today after all."

"No, master, I won't." He held out the pistol to Saffern, grip first, as he had been taught.

"We had an agreement."

He shook his head. "No, we didn't. I tried to tell you, I'm leaving the palace, and Trevynisle."

The weapons master didn't respond. He had known. It was Mara who asked, "Leaving for where?"

Saffern had yet to take the pistol. Tobias let the hand holding it drop to his side. "Hayncalde, in Daerjen."

"Mearlan's court?"

"Yes."

"Why you?" This from Nat, one of the older boys. His tone bristled with resentment. "You're no better than the rest of us, and you're younger than most."

"They want a Walker."

Which was really all that mattered, and Nat knew it. All of them did. They stared at him. Mara's expression had gone blank. Nat, Delvin, and Mara were Spanners, capable of Traveling dozens of leagues, or even more, in the time it might take Tobias to walk from one end of the courtyard to the other. Others among the novitiates were Crossers. They could pass through solid walls of wood and stone. But as the chancellor said, he was the lone Walker among them.

"I leave in the morning," he said to no one in particular. He held out the weapon to Saffern once more, but the weapons master shook his head.

"Take it. And ammunition as well. Your voyage will take you near disputed waters. You shouldn't sail unarmed."

Tobias bowed. "Thank you, master."

"Remember this final lesson, Mister Doljan. You're very good. But there's always room for improvement." He flashed a smile so fleeting that Tobias wondered if he'd imagined it. "The rest of you load your weapons," he said, showing his back to Tobias. "You all need practice, particularly with your stances. I see no one here who could have made even two of the shots Mister Doljan attempted."

The novitiates obeyed without delay.

Tobias lingered for a tencount, stunned at how quickly he had become an outsider. Only Mara continued to eye him, and when he looked her way, she turned and walked back toward the targets.

CHAPTER 3

26th Day of Kheraya's Waking, Year 647

Aside from several changes of clothes, a leather-pommeled dagger, the pistol, powder, paper, and rounds given to him by Saffern, and the sealed letter from the chancellor, Tobias had few belongings. His family had been poor, even for Redcove, and he arrived on Trevynisle wearing the only things he possessed. In nine years, he hadn't accumulated much.

Packing for his departure took him all of a quarter bell. Once finished, he had nothing to do. He considered rejoining his friends in the courtyard, but the memory of those final awkward moments stopped him.

Instead, he made his way back to the middle courtyard, and the workshop of Wansi Tovorl, the palace Binder.

Her door was shut, but at his knock she called for him to enter.

Wansi sat at her work bench, a nimbus of pearly light surrounding her head and hands, thick spectacles perched on the tip of her nose, yellow hair pulled back in a loose plait. She spared him a glance, her attention on the golden object clamped to the table.

"I thought you might come," she said, a lilt to the words. "Saying your goodbyes?"

He shut the door with care. "I suppose."

She furrowed her brow. "You suppose? Do you plan to take me with you then?"

He grinned and wandered the chamber. She continued to work.

"A new aperture?" he asked after a brief silence.

"Aye. Miss Craik damaged hers on her last Crossing. She tried to pass through a door that had iron imbedded in it. She's fortunate to be alive. Her aperture was ruined. And so a new one." She peered at him over her lenses. "I trust you'll be more gentle with your chronofor."

His eyes widened. "You have one for me?"

She shook her head. "The chancellor told me you'd be given one upon your arrival in Hayncalde. I would have made one otherwise. I was prepared to."

He answered with a small nod and resumed his pacing.

"Haplar Jarrett is the Master Binder in Hayncalde, and he's as well-respected as any of my kind. He'll Bind you a fine chronofor. I promise."

"I'm sure he will."

She sighed, put down her planer, and removed her spectacles. The glow around her vanished. "Out with it, Tobias. I haven't time for games."

He didn't answer right away, but rather scrutinized her face, her milky complexion and brilliant blue eyes. Here on Trevynisle nearly everyone was as dark-skinned as he: the palace servants, many of the masters, all of the novitiates who honed their skills in the hope of being posted to a court. Wansi stood out among them like a gull in a flock of cormorants. In Hayncalde, he would be the one who didn't blend in, who drew stares simply by entering a chamber or stepping out into the street.

"I'm not ready to be a court Walker," he said at last.

"What makes you say that?"

He lifted a shoulder, let it drop. "I've gone back a day at a time. Once I went back two, but that was the most. I know that the chronofor works the same way no matter how far back we

Walk. But I've heard people talk about the courts. Sometimes kings and queens send their Walkers back a ha'turn, or a full one. Sometimes even more. I'm not... I've never done anything like that. And whatever chronofor they give me will be one I've never used before."

An indulgent smile dimpled her cheek. "First of all, remember your studies. The chronofor is a tool. Nothing more. The Walker does the work. And Master Ojeyd tells me that you're very good. True, you have much yet to learn but, from what he's said, I gather that even your most difficult passages have been relatively smooth. You've never had any trouble crossing back. To my knowledge, you haven't missed a chosen time by more than a click or two. Am I wrong?"

"No."

"Vaisan has been teaching Walkers for a long time, and before that he served the court at Rencyr. He's good at what he does, and he wouldn't allow the chancellor to send you anywhere if he didn't think you were ready."

He stared at the golden aperture on her workbench. "I know that."

"Then what's troubling you?" She arched an eyebrow. "Lack of confidence has never been one of your shortcomings, so it must be something else."

"I– I don't know anyone there. I've never sailed beyond the Sisters and the Labyrinth." Tobias clamped his mouth shut. Already he had said more than he intended. His cheeks burned.

The kindness in Wansi's look did little to ease his thoughts. "I forget sometimes how young all of you are." She canted her head to the side and considered him through narrowed eyes. "Your training is meant to conceal it, I think. The sovereigns who buy your services are paying for diplomats and ministers, not children. And so we train the youth right out of you. Or at least we try. Perhaps we're not as thorough in that respect as we'd like to believe."

"It's not that I'm a child," he said, aware of how sullen he sounded.

"No. It's that you're normal. You're alive, you feel things, in this one small way you're terribly, charmingly ordinary."

He frowned, unsure if she was mocking him.

"What do you remember of your home?" she asked.

"You mean in Redcove?"

"Aye."

"Not much: scattered images mostly. I haven't been there since I was five."

"Precisely. This is the only home you've ever really known. I'd find it hard to leave, and I first came here as an adult. Naturally it's harder for you. It would be for any of the... any of your fellow novitiates."

Tobias had thought along similar lines since speaking with the chancellor, but hearing Wansi speak of these feelings made them easier to accept. He released a breath he hadn't known he held.

"You'll be just fine. It won't be long before you're the most famous young man in Hayncalde: the sovereign's new Walker – handsome, brilliant, exotic. People there will clamor to make your acquaintance. The greatest danger I foresee is that all this attention will go to your head, and make you even more insufferable than you already are."

A smile came unbidden. "I wish I could take one of your chronofors with me." He raised a hand, anticipating her response. "I've no doubt that Master Jarrett will Bind me a fine device. But still, I'll always prefer yours to anyone else's."

Wansi reached for her spectacles and planer. Tobias thought he glimpsed the shimmer of a tear in one eye.

"That golden tongue of yours will serve you well, Mister Doljan. Flatter the sovereign this way, and you'll have nothing to worry about."

"I wasn't–"

"I know," she said, her eyes fixed on the golden device before her. "You should be on your way. Miss Craik's aperture won't Bind itself, and I'm sure you've other farewells."

"Yes, mistress. Thank you."

He crossed to the door, pulled it open.

"I wouldn't object to a missive now and then." The soft gleam of her binding power enveloped her again. "When you've the time, of course."

"Of course," he echoed, and left her.

He returned to the Leeward Keep, the boys' dormitory in the Upper Courtyard, and sat on his pallet intending to draft a missive to his parents. He hadn't seen them in the nine years since his arrival here, but he had sent them messages now and again. For the first several years he had received gifts from them on his birthdays: toys of a sort he hadn't played with since leaving home; overshirts and breeches sewn for a smaller body, as if they couldn't fathom the rate at which he had grown; bound volumes, no doubt far more dear than they could afford, and yet written for a common child rather than for a future Traveler educated in Windhome Palace.

He sent messages of thanks each year, but despite his efforts to infuse the missives with enthusiasm, they might have sensed a growing distance in what he wrote. Last year he received nothing. No gift had come this year, either.

The note he penned struck him as inadequate to the occasion:

Dear Mother and Father,

I write today with glad tidings. I am to be posted as a Walker to the Court of Daerjen in Hayncalde. I will serve the sovereign himself.

I hope you, Bale, and Comas are well. I miss you all.

> *With love,*

>> *Tobias*

He should have written more, but no other words came, at least none that he could bring himself to write. *I am leaving Trevynisle forever. In all likelihood, I will never see any of you again.*

After staring at the page for some time, he rolled it up, sealed it with wax, and placed it in his sack. Someone at the wharf would be able to deliver it for him.

The chancellor attended the evening meal in the refectory, as he did whenever a novitiate received a posting. He spoke ever so briefly.

"Tobias Doljan will be leaving Trevynisle tomorrow morning for a posting in Daerjen. We wish him well, and ask that the Two bless him in all his endeavors."

"Hear us," intoned the rest of those in the hall.

That was all. Following the chancellor's example, everyone took their seats and began to eat. Tobias sat with the older novitiates, as always, but the conversation at their table meandered over familiar territory – the day's training, rumors of trysts among various masters and mistresses in the palace, the latest from the wars in the Aiyanthan and Herjean Seas. No one spoke of Tobias's impending departure, and he contributed little to their discussion. Mara sat across from him, but refused to meet his glance. She excused herself from the table long before the entire meal had been served.

Tobias remained through the dessert course. Ojeyd, the Master Walker, came to the table to tell Tobias that he would accompany him to the wharves at dawn. A few of Tobias's other instructors took the occasion to offer their congratulations and good wishes, but he had already said goodbye to Wansi and Saffern, who were, along with Vaisan, his favorites. When servants filed into the hall to clear the tables, Tobias fled into the night, wishing only to be alone.

Or so he thought.

Mara stood at the western end of the lower courtyard, a dark silhouette, arms crossed over her chest, still except for her hair, which rose and fell in the gentle wind blowing off Safsi Bay. In truth, it could have been any of the older girls, but he recognized the curve of her neck, the taut lines of her back and shoulders.

Torches burned on the ramparts where guards paced, but below there was only moonlight silvering the grass.

"What are you doing out here?" he asked as he neared her.

"When's your birthday?" She kept her back to him and didn't move. Her voice seemed to come from far away.

"What?"

"Your birthday? When is it?"

"I'm a Walker. My birthday is meaningless. Once I get to Hayncalde, I'll be sent back and forth so many times I won't be able to keep track. Pretty soon I won't remember how old I am."

She faced him, the moon reflected in her bright eyes. She was a year older than he, but already he stood a hand taller. "That's later. You know how old you are now. When is it? Please tell me."

He sighed, knowing better than to argue with her. "Twenty-seventh day of Kheraya's Waking."

Mara blinked. "That's tomorrow."

"Yes." He shivered, rubbed his arms. "It's cold. Don't you want to go inside?"

"Does the sovereign of Daerjen have a Spanner?"

"I don't know."

"If he doesn't, you should tell him to request me."

Tobias opened his mouth, closed it again. "Um… All right."

"I'm good. And I'm almost sixteen."

"I know you're good. And I know how old you are. I just… I thought you wanted to be posted to Aiyanth. That's what you've always said."

She shrugged, gaze wandering. "Maybe I've changed my mind."

"Mara–"

Before he could say more, she closed the distance between them with a single step, wrapped her arms around his neck, and pulled him down into a kiss. His first. He wasn't sure what to do. He touched her hair, her shoulders, and finally settled on holding his hands to her back. Her lips caressed his and he did his best to kiss her back in the same way. He was aware of her breasts pressed against him, of the pounding of his heart, and of hers.

Too soon, she pulled back, her eyes still closed.

"Tell him," she whispered. "If he needs a Spanner."

She spun away from him and ran toward the middle courtyard and the Windward Keep. Tobias could only watch her go, his head spinning, his lips still tingling with the memory of that kiss.

He swallowed past a thickness in his throat and thought he might be on the verge of tears. Yet it was all he could do not to laugh aloud. He felt himself balanced on the point of a clock hand, caught between a past that already seemed to belong to a stranger, and a future he couldn't imagine. It was an odd sensation for someone who could Walk through time.

CHAPTER 4

26th Day of Kheraya's Waking, Year 647

Tobias was still thinking about Mara and their kiss when a voice behind him said, "She's very homely."

A child's voice.

Tobias tensed, his mood shattering. "Droë."

"I think she's horrid."

He turned, keeping his movements slow, steady. She stood closer than he'd expected; he resisted the impulse to back away.

She was small, slight, dressed in a loose tunic that might have been white, and dark, worn breeches that reached to her calves. She appeared to be no more than seven or eight – an illusion, one common to her kind.

"That's not a nice thing to say," he told her.

"I don't care."

She had looked just this old the first time he met her, several years before, when he'd been but a boy himself. He'd thought her a child then. At the time, he had never encountered one of the Tirribin.

She had the palest eyes Tobias had ever seen. Her irises were faintly gray, but so light they nearly blended with the whites of her eyes. Initially, during that first encounter, he wondered if she was blind. In every other way, she was beautiful. Her yellow hair shimmered like satin with the glow of the moon, and her warm brown face was perfectly oval and unblemished. She had high cheekbones, a slightly upturned nose, full lips.

Notwithstanding the rags she wore, she looked like royalty; even her hands were elegant – slender, long-fingered. But the smell of death clung to her, cloying, noisome, though as subtle as a whisper.

When he described her for Wansi, all those years ago, the mistress had been deeply alarmed.

"A novitiate was killed by a Tirribin some time back. Before I was here, but within the last few decades. You need to be careful with them. I can't imagine how she evaded the guards."

Having seen her, Tobias could imagine it. She didn't look dangerous. To any who saw her from the walls, she would have appeared as another child among so many. Strange, to be sure, with those spectral eyes, but harmless.

"I thought Walkers were immune to their attacks," he said, trying to mask the fear Wansi's words kindled in him.

"Not immune, no," Wansi explained that day. "Time demons aren't drawn to your years the way they are to those of others. Something in the changes wrought by Walking. Nevertheless, they're still a threat. And you're certainly not immune to their charms. So you might want to have a riddle at the ready. Tirribin can be distracted with riddles. Make sure, though, that it's a good one, just in case."

Wansi's warnings had kept him wary throughout his subsequent conversations with the demon. He had come to realize, though, that regardless of whether Droë was the Tirribin who killed that novitiate so long ago, she was less dangerous than the Binder suggested, at least to him. Droë never threatened him or tried to steal his years. On the contrary: her actions suggested she was enamored of him. Too much so. She spoke with venom of anyone she believed might come between them – Mara most of all. He should have known that on his last night in Windhome she would find him.

"I don't know how you can stand to look at her," she said in the darkness and the wind. She held her hands behind her back as she circled him, her steps airy, effortless.

"I don't think she's ugly at all."

A scowl twisted her features. "Her skin is too dark."

"It's no darker than mine. For that matter, it's not much darker than yours."

"And her hair – it's coarse, like dried grass."

He brushed his fingers with the tip of his thumb, recalling the gossamer touch of Mara's hair. "No, it's not."

"She's... She's womanly." She said this with distaste.

He didn't like the turn their conversation had taken. The memory of that embrace remained too vivid.

"You'll leave her alone, Droë. Even after I've gone."

She halted, standing now near where Mara had been. "Yes, you're leaving. For Daerjen. I heard."

"You were listening?"

The demon nodded. "And then you kissed her. What was that like?" She edged closer to him.

"Did you hear what I said?"

She scowled and resumed her circling. "I'm to leave her alone."

"That's right."

A pause, and then, "Do you love her?"

He shifted his weight, stared at his own shadow on the moon-touched grass. "I don't know." *I'm leaving. I'm not even fifteen.*

Droë clapped her hands and laughed, exposing tiny teeth, white like sheep's milk and as sharp as the serrations on a bread peddler's knife. "I think you do."

"What do you want?"

She grew grave. "To say goodbye. I saw you and I wanted to chat. I like it when we chat. But now that I know you're leaving..."

"We'll see each other again."

"Will we?"

He hesitated, marking her orbit. "You tell me."

"Perhaps. I'm not bound to this island or these waters any more than you are."

He sensed her holding something back. "But?"

She stopped again, this time in the spot where she first appeared. "I choose to stay. And I think you should, too."

"Why?"

"You'll be safer here. She'll be safer with you here."

A chill pebbled his skin. "Have you seen something?" he asked. "Is something going to happen to me, or to Mara?"

She shook her head, solemn as a cleric. "Our powers don't work that way. I know you're safe here, and you'll remain so if you stay. As to the girl…" She shrugged. "You can't stop me from taking her years if you're not here. Not really."

"You promised!"

"No, you insisted. I never agreed."

Fear crested in Tobias's chest. He could beg, he could rail at her, but he couldn't bind her to his will or to any promises she made. He might be safe from her predation, but Mara was not.

"I wouldn't take all her years. Just a few, maybe enough to make her a little less pretty in your eyes. If she's too old for you, maybe you won't like her so much."

"Please don't," he said, cursing the flutter in his voice.

She laughed again, capricious as the wind. "I could spare her. For a kiss."

Tobias froze. The thought of kissing the demon sent his stomach into a lazy, unsettling somersault. "I don't think that's a good idea."

She glared. "Why not?"

"I–I won't give you any years."

"I didn't ask for any. All I want is a kiss. Like you gave to her."

"No."

The demon studied him, her pale eyes guarded. "Maybe you

don't love her after all."

If he angered her, she would take her revenge on Mara. He had no doubt. But while Tirribin couldn't attack a Walker, they could take years freely given, and he didn't know if consenting to a kiss might be construed as an invitation to feed.

"I'll kiss your cheek," he said. "A kiss of friendship."

"As opposed to passion." Her tone was mocking, but her eyes searched his. She was trying to understand. In some ways she truly was a child.

"Yes."

She considered this, her head canted to the side. "All right."

Tobias stepped forward, and Droë tipped her face up to his, eyes wide with moonlight. He leaned in to plant a quick kiss on her cheek.

At the last instant she turned her head, pressing her lips to his. They were as cold as ocean water. Her teeth grazed his. Her breath stank of decay.

Tobias staggered back, shuddering, wiping at his mouth. Her laughter spiraled into the night.

"That was fun! I might have to kiss her, too. Just to see what it's like."

"You will not take her years." He tried to sound forceful, but his voice shook.

"So you've told me," she said, imperious, a demon's rasp in the words. "You try my patience, Walker."

Tobias didn't answer. They eyed each other. A nighthawk cried overhead.

"I need to sleep," he said at last. "I leave with first light."

Droë nodded, haughty, wounded. Tobias regretted everything about this final encounter. He had enjoyed their conversations over the years. With no other Walkers in the palace, she had been the one... being aside from Master Ojeyd with whom he could discuss his abilities. Despite all that separated them, he did consider her a friend.

"I'm... I hope we'll meet again."

"If fate allows."

He frowned, turned from her with some reluctance, and started to pick his way through the courtyard toward the Leeward Keep. After a few strides, he stopped, the demon's name on his tongue. But she had vanished, leaving only windswept grass and the faint luminance of the moon and stars.

From his perch on the tower wall, he marked every movement of the two humans – the Walker and the female who had lured him into the night, as if she were doing so for him. He listened to every spoken word, took the measure of the Walker: his size, his smell, the way he moved. Distance was no matter. On a night like this, with a gibbous moon brightening the courtyard below and the air still, he could have determined their eye color from twice the distance, and heard them from twice as far. Such were the advantages of being a creature of prey.

He scented magick in both of them. They were rich with it. He could manage two kills with a single, swift stoop. He'd done so before.

But he had his instructions, and though it rankled answering to humans, his kind had found value in this alliance. He would do as they demanded.

He had already. He didn't like clinging to shadows, concealing himself from the humans who patrolled only a few hands above him. A kill or two would have made what followed much easier. Again, though, those who sent him wanted this done a certain way.

Eventually, the female ran off – an interaction he didn't entirely understand. Her departure left the Walker alone. An opportunity. He shifted, crouched, fingers splayed against the rough stone surface. He had gone so far as to spread his wings, when he heard another voice below.

A human child, female.

No. A Tirribin.

He smelled her magick as well, felt it tug at him. This he would have resisted regardless of orders. Such kills were frowned upon among his kind. Settling back against the wall, he listened again, understanding little more of this conversation than he had of the last.

Soon enough, the Walker was alone once more. The human turned to walk toward the next courtyard. Again, he readied himself for flight. Only to be forestalled a second time.

He heard scrabbling on stone, behind him, above. Then a voice – that same voice. The Tirribin.

"They don't like Belvora here. You should know that."

He turned his head to stare back at her. She sat above him, neatly fitted within a crenellation, knees drawn up to her chest, arms wrapped around them, very much like a human child. Golden hair, not unlike his, glimmered with the moon. Her eyes were so pale that even with his keen sight they seemed to glow, colorless, ghostly.

"Do they like Tirribin any more?"

"Most don't. He does."

He went still at that. "I don't know who you mean."

She pointed at the retreating figure of the Walker. Far now. Perhaps too far, at least for tonight. "I mean him. And you knew that already."

He turned his body, eyes fixed on her, wings settling against his back. He had questions, but first he checked the position of the nearest guards.

"They can't see me right now," she said. "Any more than they can see you. They'd have to be looking for us, and that doesn't seem likely, does it?"

"What are you doing up here?"

"What are *you* doing up here?"

He scowled. "A child's answer, and you've probably lived

longer than I have."

"I want to know why you've come for him."

He canted his head, regarding her, his hunter's gaze penetrating shadow. "Is it the time journeying? Is that why you would take such interest in the fate of a human?"

"I could ask the same," she said. She waved a hand, indicating the entire palace. "You can hunt any of these. You could have taken the girl. I wouldn't have minded that so much. But you waited for him. You watched him."

"My kind prey. We have appetites, desires. Spanners and Crossers are common fare. A Walker..." He let the implication hang, hoping it would mask a half-truth. Less than half, really. But she didn't need to know what he had discerned sifting through the scents that wafted up to him. "Now, will you answer my question?"

She faltered, discomfited. "Yes, we share an affinity for time. Hence my interest in him."

"I sense more than that," he said, a gambit.

The Tirribin didn't answer, confirming his suspicions.

"I compel your silence," he said. "I invoke the Distraint and demand that you tell him nothing of me, nothing of this encounter, nothing of my intentions. Do you hear and acknowledge my invocation?"

She glowered and bared her needle teeth. "You're canny for a Belvora. Most of your kind are dull-witted."

He refused to be goaded. "Do you hear and acknowledge?"

"I hear and acknowledge," she said, sullen and grudging.

"You will accept punishment if you're found to have violated this oath?"

"I will."

He stared, saying nothing.

The Tirribin heaved a sigh. "I will accept punishment if I'm found to have violated my oath."

He nodded. "Good."

"I hope you choke on him," she said. "I hope he hears your wingbeats and shoots you in the heart before you can take him."

At that he laughed. "He won't. Have you never seen a Belvora on the hunt?"

She flipped her hair in annoyance, then pitched forward out of the nook in which she'd been sitting, and scuttled like a spider down the stone wall to the grass. Once on the ground, she left at Tirribin speed. In moments, he could no longer hear her or smell her power.

The Walker was gone as well, safe within the walls of the palace. That was a small matter. The human would be out again come the morning. *I leave with first light*, he had said.

Indeed.

And I will be waiting.

He ruffled his wings, hunched against the breeze to sleep. Only as he closed his eyes, though, did it occur to him that the oath he demanded of the Tirribin had been too specific, too narrow. He hoped she hadn't noticed.

Even after she blurred through the palace gate, past guards who couldn't see her when she moved at speed, Droë didn't slow. She was too angry, too frightened.

She had sensed the Belvora the moment she entered the first courtyard. Initially her awareness had been vague, an elusive, formless presence that unsettled her. When at last she put a name to what she felt, fear seeped into her. Not for herself. Even Belvora wouldn't harm a Tirribin. But for Tobias.

This Belvora was spying on them. Once she knew what it was, she smelled it. A moment later, still speaking with Tobias, circling him, she spotted it: a pale shape pressed into the dim recesses of the palace wall.

She said nothing to the Walker, did nothing to draw his attention to the creature above them, for that would have meant his death. Instead, she bided her time, spoke to the Belvora herself.

A mistake.

It never occurred to her that a Belvora would be clever enough to invoke the Distraint. Most of them were thick-headed, and single-minded in their pursuit of the kill. Not this one, though. This one had been quicker than she.

Among creatures of their kind – Tirribin, Belvora, Arrokad, Shonla, and others whom humans in their ignorance referred to as demons – the Distraint was highest law. Punishments for violating a Distraint could be extravagantly painful. Or so she had heard. She had never fallen afoul of an invoked oath; she had been subject to only a few in the hundreds of years she'd been alive.

So how had she allowed this creature to trap her in one? If other Tirribin learned that she'd been ensnared in this way, by a Belvora of all creatures, she would be humiliated. More incentive, as if she needed it, not to violate her oath.

Fortunately, the Belvora had been quick, but not thorough. Already she saw ways around the promise he had wrung from her.

She slowed, took a breath. Yes, he had left paths open to her. She could give Tobias a chance to live without bringing harm to herself. If he died despite her efforts… well, then perhaps there was less to him than she had credited.

Halting, she found herself on a narrow lane leading to Windhome's waterfront. The Belvora would do nothing until dawn, which gave her several bells. Enough time to feed, and then return to the palace.

Footsteps echoed nearby. Another lane over. A brisk gait. A man, she guessed, young, ripe with years.

Droë eased along her lane, a hunter herself, in pursuit of this evening's meal.

• • •

Tobias's journey to Hayncalde began the following morning, before daylight. Master Ojeyd came for him, bearing a single candle, his eyes glinting with pride and flame, as if he couldn't imagine a better way to begin his day than to escort a young Traveler to the wharves.

Tobias hadn't slept at all. Thoughts swarmed in his head: Droë and Mara, Wansi and Saffern, memories of his parents and anticipation of the Daerjen court.

Upon hearing the master's approach, he swung himself off his pallet and grabbed his sack from the floor. He paused to scan the chamber. Most of the boys slept still, but Delvin was awake and had propped himself up on one arm. He nodded once, offered a small smile, which Tobias returned.

"Come on, then," Vaisan whispered. "Your ship sails with first light – a merchant ship, and I doubt the captain will wait."

They stepped out of the Leeward Keep into the murky light and cool, damp air of dawn. The moon still shone low in the west, and a few stubborn stars clung to a clear, brightening sky.

"A fine day to begin your voyage," the master said, flashing a smile. "I envy you, Mister Doljan."

Tobias glanced his way, intending to thank him. For the kind words, for years of guidance and wisdom and friendship.

He never got the chance.

Someone shouted a warning from across the courtyard. Tobias couldn't say why he looked up, instead of behind or to the side. He did, in time to see a huge, pallid shape dropping toward him. Tapered falcon-like wings, membranous, aglow with moonlight. Arms stretched toward him, clawed hands reaching.

Tobias couldn't bring himself to move, or scream. He had time to think, *I'm dead.*

A hard shove from Master Ojeyd unbalanced him. He sprawled to the ground. The creature shrieked, rage and thwarted desire in the sound. It swerved, a slight twist of its body. Another scream, and Vaisan went down in a fury of limbs and wings.

A rush of air from the creature's dive battered Tobias, carrying the stench of rotted meat. He heard another cry, truncated. Then the rending of flesh.

He rolled to his knees.

"Stay down!"

That voice again, closer this time. Then a spurt of flame and the deafening roar of a musket. The creature shrieked again. It tumbled off Vaisan, spread its wings.

A pistol shot followed, and the creature fell.

Saffern strode past Tobias, tossing his firearm aside with one hand and drawing a sword with the other. Reaching the winged form, he hacked at it with the blade once, twice. Its head rolled free, trailing dark, noisome blood.

Saffern straightened.

Shaking, Tobias crawled to where Master Ojeyd lay. The man breathed still, each gasp shallow and desperate. Blood coursed from a ghastly wound on his neck, and from five long, parallel gashes along each side of his face and jaw. Tobias swallowed hard to keep from vomiting. Tears blurred his vision. The master's wide eyes found Tobias's. Vaisan groped for his arm with a bony, trembling hand. Finding it, the master pulled him nearer.

"We'll get a healer," Tobias said. He looked up. People were emerging from the towers, drawn by the weapons fire and shouting. "We need a healer," he said, raising his voice.

Vaisan's fingers gouged his arm. "No. No healer. I'm dead."

"That's not–"

"Listen!" the master said, the sharpness of the word shocking Tobias silent. "Belvora... don't choose."

Tobias frowned. "I don't understand."

"Predators. Mindless. They don't choose." His voice had fallen to a whisper. The gush of blood from his neck had slowed.

"They don't wait. No subtlety. But this one..." He closed his eyes, then forced them open again. "This one, I fear, wanted you."

Loath as he was to believe this, Tobias knew better than to doubt the man. Belvora were also called Magick Demons, because they preyed mostly on those who possessed powers – Travelers, Seers, even Binders. It was no surprise that one would hunt in Windhome Palace. Except they rarely did. They had been driven from Trevynisle long ago; they were said to be extinct here, which meant that this one had come from elsewhere. For him?

He sifted through his memory of the attack. The warnings, the shove, the booming reports of Saffern's weapons, and the violence of the Belvora's collision with Ojeyd. The master had saved his life. So had Saffern. And now Ojeyd was dying. Because that creature had wanted Tobias dead? None of it seemed real. Yes, he was a Walker, and bound for the court of a powerful isle. But he was one man, and barely old enough to be considered that much. Why would his life and death matter so?

The palace healer reached them and dropped to her knees on the other side of Vaisan's body. By then, the master's grip on Tobias's arm had slackened. The healer felt for a pulse, her lips thinned. She placed a hand on Vaisan's neck wound, and was enveloped in a faint halo of magick, not unlike the glow Tobias had seen on Wansi. After a tencount, she glanced up, looking past Tobias and above him. She gave a small shake of her head, and the light of her power faded.

Vaisan's hand dropped to the ground.

"Blood and bone," Tobias breathed, shaking again. A tear fell from his cheek, darkening the master's overshirt.

A hand grasped his shoulder.

"Come on then, lad," Saffern said. "There's nothing to be done."

Tobias stood, but didn't follow the weapons master. Not yet. He walked to the body of the Belvora. He had never seen one before, and hoped never to again, though he sensed that these creatures might well be part of his future.

It was muscular and would have been tall if it stood. One of its wings lay open at an odd angle. Blood, black in the dawn light, glistened on its side and chest where Saffern had shot it. The head, golden-haired, with elongated, pointed ears and blunt features, had come to rest some distance from the corpse, a spiral of blood leading from one to the other.

"The guards should have killed it," Saffern said from behind him. "He should never have gained entry to the courtyards."

Tobias offered no reply.

"Come along, Tobias."

He turned at that. He couldn't remember the last time Saffern had used his given name.

"We still have to get you to your ship."

Tobias surveyed the grounds again. It seemed every person in the palace stood around them, staring at Ojeyd and the Belvora, shocked silent. Or not quite every person, not yet. Even now Chancellor Shaan strode in their direction, his robe billowing behind him, guards before him and behind.

He spotted Mara, her eyes puffy, her arms crossed over her chest. She stared back at him, lovely and grave. He gazed at her for another fivecount, then shouldered his sack and followed Saffern away from the blood and toward the palace's lower gate. The weapons master paused to retrieve his pistol, and the musket he had fired and discarded.

"You still have that pistol I gave you?" he asked Tobias.

"Yes. It's in my sack."

"What good is it doing you there?"

He glanced at the man before pulling out the weapon. He loaded it while they walked.

As they entered the middle courtyard, Tobias spotted a small form watching them from an archway. Droë.

At the same time, Saffern said, "The Two take my eyes, there she is again."

"You've seen her before?"

"Aye. Have you?"

Tobias faltered, fearing Saffern's reaction. "She's a Tirribin, and… and a friend. I've known her for a long time."

"Well, I had never seen her before this morning, and would never think a bloody demon could be friend to anyone in this palace. She woke me with her knocking. When I finally got up to open the door, she told me to follow her and bring a weapon. Then she ran away without giving me time to ask questions. I dressed and grabbed these–" he hefted his musket and pistol, "and went after her, but she kept her distance. Led me to the upper courtyard." He regarded Tobias again. "She's your friend, all right. She saved your life."

Tobias halted, as did Saffern. They both turned to look Droë's way again, but of course by then she was gone.

CHAPTER 5

27th Day of Kheraya's Waking, Year 647

He made his way to Windhome's waterfront in a stupor, images of the Belvora and Ojeyd flashing through his mind. Every few strides he scanned the sky, expecting to see more of the winged demons stooping toward him, clawed hands extended, teeth bared.

Saffern watched him, and Tobias hoped the weapons master would tell him to relax, that another attack was unlikely so soon after the first. He didn't.

The chancellor had arranged passage for him aboard the *Gray Skate*, a merchant ship out of Belsan, on Aiyanth. Upon reaching the ship, Saffern sought out the captain, a tall, spear-thin, taciturn woman named Seris Larr, and spoke to her in low tones. Tobias couldn't hear what they said, but he guessed that the weapons master told her of the attack at the palace.

When Saffern concluded his conversation with Captain Larr, he approached Tobias, proffering a hand and, when Tobias gripped it, laying his other hand on Tobias's shoulder.

"You'll be all right," he said. "Remember all you've learned, and do me proud. Do Ojeyd proud."

"I will." Emotion thickened the words. He had to blink back tears.

After Saffern left, the captain greeted Tobias in the most perfunctory manner, saying nothing about the Belvora, but making it clear that he should stay out of her way, and do nothing to distract the men and women of her crew.

That suited him. He wished only to stand by the rails near the bow, take in the seascape, and watch the sky for threats. The sun was still low in the east when they slipped out of Windhome Inlet on oars, passing laborers in broad-rimmed straw hats, ankle deep in mud, shaping *gaaz*, the mud bricks for which these isles were renowned.

Once beyond the shallows, they raised sails, and began to carve through the waters of Safsi Bay and then the Oaqamaran Sea. Tobias had but the dimmest memories of his voyage to Windhome so many years before, but now, as the pall cast over his mood by the morning's events lifted somewhat, he discovered that he enjoyed sailing. His body adjusted with alacrity to the pitch and roll of the sea.

Too much of his time in the palace had been spent indoors, poring over maps and texts. He savored the warmth of the sun on his face, the briny wind that swept back his hair and made the gold and blue flag of Aiyanth snap above the swelling sails. Once out on open water, there was little to see. Occasionally he spotted schools of fish leaping clear of the ocean surface, flashes of silver twisting in the sunlight. Or long-winged birds skimming over the swells, swooping up into the blue before tucking their wings to dive for food.

He had feared feeling exposed on open water, an easy target for another Belvora. Instead, he took comfort in the endless stretch of swells and troughs. For now, he or some member of the crew would see any attack coming. But he dreaded the setting of the sun.

The crew, which numbered about twenty, joked and teased, but they worked with quiet efficiency and responded instantly to the captain's commands. As far as Tobias could see, no tasks were assigned to one sex to the exclusion of the other. Men and women worked together, dressed similarly, swore with equal eloquence. The same had been true among the novitiates in Windhome, but he was surprised just the same.

Late that first day, one of the crew shouted from the rigging and pointed to the southwest. Crossing to the starboard side of the ship and following the line indicated by the sailor, Tobias picked out the outline of a large ship on the horizon. He glanced back at the captain, who had raised a brass spyglass to her eye. The rest of the crew fell silent, waiting for her next command. He had been taught in the palace that privateering ships operated in waters farther south and west. Chances were this was an Oaqamaran marauder, one of the huge warships that had menaced the Aiyanthan and Herjean Seas and inflicted heavy damage on the navies of Daerjen, Vleros, and Aiyanth.

He doubted the marauder's crew would look kindly on a Walker from Trevynisle newly assigned to the Daerjeni court. His stomach tightening, he eyed Captain Larr.

For her part, the captain studied the ship for some time, and though she didn't call for a change in course, she continued to check its position until it disappeared from view just before sunset.

A short time later, a bell rang belowdecks, and the crew converged on the hatch leading down to the hold.

"Come on there, young master," one sailor called, beckoning to Tobias. "Mess time."

Tobias hadn't realized how hungry he was. He followed the woman belowdecks where most of the crew had already tucked in to a meal of hard biscuits, salted meat, and wrinkled apples. He had heard that sailors put up with abominable food. This supper was edible if not elegant. His meals aboard the *Gray Skate* wouldn't compare well with the fare he had enjoyed in the palace, but he knew better than to complain.

"The meat's fresh," one of the men said. "If'n you don't mind dog." Several of the others laughed.

Tobias didn't want to believe him, but he also didn't want to scoff, just in case it really was dog.

"It ain't dog," said another sailor, looking his way.

"I was just having a go," the first man said. "Coulda played along a bit."

"And let him puke on me? Not a chance."

Everyone laughed again. Even Tobias grinned.

"It's stag," said the second man. "And it *is* fresh. Got it in Windhome. The apples..." He eyed the one in his hand and then took a bite. "They still eat fine," he said around a mouthful of fruit, "no matter how they look."

Someone placed a full tankard of ale in front of him – something the chancellor would never have allowed. Tobias took a sip, decided he liked it, and began to eat. He said little, and blushed at many of the stories told by the men and women around him. For what remained of the supper, the crew and captain largely ignored him. By the time the meal ended he was sated and slightly dizzy from the ale. The crew cleaned up and began to arrange themselves around the hold on pallets and in hammocks. A few couples – men and women, women and women, men and men – retreated into darker corners away from the hatch.

The second mate, Melsed Carina, led him to a pallet under the stairway and handed him a rough woolen blanket.

"This is yours, such as it is. Rest well."

"Thank you."

Conversations continued. Low laughter and the occasional taken breath emanated from those dark recesses. Someone began to play a mouth harp. Tobias didn't think he could fall asleep with so much noise. Once lanterns were extinguished in the Leeward Keep, the boys were expected to remain silent. But he was already a long way from the palace. He lay on the pallet, covered himself with the blanket and closed his eyes, thinking he should try to sleep, fearing that winged demons would haunt his dreams. He kept his loaded pistol beside him.

Next he knew, the peal of a nearby bell woke him from a

sound slumber, and morning sun spilled through the hatch onto the stairs above him.

Most of the others were already awake and on deck. He rubbed a hand over his face and blinked. He could have slept more, but his bladder was full to bursting. He went forward in the hold to where the heads – as the sailors called the ship's privies – were located and relieved himself. Then he climbed the stairs to the deck and took his place near the bow. The sky had clouded over during the night, a freshening wind out of the west carrying the scent of rain and the threat of heavier seas. Tobias kept his place along the rail for as long as he could, but by midday rain and spray from the surf had forced him back into the hold.

The storm lasted into the night, testing his newly-discovered affection for sea travel. He felt queasy for much of the day and evening, and had no interest in eating his supper.

"You'll be better off if'n you do," one of the sailors, man named Trem, told him, offering another of the wrinkled apples. "These 'n particular might help."

He was right. An apple, a bit of bread, a few sips of ale: by the time Tobias finished, his stomach had settled. He took to his pallet, damp though it was, and soon managed to fall asleep despite the rocking and creaking of the vessel.

By the following morning, the weather had passed, gentling the *Skate*'s motion, and allowing Tobias to reclaim his spot at the ship's bow. Dark clouds retreated to the east, shadowing the waters there. Clear skies in the west stretched to the horizon, a welcome sight.

Near midday, they sighted Craeda and several other isles of Sipar's Labyrinth. The storm had cleared the air, and at first Tobias thought the isles closer than they actually were. It took the ship another four bells to reach the first. All the while, the isles grew, darkened, came into relief: towering stone cliffs, capped by lush forests and striated by silver cascades. Clouds obscured the highest peaks of the larger islands, and white ernes circled above the coastal crags, their cries echoing weakly across the water.

The captain steered them into the Labyrinth and to a small port village on an island just past Craeda. The closer they drew to land, the more watchful and nervous Tobias grew. He scanned the sky continuously, his pistol tucked into his belt.

A boy about Tobias's age had swabbed the deck for much of the day, gradually working his way from stern to bow. Despite the captain's instructions, Tobias had been tempted to speak with the lad. At last he had an excuse.

"Why here?" he asked, his voice low. "Why not Festown?"

The lad cast a wary look back at the captain, who called instructions to her bosun. "She can't moor at Festown," he whispered in a lilting accent. "Nor anywhere in Craeda. Word is, she killed a man there. Tha's what they tell me, anyway. They could be havin' a go with me, though."

"And you could be having one with me."

The boy's eyes widened. "No! I'm not! I–"

Tobias stopped him with a grin. The boy smiled as well.

"That was pretty good."

"I'm Tobias."

"Evan," he said, checking on the captain again, and shifting his attention back to his mop and bucket. "Gotta keep workin'."

They didn't remain in the port town for long. Only Captain Larr left the ship, and she returned within half a bell, bearing a small parcel that she took directly to her quarters. Soon they were back in open ocean, their sails full, the setting sun to starboard.

One bell out from port, they came upon a large drift of ships, large and small, all of them heading east, their decks crowded with men and a few women. They were short and tall, fair-skinned and dark, with hair of yellow, red, brown, and black. Some bore elaborate skin etchings on their cheeks and brows, necks and arms, and a few had shaved heads, save for a single plait growing at the nape of their necks. Most wore rags: torn breeches, tired, tattered shirts. None appeared to have bathed in some time.

Still, they were anything but downtrodden. Torches burned in sconces mounted on the vessels' masts, and on several of the ships men and women played stringed instruments, sang, and danced. Tobias heard many of the languages he and the other novitiates had been taught in the palace: Oaqamaran, Aiyanthan, the common tongue of the Ring Isles, even Milnish.

"Prospectors," Tobias heard from behind him. Another of the ship's crew, a burly bearded man, stood a few paces away, leaning on the rail. "They're heading for Chayde, or maybe Flynse. Word is, folk are practically tripping over gold and silver up there. Gems, too. And lesser metals."

"So how come you ain't there already, Ben?" came a voice from the rigging above.

The bearded man answered with a grimace. "Mining work's too hard for me. I prefer the easy life of a sailor."

That drew laughs from the sailors around them.

"I heard that," the captain called, eliciting more laughter.

"Where are they from?" Tobias asked, eyeing the vessels once more.

"All over, from the looks of them. Some it's easier to tell than others. Those with the skin art – they're from the western lands: Jsorde, Herjes, maybe even Westisle itself. And the shaved heads come from the Knot."

That much Tobias had learned, though he didn't say as much to the sailor.

"Them with red hair probably come from around the Bone Sea, and the yellow-heads are likely from the Inner Ring, though you can't be sure with any of them."

"Some of those places are at war. Westisle? And the Bone Sea islands?"

The sailor dismissed this with a wave of his meaty hand. "Wars are for kings and queens. The rest of us just want a bit o' gold to keep the demons at bay."

"But surely—"

"That's enough prattle over there," the captain said.

The sailor pushed away from the rail and pulled himself up into the rigging.

The captain sauntered forward from the quarterdeck, the last golden rays of sunlight on her tanned face.

"I believe I instructed you to stay out of the way of my crew," she said, her voice a gravelly alto.

"Yes, captain. Forgive me. I was… curious."

She crooked a smile. Her face was all sharp angles and overlong features, but when she grinned it coalesced into a mien both friendly and winsome.

"Curiosity can be good. I find myself curious about you."

"Me?"

"Your chancellor paid me ten Oaqamaran rounds to take you on. That's quite a lot for any passenger. He also forced me to change my route. I had planned to stop at several ports, but he didn't want that. It had been my intention to anchor at Belsan and pass you off to another captain. The chancellor made me swear I'd see you all the way to Hayncalde."

"I had no idea."

"I don't doubt it. But I wonder if you know what makes you special, what would make him spend so much gold, and take such care with his instructions to me." She tipped her head. "What would bring a Belvora to Trevynisle?"

Tobias's cheeks warmed, and he was abruptly aware of the weight of his pistol on his hip. His gaze swept the sky again.

"I've noticed you do that a lot. Watching the sky, I mean. Do you expect another attack?"

"I don't know," he said. "I find myself more comfortable on open water. I hadn't expected that."

"Interesting," she said, her tone making him turn. "And worth discussing. First, though, I'd like an answer to what I asked. Do you understand your value?"

Since the age of seven, Tobias had been trained in the art of diplomacy, the first rule of which was quite simple: no matter the currency – gold, land, authority, information – never give away more than necessary.

"You've taken passengers from Trevynisle before, haven't you?"

Her grin ossified. "I don't like impertinent children."

"I wasn't trying to be impertinent. Forgive me if I was."

She gazed eastward, after the drift of vessels. "Yes, I've had previous dealings with Windhome. You're a Traveler. I want to know what kind."

Tobias faltered, caught off guard by the directness of her response.

Her smirk was thin, reflexive. "For all your training, you're not ready to match wits and will with the likes of me. Remember that, boy."

"Yes, captain."

"So?"

She might have been a merchant – legitimate in the eyes of the chancellor – but there was a hardness to her. How much trade did she do with the privateers of the western waters? Or, for that matter, with the Oaqamaran autarchy? Someone with his talents might fetch a price that would dwarf the ten rounds the chancellor had paid for his passage. Without a chronofor, he could do little, and securing such a device would cost a good deal of gold. But hardly enough to dissuade the autarch, or privateers.

"You don't trust me," she said. "That's probably wise, albeit unwarranted. Besides, your reluctance to answer gives you away."

"I'm a Walker."

"I assumed as much. I could make good use of a time Walker. Any merchant could."

The blood drained from Tobias's face.

"Not against your will. I would pay you. Far more, no doubt, than will the Daerjeni sovereign."

"The chancellor gave his word, and the sovereign has paid for me already."

"Paid *for* you? So you're chattel."

He recoiled. "I am not. I've never been asked to do anything against my will."

She raised an eyebrow. "Really? How old were you when they took you from your home?"

"Five," he said, an admission.

"Were your parents paid?"

He lifted his shoulders, nodded. "I believe so."

"That's twice you've been sold. And however you feel about going to Daerjen, I doubt you were so pleased with the first instance."

"I was fed, clothed, housed, educated, given a future. Most children who grow up in Redcove fare far worse."

"So you're a slave, but a happy one."

"Don't call me that!"

The captain raised her eyebrows.

"Please," he added.

"I would pay you better, feed you, take you to lands you've never seen, never even dreamed of. With me – aboard this ship – you'll experience sights, tastes, pleasures..." she smiled in a way that made him blush again, though in an entirely different way, "...the like of which you can't imagine. In return, you'd provide me with the means to reconsider negotiations that don't go as I please, or to take advantage of opportunities that I regret passing by, or, perhaps, to avoid boardings and other encounters that prove... unprofitable. And when you aren't Walking, you'll make yourself a valued member of my crew. In short, I get a sailor and a Walker. We both gain."

He cleared his throat. "I'd be negating a contract."

She laughed, and not kindly, brushing strands of raven hair from her brow. Silver mixed with the black at her temples, but her skin remained smooth. Tobias wouldn't have hazarded a guess at her age.

"You wouldn't be the first," she said.

He started to answer, shook his head. He knew he should say something, but no words came.

"Silenced you, have I? Good. Come with me."

She gave him no time to agree or object, but merely strode back toward the quarterdeck and her cabin. Tobias hurried after her, only pausing at the threshold. One didn't simply enter a captain's quarters.

"It's all right," she said, waving him inside. "Close the door."

She stepped behind the low desk beside her bed, opened a drawer, and pulled out what he thought was the parcel she had brought back from the port town.

It was a bit larger than her hand, flat, wrapped in stained sacking that had been tied with twine.

"What do you think this is?" she asked, holding it in her palm.

"I... I have no idea."

She flipped it to him, and he caught it. "Open it."

Tobias hadn't expected it to be so light. It felt almost fragile in his hands. He stared at it, glanced at her.

"It won't explode. You have my word."

He remained uncomfortable under her gaze, but did as told. The knot in the twine gave grudgingly, but once Tobias managed to untie it, the wrapping fell away with ease, dropping to the floor, and revealing a circlet of gold. An aperture. Tobias held it in both hands, as he would a hymnal, scrutinizing the curved, overlapping blades, the rounded outer edge, the sectioned arcs of the inner contour.

"Is it real?" he asked, without thought.

The captain didn't answer. He tore his gaze from the circlet to find her glaring at him, dark eyes as hard as onyx.

"One can find imitations of all Bound devices," he said. "Worthless fakes. Surely you know of these."

"You have ventured into very dangerous waters," she said, her voice silken. "Do I look like someone who would traffic in counterfeits and forgeries?"

Tobias shook his head, fear rising in his chest. "No, captain, not at all." He opened his hands. "I'm a Walker. My power is different from that of Crossers. I can't tell you whether or not this is real."

She considered him, then threw back her head and laughed again. "That's why you think I've shown you this?"

Heat rose in his neck and face. She had a talent for disconcerting him. "It wasn't an unreasonable assumption," he said, knowing he sounded prideful and sullen.

She reined in her mirth with visible effort. "No, I don't suppose it was." He sensed she was humoring him, which angered him that much more. "I know the aperture is real. I purchased it from the family of an old Crosser who recently died. It's as real as you and I. And if we had a Crosser with us, he or she would be able to use it to pass through the walls of this cabin as easily as we can use the door. I'm showing it to you because I want you to understand that my offer of employment is real. I'm a merchant, and a successful one. I've been at sea for twenty-five years, and I've captained my own ship for nearly twenty. Over that time, I've come into possession of apertures, sextants, and even a few chronofors. Consent to work for me, and I won't rest until I've found you a device. You have my word on that."

"I... I don't know what to say."

"Say you'll consider the offer, that it's generous and attractive, but you need a bit of time."

She grinned again. Tobias did, too.

"Yes. That's... All of those things."

"Very well. Belowdecks with you. The crew should be eating by now."

"Yes, captain." Tobias handed her the aperture and made to leave.

"Walker," she said, stopping him before he could let himself out of the cramped quarters. "I would prefer that no one else know of this." She held up the circlet.

"I understand," Tobias said, though he wasn't sure he did.

He left her, and joined the crew in the hold for the evening meal. But their conversation haunted him all the rest of that night, and throughout his slumber.

CHAPTER 6

10th Day of Kheraya's Ascent, Year 647

Two mornings after his exchange with the captain, they encountered another Oaqamaran marauder. This one took notice of the *Skate*, and changed course to intercept her. As the ship neared, Captain Larr called Tobias away from the bow, meeting him at the hatch.

"I want you below, in shadows."

Tobias cast a leery glance at the warship. "Will they board us?"

She eyed the vessel as well. "I'd be shocked if they didn't. Ships of the autarchy make it a practice to confiscate goods, calling it tribute. Like it or not, you're a good, and a valuable one at that. And I'd imagine you have documents with you that indicate you're bound for Hayncalde."

He nodded, remembering Chancellor Shaan's letter of introduction.

"I feared as much. You might as well be wearing a Daerjeni naval uniform. If they don't kill you, they'll take you. Now go below, and hide. Do you have a weapon?"

His heart pounded, and he could barely summon enough spit to speak. "Yes."

"Keep it with you."

He ran down the stairs and retrieved from his pallet the letter from the chancellor. He also grabbed the pistol, powder, paper, and ammunition Saffern had given him before picking his way to the darkest, most remote corner of the hold. Crouching there behind barrels and crates, he covered himself with old sailcloth, and loaded his pistol blind, something the weapons master had insisted all novitiates learn to do.

Sooner than he expected, something scraped along the side of the ship. Above him, men shouted and heavy footsteps thudded on deck. Something scuttled near him in the darkness and stuffy heat. A rat? Tobias clutched his weapon in sweating hands and willed himself to remain still. Judging from what he heard above, many men had boarded the *Skate*. They were on the deck, then on the stairs, and finally in the hold with him. Torchlight glimmered through the weave of the cloth.

Tobias's breath sounded loud to his own ears. As the torches loomed closer he was certain the Oaqamarans would find him. He raised his weapon, braced his shooting hand on his knee. He'd die before he allowed them to capture him, and he was determined not to die alone.

They remained in the hold, shifting barrels and crates, laughing and speaking in their language. Their words came too quickly, and Tobias's breathing was too loud for him to make out what they said.

After what seemed an eternity, the torch flame retreated and then disappeared altogether, plunging him into shadow again. Not long after that, the noise above abated. Another scrape along the hull, and Tobias assumed the danger had passed, though he remained hidden until Captain Larr descended the stairs and called to him.

He emerged from his hiding place soaked in sweat, but otherwise none the worse for wear. He learned from one of the sailors that the Oaqamarans took three barrels of ale, and most of their remaining meat. Later that day, they made an unplanned stop at a small isle to replenish their stores. The sailor and her mates agreed their losses could have been far worse.

• • •

A few days later they entered the Outer Ring through the passage between Aiyanth and Ensydar. Warships patrolled these waters: sea eagles flying the red and white of Daerjen, and the similar Aiyanthan frigates, flying blue and gold. They were large vessels, three-masted and armed with forty guns. They cut an impressive line in the coastal waters and were nearly as numerous as merchant ships. Smaller warships bore other colors: green and silver for Herjes, black and purple for Rencyr, and yellow and red, which Tobias could not place. His diplomacy master in Windhome would have been displeased.

More open seas might have attracted privateers or Oaqamaran marauders, despite the presence of the Daerjeni and Aiyanthan vessels, but these waters were safe, at least for now.

"It's a lot more dangerous up near Oaqamar and the Bones," Evan told him, as he mopped the deck again. "We fly Aiyanthan colors, so we're all right here. Near those others, the captain strikes the banners before we get anywhere close. She has another set – from one of the isles in the Knot, I think – that she flies when we're in the northwest."

"Why not fly those all the time?"

"Because sometimes being from the Axle is good for business." Evan said this with pride, leading Tobias to guess that he hailed from Aiyanth.

As they tacked along Aiyanth's southeast coast, Tobias's excitement mounted. The threat of another Belvora attack had lessened. Magick demons were found almost exclusively in the northern isles, from which Seers and Travelers hailed. He had less to fear and more to anticipate.

The captain joined him at his customary position by the rail.

"You seem impatient," she said.

"Excited mostly. But yes, I'm eager to reach Hayncalde."

"I take it then you've decided to refuse my offer of employment. Or had you forgotten our conversation?"

He hadn't. Far from it. He had dreaded this return to the subject. He admired the captain and her crew, and had enjoyed their voyage. But he had trained all his life to serve a court. He was loath to give up what he had long considered his destiny. Or maybe that was merely an excuse.

So you're a slave, but a happy one. Captain Larr's words had haunted him since their last exchange, goading, even offensive, but as blunt as anything anyone had ever said to him.

Was that the source of his ambivalence? He had spent his life meeting the expectations of others, going where his parents sent him, where the chancellor sent him, excelling in his studies and in his training. For as long as he could remember, he had been dutiful and compliant. He had been rewarded for this; meeting those expectations – exceeding them – had brought him attention, praise, both of which he coveted.

"Perhaps you thought *I* had forgotten," Captain Larr said, filling a lengthening silence.

Tobias forced a smile, his thoughts still churning.

Refusing the captain's offer felt like another capitulation to what was expected of him. He was clever enough to wonder if this had been her aim when she compared him to a slave.

He wondered as well if his training had been too complete. For taking this alternative path still seemed unthinkable. Negate the contract? Turn his back on nine years of instruction? Deny the sovereign his service so that he might journey the seas with the crew of the *Skate*? It seemed the height of folly, of irresponsibility.

It was also deeply attractive.

His thoughts had followed this circular path for days as he careened from impulse to impulse. *I can't accept her offer. I want to accept her offer. I can't accept her offer…*

He wanted adventure. Even as he sweated and trembled beneath that old sailcloth, wondering if he might have to kill the Oaqamaran sailors searching the hold, he also thrilled to be in such circumstance. Life on the *Skate* might be filled with moments like that one.

On the other hand, for years now he had anticipated going to one of Islevale's great courts and living each day at the center of world-shaping events. Could he abandon that dream for life on the sea? Would the captain feel bound by the limitations on Walking set out in the contracts agreed to by sovereigns? More to the point, he had grown up hating and fearing the Oaqamarans. Giving up his posting in Daerjen to stay on this ship would feel like he was fleeing the autarchy. That was what he would do as the ship's Walker. He would hide in the hold, or hope that the captain avoided marauders entirely. For all he knew, the sovereign needed him to play some role in Daerjen's war against Oaqamar. How could he refuse this summons to Hayncalde?

This thought, as much as anything, finally gave him the courage to speak.

"I'm sorry, captain. The life of a court Traveler is what I've been preparing for since I was five years old. It's the path my parents envisioned for me when they gave me over to the palace. Your offer is tempting, truly it is. But..." He broke off, shaking his head, fearful of saying something insulting.

"I take no offense, Walker. Indeed, I believe I understand."

"Someday maybe–"

"Someday," she repeated. "I don't wish to wait so long. Well before you grow bored with your sovereign, I hope to find another Walker who better appreciates the opportunity I'm offering." She smiled to soften the words, then started away from him, back toward her cabin, her boots clicking on the wooden deck. "We should enter the Inward Sea tomorrow," she said over her shoulder. "I'll have you in Hayncalde in a few more days."

He walked after her. "What would you have done had I said yes?" he asked, his voice low.

She halted, scrutinized him once more. "Was there ever a chance of that?"

"I don't know. I'm curious about what might have happened."

Her shrug was eloquent. "Obviously, we wouldn't go to Daerjen. I'd take us west, make it seem that we came through the Aiyanthan Sea. From there, I'd send word of a privateer assault. A tragedy. So many hands lost, including the young man entrusted to us by the chancellor. I would, of course, make restitution the next time I land in Windhome. I don't keep money that isn't mine. And I would beg that the chancellor extend my deepest condolences to the lad's parents."

"Lies, layered one on top of the other."

"A tale. You could take on a new name, a new appearance."

"And your commerce with the palace? You'd never again be able to transport Travelers from Trevynisle to the courts."

"I'm not convinced of that, but even if it were so, those are profits I can make up elsewhere, especially with a Walker by my side." She raised an eyebrow. "There's still time. Not much, mind you. It would be more complicated once we reach the Inward Sea. But it's not yet too late."

"I think it is," Tobias said, surprised by the pang of regret that accompanied the words. "I'm sorry."

The captain laughed, dismissing his apology with a flutter of her fingers. She had a talent for making him feel belittled, as if she was always aware of his youth.

"You needn't apologize," she said. "I've survived very well without a Walker on my ship, and I'll continue to do so. Yes, there would have been gain – for both of us – but I'm in no danger of going hungry, and I'm sure you'll do just fine with your sovereign."

He nodded, stung by her tone more than her words.

"You still seem unsure. Are you certain you know your own mind?"

Stubbornness more than surety made him say, "Yes, quite certain."

"Very well," she said with another shrug. "I'll send a bird today informing the sovereign of our impending arrival." She turned and left.

Tobias watched her go, feeling he had allowed something precious to slip through his grasp, and wondering at himself that he should regret turning down an offer he would never have considered a turn before.

Still, he knew he had made the right choice, the only choice, really. For better or worse, he would go to Daerjen, and serve as he had long intended. If this meant less adventure in his life, so be it.

The following day, the *Skate* stopped in Codport on the north coast of Qyrshen. After that she cut eastward into the Inward Sea. A day later, they rounded the wooded north promontory of Daerjen itself.

Here, warships gathered in clusters of three and four. At least twenty patrolled near the mouth of the Gulf of Daerjen, all of them flying Daerjeni colors.

Captain Larr steered them among the ships and into the gulf. Tobias felt safer with the sovereign's navy nearby, but he sensed that the captain and her crew disliked being so close to any warships. Forests on the Daerjeni Promontory gave way to open moors, and then to the lofty, jagged peaks of the Saltwind Range, which loomed over the inlet, dwarfing its gray cliffs and rugged coast.

The *Skate* bypassed the wharves of Sheraigh on the south shore and sailed into the heart of the isle, passing other merchant vessels, a few as large as she, most smaller, more agile, better suited to the narrow straits of the Inner Ring.

With every landmark Tobias identified – the Thirogan Mountains to the south, the uplands of the Hayncalde Narrow ahead of them, the hills of the Faendor Highlands at the southernmost end of the gulf – his excitement grew. If he could see the highlands, albeit from a distance, surely Hayncalde couldn't be far.

The captain had to navigate with more care in the gulf, however, and before long she ordered the sails furled and the sailors onto sweeps. When night fell and Larr instructed her crew to drop anchor until morning, Tobias nearly groaned aloud.

Once the ship had halted, Ben, Trem, Evan and the rest of the crew went below for the evening meal, urging Tobias to join them.

He followed them into the hold, where they had prepared a small surprise for him. Fresh crane fruit, brought aboard during their stop in Codport, had been piled in front of his usual seat, along with two pieces of hard bread, salt meat, and five tankards of ale.

"There's no getting up till the ale's gone," Ben said.

"And the food?"

"Eating'll take some of the sting out of the ale. We don't want you too badly off when we give you to the sovereign."

Everyone laughed, including Tobias.

It was a late night.

CHAPTER 7

13th Day of Kheraya's Ascent, Year 647

They fell out of the Spanning gap onto a broad, cobblestone courtyard. Orzili blinked against the glare of high haze and midday sun, his skin abraded by the gap wind, his vision blurred and unsteady.

Still, he saw well enough to make out the soldiers surrounding them, muskets at shoulder level. Clutching his sextant, he raised both hands, indicated with a lift of his chin that the three men with him should do the same.

One of the soldiers, a stout, pock-faced woman with hair so pale it could have been white, shouted a command in Oaqamaran. Two more soldiers hurried toward them, lowering their bayonetted weapons to waist level.

"Let them take your weapons," Orzili said in the Ring tongue. "But hold on to your devices."

His men glanced at him, but said nothing. It was a precaution, in this instance a provocative one, but necessary. He had no intention of threatening the autarch; he wasn't stupid. So he had no compunction about giving up his weapons. The devices, though, were their only means of escape should his conversation with Pemin not go as planned. In the event, chances were they wouldn't get away at all, but with the sextants in hand, they'd have opportunity.

The two soldiers took a blade and a pistol from the first man, and then reached for his tri-sextant.

"No," his man said.

After a flurried exchange in Oaqamaran between the commander and her soldiers, the woman turned to Orzili.

"You are their leader, yes?"

"I am."

"Tell them to give up these objects, or they will be killed."

Orzili lowered his hands fractionally. "No. I just ordered them not to give them up. You can hold our weapons for as long as we meet with the autarch, but the devices are ours, and they pose no threat to His Excellency."

"You give them up, or you do not see him."

He'd had similar exchanges with the autarch's guards, though not with this commander in particular. He had asked Pemin to speak of the matter with the captain of his guard, but of course the autarch hadn't done so. Pemin liked to keep those who served him off balance, and he often seemed to foster suspicion and rivalry among his various generals and ministers, and, yes, his assassins as well.

"All right," Orzili said, eliciting a frown from the woman. "Then we'll leave. I'll need you to do me a favor though. His Excellency summoned me here, and he'll want to know why I wasn't allowed to see him. If you could explain, I'd be most grateful."

She watched him, perhaps to see how far he would follow his own ruse.

He nodded toward the Spanner closest to her. "If you could have your soldiers return his weapons, we'll be on our way."

She hesitated before nodding to her soldiers. Orzili's man took the offered weapons, holstered his pistol and sheathed his dagger.

"Gentlemen," Orzili said, "please set your sextants. We return to Aiyanth."

The three men around him made a fine show of recalibrating their devices and aiming them to the southeast.

"On my count," he said.

"No." The commander lowered her musket. "You stay."

He turned back to her, a question in his gaze.

"No weapons, but you can keep those..." She gestured at his sextant. "Those things."

"Thank you, commander." He flashed his most pleasant smile and slipped his sextant onto his belt. "You're most gracious."

He had his men turn over all of their weapons, including a hidden dirk the first man hadn't relinquished initially. This served to deepen the commander's displeasure. Moments later, however, he and his men, now disarmed, followed the commander and a small company of guards into an arching gateway at the end of the courtyard. They passed through a set of doors and climbed a wide, pink marble stairway to a round antechamber. The floor here was pink marble as well, the walls white, and covered with portraits and landscapes by some of Oaqamar's finest artists.

Whatever one might think of Pemin – and Orzili disliked the man nearly as much as he feared him – there could be no faulting his taste in art. Or, for that matter, in music, food, wine, or literature.

The twin doors to Pemin's chambers were inlaid with a myriad of woods, all in different shades and styled to resemble a barred lion, like those found in the Oaqamaran highlands. Its eyes were amber gems, and its extended claws were gold.

Two heralds, both armed with curving swords, stood guard beside the doors. While Orzili waited, one of them entered the chamber. He reappeared a tencount later and indicated that Orzili could enter. His men, as well as the commander and her soldiers, were to remain in the antechamber.

Orzili took a measured breath and stepped through the doorway, his hand straying to the empty sheath on his belt, which was hardly reassuring.

He had been in the chambers of kings, queens, and sovereigns, not to mention dukes and other minor nobles too numerous to recall. Over the years he had grown accustomed to royal extravagance in all its incarnations, subtle or crude. Pemin's chambers didn't lack for opulence, but the embellishments here, as in his antechamber, were elegant and restrained: a few fine paintings, tapestries in muted tones, furniture carved and finished with practical refinement.

These touches were, Orzili decided, much like the man himself.

Pemin had ruled Oaqamar for nearly thirty years, following in the footsteps of his father, who had been autarch for more than four decades, and who had lost two sons to war before siring Pemin with his third wife. In the nearly twenty years Orzili had served Pemin the autarch hadn't changed much. There was now more silver than brown in his hair, and the skin around his eyes and mouth was etched with thin lines. But he remained trim and tall, straight-backed and graceful, handsome and supremely confident. His eyes were cold, gray, watchful, and unrevealing. He wore dun breeches and a white shirt, his one concession to finery a gold and brown embroidered waistcoat that he kept unbuttoned. The entire effect was at once welcoming and intimidating. Only a man utterly at ease with himself and his authority could eschew so completely the trappings of power embraced with such ardor by lesser rulers.

He stood now by a desk – tidy without being fastidious – near the glazed windows, a scroll in his hand, spectacles perched on his nose. These were new, and as Pemin turned at the sound of Orzili's entry, he removed them, held them up with a self-effacing smile.

"A conceit to age. Do you wear them yet?"

Orzili bowed, straightened, and shook his head. "Not yet, your excellency. But I make it a point to read as little as possible lest I find them necessary."

Pemin's laughter was as warm and rich. He gestured to a pair of chairs set before a second bank of windows. Taking the nearer of the two, he watched Orzili lower himself into the other.

"You bear tidings," he said. "And not the ones I wish to hear."

"You know me too well, your excellency. You always have."

Pemin's features resolved into a frown. "The demon?"

"Our contact in Daerjen says they have heard nothing. The last missive they received from the chancellor in Windhome – by way of ship and pigeon – had the Walker departing for Hayncalde within a day. That message arrived a qua'turn ago. If the attack had succeeded, Mearlan would surely have received word by now."

"I'm sure you're right." Pemin offered a thin smile. "Indeed, I believe you predicted as much."

"That isn't–"

"Important? No probably not. Just the same, I'm grateful to you for not gloating."

As if he would have dared. The truth was, he had argued against sending the Belvora, but he had also understood Pemin's decision to ignore his counsel. An assassination would have been too transparent. Everyone in Islevale would have known the order came from Oaqamar. Such a blatant attack on Windhome itself might have further inflamed passions in the Ring Isles. For now, due to Daerjen's relative isolation, the wars in the Herjean and Aiyanthan Seas continued to go well. Any provocation might convince leaders in Kantaad, Rencyr, and even Liyrelle to join forces with Mearlan, threatening Oaqamar's advantage. That was why Pemin had built the Travelers' Academy in Sholiss some years back rather than simply taking the palace in Windhome.

"So, what do we do now?" the autarch asked a moment later.

"I'll do whatever you wish, your excellency, as always."

"Do we know when the lad will reach Mearlan's court?"

"They expect him any day."

"And you would have me send you and your assassins."

Orzili hesitated.

"It's all right, Quinnel. Speak your mind."

"Very well, your excellency. You pay us a good deal of gold for this very reason. You built the facility at Sholiss to provide the autarchy with the means to combat Windhome and its Travelers. Let us do what you brought us here to do."

Pemin's brow knitted. "Killing the Walker in Hayncalde is barely a step shy of killing him on Trevynisle. It could bring a response from within the Ring." He cast a glance at Orzili, tapping a finger against his lips. "Mearlan's navy barely has a pulse. I don't want to give him any hope. Not now, when we're so close."

"All the more reason to kill the Walker."

The autarch conceded the point with a twitch of his lips and the dip of his chin. "You trust your assassins to do this?"

"I trust myself."

"So you would go," Pemin said, a statement, but clearly one he wanted confirmed.

"For something so important? Of course."

"It would have to be done quickly."

"I expect word from Daerjen will be sent the moment his ship docks. We can be there that night."

"Fine," the autarch said, sounding less than pleased. "Make your arrangements. But I want plans in place in case this doesn't work. The woman is prepared to follow this lad back in time?"

The woman. "You mean my wife?" Orzili said, none too wisely.

Pemin stared, his expression icy. "I mean *my* Walker," he said, the words honed like steel.

Orzili looked away first. "Yes, your excellency, I believe she is."

"Make sure of it." His tone hadn't changed. "It might be better to do this in the past. The boy will be careful when Walking not to interact with too many people, and Mearlan will be cautious as well. A killing in another time would suit our purposes best."

Orzili bit back his first response. Angering the autarch once had been foolish. Doing so twice could be fatal.

"You disagree?"

I don't want her to lose any more time. "I would prefer to put my planning to the test," he said. "We have the tri-devices. We can find the boy, kill him, and be gone before anyone is the wiser. Perhaps blame will fall on someone within the castle."

Pemin's glare sharpened.

"Not our contact," Orzili continued. "A guard perhaps. They don't like Northislers in the Ring."

"Their queen is dark-skinned. You think they'll resent a court Walker more than they do her?"

"I think resentment of the queen might be expressed in many ways."

The autarch smirked. "Not your most compelling case, Orzili. You wish to spare your wife a lengthy Walk. I understand. I even sympathize."

He'd been too transparent – never wise in conversation with anyone as perceptive and shrewd as the autarch, especially when allowing personal considerations to twist his counsel. He expected a "but" to follow what Pemin had said, but the man surprised him.

"Very well. Take your assassins. But be clear: I want the boy dead within a day of his arrival in Hayncalde. Later than that and we might as well send her back now. I understand your concerns, but if this attempt fails I want her ready to follow the boy into the past, wherever – and whenever – Mearlan sends him. Even if that means going with you and your men to Daerjen when you make your attempt."

Brilliant though he was, Pemin had limited understanding of the rudiments of Walking and Spanning. Again, though, pointing out his lack of knowledge would have been a grave mistake.

"I don't believe that will be necessary," was all Orzili said.

Even that turned out to be too much.

"And I don't care what you think," Pemin fired back, voice rising. "If it means she catches up with the boy sooner, if it gives him less of a chance to do what Mearlan is sending him to do, then she will go with you. Are we clear?"

"Yes, your excellency."

Pemin glared a moment longer before his expression eased.

"Do they know of your tri-devices?"

"Does who know, your excellency?"

Pemin waved a hand vaguely toward the window. "Mearlan and his people? The Travelers in Windhome?"

"I don't believe Mearlan knows, though our contact in his court might. I think it likely that some in Trevynisle know, but I can't say how widely that knowledge is shared, or how detailed their understanding might be."

"Are you prepared for that to change?"

It might have been a more complicated question than Pemin knew. The development of the tri-devices had been fraught with mistakes and dead ends. They should have been known to the wider world years before now, and Orzili was impatient to show all of Islevale what he and the others in Sholiss had accomplished.

Yet he also knew that the moment other Travelers and Binders learned of the devices, and recognized the truth of their relative simplicity, they would race to replicate them. The initial invention had consumed more than a decade. The spread of tri-sextants and tri-apertures to every isle between the oceans would take a fraction of that time. Such was the nature of advances like these.

"I am, your excellency," he said, answering Pemin's question. "I suppose the real question is, are you? They were developed at your expense, by those in your employ. Once others know of them, they'll build their own, and your exclusive access to them will be gone."

The smile that curved the autarch's lips could have rimed a window in mid-summer. "If you and your assassins do what I ask of you, in the manner I demand, it won't matter what those others do. A year from now Oaqamar will be the preeminent power in Islevale, and all the tri-devices in the world won't make a bit of difference."

Orzili and his men Spanned back to the open pasture outside Aiyanth's royal city, whence they had initiated their journey to Oaqamar. He collected their tri-sextants and concealed them within a sack he'd left in a corner of the field, and the four of them returned to Belsan.

As they neared the central gate, the road grew more crowded with farmers, day-laborers, and peddler's carts.

"Time to separate, lads," he said, his voice low. "Beginning tonight, we gather at the Whistle by sundown each evening. Don't expect to leave before midnight bell. We might only get one chance at this, and I don't want to go back to Qaifin with word that we missed our opportunity because one of you was out whoring."

He flashed a smile to soften the words, drawing grins from his men. But they knew he spoke in earnest, just as he knew they would be at the tavern as ordered. He'd chosen this small company with care.

They walked on, but strung themselves along the column of traders and workers streaming toward the city. Within a spirecount, no one would have guessed that they knew each other. By the time Orzili passed through the gate and into the city, he had lost track of the others.

He wound through the crooked lanes west of the castle, to the flat he and Lenna had leased for the past year. It was empty when he arrived. Lenna would have been at the market, or perhaps at the waterfront. Their true occupations, and the autarch's insistence that his Traveling assassins remain a mystery to the rest of Islevale, required that they have secondary talents. He had some skill as a binder of books, and she kept bees in a field near the one to which he had spanned a short while ago. She sold her honey to several of the brewers here in Belsan, a city renowned for its fine mead. No one who knew them, not even those who lived in the apartments directly above and below, would have guessed that they made most of their coin as assassins.

He'd barely had time to stow the sack holding the tri-sextants when the door to the flat opened and closed again.

Lenna set a jar of honey on the table in the common room, her cheeks flushed to a warm russet. Strands of silver blended with the bronze of her windblown hair, and lines crinkled the corners of her eyes, but she remained as lovely as he remembered from their tumultuous days in Windhome so long ago.

"I saw you come through the gate," she said, music in the voice.

She was his love, his desire, and, as he'd been reminded more than once during this day's encounter with the autarch, his greatest weakness, the one element of his life that could unman him at any moment.

"It went well with Pemin?"

"Well enough," he said, trying to keep his tone light. And failing. Of course. No one knew him as she did.

"Which is to say, not well at all."

"It wasn't that bad. He wants it done quickly, as soon as the lad reaches Hayncalde, which could be any night. And he's willing to risk having us seen with the tri-sextants."

"Well, we knew that would happen eventually. Surely that's not..." She trailed off, the sadness of her smile reaching her dark, liquid eyes. "It's me, isn't it?"

Isn't it always?

"He wants me to Walk?" she went on.

"Perhaps. If we fail."

She quirked an eyebrow, sauntered closer to him, and draped her arms around his neck. She smelled of grass and honey and sunlight.

"Do you intend to fail?"

"You know I don't."

She kissed him, her lips soft and cool. "Then why do you look like a boy who's lost his favorite toy?"

"He wants you to come with us when we Span to Daerjen, so that if we can't kill the lad, you'll be ready to follow him back in time."

Lenna shrugged. "He's not a Traveler, and he's always been impatient. Truth is, I wouldn't necessarily need to find you in the past. I can kill the boy myself. It might not be a bad idea to take me along."

"This is no festival we're going to," he said, voice dropping. "And Hayncalde's soldiers won't exactly welcome us with open arms. Now or in the past."

The angles of her face hardened, though this made her no less beautiful. "You doubt my abilities?"

"Of course not. But–"

"But you'd be happier if I kept to my bees and never put myself at risk."

That coaxed a smile, despite his fears, his lingering anger at the autarch. "That would be preferable."

"Not for me. I'd get dreadfully bored, and while you were off plying your trade, I'd probably need to find another man. Or two."

He laughed, and she kissed him again.

"This is what we do," she said. "And if I didn't, I *would* get bored. You know I would."

He sighed. "Yes."

"You're meeting your men tonight then?"

"At the tavern. Sundown. Every night until word comes from Mearlan's court."

"Which means we'll be busy all night, every night." She stepped past him, toward the alcove that held their bed. As she walked, hips swaying, she began to unlace her bodice. "Come along then." She glanced back, smiling once more. "And bring the honey."

Later, as they lay together in a tangle of bedding and limbs, the golden glow of late day angling through the open window, he told her what he'd said to Pemin, his foolhardy challenge to the autarch's authority over her.

She laughed, but concern shadowed her gaze. "You can't speak to him that way. Not even about me."

"I know that. But you should know by now that I can hardly help myself. Love turns all men into idiots."

"I've noticed."

"What can I say? As we get older, you and I, I grow ever more jealous of our time together. I don't want Pemin spending even a bell of it."

She touched her lips to his brow. "Foolish man. I'm a Walker. This is what I'm meant to do. And really, even if he is the most powerful man in Islevale, how much of my time do you think he can take?"

CHAPTER 8

16th Day of Kheraya's Ascent, Year 647

The gentle roll of the ship on sweeps, to which he'd grown accustomed over the course of the journey, didn't seem quite so gentle this final morning. Sunlight angling through the hatch onto the steps above Tobias's pallet stabbed into his eyes like needles. Every footstep on the deck above echoed in his head like a war hammer. He levered himself into a sitting position, his movements deliberate, and still the motion proved too much. His head spun, and a queasy tremor roiled his stomach.

He had enjoyed the ales and the warm, giddy feeling that came with them. Only now did he understand what the priest in the palace temple meant when he railed against the evils of drink.

"Time to rouse yourself, lad!" someone shouted from above at ear-splitting volume. Several of the crew stomped their feet on the deck, rattling his brain.

The laughter that followed served to further darken his mood.

He stood, swayed, was nearly sick. Steeling himself, he stepped around to the stairway and dragged himself onto the deck. The crew greeted his emergence with applause, whistles, shouted gibes – "You look half-dead!" "Dead? Nonsense, he's a healthy shade of green!" "That side of the ship, sonny. A true sailor vomits to larboard!"

"Enough!" The captain's voice. "He goes before the sovereign of Daerjen today. Give him some peace."

A couple of the sailors patted his shoulder as they hurried back to work. A few offered encouraging words. Despite his current state he knew the teasing had been meant kindly.

"How badly off are you?" the captain asked, coming forward from the quarterdeck.

Tobias assayed a small smile, but wasn't sure he managed more than a grimace. "I'll be all right."

"I know that. I've seen hangovers worse than this. But I'd prefer the sovereign didn't tell your chancellor that I corrupted his new Walker. You do remember me telling you that we would arrive in Hayncalde today."

He could hardly have forgotten. "Yes."

"Well, that's something, at least." She narrowed her gaze. "You know, you didn't have to drink it all."

"No?" Tobias said. "Would you have stopped, with all of them watching?"

"I'm their captain."

"Even if you weren't, you would have done what I did."

She offered a shrug that conceded little, her eyes wandering over the shoreline. "Perhaps." She pointed to something behind him. "There's Hayncalde."

Tobias whirled, nearly overbalanced. At the end of the gulf, nestled against a cove on the western coast, stood a wall of gray stone. Behind it, strewn over the gentle slope of the inlet, buildings large and small – some made of wood, others of white stone – lay together in a jumble, their red and gray rooftops creating a haphazard tableau. A large structure at the northeast corner of the city dominated the view, its towers and battlements made of that same white stone. The castle loomed over the coastline and the broad delta of a slow river. Above its ramparts, banners of red and white rose and fell in the warm breeze.

"The sovereign lives there?" Tobias asked.

"Yes. Hayncalde Castle. And that," the captain said, indicating a gray stone structure with soaring narrow steeples that stood near the center of the city, "is the Temple of Sipar."

He stared. Outside of Trevynisle, the temples were more apt to split, some worshipping Kheraya, the goddess, and others Sipar, her mate. Tobias and the rest of the novitiates had been drilled in the divisions. He had known since speaking with the chancellor that he would be living in a Siparite city.

You're not a novitiate anymore.

He heard the words in Mara's voice, and gave a small shudder, fear and excitement warring for supremacy in his thoughts.

"We'll dock before the next bell," the captain said. She started back to the quarterdeck. "Ready your things. I expect the sovereign will have someone at the wharf to greet us."

Tobias hurried into the hold to retrieve his sack. At the sight of Hayncalde, his headache had subsided to a dull throb, and the queasiness in his gut had diminished. He soon climbed back up to the deck and took his usual spot by the rail, his sack at his feet.

The crew oared a powerful rhythm through the calm waters, propelling the *Skate* toward the middle of three wharves that jutted into the gulf. All three docks teemed with sailors and wharf workers. Several ships were moored to each wharf and dozens more bobbed on the waters beyond the pier, awaiting their turn to dock. Tobias had never seen a busier port.

A ship on sweeps maneuvered away from the middle wharf, creating space for another ship. None of the others moved to take its place, allowing the *Skate* to make its approach.

They're doing this for you. They're letting the ship dock so that you can join the sovereign in that grand castle.

It was as alien a thought as he'd ever entertained, yet he knew it was true. His life had changed – was in the process of changing – in ways that thrilled and terrified him.

Before long, the crew had guided the *Skate* to the wharf. Two sailors jumped from the deck to the dock and tied the mooring lines to blackened metal bollards. Two others lowered the gangplank to the wharf.

Once the plank was in place, a young man in livery of white and red stepped away from a crowd of onlookers and positioned himself at its base.

Also for you.

Tobias glanced the captain's way, but she was deep in conversation with her second mate. He searched the deck for Evan, or Ben, or Trem, or any of the others who had befriended him, but everyone was occupied with one task or another. He tried to catch the captain's eye, and succeeded at last. She acknowledged him with a curt nod and a perfunctory smile, but otherwise didn't interrupt her discussion.

He couldn't say what he had expected, but this final exchange disappointed him. He knew he was being foolish, immature. He had been on the *Skate* for a bit more than a ha'turn, and would probably never set foot on her decks again. He had refused the captain's offer of employment. Why should she care about him one way or another?

He shouldered his sack, hopped onto the gangplank and walked down to the dock. His pulse raced, and he had to resist the urge to wipe his damp palms on the legs of his breeches.

The uniformed man watched him, grave and attentive.

After all his years on Trevynisle, and so many days aboard the *Skate* with men and women browned by the sun and wind, Tobias thought the man's skin unnaturally pale. His light blue eyes and straw-colored hair gave him a ghostlike appearance. Most of those on the wharf looked much the same. Tobias saw no one as dark as he was. Even having anticipated this, it made him self-conscious.

"You're the Traveler?" the man asked, as Tobias stepped off the plank.

Tobias smiled at the dual meaning of the question. "Yes. Tobias Doljan, of Trevynisle."

"Welcome. I'm Palry Farniss." He spoke with a lilt that put Tobias in mind of Wansi. A pang of homesickness slid like a dagger through his ribs. "I'm the sovereign's sub-minister of protocol."

The title sounded impressive and it made Tobias wonder how many ministers and sub-ministers the sovereign employed. "It's a pleasure to meet you," he said. He swung the sack off his shoulder and dug through it for the rolled parchment bearing the chancellor's seal. "I have a letter of introduction…"

"I believe that's meant for the sovereign."

Tobias straightened, his cheeks coloring. "Oh. Yes, forgive me."

"Do you have other possessions?"

"No, just this."

"Very good." The man gestured toward the city. "Shall we?"

He strode away from the ship and Tobias followed. Two soldiers, tall and brawny, fell in step on either side of them, seeming to materialize from nowhere. Their uniforms resembled Palry's in color, but were less ornate. Both men carried swords, daggers, and muskets. The people on the wharf gave all of them a wide berth.

At the mouth of a cobbled road leading from the end of the wharf to the city, stood a white and red carriage harnessed to two large dun horses. Another man, also dressed in Daerjeni colors, sat atop the carriage box, reins in hand.

Palry opened the door and waved Tobias inside.

Tobias took a seat facing forward and was joined by the minister. The soldiers sat opposite them, the breadth of their shoulders making the generous seat look cramped. One of the men reached out through the open window and rapped twice on the roof. With a shout and the snap of leather, the carriage lurched forward.

The cobbled lane wound toward the massive city wall, which stood as tall as the keeps of Windhome Palace and was thick enough to accommodate the dozens of armed guards who walked its ramparts. The road itself was choked with men and women making their way to and from the wharf. Some carried wares from ships; many led crude wagons, drawn by horses or asses and loaded high with foodstuffs, or bolts of cloth, or wooden cases containing bottles of wine.

The carriage rumbled through an arched gate that was deep enough to shelter the carriage from the horses' snouts to the rear of the coach. As the rattle of the carriage wheels echoed to a roar, Tobias eyed the walls and arch of the gate, noting the two oak and iron portcullises and the murder holes built into the stone.

Emerging from the gate into the city proper, Tobias was afforded a better view of the houses and businesses he had glimpsed from the ship. So close to the outer walls, the buildings were constructed of wood, gray and weatherworn. Most stood at angles, their roofs sagging, their walls leaning together like rows of drunkards supporting each other to remain upright.

The scent of brine and fish, so strong near the wharves, was overwhelmed here by the stink of urine, excrement, and rotting food. Rank water filled the spaces between cobblestones and flies swarmed around fresh piles of horse dung.

Several lanes – many cobbled, a few no more than dirt tracks – spread like tree roots from the main road, snaking into shadowed neighborhoods where a few lone figures walked. The minister's carriage, though, angled northward, climbing to the castle. Wood gave way to white stone, strained walls and tired lines gave way to clean angles and tiled rooftops, silks and refined wools replaced rags and tatters. The fetor of the lower lanes receded.

Still they climbed, steadily closing the distance between their coach and the lofty white towers of the sovereign's palace. Ravens circled the turrets, black as pitch against the azure sky, their rough calls nearly lost in the noise of the carriage wheels.

The lane rounded one last curve and straightened, revealing a second stone wall around the palace, this one nearly as thick and high as the city battlement. Soldiers patrolled these ramparts as well. The portcullis of the gate ahead of them was down.

The coach slowed, then halted. The portcullis rose with the clatter and growl of iron gears.

Once the barrier was up, the carriage started forward again, rolling through the palace gate and emerging into an open ward of grass and stone, a defensive perimeter. The carriage followed a narrow path to an inner gate, as well-fortified as the first. This one spilled onto a courtyard the size of those in Windhome Palace, and yet nothing like them. Tobias stared out at the ward, hardly daring to breathe.

White stone, as bright in the sunshine as fresh snow, surrounded the coach. At the center of a round plaza defined by rainbow tiles laid out in concentric circles, a fountain danced and gurgled. Gardens framed the plaza, the petals of their flowers a match for the tiles, and beyond these plots, rows of stone arches marked a walkway that encircled the entire courtyard. Tobias had never seen any place more beautiful.

The carriage halted beside yet another arched gate in the gleaming stone, framed by a mosaic of blue, gold, and red tile. The minister pushed open the carriage door and stepped out into the plaza.

Tobias grabbed his sack and followed.

"This is Trygar's Ward, named for–"

"The leader of the Hayncalde Reassertion," Tobias said. "We studied him. And his son."

"Very good. The sovereign will be pleased to know you have some knowledge of our history. Shall we take you to him?"

Tobias's heart thudded against his ribs. "Now? Can't I have a little time? At least to change my clothes?"

"I'm afraid his instructions were quite clear in this regard. I'm to present you to him without delay."

I'm not ready!

He didn't say this. If he couldn't so much as meet the man, how was he to serve him, and justify all the gold the sovereignty had already spent on his behalf?

He straightened, hoping his posture would convey confidence. "Well then, we shouldn't keep him waiting."

They entered the keep through the archway, and climbed a winding stairway of black marble to the third and highest level. Palry led Tobias out of the stairway and down a lengthy, arcing corridor. An array of artwork hung on the gilded walls – portraits, landscapes, still lifes – and white marble busts of men and women rested on occasional wooden plinths. Slotted windows, clearly intended for archers, allowed in some light, and candles burned in sconces.

Tobias walked by the paintings and sculptures, resisting the urge to stop and admire them all.

They halted before a ponderous door at the end of the corridor. Palry knocked and at a summons from within opened the door and gestured Tobias inside. Tobias entered. Only when he heard the door close did he realize the minister hadn't followed.

The sovereign's chamber was twice the size of Chancellor Shaan's quarters back on Trevynisle. Sunlight streamed into the room through a bank of glazed windows, brightening the white walls, which were mostly bare, save for a few portraits behind the sovereign's desk. A round rug depicting a vast battle scene covered most of the marble floor, its threads vivid and colorful enough to bring the violent tableau to life with disturbing clarity. As in the chancellor's study back in Windhome, a cage crowded with messenger pigeons rested on a shelf by the windows.

A man Tobias assumed must be the sovereign stood beyond the desk, his form framed against the daylight, his back to the door, his hands clasped behind him. He was of medium height and build, his hair light and closely shorn.

He didn't turn at the sound of the door's close, nor did he speak.

Tobias waited, still and silent, wondering if he ought to clear his throat and let the man know he was there. He drew breath to speak, then stopped himself, fearing he might give offense.

Finally, he said, "Good day, sovereign. I am–"

"Tobias Doljan, Walker. Fifteen years of age, though only just. Yes, I know."

"Y– Yes. I have my–"

"You may place your letter of introduction on the desk. Beside the chronofor waiting for you there."

Tobias all but leapt to the desk, his gaze alighting on the chronofor. He reached for it, but stopped himself, remembering his letter. He swung the sack off his shoulder and pulled out the chancellor's missive, which he set beside the device. His hand trembling, he then picked up the chronofor by its shining chain.

Like all bound devices, its casing and hands were forged of gold. It resembled a gentleman's chainwatch. It was round, and fit neatly in the palm of his hand. As soon as Tobias touched it, he sensed its power. It would work for any Walker, but this one was his, the first he'd ever called his own. Did he simply imagine that its power twined itself with his, or was that connection real, something other Walkers experienced upon being presented with their chronofors?

The lustrous face of the device was divided into three equal, graduated circles, each with a sweep hand, for bells, days, and turns. Each dial had a corresponding stem, which allowed the user to set the hands to the desired target time. A fourth stem, larger than the others, jutted from the top of the chronofor. This activated the device once the target time had been entered.

Wansi had promised Tobias that Haplar Jarrett, the sovereign's Binder, would build him a fine chronofor, and Master Jarrett didn't disappoint. The workmanship on this device was as fine as that on any of Wansi's chronofors. The golden face had been buffed to a mirrored shine, and a stylized eagle, sigil of Hayncalde, had been carved into the gold on the reverse.

"Thank you, sovereign," Tobias said in a whisper. "I'm–"

"You will set the chronofor for twelve days and two bells ago. I think that ought to do it."

Tobias gawked. "You want me to Walk now?"

The sovereign shifted fractionally, enough to reveal a straight nose and rounded cheeks. "Is that a problem?"

"Well, I–"

"You were sent here to Walk at my bidding. I am asking you to Walk now. If you can't do this, I may need to rethink my arrangement with your chancellor."

"No, I can... I just wasn't... I'll do it right now, sovereign."

"You'll address me as my liege, or Lord Sovereign."

"Yes, my liege."

Twelve days! In all his training, he had never gone back more than a day or two. Every journey – to the past and back to the present – cost a Walker the amount of time he Traveled. And so the palace masters hadn't taxed him too heavily in his training. The cost of too many practice Walks would have been considerable.

He knew his trade, though. He knew what to do, and how

to do it. Still he was afraid. *Twelve days*. He stripped off his clothing – aside from the chronofor, he could take nothing back with him. Any other object, even something as small as a ring on his finger, would keep the chronofor from working.

Once he was naked, he picked up the device again. His hands still shook, and a trickle of sweat tickled his temple. He pulled out the middle stem and set it back twelve clicks. Using the left stem, he added two more bells. He took a deep breath, and pressed the top stem.

The instant he heard the stem catch he felt himself pulled backward and up, as if some great hook had pierced his heart from behind. The light changed, became inconstant, uncertain. Sounds pounded at him – a din of voices, a cacophony of music, an incomprehensible roar of ocean breakers, birdsong, clashing weapons, wheels on stone, and so many other noises he couldn't separate amid the clamor. His skin prickled with sensations subtle and gross. A melange of smells assaulted his nostrils; he gagged on a hash of a thousand flavors. He hurtled through a riot of sensory experience, guided always by that invisible, uncompromising barb.

When he had Walked under Wansi's supervision – in a distant corner of his mind it occurred to him that "Walked" was too benign a term for this abrupt, violent experience – the tumult lasted but a few heartbeats. This time, with his target a dozen days away, the time between dragged on much longer. In his fear and discomfort, he tried to draw breath – a novice's mistake. Despite all he perceived, there was no air here. As the between stretched on, panic took him. He gulped for breath again. Nothing. He couldn't even fill his lungs to scream.

As abruptly as it had begun, his journey back ended. He staggered, braced himself against the sovereign's desk, breathed in blessed air. His pulse raced, and his vision swam, but otherwise he had come through the journey unscathed.

The sovereign sat at the desk, startled amusement on a face that was not nearly as fearsome as Tobias had anticipated. He was clean-shaven, with bright blue eyes and a dimpled chin. Tobias had thought the sovereign of one of Islevale's great powers should be imposing or dashing or at least unusual in appearance. This sovereign was none of those. He might have been a peddler or a farmer or a common soldier.

"You're the Walker, I presume."

"Yes, my liege."

"Your name?"

"Tobias Doljan, my liege."

"Very well. There are clothes on that chair." He indicated a chair against a near wall. "Dress yourself and we'll speak." The sovereign's voice followed him to the piled clothes. "I'm afraid they might not be a good fit. I didn't know what age Walker your chancellor would send, or even what gender."

"I'm sure they'll be fine, my liege."

"Do you prefer to be called by your name or by your title?"

I have a title! "I'll answer to whatever you decide is most appropriate, my liege."

"Very well."

The white silk shirt fit well enough, but the breeches, made of brown flax, were too short in the legs and too wide in the waist. Tobias managed to cinch the belt tight enough to keep them up. He hoped he wouldn't have to wear them for long.

Once dressed, he crossed back to the desk and stood before the sovereign, his hands at his side. "I have a letter of introduction, but it's back in the time from which I Walked."

"And when was that?" the sovereign asked. "How long from now will you arrive?"

"Twelve days, my liege."

A frown flickered in the plain features. "More time than I would have liked. I sent payment more than a full turn ago. My original thought was to have you Walk back to that day. I think I'm glad I didn't. Your arrival in this time was... rough?"

Tobias hesitated.

"No harm can come of a frank answer. You're here now; there's nothing for it. I'm not going to toss you over for another Walker, like you're a hat that doesn't fit right." His smile and boyish shrug put Tobias at ease. Perhaps there was more to being sovereign than looking the part.

"It was worse than I thought it would be," Tobias said. "We train with journeys of a few bells, at the most a day or two, and the between is short, almost nothing. But this was... It took a long time."

The sovereign didn't answer right away, and when he did, it was with a question. "How old are you, Tobias?"

"I've just turned fifteen, my liege."

Mearlan exhaled, stared off to the side. "I thought they would send someone older," he whispered.

"I don't know what the chancellor's letter says, but I excelled in all my studies. I might be young for a court Walker, but I was no less advanced a student of history, theology, mathematics, the arts, philosophy, diplomacy, or the natural sciences than any of the other novitiates. And I was as good with a blade or a firearm as any of my cohort."

"I have no doubt as to your competence, Walker. Still, I must ask: were there no disciplines that gave you trouble? None at all?"

Tobias blushed, thinking of what the chancellor had said during their final encounter. *You're brash. Royals don't like that, especially in green travelers...*

"I sometimes struggle with mathematics and the sciences."

"My demon was philosophy." The sovereign indicated a nearby chair. "Please sit. I found all the old philosophers to be an utter bore," he went on, as Tobias lowered himself into the seat. "And I was more than convinced that they were full of ox dung."

Tobias laughed.

"I didn't mean to suggest that I was questioning your credentials. Chancellor Shaan wouldn't have sent anyone he didn't believe was up to the task. I merely..." He shook his head. "You're young. There's no other way to say it."

"Yes, my liege. And I intend to serve you and your house – if you'll have me – for many years to come."

"That's well said, Walker. But I'm afraid we don't have that kind of time."

CHAPTER 9

4th Day of Kheraya's Ascent, Year 647

A cold, unsettling frisson ran through Tobias's body.

"I don't understand," he said. "We don't have time for what?"

"That's a difficult question to answer." The sovereign raised a hand, forestalling Tobias's reply. "I'll do my best, but I have more questions first. The truth is, I've had Travelers in my court for some time. I have a Spanner and a Crosser. But you're my first Walker; I want to be sure I grasp fully the implications of your power."

Tobias acquiesced with a stiff nod.

"You said you traveled back in time twelve days to get here. Am I right in assuming this means you're now twelve days older than you were when you arrived in Hayncalde?"

"Yes, my liege."

"And when you return to your correct time, you'll have aged yet another twelve days." He offered this as a statement.

"That's right."

The sovereign blew out another breath. "As I suspected."

"Why did you send me back here, my liege? Couldn't we have had this conversation the day I arrived?"

"We could have. I was testing you. As I say, I've never had a Walker before, and I wanted to see how it works, what the... the journey does to you."

"May I speak candidly, my liege?"

"Please."

"That shouldn't be your concern. I was sent here to serve Hayncalde as a Walker. I understand the nature of my power, and the costs of it. I was trained for this. For as long as I can remember, I've wanted to serve in a great court. Now I have that opportunity. You should simply use me, and my talent, as you see fit."

The sovereign's smile couldn't mask the concern in his eyes. "Would that it were so easy." He walked to the window at which he'd been standing when Tobias first saw him, twelve days hence. "You know that we're at war."

"Yes, my liege."

"On two fronts, actually. With the Aiyanthans, we're fighting the Oaqamarans in the Aiyanthan Sea. And we're also fighting privateers in the waters around Westisle. Two wars at once. That's my fault. It takes a certain amount of hubris to undertake such a thing, but arrogance was ever the sin of my forebears, and it seems I'm not immune."

"How go the wars, my liege?"

The sovereign cast a long look his way. "That's the question, isn't it? No one would find fault with fighting two wars if we were winning them both."

"I take it we're not."

Mearlan's brow smoothed. "'We.' Already you consider yourself one of us?"

"I didn't mean to presume–"

"You didn't. I'm grateful to you. To answer your question, no, we're not. The privateers… They're canny and elusive, but we can afford to be patient. They're a threat to commerce, but not to the stability of the isles. The Oaqamarans are the greater danger by far, and that war has not been going well. I'm waiting for a report from my admiral in the waters off Aiyanth, but I don't expect good news."

Tobias kept his silence, but he thought of his initial

encounter with the sovereign: the man's terse instructions, his refusal even to look Tobias's way. Had he received bad news from the Aiyanthan Sea?

"I'm still confused, my liege. You wanted to test me. Why? What is it you want me to do?"

"I can't answer that. Not yet, at least."

"But you have an idea. Obviously testing me in this way wasn't something you did without forethought. You were awaiting my arrival; you had clothes for me." He paused, thinking the matter through. "You want me to go back farther, don't you?"

"I honestly don't know yet."

The journey back to this time had been harrowing. Going back several turns or more would be even worse. Nevertheless, if that's what the sovereign asked him to do, he'd do it.

"I will, if you require it. That's why I'm here."

"And I'm glad you are. Now, though, I think it's probably best if you make your way back to the time in which you belong."

Tobias faltered. He liked this version of the sovereign better than he did the glum man who greeted him the day he arrived in Hayncalde.

"Is something wrong?"

"No, my liege. I'll... I'll set the device and be on my way."

He set the chronofor ahead twelve clicks and two, and pulled off the clothes he had been wearing. The sovereign continued to gaze out the window, granting Tobias a modicum of privacy.

He inhaled deeply, filling his lungs, and then depressed the top stem. The hook grabbed him again, this time pulling him forward into the maelstrom of light and color, noise and smell, flavor and feeling. He resisted the urge to draw breath, but in every other way this Walk proved as much a trial as the previous one.

He stumbled out of the between, once again catching

himself on the desk, which shifted under his weight with a scrape of wood on marble.

"Welcome back," the sovereign said, standing much as he had when Tobias first arrived.

He murmured a thank you and dressed with haste.

His letter of introduction still sat on the desk, unopened. Tobias wondered how much time had elapsed between his departure and this second arrival.

"Was the journey any easier this time?" The sovereign faced him at last. A mere twelve days had gone by, but clearly they hadn't been kind to the man. Dark rings lurked under his eyes and his skin had a pasty quality.

"Not much, no," Tobias said. "You've had bad news from the north?"

His smile was thin, mirthless. "You're observant. I like that. Yes, the war goes poorly."

"I passed your test. I can go back in time and return. That's what you wanted to know, isn't it?"

"It's one of many things. Forgive me for the abruptness of your welcome. These are difficult days, and I sense my options dwindling. I have less time for social niceties than I'd like."

"I think I understand."

"You're kind. We'll have a chance to speak of this at greater length tomorrow. I… I haven't made any final decisions. For today, as you say, you've passed this test. I have another one for you, of a different sort. I'd like you to dine with my family and me this evening. A few of my ministers will be there as well, and so will my Spanner. All of them are eager to meet you."

"I'd be honored, my liege."

"Good." Mearlan scooped up a silver bell from his desk and gave it a single, hard shake. It chimed once, and while that ring still faded, the door to the chamber opened, revealing a young page. "Take Walker Doljan to his quarters. See to it that he's comfortable and has everything he needs. If he requires anything you can't provide, talk to the steward."

The page bowed and with a quick look Tobias's way, stepped back into the corridor.

"Until later, then," the sovereign said.

"Yes, my liege."

He left the chamber and followed the page, who led him down the same stairway he'd ascended earlier, and across the round courtyard to a second, deeper within the palace. This one was square and contained neither a fountain nor gardens, though with its white stone archways and carved masonry, it held a subtle beauty as well.

The page said nothing as they walked, and Tobias, preoccupied as he was with his encounter with the sovereign, made no effort to start a conversation. Just how far back did Mearlan want him to go? And to what end?

Sovereigns and monarchs were said to use their Walkers much as Captain Larr had proposed to use him: to correct past errors in judgment, to change poor decisions or take advantage of squandered opportunities. Through Tobias, Mearlan might send a message to himself a turn ago, or more. Although not much more. With a twist of grief in his heart, Tobias remembered Vaisan Ojeyd telling him that any journey longer than three turns could be dangerous. Having endured the between of a twelve day Walk, he understood.

He knew as well that an ancient decree from Windhome barred royals from sending their Walkers back more than a year. Any sovereign who demanded such a journey of his or her Walker abrogated the contract binding Walker to court, and risked sanctions from Trevynisle. A century ago, an Oaqamaran autarch sent his Walker back nearly three years. The chancellor at that time learned of the transgression – in a message from the Walker – and proclaimed that Oaqamar would receive no Travelers of any sort for five years.

That same year, Oaqamar severed its ties to the palace in Windhome and built its own training facility for Travelers. The autarch also had the Walker executed for what he saw as the woman's betrayal. The isle hadn't summoned a Windhome Traveler since.

Mearlan could only send him back so far. Tobias should have taken comfort in this, but he didn't. Something in the sovereign's manner told him that Daerjen's need was great and that whatever Mearlan required of him would tax him to the limits of his abilities and the bounds of what his contract allowed.

He followed the page into another tower, climbed to the second story and followed a corridor to a plain oaken door. The page unlatched the door, pushed it open, and stepped aside so that Tobias could enter.

Tobias faltered. He hadn't paid attention as they walked. He wasn't at all certain he could find the chamber on his own. That, he decided, was a problem for later. He stepped past the lad, and surveyed his new quarters.

Light from a single, glazed window illuminated a chamber both smaller and more sparsely furnished than those of the masters he had known back in Windhome. Yet, here was more private space than he'd ever called his own.

A simple pallet, with a pillow and woolen blanket, stretched nearly from the far corner to the front wall. A stand bearing a wash-basin stood near the head of the bed. A desk and plain wooden chair were set against the opposite wall, which was unadorned, and a wardrobe loomed beyond them, opposite the bed. Already clothes hung there – formal robes from the look of them. Several, all identical. He assumed they were of different sizes.

"Is there anything you need, m'lord?" the page asked.

Tobias nearly corrected him. Never before had he been addressed so. But likely the lad knew the ways of this court better than he. "No, thank you."

The boy bowed and left him. Tobias placed his sack on the pallet and stepped to the window, which offered a striking view of the city, the river, and the waters of the gulf. He wondered if the *Skate* had already left the wharf for open sea. He crossed to the wash-basin and removed his shirt. A knock at the door stopped him. Before he could put the shirt back on, or tell whoever had come to enter, the door opened and a man bustled in.

"Ah, good. You knew I was on my way." He was bald, short, rotund. He spoke with a deep voice and didn't hesitate to enter the chamber and stride to Tobias's wardrobe. Two young women, both yellow-haired, hovered near the door.

"Um… No, I… Who are you?"

"I'm Lars," the man said, looking through the robes, "the sovereign's head seamster. He's directed me to see to it you have suitable clothing for tonight's banquet." He pulled out one robe and handed it to Tobias. "I believe this is the best fit. Try it on."

Tobias took the robe, but didn't put it on. "Banquet? The sovereign said I'd be supping with his family. He didn't mention a banquet."

The seamster snatched the robe back and held it up, clearly intending for Tobias to put it on. Tobias turned and slipped his arms into the sleeves.

"Anytime the sovereign sups, it's a banquet. That's how royals are. One of many lessons you'll learn in coming days." Lars grasped Tobias by the shoulders, spun him, and buttoned the robe. He stepped back, and appraised him with a critical eye. "Yes, I think that will do."

"But I'm to wear it with a shirt, right?"

Lars stared at him, impassive. "I really haven't the patience for poor humor."

"I wasn't trying to be funny."

"I suppose that's reassuring. Yes, you'll need a new blouse, not to mention breeches, hose, and shoes. Thank goodness we're in Her Waking. If this were one of the colder turns, I'd need to find you a cape, scarf, and gloves as well. As it is, we've only a few bells." He unbuttoned the robe again, pulled a chalk from behind his ear and made a few quick marks and notations on the waistline and cuffs of Tobias's breeches.

He beckoned to the women with a flutter of his fingers. "Take the shirt and breeches and shoes. We'll get him fitted–"

"No!" Tobias said, clutching the top of his breeches. "I mean, at least let me put the robe back on!"

Lars rolled his eyes. "Gods give me patience to endure the foolishness of children."

Tobias straightened, stung by this. One of the young women laughed. The other covered her amusement with a slender hand.

"Yes," the seamster said, voice dripping with irony, "by all means; cover yourself with the robe. These poor virgins have never before seen the male form in all its naked glory."

He resented being mocked, but still he took back the robe, unable to bring himself to remove his breeches without first covering up. When he had undressed, he handed the breeches to Lars, who passed them to the nearer of the two women.

"Do you have anything to wear in the meanwhile?"

"No," Tobias said, still sulking.

"Then you'd best remain here until we return." He crossed back to the door. "Next time, I'll have the ladies wear blinders."

They left, and Tobias could do little more than sit in his room and stare out the window. After a time, he stretched out on the pallet. The next thing he knew, Lars was back, shaking him gently.

"Time to get up, bashful."

Tobias opened his eyes. The seamster stood over him, the same two young women behind, their arms laden with clothes. The light from the window had faded, and the patch of sky he could see from the pallet had shaded toward indigo.

He sat up. "How soon until the banquet?"

"Half a bell, at the most." Lars pointed to the wardrobe. "Put his things in there."

The women did as instructed and exited the chamber.

"Those should last you for a time, provided you don't gorge yourself at tonight's meal, or do something else foolish." He smiled, perhaps to soften the words. "The cobbler had time only for a single pair of shoes. He promises boots in the days to come. I can't help you impress the sovereign – or his daughter for that matter – but at least you'll look the part of the young noble."

He started toward the door.

"Thank you, seamster."

Pausing on the threshold, the man said, "Stay away from the Miejan reds. They stain." He pulled the door closed.

Alone again, Tobias chose a pair of pale blue breeches and a white silk shirt from the items the seamster had brought him. He dressed in haste, but had to pause as he pulled on the robe. Somehow these new clothes fit better than had his old rags. So did the shoes. He wasn't usually given to vanity, but he would have liked to see himself in a looking glass, just this once.

He wasn't sure how to find the hall in which they would be dining, but he expected a guard would be able to direct him. When he opened the door, however, he found the page sitting against the opposite wall of the corridor. The boy scrambled to his feet.

"Have you been there all this time?"

"Nat'rally, my lord. I wouldn't sneak off!"

"No, I didn't... I didn't know."

The boy frowned.

"It doesn't matter. What's your name?

"Grig, my lord."

"Very well, Grig. Can you lead me to where we'll be eating?"

"Yes, my lord."

This time as they walked, Tobias paid more attention to the twists and turns of the corridors, stairways, and tiled paths. The hall was on the ground floor near the stairway to the sovereign's quarters. It was enormous, the largest chamber Tobias had ever seen. Its windows of colored glass burned with the glow of the setting sun, casting tinted ghosts of light on the stone walls and illuminating tiny motes of dust that swam in the air overhead.

Several tables and chairs had been pushed to the walls, leaving only one lengthy table in the middle of the floor. This had been set with wooden trenchers, and knives, forks, and spoons of bright silver. It was laden with platters of cheese and smoked meats, with bowls of fruits and steamed roots and greens, and with rounds of fresh bread. Any remaining space had been filled with carafes of wine, both red and golden.

The headache and sour stomach with which he'd started his day a distant memory, Tobias longed to grab the nearest bowl and gorge himself. Fortunately, the arrival of other guests saved him from himself. Several men and women entered the hall together, all of them chatting and laughing amiably. Upon spotting Tobias, they converged on him and began to introduce themselves. The flurry of names and titles overwhelmed him, but a few lodged in his memory.

A handsome older woman in a pale blue gown presented herself as Gillian Ainfor, the sovereign's minister of state, and an ancient man, his face wizened, his hair white and wild, was introduced as Mikel, the sovereign's Spanner. Tobias didn't hear his surname. Mara would have been pleased to know the Spanner was a man of such advanced years.

The one name he recognized belonged to a slightly disheveled, gray-haired man.

"Master Jarrett," Tobias said, bowing to the Binder. He

carried his new chronofor in his pocket, its weight both alien and reassuring. "I wish to thank you for the fine chronofor. I've already had occasion to use it, and it's as beautiful as any I've seen."

"Its appearance means nothing," the Binder said. "How did it function?"

"What Jarrett means," the minister of state said, giving Tobias no time to answer, "is thank you, you're most kind."

The Binder scowled, but Gillian slipped her arm through his and kissed his cheek, eliciting a wince that might have been intended as a smile.

"He's not one for compliments, nor, for that matter, does he like expressions of affection." She leaned forward, and added in a conspiratorial half-whisper, "But I don't really care."

Tobias laughed. To the Binder he said, "It worked brilliantly, thank you. I'm still learning my craft, but I've no doubt this chronofor will serve me well."

Jarrett nodded, clearly pleased. The minister caught Tobias's eye and gave a wink that bespoke her approval.

They had no opportunity to say more. The blare of a herald's horn announced the arrival of the royal family. Mearlan entered the hall first, accompanied by a slender woman, slightly taller than he, whom Tobias assumed must be his wife. She wore a simple white gown and a circlet of silver on her brow, and she favored those in the hall with a dazzling smile. Her hair was dark and long; some of it had been tied back in an elaborate plait. Her complexion was very nearly a match for Tobias's; she stood out in this hall as much as he must have. He wondered if she came from the Labyrinth or perhaps Trevynisle itself.

Behind the royal couple came two more figures. One wore ministerial robes similar to Tobias's. Tobias noticed little else about him. His gaze had locked on the face of the young woman walking half a pace ahead of this man.

What had Lars said? *I can't help you impress the sovereign – or his daughter for that matter...*

At the time, Tobias had paid little attention, consumed as he was with preparing for the banquet. Now he wondered how he could have cared about anything else. She was the perfect blend of her parents: shimmering black hair and mahogany skin from her mother; startling blue eyes and an open, oval visage from her father. She stood nearly as tall as the sovereign, and so was Tobias's height as well. Her gown was as elaborate as the queen's was plain, with layered skirts of shimmering gold, purple, and black, and a bodice of matching purple embroidered with fine gold stitching. The effect – the gown, the hair, the complexion, the eyes – was intoxicating.

"That's Sofya," Minister Ainfor whispered.

"Sofya," he repeated.

"Careful, Walker. That bloom has thorns."

He glanced her way. "I'm–" He gave a small shake of his head, and looked away once more, back to the sovereign's daughter. *Sofya.* "I'm just a Walker."

"Normally, I'd build you up with a word or two of praise, but in this instance, that's the right approach. You're a Walker, and she's a royal you want nothing to do with. Trust me on this."

"Walker!" the sovereign called, waving him over.

"Time to take stage," the minister whispered.

Tobias walked to where the royal family waited, feeling every pair of eyes in the hall upon him. In Windhome, he had welcomed the attention of Mara and his teachers, though it invited the envy of others. This felt different, undeserved, at least for the time being.

The skin under the sovereign's eyes was still bruised with fatigue, but his pleasure as he addressed his wife appeared genuine. "I present to you Tobias Doljan, of Redcove on the isle of Onyi, by way of Windhome in Trevynisle. Hayncalde's new Walker. Tobias, this is my wife, Keeda, sovereign queen of Daerjen."

Tobias bowed low. "It is an honor to make your acquaintance, your majesty."

"And a pleasure to make yours, Walker. I hail from the Labyrinth, not so far from your home. I look forward to speaking with you of the northern isles. I miss them."

"Yes, your majesty."

With a light hand on Tobias's shoulder, the sovereign steered him where he already wished to go.

"This is my daughter, Sofya, sovereign princess of Daerjen. Sofya, this is Walker Tobias Doljan."

The princess curtsied, her hard stare never leaving Tobias's face. He bowed, breaking eye contact. "It's a pleasure to meet you, your highness."

She offered no reply.

"I wish I could introduce you to my son," the sovereign said, "but he's currently serving in the Herjean, pursuing privateers. He's a commander aboard the Daerjen ship *Fulmar*."

"You and the queen must be very proud, my liege."

The sovereign thanked him; Sofya rolled her eyes.

"And finally," the sovereign said, steering Tobias again, "I present to you my Seer, Osten Cavensol, who hails from the isle of Wyehrel in Sipar's Labyrinth. Seer, our new Walker, Tobias Doljan."

As he neared the man, an odd smell reached him. At first Tobias thought it merely the smell of drink. Maybe the Seer had partaken of too much wine before coming to the hall. But another scent underlaid that hint of spirit. It was both cloyingly sweet and subtly bitter. The man was dark-skinned as well. Maybe Tobias wouldn't stand out in the court as much as he had feared.

"Walker Doljan," the Seer said in a slow drawl. "A pleasure." He wore a vague smile on his thin lips and his dark eyes had a glassy cast to them.

"The pleasure is mine, Seer."

The queen led them to the table, and took some care with the seating. She and the sovereign were to sit at the center, naturally. As the honored guest for the evening, Tobias was positioned just to the left of the sovereign, with Sofya on Tobias's other side, an arrangement that both thrilled and terrified him. The queen placed the Seer, Gillian, and the Binder nearest to her seat.

Tobias started to sit, but the sovereign stopped him with a sharp clearing of his throat. At the same time, a short, lean woman rose from a seat at the end of the table and raised both arms in supplication, her white robes marking her as a priestess from the Temple of Sipar. Tobias lowered his head with the others, embarrassed to have allowed his hunger and excitement to distract him so. Back in Windhome every meal began with a show of obeisance to the God and Goddess. He had spent too many days aboard the *Skate*.

The priestess finished her prayer, and the sovereign and his guests punctuated it with a ringing "Hear us."

With a rustle of cloth and the grating of wood on stone, the diners sat and began to eat.

Mearlan peppered Tobias with questions throughout the meal, and when the sovereign paused to eat, the queen took up where he left off. They wished to know about Windhome and life in the palace. The queen in particular had questions about his training, and the skills he had learned from the palace masters.

On occasion, Tobias chanced a glance to his left, to see if Sofya was listening. The princess, however, gave no indication that she cared a whit about his former life; she maintained an implacable silence for much of the evening.

As servants brought out a confection of chocolate, wild berries, and sifted sugar, the queen finally leaned forward to address her daughter.

"Sofya, don't you have anything to ask our guest? He's no older than you, and already he's lived such a fascinating life."

"Actually, yes," the princess said, her voice lower and stronger than Tobias had expected. She raised her gaze from her trencher. "I find myself wondering if he ever grows tired of speaking about himself."

"Such comments ill-become you," her father said, his voice low.

"It wasn't directed at him, Father. The two of you haven't let the poor boy do anything more than speak. His trencher is still half-covered with his supper."

She was right; he had been too busy answering questions to eat much of his meal. Yet Tobias couldn't decide which bothered him more: her first comment, when he thought it directed at him, or her referring to him as a boy.

The sovereign stared at Tobias's trencher, and then at his daughter. At last, he hung his head and laughed.

"Forgive me, Walker. Forgive *us*. We haven't had many visitors of late, and it's refreshing to speak of something other than provisions, alliances, and battles."

Around the table other conversations faltered.

"I don't mind, my liege. Before this evening, I'd never been given reason to think myself particularly interesting. It was a pleasant fantasy while it lasted."

Mearlan and his queen laughed. Even Sofya looked amused. She didn't actually give in to laughter, but she regarded him, seeming to consider him anew. The rest of the sovereign's guests resumed their discussions.

Mearlan leaned toward him and said in a low voice, "That was well done, Walker. You rescued an evening that I nearly ruined. I'm grateful."

"Thank you, my liege."

Tobias turned to Sofya once more, but as he did, she pushed back from the table and stood.

"I grow weary," she said. "Goodnight, Father, Mother."

The sovereign and queen frowned at this, but made no attempt to stop her. Sofya left without sparing Tobias another glance.

CHAPTER 10

Tobias thought Sofya's departure might signal an end to the evening. It didn't. The sovereign's other guests lingered over dessert and cups of black tea from the Labyrinth. Jarrett and the minister of arms engaged in a spirited argument over the question of which isle produced the finest weapons, the minister arguing for Aiyanth, and the Binder championing Oaqamar, albeit reluctantly. The sovereign followed every word, occasionally adding a remark himself.

As they continued their debate, the minister of state rose from her seat, walked the length of the table, and sat where Sofya had been.

"I hope you'll forgive me," she said to Tobias. "I'm not as stimulating company as the princess, but I was fascinated by what I heard of your history, and I have more questions for you."

"It would be my pleasure, minister," Tobias said, his enthusiasm genuine, his interest in the arms conversation long since gone.

Most of the minister's questions pertained to his training in diplomacy. She wanted to know which of the great thinkers in statecraft he had read, and responded with enthusiasm when his list included men and women from so many isles: Bentner from Daerjen, Fetgarth from Oaqamar, Goraan from Rencyr, Muul from Safsi, the Tev sisters from Liyrelle.

"Muul was always my favorite," she said, sipping gold wine from a freshly filled goblet, the blue in her eyes a perfect match for her gown. "Some think him fusty, but I find his treatise on war and alliances simply brilliant."

Tobias held his tongue, but couldn't help wrinkling his nose.

"You disagree?" She sounded delighted rather than offended.

"I don't know nearly as much–"

"Stop," she said. "I'm asking your opinion. Colleague to colleague."

All right. "I think Muul's an idiot."

The minister clapped her hands, her delight evident. "Excellent! Why?"

"War is a symptom," he said. "Extreme, yes, but not different in kind from any other diplomatic conflict. In the end, it all comes down to commerce, the quest for gold."

"Talk about fusty! You sound just like Fetgarth."

Tobias lifted a shoulder. "Even an Oaqamaran gets something right now and then."

Her smile tightened. "You're right, of course." Her voice dropped. "But that's dangerous talk around here these days."

"Forgive me."

"Nothing to forgive. Just beware."

Tobias glanced past her to the far end of the table, where the discussion droned on. The Seer eyed his companions, but appeared to add nothing to the debate.

"What can you tell me about the Seer?" Tobias asked.

The minister looked that way as well. "What do you want to know?"

"He strikes me as… odd. I almost had the impression that he'd been drinking before he arrived."

"Well, that's the Tincture, isn't it?"

As soon as she said this, Tobias realized how foolish he must have sounded asking the question. Of course he knew of Tincture, just as he knew about Seers. He had never met one of the Magi before this night, and so had never been assailed by the smell of the drug they used to induce their powers. Still, he should have worked this out for himself.

Just as every major court between the oceans had Travelers, so did they have Seers, men and women of varying talents. Some could recall word for word all that they read and heard. Others could divine the future, or discern truth or lies in the words they heard.

"I should have known," he said. "Forgive me for asking."

She raised a shoulder. "There's nothing to forgive. Still, I'm surprised. Were there no Magi in Windhome? No one to teach you and the other Travelers about Seer magick?"

"No, none."

"Let me guess," she said. "The chancellor of Windhome is a devout follower of the Two."

"Well... Yes."

"Naturally." Seeing the confusion on Tobias's face, she added, "The Temples, especially their most fervent adherents, have long been uncomfortable with the Magi's particular brand of magick. Traveling through time, or instantaneously across great distances, doesn't seem to trouble them. But the knowledge that Seers bring – somehow that's more than they can tolerate."

"What I do isn't magick," Tobias said. Even as he said this, though, he thought of the Belvora. He had been hunted by a magick demon.

"Isn't it?" She raised her eyebrows. "I can't do it. No one at this table can, except for you."

"Without my chronofor–"

"The chronofor is an instrument, nothing more. The magick resides within you. You have a power possessed by few. You can call it science, or craft, or even artifice, as some call the Seers' abilities. In the end, it's magick."

He wanted to argue, but he heard in her words an echo of

what Wansi had told him before he left Trevynisle.

He would need time to consider this. "We were talking about Tincture."

Her smile deepened, conveying an understanding of his thoughts that made him uncomfortable. "Yes, we were. What do you care to know?"

"Does it always smell so strong?"

"I don't even notice it anymore. And it's not as though the smell would keep any Seer from using it."

Tobias frowned at this.

"It's terribly addicting. More so than drink." Amusement flitted across her square face. "More so even than love. And it leaves him much as you see him: withdrawn, contemplative, clouded in a way. It's essentially a narcotic, but it enhances his innate abilities, just as the chronofor enables yours."

"And the Temples object to the drug?"

"You'd have to ask your chancellor," she said. "But no, I don't think it's the narcotic." She paused, eyeing her wine. "I believe it's the knowledge. What you and other Travelers do is physical. You go places, or to different times. Binders and healers – their abilities are different as well. With the Tincture, diviners like our Osten Cavensol, or any other sort of Magi, gain access to knowledge only the Two are supposed to possess. I think the Temples view the Seers as a threat to the primacy of Kheraya and Sipar. If mere mortals can know such things, what use have we for the God and Goddess? More to the point, what use do we have for those who serve them?"

"What nonsense are you spouting now, minister?"

They both turned to the sovereign, who apparently had abandoned the argument about weapons.

"Nothing of consequence, my liege," she said smoothly.

"Now, why do I doubt that?" He shifted his gaze to Tobias. "I hope your meal was satisfactory, and the conversation to your liking."

"Yes, my liege. It's been a fascinating evening."

Mearlan eyed the minister again, though only for an instant. "I'm sure. But it grows late, and you and I have much to discuss come the morning."

Tobias heard a dismissal in the words. He stood. "Yes, my liege."

"Goodnight, Walker."

He bowed to the sovereign, nodded once to the minister, and left the hall. He hadn't taken two steps into the courtyard when he heard a light footfall behind him. He spun, recognized the slight form of the page, Grig.

"You startled me."

"Forgive me, my lord."

Tobias walked on and the boy fell in step a pace behind him. Despite having drunk more wine than he intended, Tobias remembered the way back to the inner ward and his quarters. As he approached the arched entrance to the stairway, he spotted another figure standing in the darkness.

The princess.

Seeing her, he thought of Mara standing in the moonlight the night before he left Windhome. He recalled as well his reaction to seeing Sofya, and he endured a pang of profound guilt. Droë might have been amused. Mostly, though, he wondered why now two girls had waited for him in the darkness. Wansi had called him handsome. Was he really?

"I know my way from here, Grig. Thank you."

"Do you need anything else, my lord?" the boy asked, his eyes on the princess.

"No. I'll see you in the morning."

He didn't wait for the page's reply before approaching Sofya, who stared up at the sky, a dark cape around her shoulders.

"Are the stars the same in Trevynisle as they are here?" she asked as he drew near.

"Some are, your highness. Others..." He gestured at the sky. "Others are unfamiliar to me."

He halted a short distance from her and gazed up at the moon, a half disc in the western sky. A few clouds scudded overhead, but otherwise the night was clear.

"How old are you?" Sofya asked.

"I've just had my fifteenth birthday. And you?"

She glared at him. "That is a presumption," she said, her voice as cold as the Southern Sea. "My asking a question of you does not convey permission for you to do the same of me."

"Yes, your highness. Please forgive me."

She tipped her face to the night sky once more. "I'll be sixteen in a little more than a turn. The fourth day of Kheraya's Descent."

Not knowing what to say, he decided it was safer to say nothing at all.

"It will be a grand celebration, this year especially. Father imports skybombs from Kantaad just for the occasion."

"I look forward to it."

She sidled closer to him. The air around them was redolent with her perfume. "Can you keep a secret?"

"You have my word, your highness."

"The night of my birthday, Willem of Ysendyr intends to ask my father for permission to court me."

He wasn't certain how to respond to this either. Fortunately she didn't pause for long.

"He's heir to the house; one day he'll be duke. Our fathers haven't yet worked out the details, what with me not being of age, and all. But Willem and I have spoken of it often. Our houses have always been close; Ysendyr has supported us against Sheraigh insurgents in the past, and would again, I'm sure. Willem loves me very much. He's seventeen, you know." She gave him a sly look. "Do you have a girl? Back in Trevynisle, perhaps?"

Was Mara his girl? He pondered the question for the span of a single breath and decided she was. "Yes, I do."

Sofya arched an eyebrow. "Really? What's her name?"

"Mara. She's still a novitiate, though she's nearly sixteen. Someday she'll be Spanner in a court." He nearly mentioned her desire to come to Daerjen, but decided that might be impolitic.

"Have you kissed?"

"Yes."

"Do you love her?"

He felt his color rise and was glad for the darkness. The Tirribin had asked him the same question, and he found it no easier to answer the princess. "I miss her," he said, knowing it wasn't the same.

Sofya didn't seem to mind. "Of course you do." She put a hand to her heart. "Star-crossed loves are the most romantic, don't you think? I do." She let out a small gasp. "Wouldn't it be wonderful if she could come here? I mean, old Mikel can't live forever, can he?"

Tobias laughed. "I'm not sure your father would appreciate the sentiment."

She dismissed this with a wave of that same hand. "He'll never know. This will be our cause, yours and mine. Agreed?" She held out a hand, which he grasped. Her skin was cool and smooth. "I wasn't sure about you, Walker," she said, dropping his hand. "The last thing I wanted was another moon-eyed boy following after me all the time. But you're more than that, aren't you? Yes, I think you and I shall be good friends. You with your secret about Mara, and mine about Willem."

"I'd like that, your highness."

She started away from him. "Goodnight."

"Were you out here waiting for me?"

He regretted asking the question as soon as the words crossed his lips. He was sure Sofya would take offense again and renounce the friendship she had only just bestowed. She surprised him.

"It's possible," she said, a coy smile on her lips. "As I say, there are too many boys in this palace who stare after me, no doubt hoping that I'll declare my undying love, or some such foolishness. I hoped you might be different. After all, it's not every day that a Traveler comes to Hayncalde, particularly one who's nearly my age." She flipped her hair off her shoulder. "In other words, I was curious." She cocked an eyebrow, and walked away.

Tobias watched her go before entering the tower. With every step on the stairway and through the corridor he grew wearier, until he could barely drag himself through the door of his chamber. He would have liked to throw himself onto his pallet, but the finery he wore didn't really belong to him. He undressed, hanging the robe and folding the breeches and shirt with care, and opened the shutters on his window to allow in the cool night air. Only then did he fall onto his bed.

It had been as full a day as any he could recall. Tomorrow promised to be much the same.

Tobias drifted into a deep, dreamless slumber that might have carried him all the way to morning. Instead, he jerked awake some time later, to a velvet black sky and the tolling of a bell in the courtyard. The moon had set and stars burned like white fire. A second bell echoed the first. Or were more ringing? He couldn't tell for sure. He forced himself up, his thoughts thick, too tired to do much more than sit and wonder why bells would peal in the middle of the night.

It can't be anything good.

The thought came to him in Saffern's voice. It drove him to his feet and across the chamber's cold stone floor to the wardrobe.

His sack rested on the floor in the back. He couldn't see much, but he didn't think it wise to light a candle. Rather, he rummaged through his things until he found the pistol the weapons master had given him. He hadn't fired it on the morning the Oaqamarans boarded the *Skate*, so it remained loaded. He primed the pan again, a process made only somewhat harder by the inky dark.

When he had the weapon full-cocked, he stood, intending to check the window again. As an afterthought, he grabbed his dagger as well.

The bells still echoed, and now he heard shouts, footsteps, and the jangle of armor and weapons. Guards converged on the sovereign's courtyard, as he would have expected.

Tobias also heard the echo of a door opening and closing nearby. He crossed to his own door and, with the care of a burglar, opened the latch and peered out into the passage.

Two men, both dressed in black, cloths obscuring their faces up to their eyes, prowled the darkened corridor. They carried swords, with narrow curved blades, and wore daggers on their belts.

They advanced along the marble floor in near silence, each careful step bringing them nearer to Tobias's chamber.

He ducked back into his quarters, closed the door soundlessly, and backed toward the window. He had few good choices. He could call for help, but the two men would reach him before any guards did. He could run, but he doubted he'd get far. He could wait for them to reach his chamber and fight them off, but even if he managed to kill one with the pistol, he had little confidence that he could fight off the other. He was better with a blade than Delvin and Nat, but he was no match for trained killers.

Another door opened and closed. They were close.

The chronofor.

He felt for it on his desk, his shaking hand skimming over the wood with increasing desperation. His heart hammered in his chest; he couldn't imagine how the men didn't hear it.

Had someone taken the device? Had he lost it already?

No! He'd folded his new breeches and stowed them in the wardrobe. But he had forgotten to remove the chronofor from his pocket. He hid his pistol and dagger under his pillow, crept back to the wardrobe, and fished in the pocket of his breeches for the device.

Upon finding it, he shrugged off his clothes, and set the left-most stem back a single click. One bell.

The door latch clicked.

Tobias shoved his clothes into the wardrobe, and depressed the top stem. The invisible hook tugged him backwards into that frenzy of light and sound and smell. This time, though, it was over as quickly as it began. He emerged from the between in his own chamber, still hunched on the floor in the darkness. The palace bells were silent; no raised voices disturbed the night. Against his own better judgment he cast a quick gaze at the pallet. A bulky form lay curled up beneath a dark blanket. He looked away again.

It was said among Walkers that those who encountered themselves in their journeys back in time went insane. He hoped the sleeping Tobias didn't wake before he left the chamber. He took clothes from the wardrobe, feeling like he was stealing, and dressed in haste. After letting himself out into the corridor, he hurried down to the courtyard and across to the nearest gate. The guards there didn't recognize him, but after showing them the chronofor and telling them what was about to happen, he convinced them to wake the sovereign.

They escorted him to Mearlan's private quarters. After a few tencounts in the antechamber, they ushered him in to see the sovereign. Mearlan wore a red and white dressing gown. His hair was disheveled, his eyes swelled with sleep.

"What is all this, Walker? I don't know how the chancellor ran his palace, but I'm not accustomed to being woken at this time."

"Forgive me, my liege. I wouldn't have come had it not been a matter of greatest urgency."

Mearlan thinned his lips and waved off the apology. "Explain."

"I'm here by virtue of the chronofor, my liege. I've come back a single bell. Men – assassins from the look of them – are about to infiltrate the palace. Most of the guards will come here to protect you, as is proper. But these men will check rooms on my corridor. If I hadn't Walked back when I did, I believe they would have killed me."

If the sovereign found it surprising that assassins would target Tobias, he didn't show it. "Do you know who they are?"

"No, my liege. They're dressed in black, well-armed, and capable of moving with great stealth."

"All right. I'll alert the minister of arms. You should remain here. You'll be safer."

"I can't," Tobias said. "Right now the other me – the one who belongs in this time – is sleeping. He'll wake soon enough, and I can't still be here. Having two of me awake at the same time can be... dangerous, not to mention confusing."

"So you have to go back... forward, I mean?" Mearlan scowled. "You've been here less than a day, and already I find your talent confounding."

"I understand. And yes, I must go back. Once I'm in my own time, there will be only one of me."

"Very well. Do it here. Anywhere else, and we'll have a harder time keeping you safe, assuming that you are their target."

He indicated a dressing screen before leaving the chamber. Tobias took off his clothes, adjusted the chronofor for the return to his true time, and activated the device. That imaginary hook jerked him forward into the between and then out of it once more. He stumbled, righted himself.

"Is that you, Walker?" The sovereign's voice.

"Yes, my liege."

"Put on your clothes and get out here."

Tobias dressed and stepped from behind the screen.

Mearlan stood in the center of the chamber, clad now in simple battle garb: breeches, a dark shirt, boots. A sword hung from his belt, as did a holstered pistol.

Half a dozen guards stood in a tight arc behind two kneeling figures: the men Tobias had seen in the corridor. Both of them bore bruises and bloody wounds. One man's eyes were swollen shut, his lip split. He held his shoulder at an odd angle, and grimaced with every breath. His companion looked no better. Blood from a gash on his forehead covered his features and he bled from a stab wound high on his chest. Their hands had been bound behind them.

The men had Tobias's coloring: nut brown skin, bronze hair.

"Thanks to you, we captured them as they tried to scale the north wall of the outer ward. Now, I have to ask again, do you know them?"

Tobias walked forward, his eyes never leaving their faces. He hadn't recognized them in the corridor. But the light was better here, and despite their wounds he thought he might do so.

"Those might help," the sovereign said, pointing to his desk.

Two golden sextants lay side by side on the polished wood, and next to those, a pair of devices unlike any he had seen before, and yet familiar enough to chill his blood. These appeared to be sextants as well, but they had three arcs instead of just one, each calibrated like the arc of a normal device. The devices were equipped with a single eyepiece and trigger. Aside from the arcs, they resembled normal sextants. Yet Tobias was certain they were anything but.

"What do you make of those?" Mearlan asked.

"I'm not sure." Even as he said this, though, a memory stirred in the back of his mind.

The sovereign must have heard the catch in his voice. "Walker?"

"There was talk back in Windhome," Tobias said, still studying the sextants, "of new devices that had been developed in Oaqamar, at their academy for Travelers. It was said their assassins possessed the means to Travel fully clothed and fully armed. I wonder if these devices are what make that possible." He turned. "These men are Spanners?"

"As far as we can tell."

There were clothes piled on the desk, similar to those worn by the kneeling men.

"Whose are these?"

"A fine question," Mearlan said. "We found them in the courtyard, piled as if in haste. I don't know how they got there."

Tobias indicated the assassins with a lift of his chin. "And what about them? Do you know where they came from?"

The sovereign eyed the men, a sneer curling his lip. "They won't say."

Tobias eased closer to them, scrutinizing them as he had the strange sextants. The assassins returned his stare with keen interest.

"You were in the palace on Trevynisle when I first arrived there," he said to the one with the bloodied brow. "You were one of the older novitiates. I don't think I was there more than half a year before you left for... for somewhere." He stared at the man, sifting through memories, trying to place the countenance before him with more precision. "Hovas," he whispered, the name coming to him as an epiphany. "Your name is Hovas, and you came from Bellisi."

The corner of the man's mouth twitched, the only confirmation Tobias needed.

"Write to the chancellor, my liege. He should be able to tell you which court first purchased this man's services."

"Very good, Walker."

Tobias acknowledged the praise, taking his eyes off the assassin for no more than an instant. That was enough.

Somehow Hovas managed to leap from his knees to his feet, and in the same motion lash out with a kick that would have caught Tobias square in the throat had a guard not cried a warning.

He threw himself back and flinched away, so that the toe of the man's shoe missed his larynx. Still, it caught him on the cheek, snapping his head back and sending him sprawling onto the sovereign's desk. Ink, a pen, and sheaves of parchment cascaded onto the floor.

Tobias lay there, addled, unable to move, his vision marred by swimming points of white light, his jaw aching. By the time Mearlan helped him to his feet, both assassins lay dead on the floor, blood from sword wounds pooling around them.

"Are you all right?"

"I believe so, my liege," Tobias said, trying to stand on his own.

"You were right," Mearlan said. "They were after you, not me. Somehow they knew of your arrival, and sought to rob me of my new Walker before I could make use of him." He flashed a weak smile. "I fear I've made you infamous."

Tobias cringed, realizing he had withheld important information. "This isn't the first attempt on my life, my liege."

"What?"

"The morning I sailed from Windhome, before I left the palace, a Belvora attacked me. I wasn't harmed, but only because the Master Walker saved my life. He died in the attack."

"Why didn't you tell me this before?"

"I don't know. I didn't think it important enough to mention."

Mearlan scowled.

"I realize now how foolish that was. I beg your forgiveness."

"It must be the Oaqamarans."

Tobias started, looked to the side. The Seer sat in a plush chair, shrouded in shadow and appearing as dazed as ever. Belatedly, Tobias caught a hint of the sickly sweet scent of Tincture.

"We have other enemies," the sovereign said. "Westisle. Sheraigh. And others of whom we might not even know."

"Sheraigh hasn't the resources to buy one Traveler, much less two," the Seer replied. "I'm not sure Westisle does either. And no one from a southern isle would know enough about Belvora to stage an attack of the sort the lad describes. Besides, all of this is too subtle, too clever, not to mention too immediate. Noak and Gedeon are more likely to strike directly at you, my liege. In my opinion."

"And you see the necessary subtlety and cleverness in the autarch?"

"Reluctantly, my liege. Reluctantly."

Tobias's jaw still throbbed, but the dizziness had passed and his vision had cleared. "They couldn't have followed me all the way from Trevynisle," he said. "Unless they were on Captain Larr's ship the whole time."

Mearlan shook his head. "No. Perhaps they've been watching the port for your arrival. Somehow they must have learned of my missive to the chancellor."

"A traitor?" the Seer asked, his tone mild.

"Loath as I am to acknowledge the possibility, I'd be a fool to ignore it."

"Shall I make some inquiries, my liege?"

"Quietly, Seer."

"Like a mouse, my liege."

Osten rose, walked dreamily to the chamber door, and slipped out into the darkened corridor. Tobias couldn't help thinking that of all the people he had met since arriving in Hayncalde, the Seer seemed the most likely to betray Mearlan. He kept this to himself, however. For now.

"Clean this up," the sovereign said to his guards, staring at the dead assassins. "Make sure to get the blood out of the stone. And find me a new rug."

Guards carried the corpses out of the chamber. Moments after, servants rushed in bearing buckets of water, soap, and rags. The sovereign stepped closer to Tobias, eyeing his face critically.

"You'll have a nasty bruise by morning. Are you all right?"

"Yes, my liege."

"You're taking this well: being the target of assassins, not to mention a demon. Most lads your age would be in a panic by now."

"I suppose. I don't understand why these men would be after me. You're the more valuable target by far. If not you, then the sovereign queen, or your daughter. And if not one of them, then the Seer, or one of the ministers. I'm..." He shook his head, which made his jaw throb more. "I know Walkers are valuable, but I've only just arrived."

"That's the point, I think. Adding a Walker to my court changes things, makes me a more formidable enemy to those who want me dead. There's a reason I paid so much for you. I'm not saying you're worth more than I am, or than my family, or those others you've mentioned, but you're worth a good bit." He grinned. "At least I hope you are."

Tobias's answering smile didn't last. "Do you agree that they were probably sent by the Oaqamarans?"

"The Seer makes a compelling case."

"And they think killing me would tip the balance of the war?"

"I don't know," Mearlan said, rubbing the back of his neck. "Perhaps they know how I intend to use you."

Tobias's gaze snapped to the sovereign's face. "Then they know more than I do."

He regretted this the instant he said it.

"Is that a complaint, Walker Doljan?"

"No, my liege. I beg your pardon."

Mearlan frowned. "Go back to your chamber. Try to sleep. There are a few bells left until dawn. Guards will escort you, and they'll keep watch on your door, though I doubt we need worry about another attempt on your life tonight."

"Yes, my liege." He bowed and crossed to the door.

"I won't keep you in the dark for long," the sovereign said, stopping him. "I've made no decisions yet and I've no intention of doing anything rash. But I must entertain all options. I hope you understand that."

Tobias could do naught but nod. "Of course, my liege."

CHAPTER 11

17th Day of Kheraya's Ascent, Year 647

Even after returning to his chamber and his pallet, and despite knowing that armed men guarded his door, Tobias didn't expect to sleep.

He did. When finally he woke, once more to the tolling of the tower bells, he sensed that he had remained abed far longer than he intended.

He splashed water on his face, wincing at its first cold touch. His jaw ached, and the muscles in his back, neck, and shoulders were stiff and sore. Moving like an old man, he washed, donned fresh clothes, and slipped on his court robe. Upon opening his door, he found Grig in the corridor, dwarfed between the guards.

"I could have helped you dress, my lord."

Tobias cast an embarrassed glance at the soldiers, but their expressions remained neutral. "I've no doubt you could," he said, having some difficulty forming his words. "But I've been dressing myself for a long time now. I think I can manage."

The lad's expression bespoke disapproval more than disappointment. Tobias wondered if he had erred in some way.

Grig led him to the kitchen, the soldiers flanking them. There Tobias enjoyed a quick breakfast of fried bread, eggs, and an apple. When he had eaten his fill, they walked to the sovereign's quarters.

The sky had grown overcast, and a stiff wind blew out of

the west, making the flags atop the towers ripple and snap. Reaching Mearlan's door, Tobias hesitated, reluctant to enter uninvited. Voices came from within; he didn't wish to interrupt a conversation that didn't concern him.

"I believe he's expecting you, my lord," Grig said.

"Are you certain?"

"Yes. I have it from one of the steward's boys. He wants you to join him as soon as possible."

"All right." Tobias raised his hand, faltered again, but finally knocked.

"Enter."

Mearlan sat at his desk, his shoulders slumped. The Seer and the minister of arms sat in chairs facing him, though they peered over their shoulders when they heard the door open. The air reeked of the Seer's Tincture.

"Ah, good. Come in, Walker." Mearlan pointed to a third chair near one of the windows. "Join us. We were discussing last night's events. I trust you're well?"

"Thank you, my liege. I'm fine."

"You met my minister of arms last night, didn't you? Isak Moar."

"It's good to see you again, minister," Tobias said, as he retrieved the chair and set it beside the man.

"That's an ugly bruise," Isak said. He was burly, compact, his cheeks ruddy and full, his head shaved, save for a thin plait of red hair, salted generously with white, that hung from the nape of his neck. He spoke with a burr characteristic of the Knot. "You might see a healer. A poultice will bring down the swelling a bit."

"I will. My thanks."

Only when he was seated, did Tobias realize he had positioned himself as far from the Seer as possible.

"You know, I'm curious," the minister said to Mearlan. "If our Seer is tasked with glimpsing the future, how did he not anticipate this attack on the castle? I would think this a fairly important event, the sort of thing his powers ought to catch, if you get my meaning."

The sovereign glowered back at him, seeming more angered by the question than by any possible failure on the Seer's part.

"I've told you before, minister," the Seer drawled, sounding bored, "I See hints and portents of occurrences that may or may not happen. The future is as changeable as the present; it is a pattern woven on an ever-shuttling loom. Our new Walker arrived only yesterday, after an uncertain voyage. His would-be assassins came to the castle last night and their futures were altered by what I must say was a clever and entirely novel gambit undertaken by our young friend." He favored Tobias with an unctuous smile. "Thus, there was little opportunity for these events to come to my attention, and there never was any specific future fixed in time. I don't know what kind of vision I might have received, or even whether I would have recognized it as an outcome of last night's events." He fixed the minister of arms with a cold eye. "Does that satisfy your... curiosity?"

The armsman cleared his throat. "It might have. I'm not sure. I nodded off during your explanation."

"That's enough, Isak," the sovereign said.

"Yes, my liege."

"But his point is taken, Seer. Tobias is part of my court now. I expect to be made aware of any future threats to his safety."

"Naturally, my liege, as the God allows."

Annoyance flickered in Mearlan's eyes. "You've made inquiries as to Oaqamar's involvement?"

"I've sent messages, encoded, of course. I don't know how long we shall have to await replies."

"You think the Oaqamarans were behind last night's attempt?" Isak asked.

"The Seer believes so."

The minister glared at Osten. "When were you going to

inform me of this?"

The Seer stared back, giving no indication that he was cowed by the minister's expression. "Just as soon as there was something for you to attack."

"Would it be possible for the two of you to pretend, if not for my sake then for the Walker's, that you are capable of being in the same chamber for more than a quarter bell without behaving like children?"

Tobias shifted uncomfortably. He didn't know the minister well, but he sensed that he could come to like the man, just as he liked Gillian. It hadn't escaped his notice that neither had much good to say about Osten. Was Mearlan the only person in the castle who trusted the Seer?

"Do you think it's possible?" The sovereign went on after a weighty pause. "The Oaqamarans, I mean."

Minister Moar shifted in his seat. "I suppose." The admission appeared to come at some cost. "They have the resources, the motivation, the moral turpitude."

"You see? Stop baiting each other, and the two of you might find that you agree more often than not."

Neither man answered.

Mearlan frowned once more. "What's the latest from Aiyanth?"

"Little has changed, my liege," the minister said, standing and walking to a large table near the back wall of the chamber.

Osten and the sovereign followed.

"Come along, Walker. You should see this, too."

A large map of the Aiyanthan Sea and its isles had been pinned to the table. Small wooden blocks rested on the map in clusters; some had been painted red, others black, green, and gold.

"The red blocks represent our fleet," the minister told Tobias as he joined the others. "The gold are Aiyanth, the black Oaqamar, the green Milnos."

"What about Vleros, and the Labyrinth?"

Isak's laugh was as brittle as old parchment. "When they deploy enough ships to make a difference, we'll give them a block. Until then…" He broke off with a shrug.

Tobias scrutinized the map and blocks, noting that the black and green outnumbered the red and gold by nearly two to one. Most of Aiyanth's fleet remained close to its home isle, and the red blocks formed a broad arc around those golden ones: a defensive position. Green blocks gathered in number to the southwest, near the shores of Milnos, and a horde of black blocks menaced the red and gold from the north. That defensive posture looked tenuous at best.

"We haven't seen much movement from the Oaqamarans," the minister said. "I think they like things where they are. It's the ships from Milnos that worry me. The Vleros fleet is penned up in their waters, and according to our admirals, the ships of the shield have grown more aggressive."

"Have we engaged them?"

"Not yet, my liege. I fear that if we do, the Oaqamarans will strike directly at Aiyanth. And if the Axle falls, the Outer and Inner Rings could be next. We need more ships. We need more allies."

"We're building more ships, but I fear they won't be ready in time. As for more allies… well, who wants to ally himself with the weaker party in a war approaching its decisive battle?"

"Anyone who fears an imperial Oaqamar," Tobias said.

The others eyed him.

"You're right," Mearlan said, "at least in theory. I've tried to make that case with the leaders of the Outer Ring isles. The Aiyanthan king has done the same. But we're weak, and we have little to offer by way of assurances. If they join our cause and we lose, they'll bear the brunt of the autarch's vengeance."

"It doesn't help," the minister added, "that most young folk in Rencyr and Kantaad, and lately Herjes, too, are chasing gold and silver in Chayde. Even if the isles had enough ships to turn the war, they wouldn't have the men and women to crew them."

"What do you have to say, Seer?" Mearlan asked. "What ending have you visioned for this war?"

"Well, my liege, the future is ever-changing, as I've told you before."

"Too many times," Isak muttered.

The Seer's gaze slid his way for a moment, but he offered no other reaction. "The truth is, I've Seen few conclusions to the conflict that bode well for us. If we withdraw, we leave Aiyanth to the autarch. If we remain, we risk our fleet and leave ourselves open to a devastating attack. We can sue for peace, but no doubt the autarch's terms—"

The minister smacked his hand on the table, jarring the blocks. "He didn't ask you for options! He asked what you've seen! And the truth is, you've seen nothing at all, have you? You don't know what's going to happen, just as you didn't know those assassins would come for the lad. You're dried up, Seer. It's time you admitted it."

"Isak!"

Osten's glare would have kindled damp wood. His cheeks had gone white, his lips a thin gash. "Forgive me, my liege, but I cannot work with this man. If my visions have failed you as of late, it is because of his constant questioning of my competence and loyalty. I will withdraw to my quarters, but will, of course, be honored to speak with you in private." He directed a stiff nod at Tobias. "Walker."

He strode from the chamber, his steps clicking like a pendulum on a clock.

When he was gone, Mearlan rounded on the minister, ire manifest on his face. "Was that really necessary?"

"You depend on him, now more than ever. And he has nothing to give you. Nothing at all."

"He has wisdom, he has vast knowledge of Oaqamar, of the Axle, of the isles of the Outer Ring. You make him sound useless, and he's not."

The minister gaped. "I'm right, then. He is dried up. And you've known all this time?"

"I suspect. Nothing more. But he still has a good deal to offer. He's served me for all my years as sovereign. He served my father."

Isak's mouth twitched. He looked off to the side. "I know that, my liege."

"Then respect my wishes, and ease up on him."

"Yes, my liege."

Mearlan eyed the map again. "We'll speak of this later. For now you're dismissed."

"Yes, my liege."

The minister started toward the door, as did Tobias.

"Walker, I'd like you to remain."

"Of course, my liege."

Isak opened the door, but paused there and faced the sovereign once more. "You have my deepest apologies, my liege."

The sovereign watched him leave. "I'm sorry you had to see that," he said when they were alone. "They've never gotten along."

Tobias held his tongue.

"The truth is, even when he still had his powers, Osten was a pompous ass. But as I say, he's served Daerjen since I was a boy."

"Yes, my liege."

Mearlan gave a wan smile. "You're right in the middle of it all, aren't you? One day in my court and you've been feted, hunted, and drawn into a personal rivalry that's older than you are. You probably wish you were back in Windhome."

"Not at all. Windhome's boring. No one would ever say that about this place."

The sovereign laughed. "No, I don't suppose they would." He leaned over the map, adjusted a few of the blocks that Isak had upset with his outburst. "So, what do you make of all this?"

"The war, you mean?" Tobias shook his head. "I don't have the minister's expertise, or the Seer's experience. I doubt anything I could offer–"

"Don't. I have no time for doubts or modesty. You were educated in matters of warcraft as well as statecraft, were you not?"

"I was."

"Then tell me what you see here."

Tobias studied the map. "How many ships per block?" he asked.

"A dozen."

He exhaled. Matters were worse than he thought. "What of Ensydar, my liege? Have they contributed at all to the effort?"

"Not in a meaningful way. Why?"

"Because they would fall after Aiyanth. If Oaqamar controls both isles, it can cut off all northern routes to Daerjen. So if Ensydar's king can be convinced that his own survival is at stake, he might add his ships to your fleet."

"Or he might choose to negotiate a peace with the autarch, then sit back and allow Aiyanth to fall."

"Do you believe that's likely?"

"We've had word of Oaqamaran envoys in the royal city."

"Oh." Tobias considered the map again, chewing his lip.

"You see my problem." Something in the way Mearlan said this drew Tobias's gaze. "We're on a precipice, and I see no way off save one. We can't win. We can't afford to lose. The autarch has no incentive to end the war now, unless we concede everything, which would be much the same as losing." He picked up a red block and rolled it in his fingers. "We can fight on, and hope for a miracle, but at what cost in lives and treasure?"

"Yes, my liege. I suppose it would have been better..."

Tobias stopped himself, his face going cold as the blood rushed from his cheeks.

The sovereign watched him, his eyes appearing darker than they had the previous day, as if the blue were shrouded in storm clouds. "Better what, Walker?"

"Nothing, my liege." He could barely whisper the words.

"It wasn't nothing. Tell me."

"I was... I was going to say... Better you shouldn't have fought the war at all."

"Yes, lately I've been thinking much the same thing."

Tobias backed away from the table, found a chair, and lowered himself into it. "That's why you wanted me. That's where – when – you want me to go."

"You have to understand. If I saw any other path, I'd take it. Even before you reached the palace, I was searching for other options. But I felt it was my only choice. And then you arrived, and you're so young. I... I'm not ready to ask this of you yet. I'm still looking for another way out."

"The autarch knows you're considering this?" Tobias asked. "That's why he sent the assassins?"

"He knows I petitioned the chancellor for a Traveler, and I suspect that at some point he learned you're a Walker. Or else he just assumes it. Knowing or assuming that much, it wouldn't take him long to piece together the rest."

"And it frightens him."

"Yes, I expect it does."

"You know it does, my liege. That's why those men came for me." He slipped his hand into his pocket and found the chronofor, smooth and cool against his fingers. "The Seer is right, you know," he said. "The future changes constantly. If I do this – if I go back and stop you from going to war – it doesn't assure Daerjen's prosperity. Any number of other wars might take the place of this one. Or rather than war, the autarch might resort to assassinations or other strategies."

"I understand."

"I wonder if he does?"

"The autarch?"

Tobias nodded.

"To be honest, I can't begin to imagine what might cross the man's mind. The more important question to my mind is, what will you do? I can't make you go, I'm sure you know that. This would breach my contract with Windhome."

Tobias hadn't thought of this, but Mearlan was right. This was his way out, if he wanted it. The laws governing the Travelers' palace were clear in this regard. If the chancellor were to learn of Mearlan's intentions he would abrogate the contract and demand that Tobias be returned immediately to Windhome.

"If you don't want to go back," the sovereign continued after a brief silence, "I can't make you. And even if I could, I wouldn't make you. This is your decision."

That made it worse. Tobias feared what the sovereign might ask of him. He was far more afraid that Mearlan's desire to spare him would lead to the conquest of Daerjen and Aiyanth by the Oaqamarans. He liked this sovereign, and he had grown up in Windhome, in the shadow of the autarchy. Fear of Oaqamar, and resentment of its aggression, its hectoring, ran deep in the northern isles. Tobias had been weaned on it.

Trevynisle and the Sisters remained free because the autarch knew that the other sovereignties would unite to thwart any attempt on his part to annex the isles. All the courts depended on Trevynisle for Travelers. They might stand by and allow the autarch to take Aiyanth and Ensydar. Some might rejoice in the fall of Daerjen. But all would band against him if he moved against the chancellor and his palace. Oaqamar was strong, but the combined might of all the isles had long been enough to hold it in check. If Oaqamar won this war, Trevynisle and the Sisters would fall as well.

"I wouldn't refuse you," Tobias said, the words coming out as a whisper.

He had expected to see relief in Mearlan's expression. Instead, the sovereign winced, as from a blow. "You honor me, Walker. You honor all of us."

Tobias didn't respond.

"So, you're willing to go. Do you think it would be wise to send you back?"

"I think it's the only solution. What's more, you agree with me, and so does the autarch."

"Walker–"

"Forgive me, my liege, but if the Oaqamarans are willing to risk two Spanners for one Walker, they're afraid. And you've already told me that you have no other options."

"When did I–"

"We're on a precipice, and I see no way off save one."

It was a risky thing, throwing the words of a sovereign back at him. If this angered Mearlan, though, he gave no indication of it. Rather, his shoulders sagged.

"I might have been rash in saying that. I'm not sure I've exhausted all possibilities."

Tobias didn't argue the point further. Instead he asked, "How long?"

"What?"

"The war. How long has it been going on?"

Mearlan hesitated, his gaze slipping to the side. "Fourteen years."

The world around Tobias seemed to lurch and fall away. Fourteen years. He would be twenty-nine when he arrived in that time. He would be forty-three after he Walked back. Not much younger than the sovereign himself. Older by far than his father had been when Tobias left home for Windhome. A boy in the body of an aging man.

"Nothing has been decided, Tobias."

He could only nod.

The silence that followed was as oppressive as black smoke; he could have choked on it. The sovereign regarded him still, concern etching lines in his brow.

Tobias pushed himself to his feet. "Perhaps I should leave you for now, my liege."

"You don't..." He released a breath. "I'm sorry."

"You have no reason to be."

"Don't I? Would you have come had you known what I intended to ask of you?"

He didn't know how to answer. He felt as though he had already Traveled to a new place, one in which he could contemplate Walking back nearly as many years as he had lived. Would he have come here knowing what he did now? Maybe. Or perhaps he would have given more thought to Captain Larr's invitation to join her crew.

"Your silence tells me all I need to know," Mearlan said.

"When the chancellor told me I'd be coming here, I was thrilled. I wanted to serve your court in any way I could."

"Even if it meant losing so many years?"

Another question that was too hard to answer just then. "Please, my liege, may I go?"

Mearlan pursed his lips, his eyes on the desk. "Yes, all right."

"Thank you."

Tobias hurried from the room.

Sofya waited in the antechamber. She wore a simple gown of white, much like the one her mother had worn the previous evening. Her hair hung loose, and a blue gem, set in silver, flashed at her throat. She looked lovely, and Tobias wanted nothing more than to walk past her without exchanging a word. He kept his face angled so that she wouldn't notice his bruised jaw.

"Good morning, Walker."

"Good day, your highness."

"Did you hear all the commotion last night? I heard voices and shouting. It was all most strange."

"Yes, your highness."

"Yes, you heard it, or yes, it was strange?"

"Both, I suppose."

"Do you know what happened?"

Tobias faltered, not wanting to lie, uncertain as to whether the sovereign would want him to tell the truth.

His failure to answer told her much. "You *do* know," she said, eyes narrowing. She stepped closer, took hold of his chin, and turned his head so that she could examine his bruise.

He hissed through his teeth at the pain.

"What happened to you?"

He pulled back from her grasp, unwilling to meet her gaze. "I'm fine."

"You don't look fine. Does this have something to do with what I heard last night?" Before he could reply, she answered her own question. "It must. You didn't have that bruise when we spoke in the courtyard. Did you get in a fight?" She eyed him critically. "Were you drunk?"

At that, he did meet her glare. "Certainly not!"

"Then what happened? Was it a fight?"

"What do you mean?"

"A fight!" she said again, raising her voice. "Did you have an argument? Did it become violent?"

"No, it wasn't like that."

"So, no fight. And no drinking." She blinked. "Was there an attack on the castle? But no, that would… It couldn't be."

"I think," he said softly, "this is a conversation you should have with your father."

"Why not with you?"

"I'm not sure what I can tell you and what I can't."

Her expression turned flinty. "I see. Last night you declared yourself my friend. And now you treat me like I'm a child, and you're suddenly ten years older. I don't give my friendship lightly, Walker Doljan, and I certainly don't expect it to be spurned by a little poor boy from Trevynisle."

The prescience of her remark – *ten years older* – left him mute. He probably should have been insulted by the rest of what she'd said, but little of it reached him.

"I meant no offense, your highness," he muttered at last, because she expected him to. "Truly."

"Nevertheless, you've given it." She walked past him, knocked once on her father's door, and entered, leaving Tobias alone in the antechamber.

CHAPTER 12

17th Day of Kheraya's Ascent, Year 647

Tobias dragged himself through the corridor, down the stairway, and out into the gray morning. Whether due to the events of the night, or the prospect of Walking back so far in time, fatigue weighed on him more heavily than he could remember. He wished only to retreat to his chamber and the comfort of his pallet, and he started in that direction.

Familiar sounds stopped him, brought the ghost of a smile to his lips. The clash of steel, and shouts of instruction: somewhere nearby, soldiers trained with swords.

Tobias followed the noises to a third ward, smaller than the others and located at the west end of the castle. Compared with the other two courtyards, this one was austere. The walls were gray rather than white, and completely unadorned. Tobias saw no gardens, no fountains, no painted tile. There was naught but grass. In the middle of the space, the minister of arms drilled several dozen uniformed guards in close combat. The soldiers looked young – younger by far than the guards Tobias had encountered since his arrival.

Isak spotted Tobias and waved him over, though he continued to call out to the trainees. Out here, his ministerial robe discarded carelessly upon the grass, the minister appeared more powerful, broader in the chest and shoulders.

"A minister of arms who trains his own soldiers," Tobias said as he reached the man. "I'm surprised."

"I don't usually. But after going head to head with the Seer, or delivering bad news to his majesty–"

"Or both?"

The minister arched an eyebrow. "Aye, or both. Sometimes then, it feels good to come out here and yell at the probationers for a while."

Tobias watched the soldiers. It had been more than a ha'turn since last he held a sword. He missed it.

"Did they train you in swordplay up there in Trevynisle?"

A grin crept across Tobias's face. "A bit."

"Ho! A bit, is it? I take it you've some skill, then?"

Tobias's grin deepened. "A bit."

Isak laughed. "That's enough there," he called to the young guards. "I need two blades. Quickly now."

Two women stepped forward and handed their blades to the minister. One he tossed to Tobias, who caught it by the hilt. Isak tested the feel of the other with three vicious swipes, steel carving the air with a sibilant whistle.

Tobias held out the sword to one of the men, removed his robe, and stretched his back and shoulder muscles. He wasn't properly dressed for training, and his new shoes would not grip the turf well. Those, however, were the least of his concerns. The minister might have been past his best days, but Tobias had little doubt he remained a formidable swordsman. Tobias stood half a hand taller than the man, and probably had a longer reach. He knew, though, that this single slight advantage would prove meaningless. He'd be lucky to come out of this unbloodied. Not that he minded. A fight, a chance to sweat and match wits with a foe, was what he needed.

Feeling more limber, he reclaimed the sword and faced the minister, weapon held ready.

"Someone keep an eye on him," the minister said with a rakish smile. "Make certain he doesn't jump back in time and beat me before we've begun." He took his stance as well.

"Ready, Walker?"

"Yes, sir."

"Come on then."

When you find yourself overmatched, Saffern once told Tobias and his fellow novitiates, strike hard and fast. The longer the fight goes on, the more likely skill and experience will win out.

Tobias leapt forward, slashing at the minister's head, his neck, his chest. He didn't worry about hurting the man, trusting to Isak to block or deflect blows that might do serious damage. He did take care to remain in his crouch, to control his attack and not open himself to the minister's counters.

Restrained fury. That's what you're striving for. Anyone can swing a sword. A swordsman finds the balance between aggression and caution.

Tobias toed that fine line, his assault furious, unrelenting, yet measured. Any of the Windhome novitiates would have succumbed already and borne a gash or two. He might have managed to bloody some of the probationers observing this battle. Against the minister, he hadn't a chance.

Isak bared his teeth in a grin both joyful and ferocious, a few beads of sweat breaking out on his tanned brow. But he appeared neither winded nor overly concerned. He met every sword stroke, anticipated every advance. He didn't bother with counters, at least not at first. He parried and blocked.

Already winded, his shirt soaked through, Tobias danced away, switched the sword to his left hand, and renewed the attack, hoping to catch the minister unprepared. This earned him another raised eyebrow from the minister, who actually gave ground briefly.

Tobias's ploy was an act of desperation; he fought better with his right hand. After the initial surprise spent itself, the minister seemed to grasp as much. He began to advance. He still fought guardedly, defending himself against Tobias's blows. Now, though, he lashed out with a few attacks of his own.

Tobias backed off again, shifted the weapon to his right hand, and engaged once more, circling, fighting with less frenzy, conserving what strength he had left. In truth, though, it was too late for that.

"You're good, lad. I could use a few young guards like you."

Tobias could think of no response, and was too winded to say anything.

He lunged, trying an attack he had learned from Mara – a slash at the head, and a backhand toward the chest, so that his gleaming blade carved a bright "S" in the gloomy daylight. Isak parried both strokes with ease and flicked out his blade toward Tobias's cheek. Tobias barely blocked the attack, stumbling back as he did.

Isak pounced like a hunting cat, leveling two chopping blows at Tobias's head. Tobias parried these as well, but could do nothing about the upward stroke the minister aimed at his midriff. His flesh burned, blood blossomed from the wound, staining his shirt.

A superficial cut, but enough to decide the contest.

Tobias stepped back, breathing hard, and bowed to the minister.

The probationers whooped, whistled, and clapped. Isak answered Tobias's bow before walking to where he stood.

"You all right? I haven't delivered a fatal blow to his majesty's new Walker, have I?"

"I'm fine," Tobias said. "Thank you. I enjoyed that."

"As did I. You have a bit to learn yet, but if I'd had to fight you as a fifteen year-old, I wouldn't have stood a chance."

Tobias's smile slipped. Why did everyone talk to him about moving through time?

"The rest of you oil and stow your weapons," the minister said, addressing the probationers. "We'll meet here again on the morrow." He grasped Tobias's arm. "You come with me."

•   •   •

The minister took him first to the castle healer, who mended his wound and also used his powers to ease the swelling and tenderness of the bruise on his face.

"It's easier when the injuries are fresh," he said, a sour note to his voice. "Next time don't wait so long."

Tobias murmured acknowledgment of this, eager to be away from the man. Once the healer had tended to him, Isak led him back toward the kitchen.

"I'm really not hungry," Tobias told him.

"There's more to the kitchen than food, lad."

Isak took him to one of several small, dim, musty chambers off the main kitchen. Stacks of barrels stood shoulder to shoulder, floor to ceiling, each with a spigot attached.

"You like ale?" the minister asked.

Tobias grimaced at the memory of his last night aboard the *Gray Skate*. Or rather, his last morning. "I thought I did."

"Had too much of it a time or two?"

"The night before my arrival in Hayncalde."

"Ah, excellent. Have some now. You shouldn't wait long to oar a boat you've capsized."

He produced two tankards from a dark space among the barrels, winked, and filled the vessels. He handed one to Tobias, tapped it with his, and said, "To a fine blade match."

"Thank you, minister."

Tobias sipped his ale; the minister took a long pull, wiped his mouth with his sleeve, and perched on one of the barrels. Tobias sat on another, raising a billow of dust in the silver light from a single, high window.

"You've had a time of it since getting here," the minister said, the intensity of his gaze belying a friendly grin.

"The sovereign said much the same thing after you and the Seer left."

Isak drank some more. "I'm sorry for that – my harsh words with the Seer, I mean. I'm old enough to know better."

Tobias sipped his ale, unsure of what to say.

"So, I don't suppose you had people trying to kill you on Trevynisle."

At his hesitation, the minister lowered his tankard.

"You did?" Isak asked.

"A Belvora demon, the morning I left for Daerjen."

"Does the sovereign know?"

"I told him last night."

"Blood and bone. Twice now. I suppose I shouldn't be surprised."

Tobias eyed him. "You know why the sovereign wanted me."

This time it was Isak who hesitated. "Aye. I don't know much about Traveler magick, and until this morning, when the sovereign told me, I didn't know what it would cost you to do what he has in mind." He ran a hand over his shaved pate. "I'm not even sure what to say."

"Tell me about the war."

The minister drained his tankard, refilled it, and sat once more. "What do you want to know?"

"Are matters as dire as they seem?"

He blew out a breath. "I'm afraid they are." He straightened. "What you're really asking is, can we win? And the answer is no, probably not. And so the next question becomes, what are the consequences of an Oaqamaran victory, which is harder to answer."

"I told the sovereign I thought that if Aiyanth fell, so would Ensydar."

"You're probably right. And so will Vleros. Milnos has been waiting centuries for the opportunity to end their feud for good. This would give them that chance. Without us there – and Aiyanth – Vleros won't survive for long."

"What of Daerjen?"

"Would we fall, you mean? I don't think so. After taking Aiyanth, the autarch would turn his marauders on the Ring isles – Outer and Inner. At that point, they'd have no choice but to fight. They've been content thus far to let us carry the load. That would change. Their very survival would depend upon it. So long before the Oaqamarans reached our shores, they'd face an array of fleets intent on protecting themselves and the Inward Sea. It would be a long, costly, bloody war, but in the end I don't think the Oaqamarans would conquer all the Inward isles."

Tobias took a pull of ale. "Thank you," he said.

"For what?"

"You could have lied. You could have said Daerjen was doomed if I didn't Walk back and stop the war. That might have made things easier for the sovereign, and for you."

Isak drank as well. "That's not our way. The autarch might treat his people that way. We don't."

"No, I didn't–"

"I know you didn't mean to imply anything, lad. Don't trouble yourself." He took Tobias's tankard, topped it off, and handed it back to him. "So, now that I've said my piece, do you intend to refuse to do your magick?"

"No. I serve the sovereign, and I'll do as he asks, contracts notwithstanding. You didn't exactly paint a rosy image. Defeat for Aiyanth, Ensydar, and Vleros? Years of war in the Inward Sea? If I can prevent that, I should."

"And if you can't?"

"I should make the attempt anyway."

The minister raised his tankard. "You're a good lad."

They finished their ales and stowed Isak's tankards. Several guards converged on them as soon as they emerged from the kitchen.

"The sovereign wants to see you, my lord," one of the men said, addressing Tobias, not the minister.

Tobias and Isak shared a glance.

"I hope we can share an ale or two again soon," the minister said. "With any luck, maybe even this evening."

"With any luck," Tobias repeated. He didn't add that he'd be virtually unrecognizable, a grown man with gray in his beard and hair.

He followed the guard to the now-familiar stairway, and trod the steps as he imagined a condemned man might, climbing onto a gallows.

This is what you were meant to do.

As they stepped into the corridor, Tobias caught sight of Sofya, who stood halfway between the stairway and the door to her father's chambers. He and the guard started toward her.

"I know my way from here," he said to the man. "Thank you."

The soldier regarded the princess, then bowed. "Yes, my lord."

He turned away. Tobias continued toward Sofya, who waited for him, looking grave and proud and beautiful.

"You didn't tell me," she said, as he drew even with her. She fell in step with him. "I didn't know what Walking does to you."

"Few people do, your highness."

"Do you keep it secret? Your kind, I mean."

"No," he said. "But there aren't many of us, and our... our talents aren't well understood by most."

"My father explained it all. Why he's sending you, what happened last night, what it will be like for you when you return. I... I'm sorry for what I said earlier."

"Thank you, your highness."

"I would still be your friend, if you're willing. When you're back, I mean."

"I'd like that."

He walked on. She halted, but he knew she continued to watch him.

Reaching the door, he knocked once. At the summons from

within, he entered, crossed through the antechamber, and entered the chamber.

Mearlan stood at his window, hands clasped behind his back. He remained so even after Tobias closed the door behind him.

"I couldn't decide whether it was more merciful to give you time," he said, after a yawning silence, "to let you grow attached to the people here, or to send you sooner, so you have no time to adjust to the place. Both choices strike me as cruel. In the end, I consulted my daughter, of all people. She suggested I send you sooner rather than later. 'There's no way to do this well,' she said. 'So you should do it quickly and have done with it.'"

"She may well be right, my liege."

After another silence, Mearlan said, "I've been pondering whether I have the right to send you back – whether any sovereign has the right to bend the course of history to his or her needs and desires. I have no good answer."

"Forgive me for saying so, my liege, but don't sovereigns attempt to bend history to their needs every day? Isn't that what wars are about? And treaties? And the decrees that shape the lives of your subjects here in Daerjen?"

Mearlan chuckled. "That's well-argued, Walker."

"Actually, it's not my argument," Tobias said, remembering lessons with Vaisan Ojeyd. "In Windhome, novitiates read treatises on the use – and misuse – of Travelers. I believe that particular line of thought originated with a fourth century Aiyanthan philosopher named Serenne Fareq."

"Intriguing. Perhaps I should have read more before contracting for your services."

They settled into a third silence. Tobias's apprehension grew by the moment.

"Are your kind uncommonly long-lived?"

"I'm sorry?"

At that Mearlan turned from the window. "I'm wondering

if you'll live longer than most. I know you're about to age precipitously, but I'm thinking... you'll add the years, but the wear on your body... It won't really be like it is for the rest of us, will it? So perhaps you'll live longer than most, and the years won't be lost to you after all. At least, not all of them."

"I don't know, my liege. I've never heard others speak of it." *I've never known of any Walker who went back so far, and lost so much.*

"Well," the sovereign said, his tone too bright. "I suppose we'll have to wait and see."

"Yes, my liege."

Mearlan sat, gestured at the chair beside Tobias. He sat as well.

"You'll have to..." The sovereign broke off, let out a small, breathless laugh. "This is terribly odd. You'll have to convince me of who you are and why you've come. I won't believe you at first. I won't believe you've crossed so many years, and I'll be doubly suspicious when you tell me *why* you've come. It's hard for me to understand now, but at the time I was so very sure that war with the Oaqamarans was necessary. I thought the autarch incapable of reason, and I believed any concession to his demands would weaken Daerjen for a generation. So you'll have a rough time of it at first. I'll be hostile, dismissive, maybe even accusatory."

"All right."

He furrowed his brow and tapped a finger to his lips. "Then again, there may be a way around my stubbornness. Yes, I believe there is. My father used to say, 'Blinders don't become you, and neither does mistrust.' Say it for me."

Tobias repeated the phrase.

"Good. When I express my doubts, toss that epigraph my way." He grinned. "It should put me in my place."

"I will, my liege."

"After that, things should be a bit easier. There are a few

things we might do to avoid this war. First, we need to be less demonstrative in our support of Aiyanth. Caltha was queen of the Axle at the time. She was brilliant, but combative, and she hated the Oaqamarans. I believe her hostility toward them fed my own. You'll have to help me guard against that."

"All right."

"The second thing you might suggest is that we make some concessions in the Bone Sea. This war began as a territorial dispute between Vleros and Milnos over the isles between their shores. They had been fighting for several years by the time Oaqamar and Daerjen stepped in. And really, the isles aren't important." He grimaced, shook his head. "Let me amend that: they aren't important to us. They certainly aren't justification for war. The royal family in Vleros will scream injustice and call us traitors, but the truth is, the isles don't matter as much as I thought they did back then.

"Finally, if all else fails, we can make some concessions in the Herjean as well. This would not be my preference, even today, even knowing how poorly the war's gone. But it might be necessary."

"What kind of concessions, my liege?"

"Again, territorial. The privateers in Westisle wanted safe passage through the Bone Sea and in the waters around Herjes. The autarch was already protecting them, but the Oaqamaran fleet could only do so much, and the Ring isles refused to give the privateers any quarter."

"Well, they're outlaws. Why should they? Why did the autarch?"

"A fine question. Why do you think?"

Tobias considered the matter. "Gold," he said. "The privateers must have paid them for protection and passage through their waters. So the autarch was getting a share of their plunder."

"As much as a tierce, from what I hear," Mearlan said. "He's still getting it to this day."

"You think you should have acquiesced to this?" Tobias asked.

"No. We're fighting this second war with the privateers – and have been for two decades – because neither my father nor I was willing to surrender to piracy. The autarch demanded that we draw back our fleet. He wanted us out of the Aiyanthan Sea altogether. It's an unreasonable demand: those aren't his waters, and the shoreline buffers he was demanding on behalf of Milnos were too large. Worse, giving in here will make our war in the Herjean that much more difficult. As a last resort, though, I'll risk it."

"Very well, my liege. Pull back in Aiyanth, make concessions in the Bone Sea War, and be less aggressive in our pursuit of the privateers."

"Just so," the sovereign said. "I won't like it at first. I might grow angry, accuse you of treachery. But if you tell this younger version of me how much you've sacrificed to deliver my message, I'm sure I'll listen."

And if you don't? Tobias wanted to ask. Instead he repeated the points the sovereign had made, doing his best to commit them to memory.

The sovereign might have read doubt in his eyes. "Reasonably sure, at least. Which members of my court have you met thus far?"

"The ministers of state and arms, the Seer, your Binder and Spanner, and, of course, your wife and daughter."

Mearlan scratched his brow, a frown furrowing the skin there. "Fourteen years ago, the minister of arms had yet to come to Hayncalde. He was a captain in the fleet, exceptional, but not yet seasoned enough to be a minister. My Spanner was here, but I'm not sure how much good he would do you. I had a different Binder, but the minister of state was here, and she was a trusted advisor even then. You might enlist her aid." The corner of his mouth twitched. "And then there's the Seer." He leaned forward, forcing Tobias to meet his gaze. "I take it you don't like Seer Cavensol."

"I'm more comfortable with the minister of state."

"I can understand that. Most people are. Still, back then I relied on Osten more than anyone else, with the possible exception of my wife. I trusted Gillian, too, but if you win Osten's trust, you'll have a better chance of convincing me."

"Yes, my liege."

The sovereign's smile conveyed so much: sorrow, guilt, reassurance, confidence, even affection. "You're going to do fine, Walker. I'm sure of it. When you return, Daerjen will owe you a great debt. As will I. And I promise you this: succeed, and I will never again send you back more than a quarter turn. You have my word."

"Thank you, my liege."

A bell struck out in the courtyard. Tobias had lost track of the time, but he thought it might have been the midday bell. He whispered the sovereign's instructions a third time.

When he finished, Mearlan nodded his approval. "Good. Remember to remind me that the Bone Sea conflict is decades old."

"I will."

Mearlan dipped his chin a second time. "You should be on your way. I did some calculations after our last conversation. You need to go back fourteen years, three turns. At that time I was still contemplating how to respond to Caltha's overtures and the intransigence of the autarch. I hadn't yet committed us to any action."

Fourteen years, three turns. The very thought made Tobias light-headed.

"I can be more precise if that would help," Mearlan said, misinterpreting his silence.

"That's not necessary, my liege. With so much time... The chronofor is only so exact, and that accuracy decreases as the interval grows. Walking back a day, I can't choose the exact spirecount. If I walk back several days, I can't arrive at a precise bell. Walking back years…" He shrugged.

"I understand." He stood, forcing Tobias to do the same. "Shall I leave you, let you do this in private?"

Tobias blinked back tears, his throat tight. "That might be best, yes."

"Very well." He stepped out from behind the desk, and proffered a hand. When Tobias gripped it, the sovereign placed his other hand on top. "May the Two guide you, and protect you, and bring you back to us. Go with His glory and Her grace."

"Thank you, my liege. May the Two watch over this house in all times."

The sovereign nodded once, maintaining his grip on Tobias's hand. Then he released him and strode from the chamber.

Once he was alone, Tobias removed his clothing, taking care to fold each item and place it on the chair. For several fivecounts after he had finished, he stared at the pile, naked in the chamber, shivering slightly, though the air wasn't cold. The clothes probably wouldn't fit him after. Had the sovereign thought of that? Would he have Lars make new ones for him? No, he'd have to wait until Tobias Walked back. How would any of them know how tall or short, narrow or broad he would be?

Go. These thoughts gain you nothing.

He retrieved the chronofor from the pocket of his breeches, hands unsteady. After pulling out the turns stem to set the device, he had to pause. Fourteen years, times twelve turns, plus three. One hundred and seventy-one turns. Somehow that sounded longer, more final. If ever there were a sign that Walkers weren't meant to go back so far, this was it. One hundred and seventy-one turns. He began to twist the stem, slowly, methodically, counting with care. Better, he thought, to err on the high side, rather than find himself forced to Walk back still farther. Best to get the count right this time.

By the time he finished, his fingers had started to cramp. This struck him as funny, though he couldn't say why. Maybe it was the ridiculousness of scale. *I'm about to lose fourteen years of my life, and I'm whinging about sore fingers.*

He had delayed long enough. With one last glance around the sovereign's chamber, one last deep breath, he thumbed the central stem, and depressed it.

It caught with a faint click. The hook took him.

CHAPTER 13

18th Day of Kheraya's Ascent, Year 647

He had lost two good men. Someone in his position, in his profession, couldn't afford to grow attached to those with whom he worked, but the truth was, he had also lost two friends. Hovas especially had been a valued companion: competent and quick-witted, quiet, but willing to offer suggestions and insights.

It had never occurred to him that they would fail, much less that they would be killed. Yes, the assignment was dangerous, but they were talented, smart.

Blood and bone.

The men who would take their places were skilled as well, like all his men. But he hated to lose any of them.

That, though, was the least of his concerns.

The Span to Qaifin Palace seemed to take longer, the wind of the gap to sting more, the assault on his senses to sap more of his strength and will. When they reached the seat of the autarchy, and were confronted by yet another of Pemin's commanders and a unit of well-armed guards, Orzili and his men surrendered their weapons and tri-sextants without argument.

The guards accompanied them to the autarch's chambers. Was it Orzili's imagination, or did the Oaqamarans walk in a tighter formation than usual? Were the gazes of the autarch's soldiers always so dour, or were these guards particularly grim?

Orzili entered Pemin's chamber alone. He turned slightly at the click of the door closing behind him. A sound like the cock of a flintlock.

Pemin stood at the window, framed by sunlight, tension in his shoulders, his back, his neck. He held his hands behind him, one fisted, the other massaging his wrist.

The autarch would know from Orzili's arrival that the boy still lived. Orzili would have conveyed word of success with more subtlety, and without the urgency of another Span across so many leagues. Pemin's rage would be fresh, unbridled. Orzili would be fortunate to walk away from this encounter.

"Your excellency," he said.

He bowed, though Pemin didn't bother to look his way.

The ensuing silence lasted a tencount, more. Then, "Mearlan's Walker is still alive. You failed."

The words filled the space between them, as flat and hard as roof tile. Nothing about the men lost. No acknowledgment of the risks Hovas and Bregg had taken. Orzili expected this, but he bristled nevertheless. Only a supreme assertion of self-control allowed him to reply evenly.

"Yes, your excellency. We failed."

Pemin half-pivoted, their eyes meeting for an instant. Then the autarch faced the window again.

"I suppose that evens the tally between us. My misjudgment with the demon, yours with this attempt."

It would have been dangerous to agree, more so to argue. Orzili left the words hanging between them.

"This makes everything harder. You understand that."

"I do."

"Mearlan's people will be watching for any more attempts. And even in the past, the boy will know to be on his guard. You've made a mess of things."

Orzili bit his tongue, tasting blood.

The autarch peered back at him again, brown and silver hair

lit by daylight. "You disagree?"

"My thoughts on the matter are irrelevant, your excellency. I've failed you and you're displeased. Nothing else matters."

"Yet I would hear your thoughts."

Orzili's gaze darted away, but he made himself look the man in the eye again.

"No matter the time," he said, "this was going to be difficult and dangerous. No one regrets the loss of my men more than I do." He refused to say anything about them failing. "But none of this was ever going to be easy."

Pemin glowered. "I'm not used to hearing you make excuses."

"I don't believe you did, your excellency," he said, the words clipped.

Too much so, it seemed.

"You will send my Walker back. As soon as you know how far the boy has gone, you will send her back as far. Farther. Give her an extra turn if you must. Or two. I don't care. Just make certain she has plenty of time to locate you in whatever past Mearlan seeks to alter. The two of you will plan and execute an assassination of Mearlan, his family, and the Walker. I want all of them dead."

Orzili opened his mouth, closed it again, unable to think of anything to say. *My Walker*. A reminder of yesterday's encounter. Lenna. His Walker, but Orzili's wife. Of course, Orzili didn't dare correct the man, or refer to her in any other way.

"She will Walk back with tri-devices," the autarch added, compounding Orzili's shock. "Enough to enable you to do whatever you must to follow these orders."

"Those devices... your excellency, that is..."

"Spit it out, Orzili."

"You're playing a dangerous game with history, your excellency. We've gone to great lengths to keep these devices hidden. We've taken every precaution, because we know that if other Binders learn of their existence, our advantage will be lost. Now you want to send them back. That will change the course of history in any number of ways. Not least among them the… forgive me, but the squandering of that advantage."

Pemin shook his head, a faint, sardonic grin on his lips. "You're a clever man – as clever as anyone who serves me – but your thinking in this regard is remarkably limited. Don't you see? That advantage is already compromised. Not completely, of course. But enough. People in Windhome know of the devices; you said so yourself just yesterday. That knowledge remains vague for now, but it won't for long. And even vague, awareness of the devices serves as a warning to our enemies, which blunts the devices' effectiveness.

"On the other hand, if she goes back as I have instructed, and can equip you – a younger you – with tri-sextants, the advantage will be magnified tenfold. More. No one will stand against you. Mearlan will be destroyed. His attempt to alter the past will be crushed. And I will have won these wars, perhaps before they even begin. The world will be changed, and this autarchy will be unassailable."

It was an audacious plan, bolder than anything Orzili would have dared. Which was why Pemin, and his father before him, had built Oaqamar into the most powerful isle between the oceans.

"I know you begrudge the time she will lose," Pemin said, ending a brief silence. "I'm not insensitive to her sacrifice, or to yours. It could be a year or more. If Mearlan is as desperate as I believe him to be, it could be far more than that." He pointed to something on his desk. A large purse, swollen with coins.

"There are sixty rounds in there. Even after you pay your men, that will leave you with a handsome sum."

Orzili eyed the purse, but made no move to pick it up.

The autarch's eyebrows rose fractionally. "You want more?"

"No, your excellency. I just…"

Twice as many rounds wouldn't have been enough to compensate them for what they were about to lose. How did one value a year? Two? Ten?

Again, he knew better than to give voice to his thoughts.

"You're most generous, your excellency." He crossed to the desk on leaden legs and hefted the purse, which weighed as much as a small artillery ball.

"Mearlan will send him back soon," Pemin said. "You'd best return to Daerjen. Our contact knows to send word as soon as the boy Walks?"

"Yes, your excellency. Before he Walks if possible. As soon as Mearlan decides how far to send the lad, we'll know."

"Good." Pemin returned to the window, showing Orzili his back. "Don't fail me again, Orzili. As I said, the scales are balanced between us. Disappoint me a second time, and I will be far less forgiving than I've been today. Do I make myself clear?"

"Perfectly, your excellency."

He bowed again and left, the purse like an anchor in his hand.

He was halfway through a bottle of Miejan red when Lenna returned to their flat. She came through the door, hair tangled by the wind, cheeks glowing with the exertions of her day, oblivious of what awaited her. Or perhaps just braver than he.

Seeing him, she faltered, her smile slipping.

She glanced around the flat, approached him, her steps deliberate.

"You were thirsty," she said, dark eyes flicking to the blue bottle.

"It's a long way to Qaifin and back." He kept his voice low, tried hard to keep his diction clear.

She retrieved a goblet, sat opposite him, and splashed some wine into her cup.

"What are we drinking to?"

"Pemin," he said without delay. "May he live a long life filled with misery and loneliness."

Lenna sighed and regarded him, lips thin. She drained her goblet and poured herself more.

"He wants me to go back," she said.

"As soon as we know how far." He emptied his goblet in turn and refilled it. Soon they would need another bottle. Or he would. She wasn't likely to be here much longer.

"Maybe I should have gone with you to Daerjen, as he said."

He shook his head. "When you go back, I want you to find me, no matter how far, no matter where we were at the time. If you're going to spend these years, I want to be sure we find that other Walker and kill him. Going with me to Daerjen would have been a needless risk."

She didn't argue. Instead she asked, "Do you have any idea how far it will be?"

He had long admired her courage. Even when they were children, novitiates in the palace at Windhome, she had been the brave one. Clever, too. And always lovely. She deserved the truth.

"It will be a long way. Years, I expect."

She raised her cup to her lips again, but this time took only a sip.

"I've said all along that you prefer older women."

"Don't." It came out sharper than he intended.

She set her cup on the table and took one of his hands in both of hers. "You're torturing yourself."

He nodded, lips quivering. He refused to cry.

"I've told you before, this is what I do. You Span, I Walk. We both kill. I was going to lose the years eventually. Why should it matter whether I lose them in a trickle, or all at once?"

"Because it does, and you know it. It's all the difference in the world."

She didn't argue the point.

"I'm not ready to–" He broke off. He'd intended to say "to lose you," but that wasn't quite right.

"To be wed to an old woman?"

How old was too old? Did he love her because she was young and beautiful, or because she was Lenna? Did the years matter? After a moment's consideration he realized these questions missed the point. What he loved was their life together. He didn't want that foreshortened by Pemin's scheming.

"We can run," he said, voice dropping further. "Leave this place now and make our way north, or out to the Knot. Pemin's reach is long, but–"

"His reach is long. Too long. I don't want to live my life watching for his assassins, for younger, stronger versions of us. That's..." She shook her head. "That's not us, and it's no way to live."

She was right, which pained him as much as anything the autarch had said earlier in the day.

They sat thus for some time, his hand in hers, the goblets and mostly-empty bottle between them.

The flutter of wings made both of them jump. They turned their heads as one. A gray and white dove sat in their open window, cooing softly, ruffling its feathers. A small, folded piece of parchment had been tied to the creature's leg.

For a tencount neither of them moved. At last Lenna stood, crossed to the window, and stroked the feathers on the back of the dove's neck. As she untied the parchment, the bird raised its wings to keep its balance.

Lenna faced him, their eyes locking.

"Do you want me to open it?" he asked.

"No." She stared at the parchment a fivecount more, then unfolded it.

Her eyes widened and she braced herself on the window frame with an unsteady hand.

"Lenna?"

She breathed through her mouth, saying nothing. The hand that held the paper shook.

In two strides he was beside her. He put one arm around her and with the other took the scrap of parchment.

Even after staring at it for a tencount, he couldn't make sense of it. Surely this wasn't possible. It had to be a mistake, the answer to a different question. They couldn't expect her to go back so far.

14 years, had been scrawled on the parchment in a neat, slanted hand. The same hand that had written so many missives before. Never in error.

She would be old when she reached that past. Too old to return to him in this time.

"You can't do this," he said.

"I have to. He'll kill us otherwise."

"Running would be better. It would have to be."

She eased her grip on the window frame, stood straighter, and stepped away to look him in the eye.

"No, it wouldn't," she said. "We went to Pemin because he could do as much for us as we do for him. That's why we worked so hard to build the facility at Sholiss. I'm not going back for him. I'm going back for us, for what we've been working for. This could allow us to weaken Windhome years sooner."

As she spoke, she retrieved a small scrap of parchment from beside their dove cage. On it she wrote in black ink, *Recvd.* She tied this to the leg of the dove, lifted the bird, and tossed it gently out the window. After watching it fly off, she turned to him once more.

He couldn't move, couldn't find the words to argue. She was right in all she had said. On top of everything else, she was brilliant. And he was on the verge of losing her forever.

She smiled, a rare tear slipping down her cheek.

"My poor love," she whispered, brushing his lips with the

back of her fingers. "Come with me to bed. Make love to me. And then let me go."

Mute, forlorn, helpless against his love for her, he followed her to their room.

By the light of the gibbous moon low in the eastern sky, they made their way to the clearing from which he had Spanned to Qaifin. She undressed and set her chronofor, winding back the turns until the clicking of her device felt like the final beats of some metallic heart.

When she had finished, he handed her the three tri-sextants they had carried with them from the city. He kissed her on the lips and stepped back. Moonlight shone in her hair, on her bare shoulders, on the devices in her hand. She appeared otherworldly, a creature of light and magick and gold.

"Come back to me," he said. "As soon as you're done."

Her smile caught the glow of the moon. "You don't mean that. I'll be seventy. You won't want me when I'm so old."

He didn't know how to answer. Already she seemed to be gone from him and he wanted her back. Desperately. But he feared meeting that older version of her.

"I love you," he said after a fivecount. Because everything came back to that.

"And I love you."

He saw her thumb move on the chronofor, heard one final *click*.

Without another sound, without light or a change in the air or any kind of warning, she jerked back away from him, vanishing from sight, as if tugged into nothing.

For a long time, he stared at the spot where she had been. Finally, as he heard bells toll in the distance, he exhaled and began the long walk back into Belsan.

He left her clothes there, for her return.

CHAPTER 14

4th Day of Sipar's Settling, Year 633

Lenna bustled through the flat, pulling on her woolen overshirt, bronze hair tied back from her face.

"I won't be gone long," she said, making her way to the door. "I want to check the market again, in case they've come in."

He sat at the table, watching her, making no effort to hide his amusement. Below the tiny room they rented, the thud of the cooper's mallet shook the entire building.

"You understand that this is for show," he said. "It's like the bees. You're not going to make any more gold as a seamstress than you will cultivating honey."

She halted, set her fists on her hips. "You don't know that. And the bees will make money. Just not in winter; certainly not in Kantaad." She stepped closer to him. "And you might consider," she said more quietly, "that spending coin the way we do, you ought to have a skill that you can show off as well. I'd rather not explain to our landlord that we make our rent money assassinating court nobles."

It was a fair point.

"I don't know how much longer we'll be in Fanquir."

"That's fine," she said. She rubbed her arms. "Frankly, I'll be glad when we leave. In the meantime, I'm going to look for those bolts of cloth. I'd suggest you figure out what you want to be when you grow up."

He grinned. She stooped and kissed him on the cheek before leaving the room and descending the stairs, each step on the worn treads rattling the ancient building nearly as much as the strokes of Skav's hammer.

A few spirecounts later, he heard her on the steps again, returning to the room. The door opened.

"That was quick." He swiveled in his chair. "Did you forget—"

The rest of his question caught in his throat. Lenna stood before him, though not the Lenna he knew. Not one he had ever seen. Broad streaks of silver mingled with the bronze of her hair, and deep lines marked the skin around her mouth and eyes. She wore an ill-fitting gown, faded but thick, warm, and partially covered with a woolen cloak, also tired. She was still a beauty. She always would be. But the years written in her face, and in the skin on her hands and neck, daunted him.

Neither of them spoke. After a tencount, she turned and shut the door.

"I saw her leave," she said, facing him. "Me, I mean. I figured it was safe."

He nodded, speechless.

"Gods, I'd forgotten how beautiful you were. Not that you're any less handsome now, but when we were young..." She shook her head. "How long will I be gone?"

"You've... you've gone to the market. A bell maybe. Not much more. What are you doing here?"

"We have work to do, you and I. A Walker to kill."

"How far back have you come?"

She frowned, canted her head. He read sympathy in her eyes, loss, grief.

"I don't think I should tell you that. I'm sorry."

She didn't have to. He could calculate it in his head, adding years lived to years lost in the Walk back. Not with precision – a guess only, but close enough. If she'd come back a year she would look much like the woman who had left this room moments ago. If she had come back twenty she would be even older than this woman standing before him. So ten years. Maybe a few more.

"Don't be angry," she said, misinterpreting his silence.

"I'm not. I'm just… You've come a long way."

"Yes. In years and in leagues. I've been in this time for nearly a ha'turn. I needed passage from… from elsewhere."

"More secrets."

"More things you shouldn't know yet. It all has to unfold the way it's intended."

"Except you've come back to kill a Walker, who, I would guess, has come back to change things in ways someone doesn't like. Pemin?"

She hesitated, nodded.

"So why hide things from me?"

"I don't care about the rest of the world. Not really. I mean, I do, and that's why I'm here. But our life together, that's… I don't want to change that. Not any more than I have to. Do you understand?"

He did. "Yes."

"Good. Because we're about to tear to pieces everything else between the oceans."

She drew forth from within her cloak three golden objects.

Tri-sextants. He had never seen one before, but he knew immediately what they were. Binders were working on these in Sholiss, and elsewhere. Some worked for Pemin, some didn't. To his knowledge, none had perfected the devices. Not yet. Not to this degree.

"Do they work?" he asked.

"Yes. As I understand it, the Spanners who use them will need to be trained. I know enough to help with that. Thanks to you." She flashed a smile, and the years melted from her face.

"I lose you, don't I? You're here, and I have some idea of how far back you Walked." He dragged a hand over his face.

"The return could kill you. At the very least you'll–"

"Please don't." She drew a breath, and he regretted what he'd said. Their goodbye would have been brutal for both of them.

"I'm here," she said, "and there's nothing to be done about the years I've spent. More to the point, we haven't much time. An irony, I know, but there it is. A Walker is coming in less than a turn, and we have to be in Daerjen when he arrives. In Hayncalde."

"To kill him."

"That's right."

"And what do I tell her? The younger you."

"Tell me the truth, at least as much as you can. That you'll be spending the next turn with me, that we have a task to complete, and that you'll be home when it's done, so that we can be together for years more."

"Do you know what all this is about?" he asked. "Can you tell me?"

That, of all things, drew a laugh. The same laugh he knew so well, that set his heart on fire every time he heard it.

"It's about Pemin, of course. Pemin and his wars. Isn't it always?"

He chuckled as well. Their mirth soon spent itself, leaving them gazing at each other. Her eyes hadn't changed.

"I don't like this," he said.

She shrugged. "I can't help that. I don't like it either." She glanced toward the door. "I should go. It's dangerous for Walkers to meet themselves across the years."

"Right." He stood.

"I need a place to stay. I managed to steal some coin when first I arrived in this time, but I used most of it getting here."

"Of course." He retreated to the table by their bed and pulled several treys and a few rounds from his purse. "There's a boarding house near–"

"I remember."

He returned to her, handed her the coins. Her skin was cool.

"I shouldn't come here again," she said. "I'll wait for you in the boarding house. We should leave tomorrow. The next day at the latest. You have enough Spanners among the men who work for you?"

"I have two," he said. "For now I can be the third. I'm sure we'll find another before the time comes."

"All right, then."

They eyed each other again, as if unsure of how to say goodbye. At last Lenna pocketed the coins, turned, and let herself out of the room.

He stared after her, a dull ache in his chest. But already his thoughts churned. They would go to Qaifin first. Pemin had set all of this in motion sometime in the future. He would want to know that this Lenna was here. And the autarch would pay them before they did anything more. He and Lenna would insist.

After that, they would make their way to Daerjen and Hayncalde. He knew the city, but not as well as he should. And time was short.

CHAPTER 15

21st Day of Sipar's Settling, Year 633

A fury of light and color. Voices and notes and every variety of noises, blaring, skirling, assailing. Sweet scents, savory aromas, foul odors, all blended in a noisome cloud that enveloped him. Vile assault on his tongue, as if every morsel he had ever eaten sought revenge. Violent abuse of his flesh: battering, poking, burning, freezing; even the most gentle caress would have made him cry aloud.

If only he could draw breath.

Tobias writhed and flailed, desperate to break free, knowing all the while that no bonds held him, no walls confined him. Only time swooping past, tearing at his mind, his senses.

The deep breath he'd taken had already spent itself, and he sensed that he had years left to go. His chest ached, his heart labored. His lungs had been set ablaze.

Legs trembling, vision swimming, he would have collapsed to the ground had the between not held him in place, a mercy and a torment. And still it went on. He ached to breathe, to relieve the intolerable pressure on his chest.

The storm buffeting his senses started to fade. The light dimmed; the roar grew more distant, the smells and tastes and touches lost their intensity. He grew cold, but if the rest left him alone, he could live with that. Or die with it.

No air. Nothing. He sensed his grasp on memory slipping. Walkers, it seemed, were not meant to go back so far. It was too much. Not his fault. Giving in to the darkness was not surrender, so much as acknowledgment. He had reached too far.

All went black.

Sensation returned piecemeal. The pressure of cold stone against his back. The scratch of warm wool on his legs and arms, chest and neck. The clean scent and taste of precious air. The smooth, gold back of the chronofor pressed to his palm.

And voices. Not a clamor of them, but individuals, one speaking, and then another.

"...the question though, is from when." A man. The sovereign?

"A long time, I should think, given his condition. This was no simple journey." Also a man. This time Tobias knew the voice, the drawl, the lazy assurance in the words: Osten Cavensol.

He forced his eyes open, blinked against the brightness, tried to lift a hand to shield his eyes. He couldn't move. For a moment he wondered if, unsure of his origins and wary of his sudden appearance, they had bound him. But he felt no rope, no silk, no iron, only the blanket.

He opened his mouth, but couldn't make a sound.

"He's trying to speak," the sovereign said.

Mearlan leaned over him, peering down at his face. Tobias stared back. He looked so young! No gray lightened his brown hair. The skin around his mouth and eyes was smooth. Care had worn a line or two in his brow, but otherwise he appeared to be in the prime of youth, a far cry from the worn man Tobias knew in his own time.

The Seer was also much changed. He stood straighter, his features those of a younger man. Tobias caught the scent of Tincture hanging in the air, but Osten's eyes were clear.

"Can you tell me your name?" the sovereign asked, enunciating loudly.

Tobias wanted to tell him his hearing wasn't impaired. He

tried again to speak, managed a small sound, deeper than he had expected, but inarticulate.

The sovereign sighed, straightened. "Fetch him some clothes."

Tobias heard the door open and close.

Mearlan and his Seer continued to talk about Tobias as if he weren't there, which, he decided, was probably fair. He couldn't add to their conversation, though as their speculation about him carried them further from the truth, he grew ever more agitated. He tried repeatedly to form words, to move his limbs, to do anything more than lie there, mute, helpless, naked.

The door opened again, and someone stepped into the chamber. Footsteps approached him and a woman came into view. A beauty, short-haired, with a square face and eyes of sky blue. Tobias couldn't keep his eyes from widening.

"He recognizes you, minister," the Seer said. "Perhaps someone from your future."

She paled at this, but tossed a smirk at Osten. "I was given to understand he's from all of our futures, Seer."

The Seer answered with an enigmatic smile and a twitch of his shoulder.

"We've sent for clothes," the sovereign said. "You should wait in the antechamber."

"Can't I remain until they do? He's quite decent right now."

"Very well."

"T–Tobias," he managed, the effort leaving him short of breath. His voice definitely sounded different, lower. He should have expected this, but still it struck him as odd.

"Your presence works miracles," Osten said. "I really must wonder about you two."

"Do shut up, Seer." She looked down at Tobias again. "I'm Gillian Ainfor, minister of protocol. But you know that already, don't you?"

"S-state."

Tobias said this with somewhat less effort than he had expended on his name, and he spoke without thought. He regretted it the instant the word crossed his lips. Going back in time a bell or a day, or even twelve days, gave him little power over future events. In this instance, he had come farther than anyone in Windhome would have permitted. He was a force of history. What else might he change, for good or ill, with a careless word or deed? He would need to be more careful.

"It seems there's a promotion in your future, minister," the sovereign said. He wore a frown, perhaps concerned as well by what Tobias had revealed.

The minister's cheeks remained ashen. "How far have you come?" she asked in a hushed voice.

Tobias tried to answer, but couldn't form the words. While he made the attempt, the door opened once more, and a guard handed a pile of clothes to the sovereign.

"Minister, give us a moment, will you?"

Once Gillian was gone, the guard and the Seer propped Tobias up and maneuvered him into the clothes. Tobias could do little to help, but once they were finished, and had lifted him into a chair, he had enough control of his muscles to keep his head upright and to flex his fingers.

His hands were bigger than he remembered, his arms thicker and covered with more hair. He felt large and heavy and awkward. The sovereign walked around his desk and sat, eyeing Tobias the entire time. Tobias followed his movements with his head and eyes.

"I sense you're doing better."

"Y-yes, my l-liege."

To the guard, Mearlan said, "Bring the minister back in." Of Tobias, he asked, "Are you ready to tell us how far back in time you've Walked?"

"F-f-fourteen years, my l-liege."

"Did I hear that correctly?" Gillian asked from behind him.

"Fourteen years?"

The sovereign stared unblinking, his mouth open in a small O. Even the Seer appeared stunned.

"Yes," Tobias said. "F-fourteen."

"And I sent you," Mearlan said. "I must have. As I understand it, a Walker moves through time, but remains in the space where his journey originated."

"Th-that's right."

"So you come with a message, from me, to me."

Tobias glanced toward the guard.

"I think you all should give the Walker and me some time alone."

The soldier regarded Tobias with mistrust. "But, my liege—"

"He can barely move, and we know he's not concealing any weapons."

"N-not the minister," Tobias said. "Or th-the Seer."

"Very well."

As the guard left the chamber, Gillian and Osten took seats on either side of Tobias. His chronofor rested on the sovereign's desk, where the Seer had placed it when they dressed him. Tobias reached for it, managed to grip it and slide it into his pocket. The Seer watched him.

"All right, then," Mearlan said. "What is it you're to tell me?"

"You m-must not go to war with the Oa-Oaqamarans.

The sovereign's gaze flicked toward the Seer before settling again on Tobias. "And why not?" he asked, his voice hardening.

This was not the sovereign Tobias knew. He heard as much in the tone of the question, saw it in the dangerous flash of those indigo eyes. Youth might serve him in other ways, but it would make him stubborn, leery of any who questioned his judgment.

"It goes p-poorly, my liege."

"Poorly, in what way?"

"I expect we're losing," Gillian said.

Mearlan shot her a quick glare. "Is that it?" he asked Tobias. "We're losing? And so I sent a Walker back to talk me out of fighting?" He shook his head. "That's doesn't sound like me." He considered Tobias. "How do I know I'm the one who sent you? It could have been someone else, someone I ought not to trust."

"You told me to tell you something – a ph-phrase your father used to use. 'Blinders don't become you, and neither does mistrust.'"

The sovereign's face fell.

"At least we know who sent him," Osten said after a lengthy silence.

"You knew how hard this would be for you to b-believe." Tobias pressed on, despite the awkwardness of the syntax. "But you paid a good deal of gold to bring me to your court. And then you s-sent me back, costing me fourteen years of my life. Actually, twenty-eight."

"Costing you... What do you mean?"

"Gods," the minister whispered. "He's right, my liege. The Binder has told me this, but I'd forgotten."

"Forgotten what? Explain, please."

They watched him, expectant, all clearly unnerved by his arrival.

"When I left this chamber a short time ago – when I began my journey back – I was f-fifteen years old. The Walk aged me fourteen years. Returning to my own time will do the same."

The sovereign pushed back from his desk and stood. "You mean to tell me you're a boy?"

"I was a short while ago. I don't think I am anymore."

"And you say you'll... you'll be in your forties when you get back?"

"Yes, my liege. Your older self thought the magnitude of that s-sacrifice might convince you to take my warnings seriously."

"It certainly lends weight to what you have to say." Mearlan crossed to the window, a habit he apparently acquired in his youth. "How long can you remain with us?"

"As long as I must, my liege. Walking through so many years, my d-destination can only be so precise." The words echoed in his thoughts, reminding him of a similar conversation with this very man in this very chamber less than a bell before. Fourteen years from now. A chill ran through him. He made himself complete the thought. "Remaining here for a few bells, or even for a day or two, should make little difference."

"Good," the sovereign said. He nodded to Gillian, who crossed to the door, opened it, and beckoned for one of the guards.

A uniformed man appeared in the doorway.

"Please find Walker..." Mearlan paused and turned back to Tobias, frowning again. "I'm sorry, I didn't catch your full name."

"Tobias Doljan, my liege."

"And you were trained on Trevynisle?"

"Yes, my liege. In the palace at Windhome, under the guidance of... Of the chancellor there." He couldn't recall when Shaan assumed his position, and he thought it best to err on the side of discretion.

Once more, the sovereign appeared to read his thoughts. "Yes, very good." To the guard, he said, "Find Walker Doljan something to eat, and have quarters prepared for him, in case his stay with us extends past this evening."

"Yes, my liege." The guard left them.

"In the meantime," Mearlan said, "I'd like you to remain in my antechamber. Forgive me, but this is all quite extraordinary, and I think it best that we limit your interactions with all but my most trusted advisors. I hope you understand."

"I do, my liege," he said, and meant it. He understood better than the sovereign thought, perhaps better than Mearlan did himself. The sovereign seemed to want him gone from his sight. Tobias's mere presence here was evidence of Mearlan's future failures.

Tobias stood, and exited the chamber. The antechamber was empty save for a single guard, who watched Tobias as if she expected him to steal art off the wall. A fire blazed in the hearth along the far wall. Tobias moved a chair close to the flames and sat, knowing the woman followed his every movement. He tried to ignore her and soon found himself staring at his hands and arms, marveling at their transformation. His fingers looked too long. His forearms were those of a grown man. He wanted to see his face in a mirror, but wasn't certain he could bring himself to look.

On the thought, he raised a hand to his cheek and, to his astonishment, felt stubble. He had the beginnings of a beard! He fished the chronofor from his pocket and tried with little success to use its back as a mirror.

The first guard returned with a generous repast of bread, cheese, and wine – golden, from Brenth. He ate slowly, more because it was something to do than because he was hungry. As he did, Gillian slipped out of the sovereign's chamber and crossed to where he sat.

"He wants me to fetch the Binder, so that he might explain a bit more about the journey you've just undertaken."

Tobias nodded, but then said, "He could just as easily ask me."

"Yes, well, I'm not sure he's ready for that."

He knew she was right.

"I can't begin to imagine what you're feeling right now," the minister said.

Tobias could only shrug. "Will he listen to me? Will he do what his older self wants him to do?"

"I don't know. He's intelligent, wise beyond his years. But he's young and new to his power, still trying to emerge from the long shadow cast by his father. And he's a man, which doesn't speak well of his judgment."

Tobias laughed. "I'm a man."

"You're a boy in the body of a man. I'm not sure what that makes you."

His cheeks flushed.

"I mean no offense," she said. "I'm stating a fact. More, I'm certain that seeing both ends of this war you're trying to prevent, gives you a perspective none of us can match."

"I hope the sovereign agrees."

She studied him as he continued to eat, until he grew uncomfortable under her gaze. "Forgive me. I'm... Your appearance here is unsettling for all of us. I'll leave you."

Gillian stepped to the door, glanced back at him once more, and let herself out of the antechamber.

She returned before long with a dour, dark-eyed man in tow. He wore ministerial robes like hers, and was as tall as she – perhaps a hand shorter than Tobias. His hair was dark, as were his meticulously groomed mustache and goatee.

Again Gillian faltered at the sight of Tobias, and after a moment's thought, she led the man to him. Tobias stood.

"Walker Doljan, I'd like you to meet Bexler Filt, Hayncalde's Binder. Bexler, this is the young man I told you about."

The Binder offered a hand, which Tobias gripped. The man eyed him keenly.

"Gillian told me how far you've come," he said, whispering and eyeing the guard. "I... I have so many questions for you."

"I understand," Tobias said, keeping his voice low as well. "Sadly, I don't believe it would be wise for us to have such a conversation."

"Yes, I understand. You're wise to be cautious. And yet, I expect you've come to change history, haven't you? There can be no other reason for Traveling so far."

"I told you," Gillian said, "he's trying to prevent a war."

"Yes, I was sorry to hear that."

"Have you advised the sovereign to send the fleet?" Tobias asked.

"I have. I think it's a fight we can win. Especially if I'm able to complete a project I've been working on."

At the periphery of his vision, Tobias thought he saw Gillian give a quick, sharp shake of her head.

"It's not yet ready to be shown," Filt went on smoothly. "Especially to someone from another time. As you've indicated, your presence here creates risks none of us can fully understand."

Tobias looked from Gillian to the Binder. "Of course." After another pause, he decided that he needed to trust someone, even at the risk of revealing details about the future. "I can't tell you much, but I do need help from both of you. The sovereign – your sovereign – he wants this war. I can tell. But it will weaken Daerjen, and it will bring our allies to ruin. I swear it will."

"Can you tell us who we're fighting?" Filt asked. "In your time, I mean."

Tobias weighed the question, remembering that Mearlan had spoken to him about details of the wars. Clearly the sovereign had expected him to discuss these matters. "We fight on two fronts: against the Oaqamarans and Milnos in the Bone Sea, and against privateers in the waters around Westisle."

"And in all this fighting, have we any advantages at all? Are there any... any weapons or tools that have turned battles our way, perhaps something–"

"That's enough, Bexler."

Tobias made no attempt to conceal his bewilderment. "I'm afraid I don't understand."

She cast a hard glance Filt's way. "It's nothing. And I think we should keep in mind that history can be influenced in any number of ways. We in this time should be cautious as well."

"Yes, of course." Filt's gaze bounced between the two of

them. "You make a fine point, minister."

Gillian's smile was brittle, but she hooked an arm through the Binder's and patted his hand. Tobias had seen her do something similar. In the future, with her husband, Haplar Jarrett. Apparently, Jarrett wasn't the first Binder in her life.

"You were telling us you need our help," Gillian prompted.

"That's right," Tobias said.

"What do you want us to do?"

"To start, believe me," Tobias said. "And do what you can to help me convince the sovereign."

Gillian turned her bright eyes on Filt. "Binder?"

"I'll have to think about it. This is all quite sudden."

"I understand," Tobias said.

The minister tugged Filt toward Mearlan's door. "We should get in there. The sovereign is waiting for us."

"Yes, of course. A pleasure to meet you, Binder."

"And you, Walker. Perhaps we can speak again later."

"I'd like that."

The two of them crossed to the door, and after knocking, entered the chamber. Tobias placed another log on the fire, and returned to his chair.

He remained there for more than a bell, until at last the sovereign himself emerged from the chamber and walked his way. Tobias stood and straightened his shirt and robe, which didn't fit him nearly as well as the clothes Lars had made for him.

"You've been comfortable, I trust," Mearlan said.

"Yes, my liege, thank you."

"Your arrival has prompted quite a discussion, as I'm sure you can imagine. We're not done, but I see no reason why you need to remain here. I'd like you to avoid contact with others in the castle, but with that in mind, if you would like to repair to the quarters we've arranged for you, you have my permission to do so."

"Thank you, my liege. I would like that. I take it, then, that you'd like me to remain here tonight."

"That would be best, yes. We can speak in the morning."

"Very well, my liege."

Mearlan beckoned to the guard and told her to accompany Tobias to the chamber that had been arranged for him.

As it turned out, he had been assigned a room on the same corridor where his quarters had been in his own time. Once Tobias was settled, with a pallet, pillow, and blanket, the guard positioned herself in the corridor outside his door. With nothing else to do, Tobias lay down, thinking he would rest for a short while.

He awoke some time later to a darkening sky and the tolling of the castle bells. Panic gripped him; he was sure the castle was under attack again. But within a tencount the tolling ceased and he realized it was just the early evening bell. He rolled off the pallet and searched the darkening chamber for a candle and flint. Finding none, he returned to the bed and sat. After a time, he began to pace, and at last he opened his door.

Another guard had joined the woman.

"Yes, my lord," this soldier said. "Can we help you?"

"I would like to go outside."

The two guards eyed each other.

"I won't speak with anyone. You can watch me the entire time. I just..." He opened his hands. "I'd like to get out of here."

The guards appeared unsure, and Tobias considered withdrawing his request, not wishing to get them in trouble. An instant later, he felt himself growing angry. He was fourteen years older than he had been that morning, fourteen years closer to a premature dotage. That they would treat him as a prisoner seemed like an affront.

"I'm not sure we can allow that, my lord," the woman said.

"Did your sovereign give you any indication that I'm to be

held captive? Did he say that I had committed some sort of crime?"

"Well, no, my lord."

"In that case, I would leave this chamber. You may accompany me, but you will not hold me here."

He didn't wait for a reply. Stepping past the guards, he strode down the corridor toward the stairway. The two soldiers hurried after him.

Upon descending the stairs, and stepping outside, he paused to get his bearings. Then he struck out toward the sovereign's courtyard, with its fountain and gardens. The guards followed a few paces behind him.

He hadn't expected that evening would bring such a chill; he had failed to take into account those extra three turns he'd added to his journey. It had been Kheraya's Ascent when he left. Most lands had been in the midst of their planting seasons. Now it was Sipar's Settling, or Her Stirring at the latest. The first plantings were still several turns off. As was his birthday. His former birthday.

Tobias chuckled at the thought, surprising himself.

He lingered near the fountain for only a short time before deciding to go back inside, perhaps to another chamber with an active hearth.

He pivoted, intending to ask the guards where he might find one. As he did, though, he spotted a figure standing near the gate that led to the other courtyard. Tall, lean, clearly a man – but Tobias didn't think he was a guard. He wore no armor.

He started toward the figure.

For his part, the stranger took no notice of Tobias. He glanced about, appearing to take note of archways, towers, the position of the next ward. Tobias thought he was orienting himself.

Additional movement caught Tobias's attention. Three men stood near the stranger, arrayed around him. Still, Tobias wouldn't have given this much thought had two more guards not emerged from the gate at that moment, both of them brawny and well-armed. The figure took a step back and pressed himself against the courtyard wall. His companions did the same. The guards passed without taking notice of them.

"Who are you?" Tobias said, more to himself than to the strangers. Pitching his voice to carry, he called, "You there! What are you doing?"

The men spun in Tobias's direction. Tobias's guards hurried forward with the ring of drawn steel. Tobias pointed at the stranger. The two distant guards shouted, drew their swords as well.

The man stared at Tobias for the span of a single breath. He bared his teeth in a grin and signaled to his compatriots, who took positions around him again. In less than a fivecount, they vanished from view as if they had never been there.

Just before they disappeared, though, Tobias thought he saw something glimmer in the man's hand. He could have sworn it was made of gold.

CHAPTER 16

21st Day of Sipar's Settling, Year 633

"Tell me again what you were doing in that courtyard."

The sovereign stood with his back to his desk, arms crossed over his chest, eyes fixed on Tobias, who sat in a chair before him. The Seer and Mearlan's ministers of arms and state stood to the side, listening, their silence as weighty as stone.

The minister of arms, a tall, steel-haired woman with fine features and the build of an Oaqamaran warrior, rested one hand on the hilt of her blade. Tobias half-expected her to draw the weapon and take off his head.

"I told you," he said. "I fell asleep in the chamber that was assigned to me. When I woke, I decided to wander the grounds a bit. In my own time, I've only lived in this castle for a couple of days. I'm still curious about it."

"So you chose to ignore my orders to remain in your quarters. You even prevailed upon your guards to accompany you as you defied my wishes."

"With all due respect, my liege, I did no such thing. You told me to avoid contact with others in the castle, and I was doing that. But you never said that I was to be a prisoner in my quarters, and I told your soldiers as much. They remained with me the entire time, and I made certain not to approach or speak with anyone else."

"Forgive me, my liege," the minister of arms broke in. "Right now I'm more interested in this intruder the Walker claims to have seen. The rest can wait."

Mearlan still glowered, mistrust of Tobias manifest in his hard expression, his coiled posture. After a fivecount he nodded. "Go on, Walker."

"Yes, my liege. I was… I was walking. But it was colder than I expected, and I decided to go back indoors."

"Colder than you expected," Mearlan said, seemingly unable to stop himself. "It's Sipar's Settling. Why shouldn't it be cold?"

"Because when I woke this morning," Tobias fired back with more asperity than might have been wise, "I was in Kheraya's Ascent."

That brought the sovereign up short.

"The guards said the men simply vanished," the Seer said, filling an uncomfortable silence. "Is that what you saw as well?"

"Yes," Tobias said, a catch in his voice.

"It's not a difficult question," the sovereign said. "It either is or isn't."

Tobias had decided he didn't like this younger sovereign.

He did a poor job of keeping his growing animosity out of his voice. "It's *what* I saw; it's just not *all* I saw."

"My liege," the sovereign added for him, drawing out the last word.

"My liege," Tobias repeated. "I'm almost certain I saw something in his hand. Something made of gold."

"A jewel?" Mearlan asked.

"A device," said the Seer. "Like those the Binder makes."

The sovereign looked back and forth between them. "Is that what you meant?"

"It is." Tobias wished Gillian, or even Filt, was in the chamber with him, but maybe the Seer would prove himself more of an ally than he had anticipated.

"Might these men have followed you here?"

"I don't see how, my liege. I was alone in your chamber when I began my journey. Few people knew you intended to send me back to prevent the war, and none save the two of us knew exactly how many years and turns I'd be Walking."

The minister of arms dismissed this last with a wave of her hand. "That would be easy enough to work out. If the war is being fought in your future, others would know when it started, wouldn't they?"

"Yes, I suppose they would."

"Minister, have your guards conduct another search of the grounds. If these men were, in fact, Travelers, you probably won't find much, but let's be certain."

"Yes, my liege."

She regarded Tobias, her hand straying again to the hilt of her weapon. Tobias sensed that she didn't wish to leave while he was anywhere near Mearlan, but at last she strode from the chamber.

"Who else knew of my intentions?" the sovereign asked once she was gone.

When Tobias faltered, the Seer volunteered, "I must have. Isn't that right?"

"Yes. And also your minister of arms, who doesn't serve you yet in that capacity."

"In what capacity does this person serve me?"

"As an officer in your fleet, my liege, far away from here."

"All right, who else? The minister of protocol? Clearly you knew her in that other time."

"She might have known. I'm not sure. The only other..." He shook his head. "The only other person I'm certain of couldn't have said anything to anyone. At least not after my arrival in this time."

"I'll be the judge of that. Who was it?"

"Your daughter, my liege. The sovereign princess."

Mearlan recoiled. "Sofya?"

"Yes, my liege."

"You know her? As a young woman, I mean."

"I am fortunate in that your daughter has named me her friend."

A smile touched the young sovereign's face, and it seemed all the cares of his office fell away, leaving only the proud father. "I find myself in the odd position of envying you, Walker. I would give all the treasure of Hayncalde to catch a glimpse of that young woman you call your friend."

"I think that would be a poor trade, my liege. As you say, I know her as a young woman, but only thus. You'll have the pleasure of guiding her through her childhood."

The sovereign considered him. "Lest we forget, Seer, our friend here has been tutored in diplomacy, a skill he's obviously mastered. That was well said, Walker."

"Thank you, my liege." He paused. "Allow me to say this as well. I've only served House Hayncalde for a short while, but already I'm loyal to this land, and bound to you as my Lord Sovereign. You and the Seer have no reason to trust me, and I understand that my task here lies at cross purposes with your plans and wishes. But I'm acting on your orders, trying to do what I know to be best for your house and land."

Mearlan uncrossed his arms and stood straighter. After a moment, he blew out a breath. "For what it's worth," he said, his tone milder than it had been, "the Seer has spent much of the day arguing on your behalf. It's me you need to convince. Not him."

Tobias glanced Osten's way. "Thank you."

"That surprises you, doesn't it?" the Seer said. "I take it you and I aren't allies in the future."

"We don't know each other well enough to be allies or rivals. I'm new to the castle and you're…" *Dried up*, he heard in Isak's voice. "Practically a legend."

Osten's smile didn't reach his dark eyes. He said nothing.

"I'll dispatch a message to the Queen of Aiyanth in the morning," Mearlan said. "She'll be as mad as a sand hornet, but

I don't suppose there's much to be done about that." His smile was no more convincing than the Seer's. "I don't suppose that older version of me had any thoughts on how I might tame Caltha's ambitions."

"I'm afraid not, my liege. You simply told me that she hates the Oaqamarans, and that her hostility toward them fed your own. I was to warn you against allowing that to continue."

"Not very helpful, am I? What other keen insights did I offer?"

"You told me that the isles in the Bone Sea don't matter as much as you once thought." Tobias repeated the rest of what Mearlan had told him about the dispute between Vleros and Milnos.

"You've been telling me much the same thing for two turns," the sovereign said to his minister of state. "I've refused to believe it."

This other minister, a dark-haired woman with icy gray eyes and skin as pale as a full moon, bowed her head slightly, the gesture conveying deference without confirming or refuting the sovereign's statement. "Bone Sea politics have confounded Islevale's sovereigns and royals for a thousand years, my liege."

"An evasion."

"A simple truth, my liege."

"More diplomacy." To Tobias, Mearlan said, "Did I tell you anything else?"

"We discussed concessions to the privateers in the Aiyanthan and Herjean Seas, although you viewed that as a last resort."

The sovereign's expression soured; he didn't like this idea any more in this time than he had in the future. "Very well," he said. "If all else fails."

"Yes, my liege."

A knock drew the sovereign's eyes to the door. "Yes?" he called.

The door opened, and Tobias nearly stumbled back a step.

Sofya stood on the threshold, a dark-haired babe in her arms, and a dark-haired boy behind her. No, this couldn't be Sofya.

She entered the chamber, followed by a pair of guards and a servant who might have been the babe's nurse.

"My lady," Mearlan said. "Come in." He kissed the woman – who had to be his queen – and took the child from her.

"Walker Doljan, this is my wife, Her Majesty, Sovereign Queen Keeda of Hayncalde."

Tobias bowed. "An honor, your majesty." *In any time.* She was every bit as beautiful as she had been fourteen years hence. In youth her cheeks were rounder. She wore her hair longer as well. Aside from her eyes, which were hazel, she was the image of her daughter.

Her infant daughter, who squealed with laughter in the arms of her father.

"A pleasure to make your acquaintance, Walker," she said, puzzlement in her expression. She glanced at her husband, who gave a small, quick shake of his head.

Mearlan steered the dark-haired lad toward Tobias with a firm hand on his shoulder. The boy couldn't have been more than ten or eleven years. His features were still delicate, almost feminine, and in his own way he was as beautiful as his sister. He, too, had his mother's complexion and his father's eyes. "This is the sovereign prince, my son, Mearlan V. Mearlan, I present Walker Tobias Doljan."

"Greetings, Walker," the boy said, eyes wide. "I've always been curious about the Travelers. I hope we'll have the opportunity to speak later this evening. That is, if you have time."

Ignoring the irony in the boy's phrasing, Tobias grasped his proffered hand. "It would be my pleasure, my Lord Prince."

"And this," Mearlan said, planting a soft kiss on the brow of his infant daughter, "is my princess."

Sofya's cheeks were as round and fat as those of a forest

squirrel, and her shining black hair barely covered her head. Her face was flawless, though, and those arresting blue eyes hadn't changed.

"Good evening, your highness."

The child gave him a big grin, revealing milk teeth on her top and bottom gums.

"A friend indeed," Mearlan said, his voice low.

The queen drew closer. "I don't understand," she whispered.

Mearlan's smile tightened. "He's a Walker. And he's come some distance, with warnings of... Well, it's enough to say with warnings."

"Are we in danger?"

"From ourselves, it seems." He cupped her cheek with a hand. "You didn't come here to speak of Walkers. What can I do for you, my love?"

"We will speak of this later, my lord." She offered it as a statement.

"You know we will."

She regarded him with sly amusement and said in a voice pitched to carry, "Our evening meal grows cold, my lord, and your children and I do not wish to sup alone."

"You came to invite me to dine?"

"I came to drag you kicking and screaming to your great hall."

Everyone in the chamber laughed, Tobias included. Mearlan opened his hands in mock surrender.

"We have more than enough food and wine," Keeda said, taking Sofya back from the sovereign. "Several of my sovereign's court will be meeting us in the hall. You are all welcome to join us."

Despite the generous invitation, Tobias wasn't certain that he would be welcomed, until Mearlan made a point of telling him so.

"This has been a long and confounding day, Walker," the

sovereign said. "All of us owe you a debt for what you've done on our behalf. I'd be most disappointed if you didn't share in our hospitality."

He could hardly decline. "Thank you, my liege."

They filed out of the chamber and through the corridor toward the nearest stairway. Tobias walked alone, but as he shuffled behind the minister of state, he heard a voice at his shoulder say, "A legend, am I?"

Tobias stiffened.

"I took no offense, Walker," the Seer went on in his low, smooth tenor. "I am curious as to what I've become in your time. Something less than I am now, I fear."

"I didn't mean to imply–"

"The inference was entirely mine. Still, I believe you would be dangerous to have around for terribly long. Usually I'm the one who entices and terrifies others with glimpses of the future. Yet you can see even farther than I. I'll admit I find that... unsettling."

He gave Tobias no time to answer, but swept past him with a rustle of his silken robe.

More ministers waited for them in the great hall, including the minister of arms. Tobias searched for Gillian Ainfor. To his disappointment, he didn't see her.

The meal laid out for them resembled the one Tobias had enjoyed the evening before: cheeses and smoked meats, boiled roots and greens, bowls of creamy soup. This being Sipar's Settling, there was little fruit.

A priestess – not the same woman Tobias had seen in his own time – led them in prayer, and they settled in for their meal. Tobias sat near the end of the table, some distance from the sovereign family and between two ministers he didn't know. These two men wasted no time jumping into what sounded like an ongoing argument about the relative strengths of various armies.

Tobias ate and tried to feign interest.

He had just finished his first goblet of Miejan red, when the stone beneath his feet shuddered with what sounded like a clap of thunder.

Mearlan stood. "What was that?" He spun away from the table and strode toward the hall entrance, the minister of arms on his heels. Another explosion shook the hall. The sovereign waved his minister of state to his side and after a brief consultation, approached the main entrance.

"Find out what's happening," the sovereign said to the guards by the door.

Both men saluted.

And were blown into Mearlan and the ministers by a third blast, which shattered the wooden door as if it were glass.

Dark smoke choked the hall. Men and women shouted. Tobias heard Sofya crying, though he couldn't see her for the gray haze that had enveloped the hall. He wished he carried a weapon, but the sovereign hadn't seen fit to give him one. His pistol and dagger were stuck in the future.

He peered through the smoke expecting soldiers wearing Oaqamaran black or Sheraigh blue to stream through the ruined doorway.

Instead he felt a frisson of something at his back.

Power. Like his own.

He whirled in time to see a man – the same man he had encountered earlier – appear along the hall's back wall. The intruder carried a sextant in one hand and something in the other that belched dark smoke. He was accompanied again by three men, and also by a woman, lithe, her bronze hair generously streaked with silver. She held a pistol in each hand.

Tobias registered what he had missed before: the men around the couple carried golden devices as well. They were similar in design and complexity to the strange sextants he had seen in Mearlan's quarters the night before, after the attempt on his life. He had no chance to note more than that.

He swung his gaze back to the stranger, who spotted him as well, his expression darkening. The woman fired one of her weapons, cutting down an advancing guard. She said something to the man. He lobbed the smoking object over Tobias's head, toward the center of the table.

Tobias shouted a warning, but it was too late by far.

A blaze of fire, followed half an instant later by an earsplitting explosion.

Tobias flew off his feet, slammed into a stone wall and slumped in a heap. He could hear nothing for the ringing of his ears. His shoulder, side, and leg ached where he had hit the wall. Blood flow warmed the side of his face and neck. He could see no more than he could hear, and for a disorienting moment he wondered if the explosion had thrust him back into some twisted version of the between.

Then he saw flames. Torches. Belatedly, men entered the hall through that broken doorway. Not belatedly. They had known about the stranger and his bomb, had waited for his attack. Tobias tried to sit up. He had to find the man. This was his doing. He led these soldiers. Tobias knew it with a certainty he couldn't explain.

The man and woman were no longer where they'd been standing. Had the explosion knocked them off their feet, too? Or had they vanished, using the devices again?

Torchlight gleamed off something small and sleek. A weapon. Flame belched from the barrel. More flames blazed and vanished. Pale smoke mingled with the darker. Tobias's ears still rang, but he could make out the report of pistols. He forced himself up, charged at these men, whoever they were.

He wasn't accustomed to this body; as a boy he'd been nimble, quick. His Walk across the years had left him heavy and clumsy. Before he covered half the distance, he tripped, landed hard on the rubble strewn across the floor. He kicked at what had tripped him. It gave under the force of his boot. A body.

He crawled back and in the faint, smoke-hazed glow of those torches recognized the bloodied face of the minister of arms. Her eyes remained open, but she lay still, an iron bolt embedded in her forehead.

He grabbed for her belt, found a pistol holstered there. He located her powder-purse on the other side of her belt, and took it as well, but he hadn't time to load. Men dressed in black, like those he had seen in his corridor the previous night, made their way through the hall, shooting, reloading, shooting again.

Where were the rest of Hayncalde's guards? Dead? All of them? Surely not.

Traitors, then?

A man bearing a torch approached. Tobias tucked the pistol under his belt and covered it with his shirt. Then he pocketed the purse and grabbed the minister's blade from her belt. He lay on the floor, closed his eyes, and positioned his head so the killer would see the blood on his temple and neck.

Despite having his eyes closed, he could tell when the torch was directly above him, its glow like sunlight in the smoky dark of the hall. He held his breath, wondering if the man would shoot him. His ears still rang, but his hearing was returning. Pistol shots echoed through the hall. He heard moans, footsteps, laughter – which infuriated him – and over it all...

"Someone find that child and silence it!" a man shouted in an accent Tobias couldn't place.

Sofya.

The man above him started to move on. Tobias seized his leg and pulled as hard as he could, unbalancing him. The torch dropped from the man's hand. His pistol went off. White pain blinded Tobias for an instant. Blood gushed from his ear and covered more of his neck and shoulder.

Still, the man fell. Tobias threw himself onto the prone form, his fingers tightening on the minister's dagger. As a fifteen year-old, he wouldn't have stood a chance. But he was bigger now, stronger. The killer flailed with both fists, drew breath to scream for help. Tobias absorbed the blows, mashed his free hand onto the man's face to muffle his cry. With the other hand he hammered the blade into the killer's neck.

The man spasmed once, twice, then sagged and moved no more. Tobias pried the pistol from his fingers, hooked it on his belt, and pulled away, leaving the torch. His ear throbbed, and he could only hear out of the other one. Sofya still cried. He crawled toward the sound, following as direct a route as he could while also avoiding other attackers.

Soldiers converged on the one Tobias had killed, but before they reached him, another skirmish broke out near the wreckage of the hall entrance. Had Hayncalde's soldiers arrived at last?

He didn't dare pause to find out, but rather used the opportunity to hurry toward the princess. One of the attackers reached her first. He held his torch low, apparently searching the floor for her. Tobias saw him lift a chair and toss it aside. Then he bent and heaved something else out of his way. Abruptly, the babe's cries grew noticeably louder. Tobias could guess what had been covering the princess. He thought he might be ill.

Instead he rushed toward the man, who had straightened and pulled out a knife, his features shadowed and grim. The killer seemed to hear him. He looked up from the girl, fumbled for his pistol, which he had holstered. Before he could pull it free, Tobias drove his aching shoulder into the man's midriff, rode him down to the floor.

The torch fell. The man stabbed his dagger into Tobias's back, just below the shoulder. Tobias howled. He stabbed at the man as well. Once in the side, a second time higher up, under the killer's arm. The killer bellowed his pain, tried once more for his pistol. Tobias heard voices, knew that the killer's comrades were already running to his defense.

He pushed himself up with his off hand, creating a bit of space between them, and plunged the blade into his foe again. This time he found the man's gut. The killer arched his back, blood spouting from his mouth. Tobias pushed harder with the knife, angling it upward, toward the man's heart. Steel grated against rib. A wet gasp of breath, another gush of blood from his mouth, and the man went still.

Tobias took the dead man's pistol, which was loaded and half-cocked. He stooped and picked up Sofya. As he feared, she had been hidden from view by her mother's broken body. As soon as he tucked her to his chest, she quieted and wrapped a chubby fist in his bloodied shirt.

"Finally," someone growled from near the entrance.

It seemed the fighting there had subsided. Tobias feared the sovereign's men had been driven back. He crept backward, trying to shroud himself in shadow, watching as the torches converged on the man he'd killed.

"Nab's dead," one of the men said in that same strange accent. He bent over the body. "Stabbed, from the look of him."

"Then at least one of them is still alive," came another voice, the one he had heard earlier. "Find him. Kill him."

The men fanned out, holding their torches high, trying to light the vast hall. If not for the smoke from their bombs and pistols, they might have spotted Tobias. As it was, he managed to remain in shadow. He kept low, and retreated farther into the hall, away from the entrance.

His back throbbed where he had been stabbed. His ear and head ached. His entire body was battered and bruised. He had no idea how he and the princess might escape the hall. His best hope would have been to hide in some dark recess and wait for the assailants to leave. But he couldn't be sure Sofya would remain quiet, and if they were discovered they would both be killed. He didn't see any way past those who stood near the entrance. They were trapped; eventually they would be found.

The men advanced on him, like dogs herding sheep. He would run out of room soon enough.

The great hall in Windhome Palace hadn't been as grand as this one, but it had been large, and though it had one main entrance, it had a smaller entry near the rear. Servants used it to bring in food and carry out empty platters. There had to be a similar way in and out of this hall, and that portal was probably near this end. Tobias wasn't sure how to find it without giving himself away. He tried to orient himself, to remember where this end of the hall was in relation to the kitchen. It would have been easier with the sun still up.

He thought – hoped – the kitchen was closest to the south end of the hall, to his right. He angled his retreat, trying to step with care, praying to the Two that Sofya would remain silent for a bit longer.

Sooner than he expected, he backed into solid stone, jarring himself and the princess. She let out a soft cry.

"Wait!" said one of his pursuers. "Did you hear that?"

They halted their advance. Tobias remained motionless. Sofya made a suckling noise that sounded to him as loud as pistol fire. But the men didn't speak or resume their search.

"I don't hear anything," said another man. "My ears are ringing from that piece of shit banger you threw."

Tobias still held the half-cocked pistol he'd taken from the man he killed. He threw it now, as far as he could toward the other rear corner of the chamber, hoping with all his heart that the doorway he sought wasn't there.

The pistol struck the floor and went off with a burst of flame and a startling report.

The men turned in that direction. Sofya began to fuss, but Tobias covered her mouth with his hand and sidled along the wall feeling for the door. When at last he found it, he nearly wept with relief. Better still, it was unlocked.

He eased it open, slipped out of the hall, and closed it again with great care. He had entered a small chamber, empty save for spent carafes of wine and bare platters. The door across the tiny room stood ajar. Through it, Tobias saw a torchlit courtyard and a star-speckled sky.

"Almost safe, princess," he whispered, creeping to that second doorway. He paused there, searched the ward for soldiers and assassins. Glancing down at Sofya, he noticed in the spill of torch fire what he'd missed in the great hall. The princess bled from a gash on her chin, and another on her left temple. Neither injury seemed to trouble her much, though. She stared up at him, her eyes dry, one thumb in her mouth, the other hand still clutching his shirt.

"You're a brave one, aren't you?" he said.

She grinned around her thumb.

He scanned the courtyard again. Several men entered through the east gate. All wore black. He saw no soldiers of Hayncalde.

Another group of men crossed through the courtyard from the west and joined the first band. Together they walked to one of the stairways and entered the castle. Tobias hoped whoever lived there would manage to flee before they were found.

Tobias decided to remain where he was for now. If the castle had been taken, all the gates would be guarded, and he hadn't lived here long enough to know where he might find the castle's sally ports.

Only then did he realize that he didn't need an escape. He had something better. Without leaving this chamber, he could go back a bell or two, and warn the sovereign of the impending attack. He couldn't bring the princess with him, but he had to risk leaving her, just briefly. If he succeeded, none of this would happen, and she would be back with her family.

He reached into his pocket for his chronofor, only to have something sharp jab into a finger. He muttered a curse, felt around in the pocket more carefully. His stomach heaved.

CHAPTER 17

21st Day of Sipar's Settling, Year 633

Shards of glass bit at his fingertips. He pulled out the device and held it close to his eyes to inspect the damage. The glass casing was gone, fractured into hundreds of tiny fragments. The face had been dented; two of the three hands had been bent so severely Tobias despaired of ever seeing them fixed. He tried to pull out the stems to set the device, but two of them wouldn't budge. Worse, the central stem jutted from the chronofor at an angle. When Tobias tried to press it, it didn't move either.

He wouldn't be going back to warn the sovereign. Nor could he return to his own time, at least not until he found a Binder to fix this device, or a trader who could sell him a new one.

What money do you have for food, much less a Bound device?

Had Binder Filt been in the great hall? Tobias didn't recall seeing him, but he wasn't sure that meant anything. Might the Binder still be in his chamber? Would he have an extra chronofor?

Tobias pocketed the remains of his device and eyed the courtyard again. Seeing no assassins, he stepped out into the night, the princess held tightly in his arms. In his own time, he'd had a vague sense of where Binder Jarrett's workshop was located. He hoped that Filt used the same chamber. He started toward a tower, hesitated, unable to recall if this was the correct one. Deciding it was, he loped across the tiled expanse, his back hunched, his gaze roaming the ward. He saw none of the enemy, and gained the stairway without being seen.

He climbed with stealth, only to have Sofya remove her thumb from her mouth and give a little shriek. She jumped at the echo, but then squealed her delight and made the sound again.

"Sofya, please!" Tobias whispered, panic quickening his pulse.

From far off, he heard a man's voice.

Sofya shrieked once more and laughed, the drying blood on her face making her look like a tiny ghoul.

They reached the second level, and Tobias carried the princess into the corridor. She made her noise again, but deflated when the effect proved less dramatic.

The corridor was empty – a blessing. Still Tobias walked with care. Not that it mattered. Sofya chattered like a woodland wren.

Reaching the workshop door, Tobias knocked. It was already unlatched. At his touch it opened a crack. His limbs quaking, Tobias pushed through it.

The chamber was dark, save for the glow of starlight and the low moon seeping through a single window. Even so, he could see that he'd arrived too late. The room had been ransacked, the workbench tipped onto its side. A pool of what had to be blood stained the stone floor, as black as pitch in the dim light. To his relief, Tobias saw no corpses, no sign of Filt. Perhaps he had escaped, or maybe he had been taken. Binders were nearly as valuable as Walkers.

He paused, his breath catching, and wondered if Gillian had escaped the hall, or if she was among the dead.

No time for such thoughts now.

Tobias's first instinct was to back out the door and flee the castle. He resisted the impulse. Taking care to avoid the blood, he searched the chamber, rooting through workbench drawers and cabinet shelves, hoping he might find a chronofor. At one point he tried to lie Sofya down on the pallet near the window. As soon as he did, she began to fuss. "All right, all right," he whispered. "I'll hold you."

She grabbed his shirt again, and stuck her thumb back into her mouth.

He made as little noise as possible, and listened for voices in the ward. Someone had heard Sofya earlier. No doubt the killers were searching for them.

He soon found what he was after, in a sense. The Binder did have devices stored in the chamber: two apertures. No chronofors, though. After a moment's consideration, Tobias took the devices. He placed them in an old carry sack he found in the corner of the chamber, and slung it over his shoulder. He wasn't a Crosser. The apertures were useless to him. But someone – a merchant, like the *Gray Skate*'s Captain Larr – would pay handsomely for them.

With one last glance around the chamber, he crossed to the door intending to leave. As he did, he remembered his brief encounter with Filt earlier in the day. The Binder had spoken in vague terms of a new project, and Tobias had the impression that, if not for Gillian's warning glance, the man might have told him more. Tobias had seen nothing in the chamber that struck him as revolutionary, but was it possible that Filt's device bore some resemblance to the odd sextants he'd seen in the hands of those assassins, and in Mearlan's chamber in his own time? With that thought he considered repeating his search.

He wasn't sure when rumors of the Oaqamaran devices first surfaced, but the man he saw in the courtyard, who later led the attack on the great hall, was fully clothed when he appeared. Both times. In the second instance, he had carried the explosive in one hand and his sextant in the other. The woman who accompanied him held two pistols.

Could it be that Filt had been developing the same sort of

device for Daerjen? Had the idea originated here, rather than in Oaqamar? Tobias eyed the cabinets again, but he didn't renew his search. He wouldn't find Filt's inventions here. Someone, either the Binder or the attackers, had taken them already.

Assassins who could materialize anywhere they wanted – clothed, armed, ready to kill – and then vanish again just as suddenly: he had known of this possibility in his own time. Now, it seemed, he was being hunted by these killers. He and the princess. How did one fight such an enemy? How could Tobias evade them?

"Time to go," he said to Sofya.

Her smile returned and she whispered nonsense sounds at him.

"That's right," he said. "A game. We have to whisper."

She repeated the noises and laughed too loudly.

"Shhh!"

She imitated the sound.

"Gods, what am I going to do with you?"

He carried her from the Binder's chamber, left the door as he had found it, and followed the corridor to a different tower and stairway, in case Sofya's cries had drawn the enemy to the stairs they'd climbed.

Tobias didn't know where Gillian had her quarters, but he wished desperately to know if she had survived the attack. He assumed the rest of the royal family were dead. He knew the minister of arms had been killed. The Seer and minister of state had been in the hall, and must have died as well. He didn't care to guess how many guards were lost.

Much if not all of the court of Hayncalde had been massacred on this one night. He could think of several who would want Mearlan dead: the autarch of Oaqamar, the Duke of Sheraigh, and any number of privateering patroons in Westisle came to mind. But who had the means to plan and fund such an assault? Oaqamar might. The Seer had thought them the most likely culprits in the attack in his own time.

"Who says it has to be just one of them?" he whispered aloud, knowing as he spoke that he had his answer: an alliance of Hayncalde's enemies, bent on destroying Mearlan's court for all time.

Tobias stared at the princess as she looked around the corridor, oblivious of what had been done to her family, to her life. Unless he could find some way to Walk back in time and prevent the killings, she was all that remained of Mearlan's line. The assassins wouldn't rest until they knew for certain that she was dead.

"They must have followed me," he said under his breath. They tried to kill him in his own time, and when that failed they came back to this time. They had relied on more Travelers than any one sovereign or royal should have had at the ready.

Voices echoed in the corridor ahead of him, pulling Tobias from his musings, and forcing him to halt. He tried the nearest door, but found it locked. The next one opened. He slipped into the dark chamber and eased the door closed again. Turning, he saw a bent woman standing near the window, a sword in one hand and a dagger in the other.

Her gaze fell to the princess. Her eyes went wide and snapped back to his.

He nodded, put a finger to his lips.

The voices drew nearer. He felt as though he had been carried back to his own time, and the attempt on his life by the two Travelers.

This time, he had no means of escape. However, he did have the pistols he had taken from the minister of arms and the dead assassin.

He took the sword from the woman and gave Sofya to her. The princess complained, but the woman cooed softly, quieting her.

Tobias loaded the pistols, cocked the hammer on one, and

returned the other to his belt. He pressed himself against the wall nearest the door's hinges, the pistol in his left hand, the sword in his right. Footsteps just beyond the door told him the men were close. The latch on the door clicked and it swung open, concealing him.

The men entered the chamber. Tobias could see one of them, though only from behind. He wore black and held a pistol. Tobias assumed his friend was also armed.

"Who are you?" one of them asked the woman. "Who's the b–"

Shifting away from the wall, Tobias kicked the door with all his might. It slammed into the second man with more force than Tobias had expected, knocking his pistol to the floor with a clatter. The man in front spun, raising his weapon. Tobias was already moving. Closing the distance between them with one lunge, he struck at the man with his sword. The assassin dove away, rolled onto his back, and aimed his pistol at Tobias.

Who dove as well before the man could fire.

The second attacker had regained his feet. He'd lost his firearm, but held a long, wicked dagger. The first man and Tobias scrambled up, pistols aimed.

Something large and dark soared past Tobias's head. He ducked out of instinct. A water pitcher. The assassin didn't see it and it crashed into his chest, staggering him. Tobias pounced, hacking at him again with the sword. His blow struck the base of the assassin's neck. Blood fountained, and the assassin dropped to the floor, his head nearly severed from his body.

The second man lashed out with the dagger, its steel glinting dully in the darkness. Tobias danced out of reach, kicked the door again so that it slammed shut, and raised the pistol.

"Drop the knife."

The assassin cast a quick look at the woman and then at Sofya, who now lay on the pallet. Tobias stepped toward the man, blocking his path to either of them.

"Drop it now, or I'll kill you."

"No, you won't," the man said in that maddeningly elusive accent. "Shoot me, and my friends will converge on this place from every corner of your castle."

Tobias knew he was right. The man backed away, knife held ready. His foot hit something that scraped on the stone floor: his dead comrade's pistol. He glanced at it, took Tobias's measure again.

Tobias advanced another step. The man leapt at him, blade arm raised high to strike.

Tobias twisted away, but the man kicked out, the toe of his boot catching Tobias's arm. The sword flew from his hand, struck the wall behind him, and fell to the floor. Landing nimbly, the assassin crouched and grabbed his friend's pistol.

Having no choice, Tobias fired. The report was deafening. The assassin fell back into the door, a dark stain spreading across his chest.

Tobias straightened, let his pistol hand fall to his side. He breathed hard, and sweat dripped from his brow. Blood soaked the floor under the first assassin. More had started to pool beneath the second. A night of blood; he had never seen so much.

He flexed the arm the assassin had kicked. It was sore, but no worse than the rest of his injuries. He was still growing used to this new body, learning to move again, to fight. But he felt strong.

Sofya fussed. The woman crossed to the pallet and picked her up. White smoke filled the chamber.

"Thank you," Tobias said, retrieving the assassins' pistols and the second man's dagger. He slipped the weapons into his carry sack. His hands had started to shake. More men would be coming; they needed to leave. "Throwing that pitcher probably saved my life."

"You're a guard?" the woman asked, gently bouncing the princess.

"A Walker. I–" He shook his head. "There's too much to explain."

Voices rose to the window from the courtyard.

"We have to get away from here." Tobias retrieved the woman's sword, used his foot to push the body of the second man away from the door.

She carried Sofya to him, glancing at the corpse of the first man as she stepped over him. If the sight of bloodied bodies in her chamber bothered her, she gave no indication of it.

"The Two guard you," she said, handing Sofya back to him.

"No, you don't understand. We all have to go."

"It'll be better for all if I remain."

"If you stay, and they find you," he said, struggling to keep his voice low, his gaze flicking to the window, "they'll kill you. Your best hope is to come with us."

"An old woman, bent, useless? They won't bother. And if they try, they'll find killing me more difficult than you might think." At his puzzled look, she said, "I'm Daria Belani. I used to be minister of arms."

He saw the resemblance. "The current minister of arms..."

"My daughter. Is she still alive?"

Tobias winced, shook his head. "I'm sorry."

Daria took an unsteady breath, tears winding crooked paths down her lined face. Her gaze fell to Sofya, who sucked her thumb again. "Is this who I think it is?"

"Yes. She's the only one left."

"Then I shouldn't go with you," she said, eyes meeting his once more. "I'll slow you down. But I can help you get out."

She led him into the corridor and on toward the stairway he'd intended to use. She'd spoken true; her steps were slow, uneven. They reached the stairway, but continued past it.

"The towers will be watched," she whispered. "Every person in the castle heard that pistol."

The words stung. "I didn't have a choice."

"No, you didn't. Because you allowed that assassin to disarm you."

"He surprised me. What was I supposed to do?"

"Not allow yourself to be surprised. You can't let that happen again, or they'll kill her." She indicated the princess with a lift of her chin.

They came to a door, which Daria unlocked using a key she drew from the bodice of her gown. Beyond the door, a narrow stairway wound down into utter darkness.

"This leads to a sally port on the west side of the castle," she said. "Whoever these men are, they won't know of it. Few do. Or did. You'll need to find your way past one of the outer gates, but that end of the castle will draw fewer men. No one uses it."

"Where should I go?"

She shook her head. "I don't know. Someplace far away."

"I…" He'd intended to say that he had no money, no food, no means of leaving Daerjen. But this woman would be alone in a castle filled with assassins and soldiers. He couldn't bring himself to complain. "I'm grateful to you," he said.

He held out her sword, hilt first, but she shook her head. "You'll need that more than I." A bitter smile touched her lips. "Besides, what use would an old woman have for a battle sword?"

"Thank you, minister. May the Two protect you."

"May They protect us all. Go." With a bent finger she touched Sofya lightly on the tip of the nose, drawing a laugh from the child.

Tobias slipped the blade under his belt, shifted Sofya in his arms, and started down the stairway. He trailed his fingers along the rough wall. Within a tencount, the dark enveloped him, leaving only the touch of stone and the tight twisting of the steps to guide him. His footsteps echoed, his breathing mixed with Sofya's, sounding too loud. Above him, something clicked and his heart jumped. He realized it was Daria closing the door.

He descended, one nerve-racking step at a time. Had he missed the port? Did this stairway pass the doorway and continue into a cellar? He considered going back, but didn't. If there had been some trick to finding the port, the woman would have told him so.

The stairway ended abruptly. Tobias tried to lower his foot to a step that wasn't there, nearly stumbled. The landing was cramped, and every bit as dark as the stairs had been. He felt along the wall and soon found a small latch. He pressed it, heard a metallic click, pulled hard. The door gave grudgingly, but made not a sound.

Pausing, he set Sofya on the stone floor. He pulled out the powder purse he had taken from the minister of arms and reloaded his weapon with hands that still trembled. He hung the weapon on his belt, picked up Sofya again.

The sally port opened onto an expanse of deserted ground covered in tall, wispy grass. Directly in front of him loomed the castle's outer wall, ponderous and impenetrable in the gloom. Daria had said there was a gate nearby, but of course it would be guarded. He needed to know by whom, and by how many.

As soon as he crossed through the grass and pressed himself against the outer wall, he spotted it. It stood perhaps forty strides ahead, lit by torches mounted in sconces. He couldn't fight his way through with Sofya in his arms, but neither could he leave her lying on the grass. He started toward the portal, placing his feet with care, his gaze swinging between the arched gate and the battlements atop the castle walls.

He had covered about half the distance when a man emerged from the gate into the yard separating the castle from its outer defenses. Tobias flattened himself against the stone, thanking the Two for the shadows cast by the castle's inner wall.

A second man joined the first. They weren't dressed as the

assassins had been. They wore blue uniforms and each carried a sword and a musket. Soldiers, then. The torchlight was too inconstant for Tobias to be certain, but this blue appeared far paler than that worn by Aiyanthan guardsmen. And what would men from the Axle be doing here? That left Sheraigh, Hayncalde's chief rival among the houses of Daerjen.

He waited, hoping the soldiers would be content to survey the yard from where they stood. Soon enough, they entered the archway again. Tobias started toward them once more.

He wasn't yet certain how he would carry the princess by the men. He knew only that he couldn't remain in the castle. And Daria had said this gate would be less heavily guarded than others.

Dried blood covered Sofya's face and stained his clothes. He must have had blood on his neck, brow, cheeks, and temple, not to mention his back where he had been stabbed. His wounds grew more painful with every step. But he could do nothing about any of this until he escaped the castle.

He reached the gate and without hesitating entered the arched passage. At the echo of his steps, the men spun and raised their muskets.

"Halt right there!"

Tobias raised his one free hand.

"Who are you?"

"I'm with the Travelers," he said, thickening his native accent so that he sounded more like a Trevynisle *gaaz* cutter. As proof of his claim, he pulled out one of Filt's apertures.

The guard eyed the device, but then pointed at Sofya. "Who's that you're holding?"

"The daughter of a castle servant."

"A servant? Why's there blood on her face?"

"Her mother showed up when she shouldn't have, tried to get in our way." He shrugged, feigning indifference. "She's dead now."

"So where are you taking that one?"

"Lanes near the wharves. One like this'll fetch a fair price on the night market there. Slave traders like to get 'em young. Easier to train that way."

Tobias had heard of slave markets operating in some of the cities of the Labyrinth and Oaqamar. He didn't know if Hayncalde had a night market as well, but he guessed these men wouldn't know either.

"You Northislers make me sick," the second guard said.

Neither man accused him of lying.

"You're just jealous the gold won't be goin' in your purse."

"I should shoot you where you stand."

"How'd your captain feel 'bout that?"

The men exchanged glances. After a moment, both lowered their muskets.

"Get out of here, you shit-skinned *gaaz*-demon," said the first man. "If I see you again, I will shoot you. That's a promise."

Tobias ground his teeth. For all his fear of being ostracized because of his skin color, this was the first time in his life anyone had used such an epithet against him. It was all he could do to keep himself from pulling out his pistol.

"You're welcome to try," he said. This time he wasn't playing a role.

He pushed past the men, half-hoping they'd try to stop him.

"You should take her to a brothel instead, you bastard," one called after him. "You probably like them young and dark like that."

Tobias faltered in mid-stride, but at a small sound from Sofya walked on. Getting away: that was his goal.

He knew the men stared after him, and he refused to glance back. With a bit of luck, it wouldn't occur to them to wonder why he left the castle through this gate if the wharves were his destination. He counted on their unfamiliarity with the city, and their disgust with him, to keep them from asking questions. Those things only delayed the inevitable.

"Wait right there!"

He quickened his stride.

"Hey, you! *Gaaz*-demon! Stop where you are!"

He had almost reached a street corner, and now he broke into a run, angling across the lane, clasping the princess so closely she cried out.

The flat, hard report of a musket echoed down the lane, but the ball missed him, whistling past. Tobias ducked into the nearest side street, ran to the next byway and turned again, heading downhill into the city, away from the castle, the wharf, anything he knew. He heard the men behind him, shouting to each other, their footsteps tracking him like hounds. Every slap of boot leather on cobble betrayed him, and the princess, too.

He ran down yet another unknown alley. After a few steps, he halted and backtracked to that last intersection. The men had yet to come into sight. He crept across the lane he'd been on previously and set out in the opposite direction, deeper still into the city. He walked with the stealth of a thief, thankful for Sofya's silence. He went some distance, leaving behind the more comfortable houses nearest the castle for smaller homes with tiny yards and garden plots.

Passing a small stone house, he noticed a masonry chimney creeping up the structure's side. He left the road, walked to the other side of it. He tucked himself into the narrow niche shaped by the chimneystack and the house wall, and lowered himself to the cold ground. Sofya stared at him, her gaze glassy. She would be asleep soon.

He had no money, no food. If Sofya was half as weary and hungry as he, she would sleep poorly and wake in a terrible state.

But no one would see them here. They could rest, perhaps sleep. And Tobias could figure out what, in the name of the God and Goddess, he was going to do next.

CHAPTER 18

18th Day of Kheraya's Ascent, Year 647

It crept into Mara's thoughts while she slept, insinuating itself like a cat seeking attention. By the time she opened her eyes to the gray glow of morning that seeped at the edges of the Windward Keep's shuttered windows, it had settled at the base of her skull, not quite pain, but distracting, uncomfortable.

She rose with the others, pulled on her tunic, skirt, and robes, and filed across the middle courtyard to the refectory for the usual breakfast fare: fatted bread, tasteless hot porridge, a few ancient pieces of dried fruit. From there, they descended to the lower courtyard, where Master Saffern drilled them in their sword work and marksmanship.

All of this under the watchful stares of Oaqamaran soldiers atop the battlements of Windhome Palace, grim in their uniforms of brown and black. Some carried muskets, others crossbows. As always. As it had been every day she could remember since her arrival in Windhome as a small girl. Yet today, something about the guards bothered her. Something that had little to do with her hatred for them.

She was aware of the Belvora as well. Four of them circling over the palace grounds on membranous wings. Mara feared them even more than she did the Oaqamarans.

High gray clouds covered the sky, and a warm, heavy wind blew in off Safsi Bay. Occasionally rain fell on them in thin squalls; at other times the sun seemed on the verge of burning through. Saffern remained the same as ever: grave, determined, stern.

When he released them to their studies, Mara all but ran to the nearest tower, relieved to be free of the weapons master.

After training came their daily consultation on the latest naval and land battles in the various wars ongoing throughout Islevale: the Westisle conflict, the blockade skirmishes in the Inward Sea, the insurrection on Vleros. As one of the older Spanners, Mara would be expected to help pilot companies of soldiers the next time they were called to Travel. She needed to pay strict attention to all that Mistress Feidys told them.

The mistress's chamber smelled of mold and old paper. Dusty shelves, filled to overflowing with worn volumes, lined the walls. A map of Vleros, Milnos, and the Bone Sea isles lay uncurled on a table in the middle of the room. Feidys herself stood at her desk, shuffling through rolls of parchment, her broad back to the door as Mara and the other trainees entered, her black hair tied back and piled atop her head.

As the last of Mara's classmates entered and took their seats around the table, Feidys faced them and began without preamble. "Reports from Vleros speak of more gains by the rebels. The seat of the provisional government is safe for now, but in smaller towns and villages, the old royalists are showing more resilience than expected."

The mistress crossed to the map, and tapped a stubby finger near the southern bend in Vleros, a long, thin isle often referred to as the Bow. "This is the site of the most recent fighting," she said without inflection, "and the most likely place where soldiers will be needed. Those of you trained in the use of the tri-sextants should be ready to Span on little notice."

Mara, Delvin, and Nat shared glances.

Feidys went on in greater detail about the fighting, describing the latest string of rebel victories throughout Vleros. The former royal city, located near the middle of the isle, wasn't yet in danger of falling, but only because reinforcements sent from Milnos still reached the provisional leaders. A few of the trainees interrupted her with questions, but most listened and kept their mouths shut.

Mara wasn't the only trainee in Windhome who had been brought up hating the autarchy and their allies in Milnos. Far from it. But so long as Oaqamaran soldiers guarded the ramparts and stalked the palace corridors, none of them dared say a word. Even the chancellor was from Oaqamar.

He shouldn't be.

The thought surprised Mara, heightened her unease. Because she knew it was true.

She thought it possible that many of the masters who taught their lessons, Feidys among them, felt as she did about the autarchy. They would be even less free to speak their minds than she.

There had been a time, beyond her memory, but within the lifetimes of many in Windhome, when the palace had been independent, a bulwark, some said, against Oaqamaran aggression. Feidys would have said that was a topic for history lessons, not strategy.

In time, Feidys steered their discussion to the naval skirmishes among the isles of the Inner and Outer Rings surrounding Daerjen. As with the conflict on the Bow, the Inward Sea battles were being fought against proxies of Oaqamar's autarch. Mara forced herself to concentrate.

Yet the alien notions that had stolen into her mind overnight continued to distract her. She wrote down what the mistress told them, studied the maps she laid before them. Throughout the lesson, though, a single thought repeated itself in her head, as soft as a whisper, as insistent as the tide.

None of this is right.

She had no idea what the words meant, or what "this" might be. She was overwhelmed, though, by the sense that she didn't belong there. Not in the classroom, not in the palace, not even on Windhome, which had been her home for more than ten years. She couldn't explain what she felt, but neither could she ignore it or banish it from her thoughts.

"You all right?" Delvin whispered.

Feidys shot a glare in their direction.

Mara nodded, keeping her eyes on the mistress.

Delvin continued to watch her, and she resisted the urge to glance back. It occurred to her that even they weren't immune. She and Delvin had been a couple for seven turns now. Almost eight. In that time, she had come to care about him. Today, along with everything else, that felt... off. She should have been with someone else. She just had no idea who.

At the ringing of the late morning bell, the trainees left Feidys's chamber for that of Wansi Tovorl, the palace Binder. Delvin walked beside her, tall and arrow thin, casting looks her way, concern furrowing his brow.

"You sure you're all right?"

"Yes. I mean, I'm fine. Just... I didn't sleep well, and I feel strange today."

"Strange meaning sick?"

"No, it's not that."

"Then what?" He halted and held out a hand, forcing her to stop as well. "What is this, Mar?"

She stared past him, conscious of the other trainees walking around them as if they were stones in a stream. "I– I'm not sure I belong here."

"It's a little late for that, isn't it?"

Her eyes met his. He grinned, and she answered with a reluctant smile. "That's not what I mean. I feel..." She averted her gaze again. Standing this close to him made her uncomfortable. When was the last time *that* had been true? "Just something's not right. I shouldn't be here. None of us should. Or maybe we belong here, but not like this."

She chanced another peek at him and wished she hadn't. He regarded her as he might a madwoman, or, worse, a child with an overactive imagination.

"That sounds a little crazy. You know that, right?"

Mara scowled, pushed past him, and walked on.

"Mar!"

She refused to stop.

"Would you wait?" He fell in step with her again. "I'm sorry. But what you said... None of that makes any sense."

"You're right. I was... I'm just tired."

"It sounded like more than that."

"I know how it sounded, but now I'm telling you what it was. Let it drop, all right?"

He huffed a sigh. "Fine."

They walked the rest of the way in silence. She knew what he was thinking. They were supposed to meet in the upper courtyard after the evening meal, as they did most nights. Many of the older trainees went there to pair off and share kisses, sometimes more. She thought the soldiers watched this as well, but most of the trainees didn't care. Let them watch, Oaqamaran bastards. Closest they'd get to any of them.

Delvin wanted to ask if she still intended to meet him. She wasn't sure she did.

Binder Tovorl watched the trainees stream into her chamber, blue eyes magnified by thick spectacles, her skin pale almost to the point of translucence in the light of half a dozen oil lamps.

"Take your seats," she said as the last of them hurried to their places. "Several of you are behind in your work. We have need of more sextants and apertures. Your milling and planing tools are before you; your pieces, whatever state they happen to be in, can be found where you left them. Please get to work."

Mara retrieved her half-completed sextant from the rough wooden shelf along the chamber's back wall, took an open seat as far from Delvin and Nat as possible, and set to work, planing the leading edge of her golden sextant with care, occasionally pausing to measure the piece with a sector. Aside from the rasp of files, the ping of metal hammers, the scratch of millers and planers, the room was silent. Wansi meandered among the tables, peering over shoulders, and at times pointing out small flaws in the trainees' work.

Most days, Mara dreaded her toolwork as much as she did her time on the training grounds. Today she welcomed it. That niggling intuition in the back of her mind faded, forced into the background by the task at hand. When the midday bell rang – far too soon – she put away her work with uncommon reluctance. She cleaned her space slowly, waiting for Delvin to leave.

He took his time as well, but then seemed to realize what she was doing. Face reddening, he saw to the last of his tools with an impatient clatter and stormed out the door, flinging a glower over his shoulder as he left.

Mara replaced her tools and, as an afterthought, straightened up his as well.

"Something on your mind, Miss Lijar?"

Wansi considered her from beside the open windows, her hands tucked into the ample sleeves of her robe.

"No, mistress."

The Binder met her denial with a smirk and dancing eyes. "Might Mister Ruhj be more forthcoming?" she asked, a familiar lilt in her words. "He seemed in rather a rush to be gone today."

Mara's cheeks warmed.

"Simply a matter of the heart then," the woman said, stepping to her own workbench and picking up the unfinished tri-aperture she had there. "Forgive my intrusion."

Mara remained where she was. She had trained as a Spanner for nearly all her life; she could hardly remember anything from before she came to Trevynisle. Her early years on Kauhi, with her parents and brothers, were a blur of isolated images and sensations, inchoate and distant. She wondered if her talent, her ability to Span, was the source of the odd displacement that had plagued her all day. Maybe she wasn't supposed to be here, not in this room, not in this palace.

But did she dare confess this to the Binder, who had placed a loupe over her eye and was calibrating a portion of the device? Delvin had all but called Mara mad when she described these sensations. What would Mistress Tovorl think? *The same thing, probably.*

"You have nothing on your mind, and yet there you stand as if in a trance. I can almost hear your brain working."

Mara bit back a smile.

"You should either say something, or leave. They won't be serving midday supper forever, and I doubt that your fellow trainees will think twice about eating your rations once theirs are gone. Mister Ruhj in particular seems always to be hungry. Has there ever been a meal at which he wasn't first to finish his rations?"

Mara did smile at this. "I don't think so."

"Nor do I."

Mara sobered. "I feel like I don't belong here," she said.

Mistress Tovorl removed her eyepiece. "You've been with us for a long time, Miss Lijar. Isn't it a bit late to be questioning such things?"

"Is it? I never had the chance when I was younger." Mara shook her head. "Besides, that's not what I mean."

"You're speaking in riddles."

"I know. I feel... out of place. Or like everything else is out of place and I'm the only one who belongs." She grimaced. "I know how that sounds."

"We all have moments when everything seems to be wrong. It's not all that unusual, especially at your age."

"No, it's not that. I've never felt this way before." Mara blew out a breath. The Binder's expression had knotted into something resembling Delvin's from earlier. She wasn't handling this well. "You're probably right," she said with false brightness. "It's just my mood. I should probably go and eat. And apologize to Delvin."

"Perhaps." The Binder set the loupe to her eye again and peered down at her work. "Or maybe you should take a bit of time to work out exactly what it is you're feeling. When you have, you may return here, and we'll speak of it more."

Mara made no effort to conceal her relief. "Thank you, mistress."

"Now be on your way. I have things to do."

Mara stepped to the door, but as she pulled it open the Binder spoke her name. She halted.

"Travelers have an awareness of our world that goes beyond that of most. Sensations of the sort you describe are not to be taken lightly. Nor are they to be spoken of without care. If you must confide in others, do so with some caution. Do you understand?"

Mara wasn't sure she did, not entirely. She nodded, though, and let herself out of the chamber.

She cut across the empty courtyard and made her way to the refectory. Over the years, she had learned to accept the soldiers and winged Belvora as normal parts of her life, fixtures atop the stone walls, or in the skies overhead. Usually she ignored them.

Not today. She knew guards watched her, and she had to keep herself from staring up at them. Her skin prickled; she felt as though the soldiers had their muskets trained on her back. When she reached the refectory, she released a held breath.

Most of her friends had already finished their meals, and she was too preoccupied to eat much. She grabbed some cheese and bread before the palace stewards could remove the last platters from the tables, and she carried the food outside to eat. She kept to the covered walkways, where fewer guards could see her.

Following the meal, she and the other senior trainees attended their lesson with the Master of Finance and then their classes in protocol and language. She tried to concentrate. Their term exams were scheduled for the coming ha'turn, and she took pride in her status as one of the palace's top students.

But her mind wandered. If anything, the feeling of displacement grew stronger as the day wore on. Delvin wouldn't look at her, but his anger lingered, a palpable presence at her shoulder. She gave much thought to the Binder's warning. Who might take notice of what she said about not belonging here? The soldiers, of course. Perhaps the chancellor. Why would they care? What did Mistress Tovorl think it meant?

By the time her last lesson ended, the sky over Windhome had darkened to a steel gray, and a stiff wind howled through the courtyards. Belvora perched like white buzzards on the highest towers of the palace, wrapped in their wings.

Mara ate little more at the evening meal than she had at midday. She spoke to no one, and ignored the conversations around her. After supper, she studied for two bells. She tired of her work early and left the quiet of the common room in Windward Keep for the upper courtyard. Part of her hoped she would find Delvin. Despite their fight, she didn't wish to be alone. Still, she wasn't entirely surprised to see him with his arm around the shoulders of another girl – Hilta Craik, of course. Hilta was pretty and smart, skilled with a blade, though not so good with a pistol. Mara had always hated her. She'd said as much to Delvin many times. He was punishing her.

Mara was sure he spotted her at the same time she spied them. That didn't stop him from leading Hilta toward the bench at the end of the courtyard. The bench Mara and he usually shared.

Tears blurred her vision, making the light of the torches at the courtyard gates shift and slide. She whispered a curse and swiped at her eyes with an impatient hand. It was her own fault. The Binder was right: some people couldn't be trusted with confidences. It just hadn't occurred to her to doubt him.

She watched Delvin and Hilta retreat into the darkness, sadness and jealousy squeezing her heart like taloned hands. When she could no longer see them, she left the upper courtyard and followed the covered walkways to the lower sections of the palace. She passed soldiers every so often and kept her gaze on the pathway before her, refusing to look at them, resenting their presence as she never had before.

The guards wouldn't let her out of the palace, so she simply walked, her arms crossed over her heart. After passing more guards in the walkways, she turned onto the grass. They could watch her from the walls, and Belvora were said to see well at night, but in the darkness she wouldn't have to see them.

A cool drizzle fell once more, slicking her robe and dampening her hair. After circling the lower courtyard, she wandered back to the middle. She wasn't ready to retreat to the dormitory. Her thoughts were too roiled for sleep.

"This isn't as it's supposed to be."

Mara whirled, her heart vaulting into her throat.

She was in a remote, shadowed corner of the courtyard, away from the walkways. A child stood nearby, her face shining with the glow of distant torches. Mara didn't recognize her. She was dressed in tatters – worn breeches like those of a street urchin and a loose tunic of some light-colored cloth. She should have been chilled in the rain and wind, but if she was, she gave no indication of it. Considering her, Mara recovered somewhat from her initial fright.

"Who are you?" she asked. "Are you new to the palace?"

The girl shook her head. "No. I've been here longer than you have."

"I don't mean tonight–" Mara broke off, frowning. The girl's expression bespoke loneliness, confusion, deepest fear. "Are you lost?"

"We all are," the girl said.

"What's your name?"

"Droë."

Mara took a step in the girl's direction, but Droë backed away. Mara held up her hands. "I'm not going to hurt you."

"You don't remember, do you?"

"Remember? Have we met before?"

The girl shook her head. She was beautiful, but haunting. Even in the darkness her hair shone like spun gold, and her eyes were so pale Mara might have thought her blind had the girl not followed her every movement. There was a delicate perfection to her features.

"You wouldn't remember me, but you should remember him."

A shiver dropped the length of Mara's spine. "Who are you talking about?" The first words Droë had spoken reached her at last, an ominous echo of her own perceptions. *This isn't as it's supposed to be.* "What did you mean before? How are things supposed to be?"

The child answered with a solemn nod. "You feel it, don't you? I can tell. You're not a Walker, but you feel it anyway."

Mara gaped, unsure of what to say. Some among the masters and mistresses of the castle knew that she possessed time-sense in addition to being a Spanner. Dual talents like hers were uncommon among Travelers, but not unheard of. Nevertheless, she had never spoken of her second ability in front of other trainees. It would have sounded like bragging, and it wasn't as though she could Walk. Yet inexplicably this strange child knew. Mistress Tovorl's warning sounded in her mind again.

"Who are you?" she asked a second time, whispering the words.

"I'm Droë," the girl repeated. "I wonder if he ever mentioned me to you."

"Who is it you keep talking about?"

"Tobias. You've forgotten him, but you love him very much. Almost..." She bit down on whatever she'd meant to say.

Mara recalled another feeling she'd had earlier: her sense that she wasn't supposed to be with Delvin.

"What happened to him?" Mara asked. "Did he... Did he die?"

"I don't know. He's not here anymore, and I don't know how to find him. That's why I'm talking to you. I need your help."

"How can I–"

"You're attuned to time. I know you are. There are no Walkers here, but you're close. You're all we have."

"I– I don't understand."

The girl took a step toward her, eyes wide in the murky light. "Look at me."

Mara stared, seeing naught but a pretty young girl. At that moment, though, a gust of wind stirred her robe and the child's rags. An odd, sickly sweet smell reached her – the fetor of decay and death.

"What–"

Before she could form her question, the girl opened her mouth in what might have been intended as a grin. Her teeth were bone white and as sharp as tiny blades. Mara backed away, raising her shaking hands as if to ward off a blow.

"What are you?"

"I'm Tirribin."

"A time demon?"

"A human term. That's not a name my kind use."

Mara glanced back toward the nearest keep, looking for a path to safety. She even thought of shouting for the soldiers. She'd heard of time demons; they preyed on human life.

"If I'd wanted to feed on your years, I would have already," Droë said, sounding hurt. "Before he left, he made me promise that I wouldn't."

Mara eyed her, hands still raised, heart pounding.

"You're being rude. I'm not going to hurt you. I need your help."

"I can't help you. I don't understand what you want."

"You do understand. I know you do. This…" She gestured, a small movement of her hand that seemed to encompass the entire world, their very lives. "This isn't right. You know what I mean. None of it is as it's supposed to be."

"Can you… Do you read thoughts?"

Droë shook her head again, golden hair lifting with another wind gust. "I read time. I read those who are aware of time. You're not a Walker, and so you don't have the awareness Tobias does, and you can't sense what I sense. But you have some understanding. You know that something is wrong."

Mara set aside her fear and considered what the girl – the demon – had said. Since waking up, she had interpreted her uneasiness as a sign that she didn't belong in this place. She'd been thinking like a Spanner when maybe she should have been thinking like a Walker. Maybe her other ability was responsible for all she'd felt this day.

"Even if what you say is true, what do you want of me? What is it you think I can do?"

"I'm not sure," the demon said, an admission. "But we need to change things back somehow."

"For this Tobias you mentioned?"

Droë gazed at her, grave and lovely, her eyes ghostlike. "For all of us," she said. "For the world as you know it."

CHAPTER 19

18th Day of Kheraya's Ascent, Year 647

Mara gawked, wondering if she'd heard correctly. *For the world...* "You're saying that time has changed, that a Walker went back and altered the future, and as a result the world is in danger?"

"That's a crude way to say it, but, yes."

"How long ago?"

The demon appeared puzzled.

"The Walker. Tobias. How long ago did he leave?"

"A turn. Perhaps a bit more."

"A turn?" Mara said, her voice rising.

The demon flinched like a child responding to an adult's rebuke.

"You want me to believe," she went on, softening her tone, "that I've forgotten someone I knew a turn ago?"

The Tirribin went still, her pale gaze riveted on the nearby pathway. An instant later, Mara heard it, too: low voices and the click of boot heels on stone. The demon retreated deeper into shadow and Mara followed, hugging the stone wall in uncomfortable proximity. The smell of rot was stronger here. Mara turned her face away from the girl, fighting an impulse to gag.

The soldiers drew nearer, a man and a woman. Mara prayed to the Two that the odor wouldn't draw their notice. Strictly speaking she hadn't violated any rules by venturing into the middle courtyard, or even before, when she was in the lower. Still, any encounter with the Oaqamaran soldiers could be dangerous, and she didn't know what the punishment might be for speaking with a time demon.

The soldiers continued past. The sound of their footsteps retreated.

"They don't like my kind," Droë said, her voice low. "No one here does, but them especially." She faced Mara. "To answer your question, yes, you've forgotten him in less than a turn. He went to Hayncalde, and he Walked for the sovereign of Daerjen and changed something. He left here one turn ago. That's how recently this future became real."

Mara wanted to shout a denial, to tell the girl this wasn't possible. Even with her limited understanding of time, however, she knew better. She stared after the guards. "Who's to say this future isn't the one we're meant to have? Who's to say that other future wouldn't be even more of a disaster?"

"I am," the girl said, her tone free of irony. "And you are."

"Me?"

"Tell me what you feel."

Mara faltered, unsure of how much she wished to reveal to the Tirribin. The girl smiled, teeth catching the dim light. The expression in her eyes remained grim.

"You fear me still. And you don't trust me."

"I'm... I'm confused. My time sense isn't very strong."

"No, it's not. That's why Walkers are valued so."

Mara frowned. "Walkers are the least valued of all the Travelers."

"That's not true, at least it's not supposed to be. Tobias left here because he was the only Walker available. I heard that Daerjen's sovereign paid dearly for him."

None of that sounded right. It had been years since the court at Daerjen had the influence or resources to do much of anything. And while Walkers were rare among the Travelers of

Windhome, they were also the least in demand, in large part because the palace Binder – all Binders, for that matter – had been unable to create a device that would allow more than one Walker at a time to visit the past. The tri-sextants and tri-apertures that allowed groups of Spanners and Crossers to ply their trades at once had made simple chronofors as worthless as slingshots in a battle of flintlocks.

The demon's remarks, implausible as they were, begged another question that should have occurred to Mara earlier.

"How do I know you haven't done this to me?"

Droë's eyes widened. "Done what?"

"Confounded me. Given me this… this sense of everything being wrong. Tirribin possess powers that go far beyond whatever time sense I have. You could have done this, made me feel this way. Maybe that's why you were waiting for me here."

"Confounded you," the demon repeated, a silken chill in her voice. "To what end?" She shook her head. "I don't know why he loved you. You're nothing but a foolish human girl."

Mara flinched at the insult. She wasn't sure which bothered her more: hearing that she didn't deserve the affection of this Walker she'd never even met, or having the child-demon call her foolish and a girl.

"I didn't mean–"

"Yes, you did," the Tirribin said. "I should never have come here. Your minds are too simple to perceive the things we do, and too closed to believe them even possible."

She pivoted and walked away. After a few steps her form began to speed up and blur.

Mara strode after her. "Please don't go!" she whispered with urgency.

The demon faltered mid-step, her body solidifying once more. She was already halfway across the courtyard. She faced Mara again, blurred back closer, and waited.

"I'm sorry for accusing you," Mara said. "I shouldn't have done that." She brushed a lock of damp hair from her brow. "I don't know what you want from me. I'm trying to understand, but you have to tell me more."

"There is no more," the demon said, her tone still cold. "Tobias is gone, the world is changed, and this future is wrong. The rest…" Her shrug conveyed indifference.

"Why come to me?"

"I've told you: your time sense–"

"I'm not a Walker. You said so yourself. So what did you think to gain by speaking to me about all of this?"

Droë dropped her gaze, appearing more vulnerable and childlike in that moment than she had at any other point in their encounter. "You were the only one I could think of. You love him, and I think he loves you, too. If anyone would care – if I could make anyone remember him – it would be you."

"Is that possible?" Mara asked, exhaling the words. *I think he loves you, too.* She had never loved Delvin, and she knew he didn't love her. That very morning, she had sensed that maybe she was supposed to be with someone else. And, she had to admit, the idea of being loved by anyone, even this stranger from a different time, filled her with longing. Was she mad, pining for someone she had never met? "Can you make me remember him?"

"I don't know. I can show him to you, show you the two of you together. That could be enough."

"How?"

The demon beckoned her closer. "Come here."

Mara hesitated, drawing a frown from the Tirribin.

"I told you before: if I intended to take your years, I would have done so already, and you wouldn't have been able to stop me."

Mara suppressed another shudder. "Why are you doing this?" She was stalling, trying to decide how much she could trust the demon. "Why would your kind care so much about us, and about this one person in particular?"

Droë looked away again. "He's my friend. And the feeling you have of things being other than what they should be – that is compounded a thousand times in Tirribin." She made that same world-encompassing gesture. "This is wrong, and that wrongness touches everything. I can't escape it."

Her words spoke intimately to what Mara had been experiencing this entire day.

Mara took a long, steadying breath, making her decision. "All right."

Before she could say more, or approach the Tirribin, Droë's gaze shifted and she shrank back. "Novitiates," she said.

Looking in that direction, Mara glimpsed several pairs of trainees entering the middle courtyard from the upper. Chances were, Delvin and Hilta were with them.

"They'll go to the keeps," Mara said, turning back. "They won't bother…"

The Tirribin had vanished.

"Droë?" She turned a full circle, but saw no sign of the demon.

Mara clutched her robe more tightly, unnerved. But she lingered in the middle courtyard, hoping the Tirribin would return. When she didn't, Mara headed toward the Windward Keep. She avoided the others and took special care to steer clear of Hilta once she was in the dormitory. After shedding her robe and drying her soaked hair, she pulled on a sleepshirt and retired to her bed. She opened the shutters of the nearest window to listen to the rain, and bundled herself in blankets. Settling back against her pillow, she closed her eyes. Try as she might to rest, however, she was too agitated. She might as well have been out on the training grounds with Saffern.

Long after the rest of the female trainees had drifted off to sleep, she remained awake, her heart thudding in her chest, her thoughts riled and scattered. Two passing female soldiers laughed quietly in the corridor outside the chamber.

They don't belong here.

Already she questioned her memory of her exchange with the demon. Could she have imagined it? Or had her fellow trainees been having some fun at her expense? Perhaps the episode was real, but the girl merely pretended to be a time demon. Mara had mentioned to Delvin that she'd been feeling odd; he could have found someone to impersonate a Tirribin.

Someone who could blur into motion before my very eyes? Someone who could vanish without a trace at the first sign that others were coming?

Why had Droë called them "novitiates?" For as long as Mara could remember, the masters had called them trainees. Or was that an Oaqamaran term, imposed on them by the chancellor? Either way, she had never heard them called "novitiates."

Mara wondered what would have happened if she'd allowed the Tirribin to show her the boy, Tobias. Might she have remembered a different life, a different world? Or had the demon wished only to feed on Mara's years, a phrase that still made her quail, even in the warmth and safety of her bed.

She was, she decided, woefully ignorant in the ways of demons. She also knew too little about the history of Daerjen and the value placed on different sorts of Travelers before the invention of the tri-devices. Fortunately, she had at her disposal the finest library in the northern isles. It was past time she availed herself of the volumes stored there.

Mara finally felt slumber tug at her, like a retreating tide. The sensation of not belonging remained, but now she had some idea of what she might do about it.

She had been careless. She had allowed panic to guide her, to loosen her tongue and expose her thoughts and emotions.

Worst of all, she'd done this in front of a human girl. In front of prey!

As if she needed more proof of how scared she was.

Of course the girl couldn't remember. Not even a Walker could navigate the folds of time as Droë did. Tobias couldn't have done it. She had asked too much of this other. Her mind wasn't working as it should. She, of all Tirribin, knew the risks of venturing into the palace and interacting with novitiates. Tobias had been a friend, but he was gone. None of the rest of them could be trusted.

She should have taken the girl's years and left her. That's what she would have done yesterday.

No, she wouldn't have. Tobias made her promise. Tobias, who was lost to her.

Among Tirribin, she was considered young. A bit over five centuries, she thought. Between time spent and time taken from others, it wasn't easy for her kind to reckon years. Whatever her age, in all her time she had never experienced anything like this. She couldn't tell, though, if that was because of who Tobias was to her, or because of what he had done.

You love him very much, she had said to the girl. *Almost...* She managed to stop herself in time, before she blurted, *Almost as much as I do.*

Tirribin did not love humans. It wasn't done. At best, humans were here for but a flicker of time. They thought their lives long, because they couldn't understand what it was to bend time to their purposes. A Walker might understand – surely he would come closer than the others. But Walkers lived shortest of all. They spent their years, but couldn't replenish them as Tirribin did.

Yet she loved Tobias. What else explained the flutter in her breast when she saw him, the warmth in her gut when they spoke or he laughed at something she said, the cruel cold that gripped her when she thought of him kissing the girl?

What else explained Droë's willingness to enlist that same girl's aid to save him? Yes, it might mean that he and the girl would be together, but at least he would be found. He would be all right, and time would flow again as it was supposed to. This wrongness, like a poison in her blood, would finally be gone. Droë couldn't bear to contemplate the alternative.

She had called the girl homely when speaking with Tobias. She'd scoffed at her bronze hair and deep brown skin. The truth was, the one he called Mara wasn't ugly at all. She reminded Droë of him.

He must have gone back far – many more years than most Walkers went. That was why she had lost track of him, why she couldn't find him even now, as she cast her awareness back as far as humans might safely Travel. It didn't help that he had sailed hundreds of leagues before Walking. Time she could cross, but distance... She was as helpless before miles as a human who couldn't Span.

After leaving the girl at Tirribin speed, she navigated the sloped lanes back into Windhome and wandered its streets. She should have been hunting. She felt hollow, the way she did when she hadn't fed on years for too long. Nevertheless, she merely walked, a child in the rank streets, poorly dressed for the rain and wind, drawing stares from wharfmen returning late to their homes, and drunken sailors staggering to their ships.

Though few of them were young, any of them would have satisfied her hunger. She ignored them, and they left her alone.

As she neared the docks, and the cold, inky waters of Windhome Inlet, she slowed, then stopped. She hadn't many friends. She knew of another Tirribin on Trevynisle, but she and he kept their distance from each other. There was Tobias, of course. And one other, whom she had last seen here some months before. Treszlish. Tresz, as she called him.

She wouldn't have thought of him if not for a cloud of pale

mist that hung above the gentle swells of Safsi Bay, unmoved by the wind and undiminished by the rain. It could have been him.

"I see you in the gloaming, I beg you stop your roaming," she sang, her voice as thin as a sandpiper's whistle. "I'd a word if you'll grant it, and a song to pay if you want it."

The cloud boiled, rose, and drifted in her direction. It appeared to move slowly, but in moments it had swept across the outer piers and settled over the cobbled lane on which she stood, enveloping her, and carrying with it the smell of mold and must.

Droë was immune to most cold – even the winds and snows of Sipar's Settling couldn't touch her. This mist chilled her, though, raising bumps on her skin. She hugged herself and rubbed her arms with raw hands.

"'Grant it' and 'Want it' isn't a very good rhyme." The voice was oily, thick, the words deliberate.

"It was good enough to lure you here."

His silence seemed to concede the point.

The mist around her shifted again, and she glimpsed the figure at its center. He was taller than she, human in form, hairless. His skin was slick and gray, and as he drew nearer, his features came into relief: a flat nose, thin formless lips, a gently tapered chin, and large, round eyes that glowed faintly, like stars peeking through cloud cover.

"You say you have more song?" he asked after a time, another concession.

"Yes. I'll sing for you. First, though, I need your help."

Surprise widened his eyes, bent the broad mouth downward. "A Tirribin, asking help of a Shonla. How odd."

Droë lifted a shoulder, hoping the gesture would convey indifference. She wasn't sure it worked.

"Do you finally wish to work together? I can trap them, you can feed, I can swallow their screams. Everyone is happy."

She lifted an eyebrow. "Everyone?"

He grinned, exposing blunt, gray teeth. "We're happy."

"I feed very well, thank you. That's not why I called to you."

"Then why? Quickly. Late as it is, there are ships on the bay."

Droë peered out over the water. Lights bobbed on its surface like fireflies. "They have lamps, torches."

"Most of them, yes. But not all. There's sound and fear ripe for the taking. Now, tell me what you want."

She kept her eyes on the distant ships, unwilling to meet his luminous gaze. "A man – a human boy – left here some time ago. A turn maybe. He sailed south, toward Daerjen. I want to know what became of him."

"Do you?" the Shonla said. "What would make a time demon care so much about a human boy?"

Droë scowled. "What would make a mist demon so crass and meddlesome?"

He shrugged, acknowledging the riposte.

"Will you help me?"

"When did you say he left?"

"A turn ago. He sailed for Daerjen aboard a merchant ship. I don't know what it was called, but the captain was a tall, thin woman."

Tresz's frown deepened as she spoke, until at last he shook his head. "I remember no such vessel, and I make it my business to know all of them."

"There is… a question of time in this case."

"You know Shonla can't sense things as Tirribin do. If he is lost to time, he is lost to the mists as well."

Droë nodded, grief constricting her throat.

The Shonla canted his head to the side. "You are most curious. I forget how young you are."

"I'm not so young." She knew she sounded defensive.

"What is your interest in this human?"

She felt herself flush. Shonla saw well in the dark.

"He's a Walker, and the world has changed since his departure. I fear he created a new future, one that could bring ruin to his kind."

"And to him. This is about him most of all."

She wouldn't bother denying it. Usually, Tirribin cared no more about humans ruining their world than did Shonla. "Yes."

"Their world has been in ruin a long time, at least by their reckoning."

She lifted her shoulders, saying nothing.

His expression soured. "Allow me a moment."

Tresz closed his eyes and spread his sinuous arms wide. The mist around him thickened, or else he grew less opaque, blending with it more. He stood that way for a time. Rain continued to fall on the streets of Windhome, and small waves on the inlet slapped at the wharves.

When he opened his eyes again, his frown had deepened. "There is awareness among Shonla of this misfuture you describe. Not all are as convinced as you that it brings ruin, and for Shonla it has been profitable. More humans at sea, more nourishment for us."

"Do they know when it started?"

"Wouldn't that be a question for Tirribin?"

"Yes," she said, impatience in the word. "And if I could reach them as you reach your kind, I'd ask. I have only you."

"They say only that it has been years, a considerable number of them by human standards."

"He wouldn't have Walked so far."

"It is unlikely," Tresz said, "but it's possible, yes?"

"Yes, it's possible."

"They fight wars in the Bone Sea, the Inward Sea, the Aiyanthan and the Herjean. All of these began at similar times. Coincidence perhaps. Or perhaps your Walker is at the center of it all."

She wanted to tell him that Tobias wasn't "her Walker", but

the words wouldn't come.

"I must go," the Shonla said, casting an avid glance out over the water. "I'm grateful for the song, brief though it was. I will collect more another time. I... I wish you well with your search."

"Thank you."

His mists swirled, further chilling the air, surrounding him, concealing him. Moments later, the cloud moved off, leaving Droë alone on the warming street. The formless gray glided over the inlet. Before long, it had swallowed a ship.

She continued onto the nearest dock, her steps light as she crept toward the moored ships. Ropes creaked with the shift of water and wood. The rain had eased to a drizzle, and the wind no longer keened. Droë kept to shadows, watchful.

Reaching the first vessel, she brushed her fingers against the wood of the hull and closed her eyes, tasting the years of those who slumbered within. Many were young; she could have fed well, had that been her purpose. But she sought knowledge rather than sustenance.

Most of those she perceived through the planks of wood had trod the same path all their lives. Whatever events had transpired to bring the world to this misfuture, whatever changes had been wrought, made little difference in their fates. They would have been sailors on this ship no matter what.

A few, though, didn't belong. They had been traveling a different road, only to be shunted here without warning, without their knowledge or even an inkling. Droë pressed her palm to the wood, delicate fingers splayed, her touch deepening. She caught the flavor of the years Tresz had mentioned. He was right. Not a lot of time, barely an instant for Tirribin. For a human, however... Ten years. More.

This couldn't have been Tobias. How could a Walker go so far?

She opened her eyes, withdrew her hand, and crept to the next ship. Fingers on that hull, she tasted again and found much the same: most unaffected, a few out of place, but on a path that had carried them for more than a decade. A third ship revealed a similar pattern.

Removing her fingers from this last vessel, she held them to her lips and licked them, lost in thought.

What if it was Tobias? Daerjen's sovereign sought a Walker. Most royals used Walkers for small journeys back in time, but what if the sovereign wanted Tobias for a Walk of great length, a single, desperate attempt to change as much as possible?

She couldn't imagine why he would do this, and that was her own fault. For too long, she had ignored the affairs of humans, content to hunt and feed. Now she longed to understand a future that was forever lost to her.

If Tobias was responsible for this misfuture, and if he lived long enough to reach this time once more, he would be much changed, a grown man, someone she probably wouldn't recognize until she tasted his years.

Her skin pebbled again, and she rubbed her arms trying to keep warm. Boot heels clicked in the distance, first on cobblestone, and then wood. A sailor, hurrying back to his ship. Droë considered slipping away, but all this tasting had left her hungry after all. She licked her fingers again, smiled, and crouched in the shadows to wait for her prey.

CHAPTER 20

25th Day of Kheraya's Ascent, Year 647

Delvin avoided her the next day and throughout the days that followed, but Mara couldn't bring herself to care. He and Hilta spent each evening together in the upper courtyard. Mara refused as well to let that bother her. Her thoughts cleaved to the time demon and the implications of their exchange. The sensation of being in the wrong place – the wrong time – remained with her, undiminished. But Mara understood its origins now and had resolved to find a solution; the burden of her time sense didn't weigh on her quite so heavily.

She had no idea what her new secret purpose would demand of her, and so devoted herself anew to her training and studies, unwilling to be caught unprepared. Previously, she had studied and honed her swordsmanship and marksmanship because her teachers expected as much. She practiced Spanning because sometime soon the autarch would send more soldiers, with orders for Windhome's Spanners to use their tri-sextants to pilot them to some new battlefield.

Only now, in the wake of her encounter with the Tirribin, did Mara hone her skills for reasons of her own.

She soon learned that she had a knack for blade work. The first day after she spoke to Droë, Saffern paired her with Hilta. Mara wasn't sure if the weapons master did this intentionally, but it wouldn't have surprised her. Their instructors, it often seemed, knew more about their lives outside of lessons than they let on.

Whatever his thinking, Mara didn't waste the opportunity. The instant he signaled for them to spar, she sprang into a frenzied attack, her sword a silver blur. Hilta stumbled back, parrying desperately, her eyes wide. Maybe she thought Mara actually intended to kill her. Mara hoped so.

It took her no more than a tencount to disarm the girl and lay the edge of her blade against Hilta's collarbone. Hilta was panting; Mara hadn't broken a sweat.

"Do you yield?"

Hilta nodded.

"That was entertaining," Saffern said, joining them. He picked up Hilta's sword and handed it to her. "This time, Miss Craik, why don't you fight as well. That might make for a more satisfying duel."

"Yes, master," she said, cheeks reddening.

He stepped back. "Begin."

Mara attacked again, and though Hilta fought with more aplomb this time, it took Mara only a tencount to knock her weapon from her hand.

Saffern considered Mara through narrowed eyes. "Miss Lijar, I think it's time we paired you with someone new."

He summoned Nat, and had him work with Mara for the rest of the day. She had long thought of him as one of the best swordsmen in their group, and he proved a more formidable foe than Hilta. Yet Mara kept up with him. By the end of the session both of them were grinning, their faces and clothes sweaty.

"I didn't know you could fight like that," he said.

"Nor did I," Saffern said from behind them before Mara could answer. "Thank you, Mister Bosmi. That will be all. A word please, Miss Lijar."

Nat bowed to the weapons master, cast a warning glance Mara's way, and followed the others to Feidys's chamber.

Mara stood before Saffern, unsure of why she felt so nervous. She'd done nothing wrong. The weapons master eyed the palace walls, and the soldiers there, before lowering his gaze to hers.

"Would you care to explain?"

"Explain what, master?"

A smirk crinkled the corners of his dark eyes. "Either you dislike Miss Craik even more than I would have guessed, or you've been practicing late at night, when no one is here."

"I haven't been practicing," she said.

He laughed.

"I also haven't been working at my training as hard as I ought to. I thought I should do something about that."

"I'm glad," Saffern said, his tone free of irony for once. "May I ask what prompted this change of heart?"

"It was... about time."

He squinted again. "Very well. You may go."

Mara started away.

"I'd like to see more of this in the days to come."

"You will," she said over her shoulder. "I promise."

When not on the training ground, Mara gave particular attention to Feidys's lectures on the current wars, and her lessons in history, politics, and finance. Somewhere in the past lay hidden an explanation for all that had happened to put Islevale in this future. Mara needed to find the point of inflection, the place where it all changed.

Her newfound enthusiasm spilled over into her labors in the Binder's chamber. Her work for Binder Tovorl wasn't likely to shed much light on the mystery of what had happened to Droë's friend, but the time she spent in the Binder's workshop offered the best chance to learn more about what it meant to Walk into the past.

Delvin and Hilta had taken to working side by side, and so Nat joined Mara at her table. He was quiet and kept to himself, which suited her. Occasionally she found herself watching Delvin and Hilta, not with anger or even jealousy, but with a hint of regret. Maybe if she had found a way to make him understand that first day, he wouldn't have made her feel so foolish, and they could still be together. On the other hand, he appeared genuinely happy with Hilta, which made her question whether he'd ever been worth caring about.

Several days after speaking with Droë, Mara was once again the last to leave the Binder's chamber.

"You've done fine work in recent days, Miss Lijar," Mistress Tovorl said, as Mara tidied up her work bench.

"Thank you, mistress."

"I wonder if you've figured out whatever it was that troubled you the last time we spoke."

A sector slipped from Mara's fingers and clattered to the floor. She stooped to retrieve it, casting a guilty look at the Binder.

Mistress Tovorl watched her, expectant. "I invited you to come back and discuss the matter when you'd gained a better understanding of what you felt. Or had you forgotten?"

"I didn't forget," Mara said, setting the sector on the shelf and facing her.

"Perhaps you've discussed it with others who were able to help you."

"One other. She was... I'm not sure how much she helped."

The Binder's brow creased. "I warned you to take some care in sharing your perceptions."

"I did. I have. This... this individual approached me."

The creases deepened. "Approached you? Another trainee?"

Mara shook her head.

"Miss Lijar, if someone has approached you who doesn't–"

"It was a time demon."

Mistress Tovorl gaped at her, open-mouthed. At last she straightened, her shoulders dropping fractionally. "Well." She gave a small shake of her head. "I certainly wasn't expecting that."

"No, mistress."

"You know Tirribin can be dangerous. One is said to have killed a trainee many years ago, before I came to Windhome."

"I didn't know that."

"Surely you know that they prey on human life."

"This one… I don't think she means to hurt me."

"Most demons are clever, and Tirribin are particularly deadly. You should be careful."

The ensuing silence stretched on for several moments.

"Why would a Tirribin be interested in a Spanner?" the mistress finally asked, the question a sort of capitulation.

"I have some time sense," Mara said. "I can't Walk. At least I don't think I can. Yet it seems I know when time has been changed."

"Having time sense is not the same as…" She stopped, staring again. "'When time has been changed,'" she repeated. Her characteristic lilt transformed the words, making them sound more ominous. She crossed to the door, opened it, and peered out into the corridor. After closing the door again, she faced Mara. "What exactly did the Tirribin tell you?" she asked in a whisper.

Mara repeated as much as she could remember of her conversation with Droë, although she avoided mention of what the demon said about Tobias loving her. And her loving him.

"So the Tirribin believes that we're in the wrong future. And she sensed that you felt this as well. Is that right?"

"Essentially, yes."

"Remarkable."

"She claimed that this all happened only a turn ago," Mara said. "Or even less. For all I know, everything changed that first day. But how can that be? I have a lifetime of memories – and I have no memory of this person she talked about."

"The Walker, you mean?" At her nod, the Binder continued, "This is far from my realm of expertise. I make chronofors when they're needed, and I understand the rudiments of time Walking. Separating one possible progression of history from another is beyond me." She sat at her work bench and picked up the incomplete arc of a sextant. "Still, as I understand it, once a future has been altered, those who live in the future can't recall any other historical path. If what the Tirribin says is true, our lives have shifted, perhaps dramatically, but we would have no knowledge of that. Rather, our memories would shift to reflect this new world we're living in. Only those with the deepest time sense would be aware of the change." She regarded Mara. "Your time sense may be limited, but it's strong enough for you to perceive the disjunction between this future, and the past you once knew. And, of course, the Walker would know. He can see the changes he's wrought, and he would remember both times."

"So he'd still remember me?" The words were out before she gave thought to what she was saying.

The Binder arched an eyebrow. "Is there something you're not telling me?"

Mara blushed to the tips of her ears. "The time demon said that the Walker and I were friends."

"I see. Does this have anything to do with why Mister Ruhj and Miss Craik now spend so much time together?"

"That was because he made fun of me that first day. I only learned about Tobias later."

Mistress Tovorl smiled. "You've been busy."

"Yes, mistress."

The Binder waved a hand. "When your fellow trainees are absent, you can call me Wansi."

"Thank you, mistress. Wansi."

Using the name should have been odd. She wouldn't have dared call any of the other masters or mistresses by their given names. But saying it aloud came to her more naturally than anything she'd done since waking that first morning.

"What is it?" the Binder asked.

"I don't know. Using your name – I think we must have done that in the other time. It felt... right."

Wansi eyed her, tapping a finger against tight lips. "You're missing your midday meal, and I'm sorry for that. But I'd like to try something. Actually, I'd like *you* to try something."

She crossed to her desk and searched one of the drawers. Soon she gave a small cry of discovery and plucked an item from within. Clutching it in her hand, she pushed the drawer shut with her hip and walked to where Mara waited.

Opening her hand, she held out a round device. At first glance, Mara thought it a golden chainwatch. The burnished face of this device, however, had been divided into three circles, with three corresponding stems rather than a single one.

"A chronofor?"

"Just so."

"I'm not a Walker."

"No," Wansi said. "You're not. You're a Spanner, and an accomplished one. But there's more to you than that. If there weren't, you and I wouldn't be having this conversation, and the Tirribin would never have approached you. Their kind are capricious, at times devious, but they don't usually interact with humans, except to prey upon them, and matters of time are as weighty to them as matters of life and death are to you and me. Her willingness to speak with you tells me that your time sense is stronger even than you know." She twitched the hand holding the chronofor. "Take it."

Mara lifted the time piece from Wansi's palm. It was heavier than she'd expected, its gold back cool against her fingers.

Wansi pointed to the three circles on the face. "Bells, days, turns. Each click of the appropriate stem is equal to a single unit. If you have enough ability with time, the chronofor should work much as your sextant does when you Span. If not, nothing will happen. It really is as simple as that."

"You want me to use this right now?"

Wansi shrugged. "Why not?"

"Well, because if I go back one bell – and I wouldn't want to try more than that – I'll appear here right in the middle of our work session. That seems like a bad idea."

The Binder twisted her lips to the side. "That was well-argued. Very well. Go eat. Join me here when the last of your lessons is done. We should be able to try this then." Wansi took the chronofor from her and set it back in the drawer. "I'll be waiting for you," she said. A dismissal, and an order.

"Yes, mistress," Mara said.

"Walkers are rare, Miss Lijar, and though the limitations on their powers have been made obvious with the spread of tri-devices, they are still coveted by royals. I wouldn't want you to draw undue notice from servants of the autarch. Speak of this to no one."

Cold washed over Mara, like a sea wave in winter. She nodded and left.

As on the day when she first realized something was wrong, Mara moved through the rest of her lessons in a sort of waking dream. She struggled to concentrate. The few Walkers she'd known had long since left the palace. Except for Tobias, of course, whom she didn't remember. From what she'd heard, she gathered that the between for Walkers was much like the gulf for Spanners: a time of disorientation and sensory assault. She dreaded experiencing it.

When she emerged from her final lesson – history, as it happened – cool shadows had fallen across the courtyards and a palette of fiery hues lit the western sky. She hastened to Wansi's chamber, and after knocking and hearing the Binder call for her to enter, slipped inside.

Despite the clear skies and the lovely breeze blowing off the bay, Wansi had her windows closed. The air in the workshop was over-warm and stale. A single candle burned on the work bench. The Binder worked on that same sextant, the ever-present loupe held to her eye, a glow of magick about her.

"Lock the door," she said, without looking up. "It wouldn't do for someone to walk in on this."

Mara did as instructed.

Still Wansi didn't tear her attention from the sextant. "The chronofor is on the table at your spot. As with simple Spanning, you can't be wearing any clothes when you Walk. You can pile your things there." She pointed to the same table, keeping her gaze averted. A plain cotton robe, folded, sat next to the chronofor. "That robe has been there for some time now. If you go back a single bell, you should find it waiting for you. You can put it on when you arrive."

"Thank you."

"You have nothing to fear, Miss Lijar. I assure you."

Mara nodded, though Wansi had yet to look her way. After a moment's hesitation, she shrugged off her robe and pulled off the rest of her clothes. Warm though she was, she shivered. She picked up the chronofor with a shaking hand.

"The left-most stem is for bells," Wansi said. "One click to the left ought to do it."

Mara turned the stem, the single click sounding as loud as a musket shot in the stillness of the chamber.

"When you're ready, depress the large stem at the top of the device. The between is rather unpleasant, worse than what you've been used to as a Spanner. Be prepared."

"Yes, all right." Her voice shook.

Wansi smiled, but studiously avoided a glance her way. "Courage, Mara. This might all be for naught."

Somehow Mara didn't think so, but she swallowed her doubts. Taking a breath, she thumbed the central stem.

Nothing.

Mara blinked, her disappointment a knife in her gut: unexpected and more painful than she could have imagined. At some point since her earlier conversation with Wansi, she had decided that she wanted to go back. She wanted to find Tobias. She wanted to experience this other time she had lived and lost. More, she had believed that she could go back. Wansi was willing to trust her with a chronofor. Droë spoke to her as she would to a Walker. Surely those things meant something.

"It didn't–"

That was all she got out. The knife in her belly became a grappling hook, carving through her flesh and yanking her back away from the Binder's chamber, away from candlelight and the glow of dusk.

Images flashed through her mind like lightning; smells and tastes and noises buffeted her, a storm of sensation, different from the Spanning gulf, but familiar enough. She tried to take a calming breath, but couldn't. No air here, which was new, unwelcome. Fear gripped her. She suppressed a scream, waited for this – the *between*, Wansi called it – to end. She wasn't going far. A single bell. How long could it last?

But she was new to Walking. For all she knew, she had erred in some way. What if she was lost forever in this airless nightmare of light and clamor? Fear tipped over into panic. She tried again to cry out, failed.

It ended with dizzying abruptness. She stumbled out of the between and dropped to her knees. The floor was blessedly solid. She closed her eyes, inhaled once, twice, opened them again. The room pitched and rolled.

"Apparently you're a Walker as well as a Spanner." The Binder's voice.

Mara didn't yet trust herself to speak. She still held the chronofor, her fingers cramping around the rounded metal. She reached up to the table with her free hand, found the robe Wansi had left for her, and pulled it on.

The Binder walked around the table and squatted beside her. "Are you all right?" Concern knitted her brows.

Mara answered with a nod and tried to push herself to her feet. Upon standing, she swayed and might have fallen had Wansi not grasped her arm and steered her to the nearest stool. Wansi left her, returning a spirecount later bearing a cup of watered wine.

"Just a sip," she said. "I've seen this before. The first journey for a Walker is even worse than it is for a Spanner."

Mara drank, grimaced at the taste. Her stomach churned, but the wine stayed down. At last, she raised her gaze to Wansi's.

"You did it," the Binder said.

"I'm not sure I ever want to again."

"The version of you that will walk through that door in a short while might wish you would. From all I understand of Walkers, you don't want to run into another you."

"I can't go back yet. I need to rest."

"I understand. Sit, sip your wine."

Mara forced herself to drink some more.

Wansi crossed her arms, appraisal in her gaze. "You're rather unusual, you know. It's rare for Travelers to have two fully realized abilities."

"I'm better at Spanning."

"Of course. You've been doing it since you were a child. And still, you Walked on your first attempt, which tells me you could become an accomplished Walker as well."

Mara stared at the chronofor. "I only went back a bell. That's like Spanning from here to the courtyard outside the window. It's nothing. How do Walkers go back an entire turn or two or five? I can't imagine it."

"They practice, as you will."

She looked up at that. Wansi's stare didn't waver. At length Mara shifted her gaze and raised the cup to her lips. She was starting to recover. "To have changed the past so completely,

Tobias had to have gone back even more. Much more."

"I'd considered that. He may have gone back years, in contravention of palace law."

She could think of no reply, and they lapsed into silence. Eventually Mara drained her cup and stood. She felt steady on her feet, and her head had cleared.

"I should go back."

"Probably. We'll speak more after you do." Wansi crossed to the shuttered window.

Mara removed the robe, folded it and left it on the table where it had been.

"One click to the right. No more," the Binder said.

She turned the small stem until she heard a single metallic click, inhaled, and depressed the larger button.

The effect this time was immediate. A violent tug at her belly jerked her forward into the ferment of the between. She knew not to draw breath, and having been through it once, she endured this passage without panicking. Still, the assault on her senses left her exhausted and light-headed. She kept her feet upon emerging, but only because she caught herself on the table.

"Was that Walk easier?" Wansi asked from her stool. She had set aside the sextant and was reading from a curled piece of parchment, her spectacles shining with candlelight. Several other scrolls lay scattered on the work bench.

"Yes." Mara began to dress. "How long was I gone?"

"Not long. Moments, that's all."

"Do you remember the conversation we had when I arrived here a bell ago?"

Wansi set down the parchment, but didn't look her way.

"It's all right. I have something on."

The Binder swiveled in her seat. "Yes, I do."

"So I changed the future."

She feared Wansi might scoff. This was hardly an occasion

worthy of history. But if the Binder thought her statement grandiose, she kept it to herself. "Yes, you did. This is why Walkers have been forbidden from going back more than a year. It's also why the palace has traditionally had a Walker to train Walkers, just as we have a Spanner to teach Spanning. Had the chancellor known about your other ability, he might have replaced Mistress Karis when she died. As it is, you only have me. So I'll tell you what Karis often said: Walking carries enormous responsibilities that go beyond anything most Spanners or Crossers can imagine. If you continue to Travel back, even a single bell at a time, you have to weigh every word, every deed."

"According to Droë – the Tirribin – in the other future, Walkers were the most valued of Travelers. They were sought after by kings and sovereigns. Maybe that's why."

"That could be. Another possibility occurs to me. I'm old enough to remember a world without tri-sextants and tri-apertures. Before Spanners and Crossers could Travel in groups, theirs were considered the lesser arts." She canted her head, eyes on Mara.

"You're suggesting that in Tobias's time, there were no tri-devices."

"A likely conclusion, don't you think?"

"Then that brings me back to the same question I asked Droë: why should we think that lost future is any better than this one? Maybe things were worse in Tobias's world."

"Perhaps. His decision to Travel back in time to change history suggests as much."

Mara nodded, pensive.

"What did the Tirribin say when you discussed this with her?"

"I asked, 'Who's to say this future isn't the one we're meant to have?' And she said that she was, and I was."

"What did you think of that answer?"

A mirthless smile lifted one corner of Mara's mouth. "I didn't like it. I still don't. It comes back to responsibility. I don't want it, at least not that much of it. This shouldn't be my decision, or hers."

"It may have to be. Aside from the three of us, I would guess that few people are aware that this other time ever existed. If Tobias is dead, it could be that no one else knows."

Mara's cheeks went cold, forcing her to recognize an uncomfortable truth: she cared more about finding Tobias, a boy she didn't remember – had never met in this lifetime – than she did rescuing the world from a troubling future.

Wansi narrowed her eyes. "The easiest thing to do would be to ignore what the Tirribin told you, ignore what you've felt, and let the world continue on this path, right or wrong."

"There are a lot of wars right now... and the autarch is winning all of them. The world doesn't seem like a very happy place."

Wansi made no effort to mask the pain in her blue eyes. "I'm not sure you can do much about that. There will always be sadness and violence and death. Right now many people in this world are quite happy with their lot. A different future will surely bring joy to some, and ruin to others. There's no ledger for this, no accounting that will enable you to determine where the most happiness lies."

"Then how do I decide what to do?"

"You follow your instincts. The Tirribin was right. You've known for several days that some vague thing is wrong with the world, haven't you?"

"Yes."

"Then that's your answer. It's the only information you have."

"Is it enough?"

"I'm not a Walker. It's not for me to say."

Mara frowned, prompting a sad smile from the Binder.

"That's a coward's way out, isn't it?"

"A bit, yes."

"I'm afraid it's all I have to offer." Wansi stood. "For now, I think the best thing you can do is practice your Walking, as well as your Spanning."

Mara placed the chronofor next to the robe she'd used. "I will. Do you want me to come back tomorrow?"

"No," the Binder said. "I want you to take the chronofor and practice on your own." She answered Mara's look of surprise with a shrug. "There are no other Walkers in the palace; that device has been gathering cobwebs. Use it, make yourself comfortable with it. And by all means, be discreet. If the chancellor or his guards find out you're Walking with a chronofor I gave you, it's liable to raise questions neither of us wishes to answer."

His guards. Mara didn't miss the implication – as she'd guessed that first day of this misfuture, she wasn't alone in hating the Oaqamaran presence in the palace.

Mara stepped to the door, but paused there, her fingers resting on the handle. "Do you know how long ago tri-devices began to be used?"

The Binder hesitated. "As it happens, I was looking that up when you returned. I don't know when the first was created. As far as I can tell, they came into widespread use approximately a dozen years ago. Possibly a bit more."

Mara's knees gave way, and again she might have fallen if not for her hold on the door handle. Going back a mere bell had been punishing. Yet somehow Tobias had Walked a dozen years, or more. He was beyond her reach.

CHAPTER 21

9th Day of Kheraya's Descent, Year 647

Mara almost surrendered that evening. Knowing that time was on the wrong path would eat at her. She would regret never finding Tobias, and she dreaded telling Droë that she couldn't help her. But she could live with all of that. She would never survive a Walk back in time of a dozen years. *Or more.*

She hid the chronofor in the Windward Keep among her few possessions, between an overshirt her mother had sent for her thirteenth birthday, and a dress, also a gift from home, that she'd long since outgrown. Maybe she should have taken it back to Wansi straight away. What was the use in keeping it if she didn't intend to use it?

Later. She could give it back to the Binder tomorrow, or the next day. With a last glance at the pile of clothes concealing the device, she left the dormitory and hurried to join the other trainees for their evening rations. Before she reached the refectory, she was stopped by three soldiers who wanted to know what she was doing on her own, unsupervised. She stammered something about having to do extra work for the Binder, and they let her go, but the encounter deepened her fears. It also rekindled her resolve.

They don't belong here.

Still, she didn't try Walking that night or the next day. If Wansi was right and the invention of tri-devices was connected to something Tobias had done, he had gone far indeed.

251

She didn't have to decide anything yet. In the meantime, though, she needed to practice.

The next day at the midday meal, while the rest of her cohort ate, she left the table, drawing glances from Nat and Delvin, and approached the refectory door. She took care to walk to a male guard.

"Where are you going?" he asked in the Ring Isle tongue, his accent sharpening the words.

"I don't feel well."

"You're sick?"

She averted her gaze. "Not sick. Just… it's my time."

Mara chanced a look at the man. His face had grown crimson. She suppressed a laugh.

"Well, go on then," he said, waving her away as if he thought her ailment might be catching.

She hurried from the refectory, using the same excuse to similar effect with two more guards on her way to the Windward Keep.

Retrieving an extra robe and a candle and flint from her shelves, she tucked the items under what she was wearing, and stole into the corridor. She needed a room, a place where she could Walk without being seen, either in the present or the past.

Mara walked the hallways of the palace, trying not to make a sound, keeping her distance from open windows and arrow slots, listening for voices and footsteps. She hadn't much time before the next lessons began, flooding these corridors with trainees. At one point she had to duck into an empty lesson room to avoid a pair of soldiers.

She found what she sought on the third story of the palace, along a deserted corridor whose chambers overlooked the upper courtyard. It was a storage chamber, filled with piles of items too old to be of value, but too valuable to be discarded: ancient volumes and crumbling scrolls of parchment, worn robes coated in dust, forgotten portraits of former instructors and chancellors. Cobwebs hung in corners, shifting as her movements stirred the fusty air. A bit of light seeped into the chamber around the edges of a lone shuttered window, making her glad she'd brought the candle and flint. Yes, this would do nicely.

She hid the extra robe and candle there, under an old upholstered chair, let herself out of the chamber with utmost care, and hurried to her next lesson. Her arrival drew another glance from Delvin, but he said nothing to her, which suited her fine.

Upon finding a place to practice, however, her nerve failed her. She felt trapped, caught between her fears, and the lingering knowledge that nothing was as it was supposed to be. In the end, it was Delvin, of all people, who allowed her to break free of her indecision.

Kheraya's Ascent ended three days after she hid her robe in the dusty chamber. The Goddess's Solstice, Kheraya Ascendant, was a day of feasting and celebration. At least it was supposed to be.

Mara kept to herself. In past years, she had savored the celebration and a day's respite from lessons and training. This year, with so much on her mind, she would have preferred to muddle through a routine day.

She did enjoy that evening's meal, and as she and Nat stepped out of the refectory into a warm, misty evening, she felt little urgency with regard to Walking, or anything else.

Then she saw that a crowd had gathered at the top of the stairs leading to the lower courtyard.

She and Nat exchanged looks and hurried to join the others. As they walked, Mara spotted Hilta, but not Delvin. Her apprehension deepened.

The scene awaiting them in the courtyard made Mara's stomach heave.

Delvin knelt in the grass, his hands bound before him and staked to the grass. He had been stripped of his robe and shirt. Two men stood over him. One was the chancellor, his pale, fleshy features lit by the last silver light of day, and the warm glow of nearby torches. The other was a soldier, who held a naked blade. Two of the alabaster-skinned Belvora flanked the chancellor as if guarding him, their wings folded, their amber eyes roving over the gathered trainees.

"The Two have mercy," Mara said under her breath.

One of the other trainees, a year younger than she, regarded her and shook his head.

"Not likely."

"What did he do?" Nat asked.

"What do you think? It's Delvin."

Nat nodded, and Mara, in her horror, understood. She and Wansi had joked about it not so long ago. Mister Ruhj in particular seems to be hungry all the time, the Binder had said. Has there ever been a meal at which he wasn't first to finish his rations?

Neither of them had added that upon eating all of his rations, he spent the balance of nearly every meal time begging others to share theirs. When that didn't work, he occasionally resorted to more desperate measures. He had stolen food before. Until tonight, he had never been caught.

"This... *thing* on the grass at my feet," the chancellor said, his voice carrying, silencing them all, "is not your fellow trainee. He is not your friend. He is not even my Spanner. Not tonight. Tonight, he is a thief and traitor. Because to steal food from our kitchens is to steal from all of you, from all of us. This was no prank. This was no act of daring. His actions are a betrayal, make no mistake. As a result, you all will have less to eat tomorrow, and the next day, and the day after that. Because of what he has done, you will be hungry.

"So his punishment must be severe. You will want for food,

and so he must be disciplined. That is only right." He opened his hands, a perfunctory smile carving lines in his face. "Just as it is only right that you should watch as he is punished, so that you can be certain that your suffering does not go unavenged."

He glanced at the soldier and gave a single nod.

The man stepped forward and raised his sword, the steel shining in the firelight. For one horrifying moment, Mara thought he intended to kill Delvin. He didn't. Rather, he brought the flat of the blade down on Delvin's back with a slap that echoed across the courtyard. Delvin stiffened and cried out. Even from a distance, Mara saw a long, red welt form on his dark skin. The soldier raised his blade and struck him again. And again and again. Until the echo of the blows and Delvin's screams blended into an appalling din, and blood streamed from the flayed skin on Delvin's back. Hilta sobbed. Mara turned away, pressing her brow against Nat's shoulder. Still it went on.

It ended when Delvin passed out. The chancellor waved the soldier away before turning on his heel and returning to his keep, the Belvora a step behind. Once he had entered the palace, and the demons had flown to the tower ramparts, masters rushed forward to tend to Delvin. The other trainees dispersed singly or in small groups, all of them silent.

Mara shared a glance with Nat and stalked back toward the dormitory. Her doubts had vanished. Whatever a different future might hold, it had to be better than this.

The following morning, she rose early, dressed, and crept through the corridors to her secret chamber, the chronofor heavy in her pocket.

She lit her candle, set the spare robe where she could reach it with ease, and stripped off her clothes, shivering in the cold, still air. This first time Walking on her own, she didn't dare attempt to Travel back more than a bell. If she could accustom herself to the shorter journey, she might eventually build up to longer ones.

She set the chronofor as Wansi had instructed, readied herself, and depressed the central stem.

The pull and the between were every bit as jarring as she remembered. Upon emerging into the earlier time, she fell to the floor, toppling a stack of books into a set of upright paintings, which promptly fell over. The clatter would have been enough to wake anyone nearby from even the most sound sleep.

Her heart battering the walls of her chest, she threw on the robe, expecting soldiers and Belvora to storm in and carry her to the chancellor for a beating.

Nothing happened. After waiting for some time and realizing no one would be coming, she gathered herself for the journey to her correct time. The Walk back proved somewhat easier, which Mara took as an indication that she was already making progress. She should have contented herself with that.

Instead, she traveled back and forth twice more, a bell each time. During the second of these Walks, she realized that the chronofor was less precise than she'd assumed. Upon her arrival in the earlier time, she found the stack of books and row of portraits she had knocked over upright and undisturbed. She stared at the volumes, pondering the implications of the neat pile. At last it occurred to her that she herself might show up at any moment and knock them over again, or rather, for the first time. Terrified at the prospect of encountering herself in this past, she set the chronofor forward a bell and returned to when she belonged, hoping she wouldn't meet herself in her own time.

Her vision swimming, as much with her exertions as with her puzzlement over the implications of her different forays to and fro, she dressed in haste and stumbled out of the storage chamber into the silent corridor. She hurried back to the dormitory, entering as others were putting on their clothes.

"Where have you been?" one of the girls asked, eyeing her askance.

"Privy," she said, her voice sounding unsteady. Fortunately, the other trainee didn't appear to notice or care.

Mara followed the others to breakfast and then to training. But throughout the day, she felt exhausted, dizzy, and sick to her stomach. She fought to keep her eyes open during her lessons, and her work in Wansi's chamber was so slipshod that she nearly ruined the sextant she was calibrating. The Binder regarded her with a brow-furrowing blend of concern and disapproval.

By early evening, she could hardly keep her feet. She went to bed early, didn't wake even when the other girls repaired to the dormitory, and slept through to her normal waking time. After that, she vowed to Walk back and forward only once in a single session.

Mara practiced with the chronofor several times more over the course of the following qua'turn, always managing to avoid wandering guards as she snuck to and from the chamber. Soon, she had graduated to Walks of two and even three bells. The betweens remained trials. The three bell Walk left her gasping for breath and so addled she almost couldn't bring herself to Walk back. After a few more days, though, she had mastered that interval as well.

The first time she attempted a four bell Walk, she passed out upon reaching the earlier time, only to wake without any sense of how long she had been unconscious. No light entered the room from the gaps in the window shutters, so Mara knew that no one would be abroad in the palace, but she had no idea how to get back to her proper time. She couldn't go forward the full four clicks; that much was clear. Should she go back three, or two? Panic flooded her heart, entirely different from the fear she experienced in the between. What would happen if she met herself in another time? Wansi's warning had been vague but unsettling. She waited in the dark room, the spare robe draped across her shoulders. Eventually, she heard what she'd been waiting for: bells. They stopped after three chimes. At least now she had an idea of the time.

She waited, trying to gauge how long it had taken her to rise, make her way here, and Walk back. When she guessed that she'd waited long enough, she Walked forward three clicks.

The chamber was empty when she arrived, and her clothes were piled where she'd left them. She dressed and left the chamber, unsure of whether she wished to try again any time soon.

She hadn't spoken to Wansi in private since the Binder gave her the chronofor. On this day, however, Wansi asked her to remain after she and the others had completed their work.

"You look tired," the Binder said, as Mara stowed her tools.

She lifted a shoulder, avoiding the woman's gaze.

"You've been practicing?"

"Yes."

"Too much perhaps."

"How can it be too much?" Mara asked, facing her. "Tobias might have gone back years. Today, for the first time, I went back four bells."

Wansi's eyes widened. "Four bells is impressive."

"I fainted when I did it. When I woke, I didn't know how far I needed to Walk to make it back."

"Yet make it back you did. That, too, is impressive."

"It's nothing." Mara shook her head, straightened a plane on her shelf. "These are like the first steps of a baby. I'm far from being able to do what I need to."

"I suppose you are. That's the life of a Walker. There are meaningful limitations on the amount of training you can do. You lose the time you Travel. If you were to Walk back an entire turn, and then return here, you would lose two turns of your life. You'd be that much older. You understand this, don't you?"

"I do."

"So any Walker, even the most skilled, can only have practiced so much. We're given a finite amount of time in this world, Miss Lijar. You can't spend too much of it in training, especially not if you intend to go back farther."

A chill crept up the back of her neck. "Are you saying I've spent too much already?"

"Hardly. You look tired, not aged. I doubt you've spent more than a day or two. But those are days you can't get back. You have to remember that."

"Yes, mistress."

"Have you seen the Tirribin again?"

"No. I've been too tired at night, and I practice in the early mornings. The rest of my days are taken up with lessons and by Master Saffern."

"Of course."

"Why do you ask?"

"Curiosity mostly. I wonder if she's trying to discover when it was the Walker Traveled back, as I have been."

"Do you know anything more?"

"A bit, yes. As you may recall from your studies, Daerjen's previous sovereign, Mearlan IV, was assassinated a little over fourteen years ago, ending the Hayncalde Supremacy and giving power to Noak of Sheraigh. As it happens, that's around the time when tri-devices came into use in Oaqamar. This strikes me as an interesting coincidence."

Mara wilted. "Fourteen years?"

"I'm afraid so."

"I can't do that."

"I'd be surprised if you could. I'm not sure how this other Walker managed it. He could have divided up his journey, although doing so creates its own set of problems, not least among them the simple truth that chronofors aren't exact. There's no telling when he might have emerged from the first leg of his journey."

"I learned that the hard way – about a chronofor's lack of precision, I mean." Wansi frowned, but Mara waved off her questions. "It doesn't matter."

"You don't have to go back," Wansi said. "This remains your choice to make. I've told no one, and I trust you've kept the matter to yourself as well." Mara nodded and the Binder opened her hands. "So you are free to do what you decide is best. If you believe this time we're living in needs to be changed, and you have faith in your ability to Walk back that far, you can go. If you don't, only the Tirribin and I will know of your choice, and I, for one, won't think any worse of you."

"Thank you."

"May I see your chronofor?"

Mara hesitated, then reached into a pocket within her robe. As she'd grown more adept at Walking, she had taken to carrying the device with her. She wondered how Wansi knew.

The Binder took it from her and crossed to her work bench. Setting her loupe to her eye, she turned the chronofor over and opened its back; Mara wasn't sure how.

She examined the device, reached for a tiny flat-tip, and made a few small adjustments, glow emanating from her hands as she worked. Then she snapped the golden case closed again, placed the loupe on the table, and handed Mara the chronofor.

"It looks fine. I tightened a spring, which may correct some of that imprecision you mentioned. It should work well for you, no matter how far back you Walk."

"Again, my thanks." Mara faltered. "I can Span, and I can Walk, but only if I can take both my sextant and my chronofor with me. I don't know if that's possible."

The Binder quirked an eyebrow. "An interesting question. I don't know either. The pure gold of the devices, and the powers we Binders impart to them, allow the devices to Travel. I've never known a Spanner to carry a chronofor, or a Walker to carry an aperture or a sextant. You're rather unique in this regard. In theory, though, you should be able to carry both devices when you Span or Walk. Something for you to test before you make your decision."

"Yes. May I–"

"You require a sextant."

"Yes, mistress."

Wansi indicated the shelf on which she kept sextants and apertures. "Choose one." As Mara walked to the shelf, the Binder added, "For obvious reasons, I would prefer that no one hear of this."

They shared a look, and Mara's thoughts turned to Delvin, who remained in the palace infirmary, forced to lie at all times on his stomach or side.

"I understand." She chose a sextant and slipped it into one of the ample pockets of her robe. "I keep having to thank you."

"It may be that before this is over, we'll be thanking you." Wansi waved her toward the door. "Off with you, now."

Mara started toward the door, only to halt and look back at the sound of her name.

Wansi's features had paled. "Before you leave – if you choose to leave – please do me the courtesy of saying goodbye. Someone should know what you've done."

"I will," Mara said, and let herself out of the chamber.

That night, Mara waited for the older trainees to pair off in the upper courtyard so that she could make her way unseen to the lower. Standing alone in an archway, she marked the procession of couples, and thought of Delvin and Hilta. Her jealousy had vanished that night in the lower courtyard as she watched Delvin's beating. Now she would have given anything to see him, even with Hilta.

She didn't hear Nat approach until he cleared his throat from just behind, making her jump.

"Nat! You scared me."

"Sorry," he said, acting more nervous than she had ever seen him. "I didn't mean to. I was just… Well, I was wondering if maybe… Would you like to… I mean, I know that you and Delvin – I know you're not with anyone – at least not anymore – and I thought maybe…"

At last, suppressing a grin, Mara took pity on him.

"Are you asking me to go with you to the upper courtyard?"

He stared off to the side, his shoulders hunched. "Not very well."

She giggled.

"I was asking seriously."

"I know. I'm not laughing at that, I'm just laughing at… I don't know."

"At me?"

"What brought this on, anyway?"

His shoulders rose and dipped. "I don't know. We've been training together, and it's been fun. You're really pretty, and I just thought–"

"You think I'm pretty?"

He finally met her gaze long enough to frown at her as if she were mad. "Everyone does."

She stepped forward and kissed his cheek. "Thank you. For the compliment and the invitation."

"But you're saying no."

Maybe she *was* mad. Nat was handsome, funny, and smart. He'd always been nicer than most of the boys in the palace. And she had to admit that she'd been lonely this past ha'turn. She should have accepted the invitation. Certainly, she shouldn't have been thinking about a boy she'd never met and couldn't even picture in her mind. Yet there it was. She was going to tell Nat no because, based on a conversation with a Tirribin, she had given her heart to Tobias. If that wasn't madness, what was?

"I'm afraid so," she said. "I'm sorry. I need all the friends I can find right now, and I don't want to risk losing you the way I did Delvin."

Nat nodded, disappointment etched in the lines around his mouth and dark brown eyes. "I understand."

"Thank you."

"I suppose I'll see you later. Tomorrow, I mean."

"I'll be there, ready to out-duel you again."

A grin sprung to his lips. "We'll see about that." His expression soon sobered.

Mara left him there, unwilling to give him the chance to ask again.

She followed the contours of the walls to the lower courtyard, keeping to shadows, ducking into unobtrusive corners when she heard the approach of soldiers. Once she had convinced herself that none of the other trainees could see or hear her, that there were no masters or mistresses nearby, and that she was safe from guards, she spoke the Tirribin's name.

Sooner than she expected, Droë appeared before her, yellow hair shining in the dim glow of a thousand stars.

"There's a price for summoning a Tirribin," the girl said, wraithlike eyes fixed on Mara. She took a step in her direction. "Are you prepared to pay?"

Mara held her ground. "Not in years."

"How then? A riddle perhaps? My kind like riddles."

"I know none."

Annoyance flitted across the perfect features. "Then what? I don't like games. Not about this."

"I want to help you. I want to find Tobias and make the time line right again."

Droë eased forward another step. "You've been Walking," she said, her voice hushed. "I can read it in your years."

The fear that first struck Mara in the Binder's chamber returned in a rush. Maybe Wansi was wrong. Maybe she'd already spent too much of her life practicing. "What do you read?" she asked, her throat tight. "Am I that much older than I should be?"

The demon dismissed the question with a flick of her delicate fingers. "Of course not. You haven't gone more than a few bells at a time. I can tell. But you've been Walking, and that's something."

"Does that mean you'll accept my help as payment?"

The Tirribin's expression turned sly. "What sort of help?"

"I can Walk back. And I can Span."

"I know what you *can* do. What are you *willing* to do."

"I'll go back. Years, if I must. I'll go to Daerjen."

Guile gave way to confusion. "Why? You don't even know him."

"You say I do."

"You haven't seen him yet. I was going to show him to you before, when we talked." She smiled, shrewd again, as changeable as an ocean wind. "Would you see him now?"

Mara had been ready to consent to this when they first spoke. She wouldn't lose her nerve now. "If you'll let me."

Droë clapped her hands with a child's delight.

Mara winced at the clap, fearing it would bring soldiers or Belvora.

"Why don't the Belvora sense you?" she asked on the thought. "They're drawn to magick, but they don't seem to notice you."

"They notice," Droë said, glancing up toward the top of the walls. "They just don't care. And they're afraid of me."

That gave Mara pause.

"They don't belong here, either," the Tirribin went on, still peering at the battlements. "There was one here not so long ago, right before Tobias left. He came alone, and he was killed, despite being cleverer than most of them. Aside from him, until this misfuture, there were no Belvora guarding your kind. The old chancellors would never have allowed it." She eyed Mara again, her smile returning. "Never mind all that. You want me to show you Tobias."

"No tricks," Mara said, troubled by the demon's eagerness. "I'm not offering you any years."

Ire flashed in her pale eyes. "Rudeness again. I've already assured you that I won't feed. Do you want to see him or not?"

"I do. And… I apologize."

"Very well. Come here."

Mara closed the distance between them, her breathing uneven. As she neared the Tirribin that same elusive odor reached her: rot, putrescence. She swallowed against her rising gorge.

"Close your eyes," Droë said. "I'm going to touch your forehead. I promise I won't harm you."

She drew breath, closed her eyes. At the demon's touch, she flinched. Droë's fingers were as cold as dead fish. She steeled herself.

Then thoughts of the Tirribin fled her mind. A boy stood before her, his skin the color of hala wood. His hair, bronze like hers, shone with sunlight, as did his startling green eyes. He had smooth skin, full lips, a smile that seemed to burn a hole in her heart. The scene shifted. Night fell. She saw him in profile, his straight nose and strong chin outlined in moonlight. She saw herself step forward, tilt her face up to his, and kiss him. It was a long kiss; Mara could almost feel his lips on hers, his hands on her back.

Then she pulled away from him and said something the real Mara couldn't hear. The vision dissolved. The demon removed her fingers from Mara's brow.

Mara opened her eyes. The Tirribin stood close, gazing up at her.

"Do you remember him?"

She shook her head, still thinking about that kiss. "I don't."

"You wish you did."

Mara didn't deny it. "Will you let me help you?"

"You're asking if we can work together."

"I guess I am."

"You won't accuse me of wanting to feed on you?"

She bit back the first response that came to mind: a demand that Droë promise not to prey on her. The Tirribin had already sworn as much. "I promise."

Droë lifted her chin toward the rest of the palace. "They'll let you leave?"

"They won't know until I'm gone." She didn't mention her promise to Wansi. That was between her and the Binder.

"I can't go back in time," Droë said. "I can't Span. And no captain in Islevale will allow a... a time demon on his or her ship. All I can do for you is tell you what I know about Tobias and the path he was to follow when he left here."

"Will you know me if we meet in the past?"

"You mean will I remember you if I've **nev**er met you before?"

Put that way, it sounded foolish. "I don't suppose that's possible."

"No. But I'll be able to read your years."

"To tell me if the time I'm in is right or wrong?"

"Yes."

"That would be helpful."

"If you greet me by name, that will tell me that we've met. And if you tell me that you know my true name, I'll know you for a... a friend."

"You would share your true name with me?"

The demon looked away. "If you'll swear not to tell anyone."

"Of course."

Droë beckoned her closer with a flutter of her fingers. Mara leaned in.

"It's Droënalka," she whispered.

Mara repeated the name and straightened. "Thank you. That's pretty."

"Even Tobias doesn't know."

"I won't tell a soul. I swear it on the Two."

The Tirribin appeared unmoved by this, but after a pause she nodded.

"There's one more thing you can help me with, if you would."

The demon regarded her, wary again. "What?"

"An experiment. I need you to watch for any humans who might come this way. I can't be seen doing this."

The Tirribin faltered, nodded a second time.

Mara stepped to the nearest archway, removed her robe, and took off her clothes.

"What are you doing?" Droë asked. She eased closer, eyeing Mara's form with the curiosity of a child and the fascinated rapacity of a creature born to hunt.

Too late, Mara wondered if this was a mistake. She shrank from the demon's gaze.

"I need you to look out for others," she said again, trying to sound firm. "I want to try Spanning while holding my chronofor. If I can't do that, I probably can't Walk back with my sextant either, and that would make all that we've discussed very difficult."

"How old were you when you got those?" Droë asked, still staring, a slender finger aimed at Mara's breasts.

"Would you watch for people, please?"

The Tirribin turned, her gaze sweeping over the courtyard. "Please tell me."

Mara shrugged, though Droë no longer stared at her. "Thirteen, I think. Yes, about then."

"Did it... did it hurt?"

"Not all the time, but sometimes, yes."

"Men like them. I've noticed that."

She couldn't help but smile. This might have been the oddest conversation she'd ever had. "Yes, I've noticed it, too. I'm going to Span now. I'm just going over there." She pointed to the far side of the courtyard: another archway. "Then I'll Span back. It shouldn't take long."

The Tirribin glanced her way, her gaze flicking over Mara's body before meeting her eyes. "All right." She scanned the courtyard again.

Mara set her sextant to the proper distance – a single hash on the arc – and sighted through the gold and glass eyepiece. Clutching the chronofor in her other hand, she flipped the release on the sextant's frame to activate it.

The pull of the sextant wasn't nearly as abrupt as the hook of the chronofor. After practicing with the time piece so often over the past ha'turn, the act of Spanning came easier than usual. Still, she felt as though she were soaring in the wake of a galloping horse. Color and light rushed past her with dizzying speed, and cool wind whipped over her skin, stinging like sand blown by a coastal gale.

It lasted less than a fivecount. Then she stood on the other side of the courtyard, facing the stone wall of the palace. She turned, spotted Droë staring after her. The demon lifted a hand in a half-hearted wave. Mara waved back. She listened for soldiers, checked the courtyard and covered walkway. Convinced it was safe, she lifted the sextant again, set it for the Span back, and thumbed the release.

Soon, she stood where she'd started, her skin prickling with the bite of the Spanning wind. She still held the chronofor in her free hand. She dressed hurriedly, feeling the demon's eyes upon her.

"It worked," Droë said. A statement.

"Yes. I can Span with a chronofor in my hand. I assume I can Walk while carrying my sextant."

"Which means you can search for him."

"That's right."

"When will you go?"

"Soon," Mara said, the word coming out as a breathless whisper. "Very soon."

CHAPTER 22

22nd Day of Sipar's Settling, Year 633

Tobias woke to a low growl that stopped his heart.

A black mutt about the size of a small pony stood over him, teeth bared, spittle frothing and dripping from its retracted gums.

Every muscle ached, pain pulsed in the wounds on his face and ear. The skin around the bruise on his jaw had tightened, and the stab wound in his back burned as if someone held a torch to his flesh. Just now, though, the dog was his greatest concern.

"He'll bite if I tell 'im to." A man's voice.

Sofya stirred, her eyes fluttering, her thumb straying to her mouth.

"I don't doubt it," Tobias said, his voice raw.

"Who are you? What business you got here?"

Tobias tore his gaze from the mutt and studied the man. He was tall, lean, with dark eyes and an aspect made severe by his scowl. His breeches and shirt were worn, stained, and he wore his long red and silver hair tied back in a plait. He held a hoe in his hands the way he might a battle axe.

"No business," Tobias said.

Sofya woke all the way, glanced at the dog, and let out a shriek. She grabbed at Tobias with both hands, scrabbling at his gut with her tiny feet, trying to climb him, or hide behind him, or scale the chimney to get away from the beast.

"Who's that?" the man asked. "She yours?" He eased closer. "That blood on her? And on you?"

"We just… We needed a place to sleep. That's all. We'll leave now. You'll have no trouble from us again. I swear."

"How do I know you ain't already made trouble elsewhere? How do I know you didn't steal that wee thing from her mother?"

"I didn't."

"I'm just to believe–"

He broke off, canted his head. Tobias heard it, too. A great many footsteps approaching on the road, and the jangle of belts and weapons.

The man considered Tobias and Sofya again. Tobias stared back, praying to the God and Goddess that the man would understand, and wouldn't ask many questions.

"Stay back here," the man said, in a voice that barely carried. "Keep out of sight, don't make a sound. Crow, you're with me."

He walked toward the lane, and the mutt bounded after, ears and tail held high.

Muscles protesting, Tobias climbed to his feet, cradling Sofya, who had calmed down with the dog's departure. She felt damp and smelled rank. It hadn't even occurred to him until now, but he needed to change her swaddling, would need to do that several times each day. He had never done anything of the sort, and just yesterday he had known her as… He didn't allow his mind to go there. She was his responsibility now, and he would do what needed doing. First, though, he would keep her alive.

Keeping his back flat to the house, he eased away from the road, moving slowly so as to make no sound. The yard, like those abutting it, was enclosed by a tall wooden fence, and parceled into neat plots. Nothing grew in them at present, but Tobias was certain that come the warmer turns, they would be green with sprouting vegetables. More to his concern right now, he saw no way out of the yard save the path the man and his dog had followed.

Sofya clung to his shirt and sucked her thumb. He hoped she would remain silent.

The man spoke with whoever had come – soldiers, he was sure. Tobias couldn't make out any of what they said.

Moments later he heard more footsteps, approaching rather than retreating. He held his breath. The door to the house opened. A woman's voice from within. They had come to search these structures.

For us.

Which meant...

"Sure," he heard the old man say, in a voice seemingly intended to carry. "You're welcome to search back here, too. Just a yard, like any other within the city walls. Nothing much. Barely enough room for the wife's potatoes and carrots."

Frantic, Tobias sought a place to hide. He had maybe a tencount, if he was lucky.

A wheelbarrow leaned against the back of the house beside a pile of dried grass and clumped dirt. He hurried to it, clinging to the princess. With a glance toward the corner of the house, he crawled under the wheelbarrow and pulled dirt and grass toward the edges until little daylight entered the space from that side. He wanted to do the same with the other side, but he had no time.

The old man's legs came into view, along with the black breeches of four others.

"See?" the old man said. "Nothin' here but dirt and sweat."

"What's in that shed?" A woman's voice, hard-edged.

"Tools and such."

One of the soldiers strode to the far end of the yard. A door creaked open.

"You seen anyone unusual today? Or maybe last night?"

"You mean aside from Sheraigh soldiers?"

A pause. "Yes, aside from us. Anyone else?"

"Can't say as I have."

The old man remained where he was – where Tobias could see him. The soldiers walked around the yard. One of them went to the other side of the wheelbarrow, but didn't bother looking beneath it.

Sofya patted her hand on Tobias's shirt, but her other thumb remained in her mouth, keeping her quiet. Boots paced and scraped on the floors within the house.

Tobias's breathing sounded ragged and loud to his own ears, and his pulse pounded. When a large brown spider scuttled over his arm, he nearly shouted in surprise and alarm.

At last, the soldiers left the yard, as did the old man. Inside, the soldiers moved back toward the front of the house. Tobias brushed the spider away, but remained where he was.

A short time later, the man returned.

"They're gone. You can come out."

Tobias crawled out the other side. The arm that clutched Sofya had started to cramp.

The dog growled at them again, and Sofya whimpered. The man eyed Tobias, saying nothing. Eventually, he glanced at Sofya and wrinkled his nose. "Better bring her in. Can't have her sitting in her mess all day."

He and the dog walked away, leaving Tobias to follow.

"What's your name?" the man asked, tossing the question over his shoulder in a low voice.

"Tobias."

"And the wee one?"

He was sure the man noticed his hesitation. "Nava."

Reaching the front corner of the house, the man halted and motioned for Tobias to do the same. He peered out at the road, then nodded. "They're at the next house. Best we wait a spirecount or two." He faced Tobias. "I'm Jivv. Wife's inside. She's Elinor." He pointed at the mutt. "This is Crow. Crow don't like strangers much, but if we let you in the house, he'll calm down. Think you're family. Crow ain't too smart."

He peeked around the corner again, glanced back at Tobias with a tight smile.

As they waited, Tobias ran a hand over his face, feeling the rough growth of a beard on his chin and cheeks. He touched his neck, traced the line of his jaw with his fingertips. It had never occurred to him to shave. He didn't know how and couldn't remember watching someone else do it. He had lived with boys his own age – the age he ought to be – almost all his life.

He had a dagger but didn't know if its edge was sharp enough to remove the beard without scraping away his skin. He'd heard of men cutting themselves with a dull blade. He wondered if he ought to shave at all. A beard might disguise him. The idea bothered him; he had never imagined himself bearded.

He thought it strange, after all he had been through in the past day, that a trifle – whiskers on his chin – should bring home to him all that had changed, all he had lost. He would never be a boy again. Even if he could find a chronofor, save Mearlan, and return the princess to her family, he would only move himself further from his own youth.

Not that he knew where to find a chronofor, or how he could get away from Hayncalde alive. The life of which he had dreamed was gone. He would never see Mara again. If he was to keep Sofya alive, he might never know the simple pleasures of having a home, a family, lifelong friends. He had given up too much, for nothing, it seemed.

"Come along then," Jivv said, snapping him out of his dark musings. "They've moved on."

Tobias nodded, adjusted his hold on the princess. Casting a wary eye down the street, he followed Jivv and the dog through a battered old door into the house. His hand strayed back to his jaw. Inside, the structure was modest, to say the least. The door opened onto a cramped common room with a cooking hearth, two chairs, and a small table. A crude stone shrine stood by the hearth, the figure at its center with its arms raised and head bowed. Sipar worshippers.

Beyond the common room, through a low gap in the wall, lay a second room that might have been their sleeping quarters.

A woman stood near the fire, her clothes and features so similar to Jivv's, Tobias would have assumed she was his sister had the man not referred to her as his wife. She was tall, willowy, with dark, widely spaced eyes, and white hair, still tinged red in places and tied back under a dingy white cloth. She had straightened when the door opened and now regarded Tobias and Sofya with something akin to disapproval.

"Who are they?"

"Don't know yet. But the wee one needs changing, and I'd guess both of them need food."

"You got money?" the woman asked Tobias.

"No, ma'am."

"Thought as much. There's blood on you both. Care to explain that?"

"He will in a bit," Jivv said. "Let's you and me find some swaddling first."

He didn't wait for her reply, but walked into the back room, Crow following. The woman considered Tobias and Sofya for another instant and then entered the other chamber. Tobias knew why they had gone back there. Already he heard snatches of whispered conversation.

"...Castle last night... Sheraigh... dangerous for us... who that baby is..."

They remained in the room for some time. Eventually he heard one of them rummage through a wardrobe or chest of drawers. When they emerged again, Elinor carried a bundle of white cloth and Jivv bore a water pitcher.

"We'll get her changed," the woman said. "Then we'll clean you both up."

Tobias wanted to ask if he could watch her change Sofya's swaddling, but he feared the question would reveal too much. He simply nodded.

"We have some bread, and a morsel of cheese. Some goat's milk for the wee one."

Elinor shot Jivv an angry look, but the man stared back, all but challenging her to deny them food. She turned away before he did, crossed to Tobias, and took Sofya from his arms.

The princess fussed, but Elinor sang in a rich alto and soon had the babe laughing and cooing.

"They'll be all right," Jivv said. "Elinor ain't had a babe to play with in more years than either of us care to count." He indicated a chair near the hearth. "You sit. I'll gather a bit of food."

Tobias lowered himself into the chair, wincing at the pain in his back. As Jivv predicted, now that they had accepted Tobias into their home, Crow seemed content to do the same. He sat at Tobias's feet, his tail thumping the wooden floor.

"That a knife wound in your back?"

Tobias hesitated.

"Bar fight?"

Again, he faltered.

Elinor stepped out of the back room, still singing. Sofya had tears on her cheeks, but she smiled. It took Tobias a moment to realize she no longer had blood on her chin and temple. He stood and approached them, scrutinizing Sofya's face. Of her two wounds, the gash on her chin appeared to be the more serious. It was deeper, longer, and the skin around it was bruised and swollen.

"You need to be careful with a babe," Elinor said, her voice hard. "I don't know how they do things in the northern isles, but you can't treat them like toys, or pets."

Tobias drew himself up to his full height. Tall as she was, he stood half a hand taller. "I'm not responsible for those wounds," he said. "I've risked my life to keep her safe. Just as I would have in the north."

He held out his arms for the girl. He could see that Elinor didn't want to give Sofya back to him, but he didn't relent. At length, she placed the girl in his arms. Sofya grasped his shirt and slid her thumb into her mouth. Whatever Elinor might think, the princess gave every indication of being pleased to be back with him. Tobias took some satisfaction in the woman's frown.

Jivv crossed to the table, bearing the promised bread and cheese.

"Have a seat," he said, motioning Tobias to the table again and setting the food in front of him. "Wine?"

Tobias sat once more. "Please."

Tobias started to break off small hunks of bread and cheese for the princess.

"She can't eat that!" Elinor said, looming over him. "Not just that anyway."

She poured a bit of goat's milk into a bowl and set it before him, slopping some onto the table. "Soak the bread in this and give it to her. You can add in a piece of cheese or two once she's had some."

He said nothing. His ignorance weighed on him. But he crumbled the bread into smaller pieces, wet them in the milk, and handed them to Sofya one at a time. She tried to grab the larger pieces from him, but he kept them beyond her reach and made sure she didn't bolt down too much.

Jivv placed a cup of watered wine on the table and sat opposite Tobias.

"You were in the castle," Jivv said.

Tobias stared back at him, without nodding or shaking his head.

"The sovereign's dead? Imprisoned?"

He said nothing.

"Those soldiers were from Sheraigh. I went to work this morning at dawn, down at the wharves, and there were Sheraigh men there, too. They sent me home. The port's closed, they said. Even the marketplace is shut down. Word in the streets is that the new regional governor will be living here before long. This is no secret you're keeping."

"Someone killed the sovereign," Tobias said at last. "And his family. Mearlan's line is broken."

"You got away."

"Yes," Tobias said. He took a bite of bread and cheese for himself.

"How did you manage that?" Elinor asked, an accusation in the question.

"I was fortunate. I received help–"

"Who from?"

"I won't tell you that. I was shown a way out of the castle, one I wouldn't have found otherwise. The rest I did on my own."

"And this one?" She jutted her chin at Sofya. "How did you…?"

Her eyes went wide, and Tobias looked back at her, knowing that she had worked it out for herself. Yes, indeed he did have a secret, a huge one, as fragile as life itself, as vast as the future. She took a step back, frightened of him, of them.

"You have to leave," she whispered.

"I know. I will."

"Now!" Emphatic, but in a voice robbed of breath.

"Soon."

"I don't understand," Jivv said, regarding them both.

Elinor and Tobias kept their gazes on each other, strangers newly bound by something profound and deadly.

"This is the sovereign princess," Tobias said, trying to make the words sound ordinary. He hadn't wanted to tell them, but there was no sense now in denying it. "I got her out before they could kill her. I... I need to keep her safe."

Again, the enormity of this burden threatened to overwhelm him. *I'm fifteen. I can't do this.*

He didn't look fifteen, and that was a secret he couldn't share. Not with anyone. He couldn't say why, but he knew doing so might prove to be the most perilous revelation of all. It was bad enough that his bronze hair and dark skin made him stand out on this bone white isle. If those who sought the princess knew she was with a Traveler, his race would make them that much easier to track and find.

But more than that, he didn't wish to upset the fragile rapport he was establishing with Jivv and Elinor. There were few Travelers in the world, and they tended to remain in the royal courts, remote from the lives of most people. He didn't know how these two would feel about his powers, and the changes they had already wrought – in him, and in their world.

Jivv stared at Tobias, his arms crossed over his chest, his mouth a thin gash across his ashen face. "You worked in the castle?" he asked.

"Yes."

"As a servant? A guard? A minister?"

"A minister of a sort, I suppose you could say."

The ends of the man's mouth turned down. "Not sure I know what that means."

"It means the sovereign trusted me. It means I was there when he and the queen died, and was able to save the princess."

"You can't stay here," Elinor said.

"I understand–"

"I don't mean here in the house, though that's true as well. I mean, you have to get away from Daerjen. They'll find her here. That search this morning – it won't be the last. It's just a matter of time. Another isle, though..." She shrugged. "You might have a chance."

A matter of time. It was almost enough to make him laugh.

Except that she was right. When they didn't find the princess with this round of searches, they'd start again, and they'd be even more thorough.

Tobias gave Sofya some more bread, wondering how he could possibly escape the isle. *I have nothing.*

That wasn't true. He pulled one of the flintlocks from his carry sack and placed it on the table.

"I don't know what this will fetch in a market or from someone who deals in weapons. But it's yours, if you can help me."

Jivv eyed him, and then the weapon. He picked it up off the table and examined it more closely. "Well made," he said. "Aiyanthan, by the look of it." Seeing Tobias's puzzlement, he pointed to a marking on the barrel, just ahead of the breechplug. "Aiyanthan armsmiths put their proprietary marks here. Most others, Oaqamaran included, put them on the butt of the stock." He hefted the weapon, held it up and sighted with it. "Aiyanthan is good. Fetch a better price."

"That yours?" Elinor asked. "Or did you take it from someone?"

"It's not mine."

"Well, that makes it harder to sell, don't it? And a mite bit more dangerous."

"Have done, Ellie. The man's trying to save the wee one's life, and his own. It's not as though you and I are delighted to see Sheraigh blue walking our streets, now is it?"

Her mouth twitched, but she gave a curt nod. "What is it you need?" she asked Tobias.

"Food," he said. "Swaddling. If you can bandage my back, I'd be grateful. We'll be gone from here as soon as we can. You have my word. I have no more desire to be caught than you do to be found helping us. But with these wounds, I'm no good–"

"Where will you go?" Elinor asked. "And what will you do with her while you're running? She's a baby, not a brigand."

Tobias closed his eyes. His world heaved and spun. "I know that," he whispered. "I'm… I don't know much about children."

"That much is clear."

"I told you to let up on him."

"And I don't see what good that will do. He doesn't need coddling; he needs to have some sense kicked into his skull."

"I didn't think about any of this," Tobias said, answering an unspoken question. "I took her, because to leave her was to let her die. And I couldn't do that." He bit back the next words that came to him: *She's a friend. I've seen her as a young woman. She's supposed to live.* "I've lost a sister myself," he said instead, and for the first time in his life, he felt a pang of grief for Yolli.

"Well, you're not going to buy your way off this isle with a pistol," Elinor said.

No, that's what the apertures are for. "I know that."

"Good," she said, retrieving more bread from the larder. "Then we'll get you on the mend, and in the meantime, you and the wee one will hide here."

"What?"

Tobias and Jivv said this together, then shared a glance.

"I thought you wanted me gone. Now. That's what you said."

She broke off some bread, soaked it, and gave it to Sofya. "I do want you gone, and soon. I can't have you endangering this one, though, can I? If you go off half-crippled, and something happens to her, how am I supposed to live with myself?"

Jivv grinned.

"I don't know what you're leering at," she said, eyes glinting like dagger blades. "You'll be working just as hard as I will. This is a princess we're having in our home. And this is the last time I feed her naught but bread, goat's milk, and moldy cheese. You hear me?"

"Yes, ma'am," her husband said. The smile lingered on his lips.

• • •

Once Sofya ate her fill, and Tobias had enough to take the edge off his hunger, Jivv ordered him to strip off his blood-stiffened clothes, and tended to his injuries. The knife wound on his back was by far the most serious. Tobias couldn't see it, but Jivv told him the flesh around it was inflamed and fevered. The man cleaned the wound – a painful process – and bandaged it. Tobias couldn't do much with his left arm without it hurting terribly.

Elinor bustled through the house holding Sofya on her hip as naturally as she would her own child. She paused at one point to *tsk* over Tobias's wound, but otherwise ignored both men. When it came time for the princess to nap, Elinor set her on a pallet of folded blankets beside the small bed she and Jivv shared. Tobias took the opportunity to sleep as well. Jivv gave him a spare blanket, and he settled down on the bare floor in a corner of the common room, his sword and the other pistol within easy reach.

He didn't think he could sleep under such conditions, but he soon fell into a deep slumber.

When he woke sometime later, Jivv and Elinor were at the hearth, speaking in low tones. Almost as soon as he became aware of their conversation, they fell silent.

"You're awake," Elinor said.

He didn't try to pretend otherwise. "Yes. How long did I sleep?"

"A long time. Two bells at least. The wee one is still dreaming."

"How much of what we said did you hear?" Elinor asked.

Tobias sat up, rubbed a hand over his face. His back throbbed, and his shirt was soaked with sweat. He wondered if he had a fever. "I heard you say something about the wharves, but that was all."

"They're still closed," Jivv said. "No word on when they'll open. Ships from Sheraigh control the gulf. Some are saying they plan to choke off all trade in Hayncalde, send the merchant ships north, to the mouth of the gulf, where the new sovereign can take the gold for himself. Others think they're waiting until they can put their own customs agents in place, and then they'll offload the ships here. Either way, anyone connected with the old sovereign is bound to have a rough time of it. And no one is leaving Hayncalde by water."

Tobias found himself rubbing at his beard again, and forced himself to stop. "I'm not sure how I'd get her through any of the gates, even those near the wharves. I have to find another way." Brave words, but he had no idea what other way there might be. "Did anyone survive?" he asked. "Did any ministers get away, or maybe Mearlan's son?"

"They claim everyone is gone, the whole family."

"That's a lie."

"Maybe, but they claim it. All the court as well. Every minister, his Seer, his Binder, his Traveler."

Tobias tried to keep his expression neutral, but wasn't sure he succeeded. He needn't have made the effort. Neither of them would look at him.

"I'm not lying. That little girl in there is Sofya, sovereign princess of Daerjen."

"I'm willing to believe it," Jivv said. "More than I'm willing to believe a word that comes from some uniformed Sheraigh shit-demon."

"Jivv!"

"The wee one's still sleeping, and she ain't got a word to her tongue yet. It's not like she'll be repeating it."

"Still, there's a babe in the house. I expect a civil tongue." She cast a dark glance Tobias's way. "From both of you."

"Yes, ma'am," Tobias said, though his courtesy only deepened her scowl.

"Truth is, I believe it, too," she said at length. "If you were lying, you would have come up with something more believable. Only an idiot would come up with a story like this."

"A lying idiot, or a truthful one?" Tobias asked.

That coaxed a fleeting smile from her. "A truthful one, I expect. And a brave one."

"Thank you."

"Didn't think the Sheraighs had balls enough for something like this," Jivv said. "Old Noak's more coward than man."

"They had help. Many of the men I saw in the castle last night didn't wear uniforms, including their leader. I think they were hired assassins, and I know they were Travelers. Spanners. Sheraigh didn't do this alone."

"Then who? Who has as much to gain from the sovereign's death as the duke of Sheraigh?"

It was a fair question. The idea that Sheraigh would do all of this was both too obvious and too great a stretch. Tobias thought again of what Osten Cavensol had said in Tobias's own time: *Sheraigh hasn't the resources to buy one Traveler, much less two.* They definitely couldn't afford the army of Travelers that had infiltrated the castle the night before.

He almost mentioned Daerjen's war with the Oaqamarans, but of course, that war hadn't started yet. And now the autarch might not think it necessary.

"You can think of others, can't you?" Jivv said, reading his expression.

"I can guess. Nothing more." Eventually he would have to do better than that. When the time came to smuggle Sofya out of Hayncalde he'd have an easier time evading his enemies if he knew precisely who they were.

CHAPTER 23

The knife wound on Tobias's back proved stubborn. By the next morning, the pain had grown worse as had his fever. When Jivv removed the old dressing, he hissed through his teeth.

"This doesn't look good. You should see a surgeon."

Tobias refused, fearing the questions a physician might ask. After arguing the point, he and Jivv agreed to give the injury another day or two to heal.

He remained in the house, unwilling to risk being seen out of doors. He tried to stay out of Elinor's way, and spent much of his time with Sofya, talking to her, playing foolish games, feeding her.

Late in the morning, she soiled her swaddling, and Tobias took her to Elinor.

"She's messed herself."

Elinor didn't deign to look up from her cooking. "Then I suppose you'd better clean her up."

"I… I don't know how."

At that Elinor faced him. "Then I suppose you'd better learn." Reading the panic in his eyes, she heaved a sigh, set aside her cooking spoon, and strode into the bedroom. "Come along. I'm only going to show you once."

He followed her, the stink of Sofya's mess hanging over him like a cloud.

"Now, watch," Elinor said, laying out fresh swaddling. She

folded the cloth into a neat triangle and set it aside. Then she removed the soiled cloth from Sofya and, using another cloth, this one dampened, cleaned the babe's privates.

"You have to make certain you get her girl parts all clean," she said, glancing up at him. Tobias hoped his growing beard would hide the reddening of his cheeks. It didn't.

"It's nothing to be bashful about. Your ma did this for you around your boy parts, just like I did for my boys. Someday, you'll have children of your own and you'll do the same for them. So stop being squeamish."

When Sofya was clean, Elinor slipped the fresh swaddling under her, folded it around her legs and crotch, and tied the corners tight, her fingers nimble and sure.

"That's all there is to it." She picked up the princess and planted a kiss on her brow.

Tobias held out his hands for the girl, but Elinor shook her head and pointed at the soiled swaddling and washing cloth. "You've cleaning to do. Dump the mess in the garden, get water from the well, and rinse those cloths. When they're good and clean, wring them out and lay them near the fire. That way they'll be ready for next time. And so will you."

She walked out of the chamber before he could argue.

He did as instructed, checking the lane with care before he ventured outside, and cursing the woman the entire time. But when next Sofya soiled herself, he knew what to do, and though the swaddling he folded didn't fit as well as the one Elinor prepared, it worked better than he'd expected.

After dealing with the dressing on Tobias's wound, Jivv returned to the wharves, ostensibly to see if he could work, but also to gather information. He came back late in the day, and what he had learned did nothing to improve Tobias's mood.

The Sheraighs were continuing their house-to-house search for the princess; it was just a matter of time before they doubled back to streets they had scoured once already. Worse, they had imposed a curfew on the city – sunrise to sunset – and they were offering rewards to informants and bounty hawks.

"One fellow says they're telling folk to look for children where there hadn't been any before, and..." He grimaced. "And for Northislers. 'Dark-skinned ones,' he says. As if there's other kinds."

"Will it work?" Tobias asked.

Jivv lifted a shoulder. "There's little love for Sheraigh blue in these streets. Folks here curse the Oaqamarans every day, but they hate Sheraigh almost as much. The fact that they're Daerjeni as well? That they'd kill the sovereign like that, just to take the supremacy? That makes it worse."

"But?"

The man shrugged again. "The wharves are closed, and so's the market. I can't work. Elinor can't sell her jams and such."

"Jams? I thought she only grew carrots and potatoes."

She whirled at this, nearly upsetting a bowl of soaking beans, and drawing a cry from Sofya, who she held on her hip. "Carrots and potatoes?"

Crow barked and then growled.

"Crow, hush." Jivv held up both hands. "It's just what I told them soldiers the other day." To Tobias he said, "She does more than that, but the point is, there's no money to be made. We have some put away, and we were at market the day Mearlan died, so we're fine for now. Other folks are hurting already. Another day or two, and those rewards are going to start looking like a king's treasure."

With daylight fading, the house had started to darken. Jivv lit some candles. Elinor returned to her cooking.

Tobias remained where he was. His back ached and the injuries to his neck and ear still stung, but he couldn't afford to wait until he had healed. He was listening every moment for footsteps, for the jangle of steel blades. He could almost feel Mearlan's assassin closing in on him.

As if in answer to this thought, Crow growled again. Jivv scratched the dog's ears, eliciting a tentative wag of his tail.

"We can't stay here," Tobias said. "And we can't risk being seen in the streets. That doesn't leave us many options."

"She looks a little like you," Jivv said, looking from the princess to Tobias. "That might help when the time comes."

"She looks like her mother," Tobias said, his voice low. "That's what they're looking for. That's what they'll see."

Crow growled again. Jivv and Tobias eyed the dog at the same time. The animal stood near the door, teeth bared, hackles up.

"What is he—"

"Oh, no," Tobias whispered.

Jivv pivoted. "What—"

Tobias silenced him with a raised hand. "Keep talking," he whispered. "Loudly, about anything at all."

He crossed lightly to his carry sack, reached into it, and wrapped his hand around the handle of a pistol. He thought better of that choice, though. Instead, he grasped one of the blades he'd taken from the men he killed in Daria Belani's chamber. Had that really only been two days ago?

He slipped the blade into his belt and crept to the door. Jivv watched him, all the while speaking of the cloth trade between Daerjen and Qyrshen, and of carrying bolts of cloth between the wharves and the warehouses along the waterline.

Reaching the door, Tobias wrapped his fingers around the handle, turned it slowly, and yanked it open.

Someone to his left hissed a curse, and bolted from the yard. Tobias leapt after the figure, the injury to his back screaming. Crow ran with him, another growl rumbling in his chest.

The figure cast one look over a shoulder – a boy's face and body. Lanky. All elbows and knees, but damnably fast. His feet slapped a steady rhythm on the cobblestone lanes. Tobias struggled to keep up, following him down one lane, over to another alley, around a corner, and up a dirt track that ran between two houses.

The pain in his back worsened with every turn, every step. He felt slow and plodding in this new body. If he'd still been a boy, like the one in front of him, he might have caught up. As it was, he was losing ground.

But Crow gained on the boy, snarling now, his claws tapping out a counterpoint to the lad's gait. Emerging into another stone lane from between the houses, the boy stumbled, righted himself, turned at the next byway.

This proved to be a mistake. A wooden fence loomed at the end of the alley, dark and hulking in the gloaming. The boy leapt for the top, missed. Staggered back to try again, but by then Crow was on him.

He lunged for the lad, paws slamming into the boy's back and knocking him face first to the ground. Crow let out another snarl and tore at the collar of the lad's overshirt.

"Get 'im off me!"

The boy tucked himself into a tight ball, his hands wrapped around the back of his neck.

"Get 'im off!" he said again.

Tobias slowed, walking the last few paces to where he lay. He was panting, soaked in sweat.

"Answers first," he said. "What were you doing?"

"Nothin'!"

"It wasn't nothing. You were crouched by the door. Why?"

"I was… I was lookin' for somethin'. Thought I lost it there."

"Bite his throat, Crow."

"No!"

The boy flailed and kicked, his shoulders and neck still hunched. For Crow's part, now that he had the lad on the ground, he had lost interest.

"One last time. What were you doing by the house?"

"Listenin'!"

As Tobias had feared.

"For what?"

"What yous were sayin'. 'Bout getting out of Hayncalde, and Northislers, and taking some wee one with you."

Tobias shuddered. He didn't think the lad noticed. "Why? Who are you doing this for?"

At that, the boy stilled and looked up at him. He couldn't have been much more than thirteen or fourteen years old. *About my real age.* His skin was smooth – he probably hadn't shaved yet either. He was pale, his features overlarge, his eyes hazel or green; Tobias couldn't tell in the twilight. Long, wheaten hair framed his face and hung into the mud and filth of the lane.

From the lad's expression, one might have thought Tobias had asked the most foolish question imaginable.

"Who am I... I'm doing it for me. For my mum and da. Do you know what they're offerin'?"

"What who are offering?"

Even in this light, Tobias saw the boy's cheeks redden. He looked away, shame in his eyes.

"The Sheraighs," he said, his voice dropping. "I hate them. I swear I do. But they'll pay two rounds 'n five treys for information if'n it helps them get what they're after."

"Do you know what they're after?"

He started to answer, but stopped himself, seeming to see Tobias for the first time. *Northislers. Dark-skinned ones.*

"It doesn' matter," the lad said. "It's like that man told you: that much coin is a king's ransom. I was doin' what I had to."

Hearing the boy repeat Jivv's words convinced him. Or maybe it merely proved that he'd never had a choice.

He squatted beside the lad. "What will you do now?" he asked, though there was nothing the boy could say that would change his mind.

The boy swallowed, met his gaze, though only for an instant. "I'll forget everythin' I heard. I'll– I'll forget that I saw you or that mutt. I won't tell a soul. I swear." A weak smile crossed his lips. "I'm not even sure I could find that house again."

Tobias nodded. He didn't think the lad saw him pull the dagger from his belt.

"I don't blame you," he said. "I want you to know that. Two rounds, five is a lot. Anyone would be tempted."

The boy stared, appearing unsure of what Tobias expected him to say.

"I'm sorry. I want you to know that, too."

He didn't wait for a response. He clamped his left hand over the boy's mouth, and with the right he drove the blade under the lad's sternum and up into his heart.

The boy's back arched. His eyes widened, and he strained against Tobias's grip, an agonized wail trapped in his chest and throat.

Warm blood soaked his shirt and flowed over Tobias's hand. After a tencount, the boy's struggles eased and he slumped back to the ground. Still Tobias held him, silencing him with one hand, bleeding his life away with the other. Tears coursed down his own cheeks, but he could do nothing to stop them or wipe them away.

The boy's eyes found him. He looked frightened, confused, and terribly young. Tobias resisted the impulse to apologize again. He had killed before, in the castle on the night of Mearlan's assassination, but those deaths had been different, easier to justify. This was murder; nothing less. He had no right to seek the lad's forgiveness or understanding. He stared back, watching the boy's gaze dim until no spark of life remained, and a last rattling breath fled the slight form.

Tobias removed his hand from the boy's mouth and brushed his eyes closed. He pulled the blade from the boy's heart and wiped the blood on the rags the boy wore. He breathed hard, and his hands shook. Fresh tears ran down his cheeks, wound through his rough beard, and dripped onto the boy's overshirt.

Crow whined from nearby. Turning, Tobias realized the mutt wasn't looking his way. The back of his neck prickled.

"That was a waste of good years."

Tobias lurched to his feet and whirled, all in one convulsive motion.

Two children stood before him, a girl and a boy. Only one creature he knew had eyes as pale as theirs, so Tobias had some idea of what they were. Where Droë's irises were softest gray, this girl's were green, the boy's blue. Like the Tirribin he had known in Windhome, they possessed an unearthly beauty. Their black hair, hers to her shoulders, his short, shimmered like satin in the twilight. They were pallid where Droë had been dark, their faces identical in their perfection: delicate cheekbones, full lips, straight, aristocratic noses. They might have been brother and sister. Their clothes were as ragged as Droë's – he wondered if this was an affectation common to Tirribin, or if something in their nature, their relationship to time, made it impossible for them to keep clothes looking new.

"He looks scared," the girl said. Hers was the voice he had heard. "Don't you think he looks scared?" Her lips curved into a tight smile.

The boy answered with a solemn nod.

Voices echoed from a nearby lane, probably men and women hurrying to their homes before darkness enveloped the city. The byway remained empty save for Tobias and the demons. And the body. Soldiers would soon be abroad in the streets to enforce the Sheraigh curfew. He couldn't be discovered here, with blood on his hand and the dead lad at his feet.

"I have to leave," he said, his voice deep and heavy after those of the Tirribin. "You should, too. You don't belong here."

The girl stared at the boy's body. "So young. He had a great many years, ripe ones. Feeding on him would have been better than ten riddles."

"I didn't want to kill him," Tobias said.

She raised her gaze. "I know. I did. That's what I meant before. A waste."

Tobias had no response, and no desire to speak riddles with time demons. "I have to go," he said again.

"He's not very nice," the girl said to the other Tirribin. "He's too serious."

"He killed that boy. He should be serious."

"Does that mean we have to be, too?"

"No, not us. But allow him to be. It's only right."

"Well, fine. Still, I don't like him very much."

"What do you want?" Tobias asked. "Why are you here?"

"I think he's rude," the girl said, flipping her hair. "Like adults are. He's not at all the way I imagined. Are you sure about him?"

"Yes, I'm sure. He killed someone, Maeli. And you're the one who's not being very nice."

Her face fell, leaving her looking as grave as the boy. "I'm sorry," she whispered. "I just hoped he'd be more like us."

The girl reminded Tobias of Droë: childlike, temperamental, as inconstant as candle flame. As desperate as he was to get away, he also knew the dangers of angering time demons, and the potential value of befriending them.

He gestured at the dead lad with a blood-stained hand. "I can't be found here. I can't risk being found at all. If I've been rude, that's why." He glanced in both directions, checking the byway for Sheraigh blue. Crow shied from the Tirribin, but gave no indication that anyone was approaching.

"What are your names?" Tobias asked

"I'm Teelo," the boy said. "My sister is Maeli."

"Were you looking for me?"

The girl gave a frank stare. "You didn't tell us your name."

"I'm Tobias. Were you?"

"We'll tell you," Maeli said, smiling again. An open-mouthed smile, so Tobias could see her teeth: tiny, bone white, as sharp as a saw blade. "But you'll have to pay us."

A flutter of wind stirred the demons' hair and carried the faint stink of decay.

"Droë once told me that your kind can sense years, that you know how old a person really is. That was how she knew I was a Walker."

"Who's Droë?" Maeli asked.

"Answer my question and I'll answer yours."

The girl shook her head. "I can guess enough from what you said. She's a Tirribin. A friend. Perhaps someone you left behind when you came here."

Tobias didn't respond.

"Yes, we were looking for you," Teelo said. "We saw you running through the streets, and we sensed your years. We wanted to meet you."

Maeli glared at her brother. "You didn't make him pay. I'm hungry, and you didn't make him pay."

"You're always hungry."

"You need food?" Tobias asked.

The girl covered her mouth with both hands and laughed, a tinkling, crystal sound, like water splashing in a fountain. Even the boy smiled.

"Silly child. We feed on years. Would you care to give us a few?"

"I'm not a–" Tobias stopped himself. Not a child? Didn't he know better? Didn't these two? He stepped closer. "So what Droë told me is true. You *can* tell."

"We see," Teelo said. "That's how we know. Your years are written on you. It doesn't matter..." He waved a hand, the gesture encompassing Tobias's appearance.

"What do you want from me?"

Maeli's smile this time was too knowing for one so youthful, even if the appearance was an illusion. "We were curious. It's not every day that a Walker comes from so far."

Teelo eyed her sidelong. Tobias hoped he might say more, perhaps hint at another reason for their being here. He said nothing.

"I came for my sovereign," Tobias said, scanning the lane once more.

Maeli held a finger to her lips. "You should keep that to yourself."

He took another step. "Can you help me get back?"

"It's not so easy," Teelo said. "Too much has changed. It's…" He gestured again, this one vague, uncertain. "It's all confused. This time, your time, other times. Going back as you mean it…" He opened his hands.

"Still, we might be able to help," Maeli said. "For a few years."

Tobias shuddered. "I've given enough. I have no years to spare."

Teelo looked like he might say something, but his eyes snapped away from Tobias, to something behind him. "We have to leave. Watch for us. Or find us near the wharves."

Tobias had no chance to respond. The children pivoted in unison and walked toward the mouth of the alley. He thought their pace unhurried, but they covered the distance faster than Tobias would have thought possible, blurring as they rounded the corner.

He heard behind him the clip of boot heels on cobblestone. Soldiers, the next lane over. He and Crow ran in the same direction the Tirribin had gone. At the corner, Tobias checked the street. Seeing it empty he turned eastward, Crow at his heel, and made his way back to Jivv and Elinor's house.

CHAPTER 24

Tobias and Crow had to follow a roundabout path to the house, twice ducking into byways to avoid companies of Sheraigh soldiers, and once following a street some distance out of their way to avoid a cluster of young men bearing torches and weapons in defiance of the curfew.

The couple sat at the table when Tobias entered the house, Elinor with Sofya on her lap. Jivv stood as Tobias closed the door. Crow bounded to him, unaffected by their ordeal. Tobias faltered, his eyes flicking to Jivv's. He crossed to the water bucket near the hearth and washed his hand.

"That blood?" Jivv asked.

He kept his back to them. "Yes."

Elinor swiveled in her chair. "The Two have mercy. What—"

"Tell us what happened," Jivv said, talking over her.

Tobias could imagine the exchange of glares. He flicked the excess water off his hands and faced them. He was shaking again and he couldn't bring himself to speak.

"There was someone listening," Jivv prompted.

"A boy." Tobias's voice was unsteady. "He ran, and I followed. Crow caught him. We were in an alley, and… and I could tell that he had heard too much." He broke off, knowing he didn't need to say more.

Jivv nodded. "You did right."

"He did right?" Elinor repeated.

Jivv rounded on her. "Aye! He did what he had to do. He killed an informant who would have taken Sheraigh gold in exchange for the life of the wee one sitting on your lap. You think he did wrong?"

She stared at him for a five-count before dropping her gaze to the princess and kissing the back of her head.

"Where did you leave the body?" Jivv asked.

"An alley some distance from here."

"No one saw you?"

Tobias shook his head, saying nothing about the Tirribin. Maeli and Teelo weren't likely to report him to the Sheraighs, and Jivv and Elinor probably wouldn't know what to make of his encounter with the demons.

He knew, though, that the boy's murder only delayed the inevitable.

"I have to leave," he said. "Tonight. Now."

Elinor twisted around again, this time to look at him. "No. You can't."

Sofya began to fuss. She reached for Tobias, opening and closing her chubby fists.

He crossed to Elinor and held out his hands for the girl. The woman held her for another moment, but this only made Sofya fuss more. She let Tobias take her.

"You can't care for her, and you know it," Elinor said.

"And you can't protect her. Unless you're ready to give up your home and leave this place." He eyed her, then shifted to include Jivv in the conversation. "Is that it? You're looking to leave Hayncalde?"

"You know we're not," Jivv said, sullen, eyes on his wife. Tobias wasn't sure to which of them he was speaking.

Elinor watched Sofya, clearly wanting to take her back. "Where will you go?"

Tobias kissed Sofya's brow and returned her. "I don't know yet." He retrieved the sack holding his possessions. Metal clanked within, drawing stares from Jivv and Elinor. Tobias peered into the sack, ignoring them. The apertures were still there, as was one of the pistols, a second dagger, and his clothes from the night of the assassination. The blood stains had faded with Elinor's washing, but they hadn't vanished entirely. He fished into the pocket of his old breeches; the broken chronofor was still there. "We'll leave the city," he finally said. "Maybe the isle as well. I need to get her as far from here as possible."

"You'll never get past the gates," Jivv said. "And even if you do, the wharves are still closed, and the highways beyond the city walls are no place for a wee one at night."

Tobias heard the truth in this, but he knew he couldn't stay here. "The sanctuary, then," he said. "Maybe they'll shelter us, help us escape the city."

Jivv ticked his head to the side. "That might work."

Elinor scowled at both of them. "It might not. More likely it won't. Are you willing to take that child into the lanes, with little chance of finding anything more than the point of a bayonet? You're mad. Both of you," she added, glowering at her husband.

"I'll go alone first," Tobias said. "If I can get them to agree, I'll take Sofya there tonight. If not, I'll… I'll think of something else."

"Even that seems a risk."

Tobias threw his hands wide. "Tell me what's safe, and I'll do it. Staying here is the greatest risk of all. They're still searching for her – for us – and if they find us here they'll kill you as well."

"You don't have to worry about us," Jivv said.

"Of course I do. If it wasn't for you, we'd be dead already. You're the closest thing to family that she and I have."

He said it quickly, almost without thought, but Elinor's expression thawed.

"I should go instead," Jivv said.

Tobias shook his head. "No. I won't let you take that risk."

"It's not a risk. Supplicants from the city approach the sanctuary all the time."

"Not at night they don't. Not with a curfew in place and soldiers patrolling the streets. If we could wait until tomorrow, then maybe, but after... what I did tonight, I'm afraid to wait even that long. It has to be now, and it has to be me."

"He's right, Jivv," Elinor said, gentling her tone. To Tobias she said, "Go then. We'll take care of the wee one until you're back. And we can send you off with food and swaddling if we have to."

Tobias pulled a pistol and powder bag from the sack.

"Don't take those," Jivv said. "A blade, yes, but you're liable to get yourself killed walking the streets with a pistol on your belt."

Tobias considered the weapon, and the warning. He returned the pistol and ammunition to the sack, which he left on his blankets, and crossed to the door. He hesitated there.

Jivv joined him. "I'll check the street for you." He opened the door, peered into the night, and ducked back in. "It's clear."

"Thank you."

"If you get a bad feeling, or you see too many soldiers, turn around and come back. We'll find some other way."

"Right," Tobias said, his throat tight. He took a breath, as if about to plunge into frigid waters, and slipped out of the house.

The moon wasn't yet up, and thin clouds obscured all but the brightest stars. He hadn't far to go, and he struck out southward, intending to keep his distance from the castle and approach the sanctuary from the west.

That plan soon fell apart. He hadn't gone more than a block or two on a curving lane when he heard footsteps ahead of him. The street was dark, and he could tell that those approaching carried torches. Resisters or soldiers. Either way, they wouldn't be able to see much beyond the light cast by their flames. Tobias ducked into the yard of a modest, white stone house.

They came into view a heartbeat later: soldiers; two patrols' worth. Tobias doubled back the way he had come, keeping to shadows, making as little noise as he could.

At the first corner, he headed westward up a crooked street, retreated several paces and waited. The guards continued past and disappeared from view. Tobias walked on.

Over the next quarter bell, however, he encountered several more patrols. They might have been enforcing the curfew, but Tobias thought it more likely that they were searching for him.

Time and again, he had to change directions. He managed to keep his distance from the castle, and to navigate the web of lanes without directly confronting any soldiers, but he wasn't drawing any closer to the spires of Sipar's sanctuary.

He tried to force his way toward the center of the city, but here the patrols grew more numerous. As he neared a corner, now south and west of the temple, he heard yet another group of soldiers. He halted and turned back, only to see a second patrol enter the very lane he had been following.

Using the cover of darkness, Tobias eased into the nearest yard and crept toward the back of the house.

He hadn't gone far when a dog inside started barking.

"Who's there?" called one of the guards. He carried a musket at waist height. His bayonet glowed with torch fire.

Tobias couldn't flee, and he couldn't afford to be found. A dark-skinned Northisler in violation of curfew? They'd have him in chains before he could blink. He had no choice but to hide in the shadows. Inside the house, the dog continued to bark.

"What is it you heard?" another solder asked the man.

"That dog. It must be barking at something."

"Yeah," said another soldier. "Us."

Others in the patrol laughed.

"It started before we got close." The man sounded defensive.

"My neighbor's dog barks if I fart too loud. It's nothing."

Most of the rest muttered their agreement and started walking again. The man who'd made them stop scanned the lane for a fivecount before following them.

They continued along the lane, passing within a few strides of where Tobias hid. But they didn't see him, and he made not a sound.

The guards reached the bend and continued straight along the lane past more houses. Only when they had crossed a second street did Tobias emerge from the yard and return to the lane. The dog still barked inside the house, and a man within yelled at it to quiet down.

Tobias cut eastward at the next corner and, enjoying a few moments of good fortune, managed to draw near the sanctuary. Additional patrols – or ones he had encountered before – forced him to backtrack or hide several times more, but at last he reached the temple.

It was immense. A fortified wall, much like the one surrounding the castle, encircled the sanctuary grounds. The wall's battlements were empty of soldiers, but the gate at the northeast end was guarded by two women, both dressed in white and armed with curved swords.

They eyed Tobias as he approached, no doubt aware of the Sheraigh curfew. They might have known that the soldiers in blue searched for a Northisler.

"How can we serve you, sir?" one of the women asked in a strong alto.

"I... I seek refuge."

"Refuge from whom?" asked the second warder.

"From the soldiers of Sheraigh."

The second woman nodded, but neither of them stepped out of his way. "So you wish to enter?"

"Not immediately, no. There is another. I seek refuge for both of us. If you agree, I can have my... my companion here before midnight."

"Who is this other?"

"I'm not prepared to say. Not yet. I wish to speak with whoever is in charge."

"That would be the high priestess, Nuala."

"Actually," came a voice from behind him, "that would be me."

Tobias spun, reaching for his blade.

"I wouldn't."

The words stopped Tobias. The click of several flintlocks kept his hand frozen in place. He glanced back at the two guards, who stared at him, hands at their sides, swords sheathed. Tobias thought he saw regret in their eyes.

He faced forward again, watched as shadows advanced and coalesced in the light of the sanctuary torches. Seeing the face of the man nearest to him, Tobias let out an audible gasp.

The assassin from the night Mearlan died. Behind him came three men dressed in black, all with pistols raised, all carrying those odd sextants with the three arcs.

Mearlan's assassin took the dagger from Tobias's belt and handed it to one of his men.

He wore a ministerial robe, one trimmed in blue rather than the red Mearlan's ministers had worn. Sheraigh colors. His complexion was nearly a match for Tobias's. The same could be said of the men with him. Of course. They were all Travelers. Did the assassin hail from Trevynisle? Or from one of the Sisters? Onyi perhaps, like Tobias himself.

On the night of the killings, the man had worn his hair tied back. It hung loose now, and Tobias could see that it resembled his own. The bronze was streaked with gold, but he and this man could have been taken for countrymen. The stranger's eyes were widely spaced in a square, handsome face. He wore a placid expression, and held himself with the grace and confidence of a man who feared no one. At least no one here.

Tobias had as much reason to hate this man as anyone, and yet he could see why soldiers – or killers – would follow him, would heed his orders and fight to protect him. He had the look of a warrior king.

All of this occurred to Tobias in the span of one heartbeat.

In the next moment, he recognized what should have been obvious from the start: his life was forfeit, and if he uttered a single wrong word, so was Sofya's.

The assassin barked a command in what might have been Oaqamaran, and the men concealed their devices under the cloaks they wore.

"You will withdraw," he said to the sanctuary guards in the language of the Ring Isles. His accent was nearly perfect. "Lock your gate if you must." He glanced at Tobias. "No one will be entering the grounds tonight."

To their credit, the guards didn't flinch or jump to obey his command.

"The sanctuary is open to all who reside in this city," one of them said. "We answer to the God and his priests and priestesses."

"No one here questions the authority of your God or his servants. But in this city, until a new duke is invested, I am lord. Tonight you answer to me, and to the sovereign of Daerjen whom I represent."

"If we refuse?"

His smile was thin and icy. "I know better than to strike at Sipar's guards." He indicated Tobias with an open hand. "This man, though, whom you seek to protect, will suffer doubly for your interference."

The two women considered Tobias again, and he them.

As formidable as they might have been, they carried only swords. The three men in black still held their full-cocked pistols. Despite what the assassin had said, Tobias didn't doubt that he would order the guards killed if they hindered him in any way. He had enough blood on his hands tonight.

"It's all right," he said, pleased to hear that his voice remained even. "I have nothing to fear from these men. Do as he says."

After another moment's hesitation, they bowed to him, closed the gate with a clang of iron, and stepped to the guard house.

"This way," the assassin said, indicating with a compact motion of his hand that Tobias should follow him.

They started northward, away from the temple walls.

"That was wise of you," he said. "Notwithstanding the lie you told."

"What lie was that?" Tobias asked, though he knew. His stomach tightened painfully, and his breath seemed over loud.

"You have a great deal to fear from me, as you well know."

Back in Windhome, Feidys, the master of statecraft, had taught Tobias and the other novitiates how to control their breathing, their pulse, and their nerves in negotiations. Tobias drew upon all of that training now.

"Why should I fear you?"

The man eyed him askance, raising an eyebrow fractionally. "You truly wish to maintain this deception? No matter the cost?"

Tobias didn't respond. That phrase – no matter the cost – reverberated in his mind.

"You look familiar to me," the man said, facing forward again. "And you recognized me the moment you saw me. So drop the pretense, and tell me where she is."

This he was prepared for. Of course the man would ask about Sofya. If not for his search for her, he would have killed Tobias already.

"Where who is?"

The assassin's laughter was harsh, ugly, utterly at odds with his smooth manner and appearance. "Fine, I'll play along. I heard you speak to the guards of a companion. Where can I find her?"

"Why would you care about Mara?"

A frown greeted this. "Who is Mara?"

"My companion," Tobias said, as if this were the most obvious thing in the world. "We're to be wed–"

The blow seemed to come from nowhere. One moment he was talking, and the next he was on the ground, blood from his nose gushing into his mouth, choking him.

"Enough," the assassin said, standing over him, his fist still clenched. "Pick him up."

Two of his men grabbed Tobias's arms and hauled him to his feet. The assassin hit him again, a punch to the gut that left him doubled over and retching.

By the time Tobias managed to raise his gaze once more, the man had turned and walked away.

"Bring him," he said over his shoulder. "The castle dungeon is well-equipped. I'm sure we'll find something there that I can use to pry the truth out of him."

CHAPTER 25

23rd Day of Sipar's Settling, Year 633

The men half-carried and half-dragged Tobias the rest of the way to Hayncalde Castle. The Sheraigh soldiers at the main gate leered at him as he and his captors passed, but they didn't speak a word, knowing better than to call him "shit-skinned" or "*gaaz*-demon" in front of the assassin and his trained killers.

The assassin led them through the length of the castle, to the farthest ward, and then into a keep at the western edge of the structure. There they followed a winding, dank stairway that descended into the bowels of the fortress.

Fresh torches burned in blackened iron sconces set into the walls, but in every other way this place reeked of years of neglect. Cobwebs and ancient dust coated the stairs, clung to the rough stone, and all but concealed the piles of pale bone and disintegrating rags that littered the dirty floor.

Tobias almost would have preferred to be greeted with the stench of rotting flesh, of vomit and urine and excrement. Those, at least, would have spoken of life – broken to be sure, but lived and lost within memory. The air here stank of oblivion, of death so old it no longer mattered to anyone alive. He gagged on it.

Shifting flames threw into grotesque relief spiked cages, iron pikes and wheels, blood-stained tables fixed with gears and cuffs, and an array of blades, hammers, and hinged devices that burrowed like rats into the darkest recesses of

Tobias's imagination. All of them were rusted and filthy, yet he didn't doubt that each could still perform the precise evil for which it had been invented. He quailed at all he saw, certain that he would die in this place and terrified of what he would be forced to reveal before he did. He could barely stand for the shaking of his legs. Had it not been for the men holding him up, and his refusal to collapse onto the mouldering remains of some previous unfortunate, he would have fallen to the floor.

"It seems Mearlan and his father didn't use their dungeon much," the assassin said, the words pealing like sanctuary bells in the oppressive space. "But everything appears to be functional." He rattled a set of wall-mounted manacles, the ring of iron on stone jarring and discordant. "Chain him here."

They stripped off his shirt and clamped the chains around his wrists and ankles. Using a winch he hadn't noticed, they ratcheted him to the wall, the chains at his hands pulling until his arms were taut above his head. The manacles at his ankles, it seemed, were fixed to the floor.

"To be honest, I don't like torture," the assassin said, gazing up at him, a benign smile on his lips. "I would rather not resort to the... uglier implements at my disposal. That, though, is entirely up to you."

"I don't–"

The man raised a hand, silencing him. "Let's not begin badly. Allow me to ask you some questions. Simple ones at first. And we can work from there. Agreed?"

Tobias faltered, then nodded.

"Good. Let's begin with your name."

"I'm... I'm Bale. Bale Lijar." His brother's given name; Mara's family name.

The assassin's lips twitched. He glanced at the man by the winch and dipped his chin.

The gears of the winch creaked and shifted. A single snap

of the rusted gear, but that was enough to jerk Tobias's arms higher still, wrenching his shoulders, his neck, his back. He gasped.

"I asked for your name. That was as simple as any question you'll face in this chamber. And you couldn't answer that without a lie. This bodes poorly. Shall we try again?"

Tobias told himself it wasn't surrender. Quite the opposite. If he was to be whole enough to withstand questions about Sofya, he would need to accede to the man's interrogation early on.

"Tobias Doljan," he said.

The assassin's smile appeared genuine. "Much better."

Again, he nodded to the man by the winch. Another creak and echoing click, and it seemed to Tobias that hot steel pierced his shoulders.

He cried out, squeezing his eyes closed. The pain crested and slowly receded, like a moon tide. "I told you the truth," he panted, glaring down at the man.

"And I'm glad. But I felt the need to impress upon you that lies will not go unpunished. I assume I've made my point?"

Tobias swallowed, nodded.

"Excellent. Where are you from?"

"Redcove. It's–"

"On Onyi. Yes, I know of it. You lived most of your early years in the palace at Windhome, isn't that so?"

His first instinct was to deny it, but already he dreaded the turning of those gears.

The assassin faced his man again.

"Yes," Tobias said quickly. "I grew up in the Travelers' palace."

A smirk tugged at the man's lips as he turned back to Tobias. "You're a Walker, yes?"

"That's right. And you're a Spanner."

White teeth flashed in the dark face. "Yes, I am, and a good one. Don't interrupt me again." The threat of pain hung in the words. "What are you doing here?"

"Here..."

"This time, this place."

"I was summoned from the palace to the court of Mearlan IV, and upon my arrival the sovereign sent me back to this time."

"Why?"

This time, his hesitation lasted too long. The assassin gave a flick of his fingers, and the winch groaned and ticked. Something in Tobias's shoulder popped and he howled, unable to stop himself.

"You seem to believe that with each question, you have a choice as to how to answer, whether to answer." As he talked, he stepped to the nearest sconce, and retrieved the torch it held. "You don't." He returned to his spot in front of Tobias. "I ask, you answer with the truth. That's all."

He thrust the torch at Tobias's chest, allowing the flame to lick at his skin.

Tobias screamed and writhed, straining against the chains, twisting his abused shoulder. All to no avail – the chains held him fast.

He couldn't have said how long the assassin held the fire there. It might have been a tencount. Maybe less. It felt like an eternity. When at last the man lowered the torch, tears streaked Tobias's face.

"Why did he send you back? It was a long time, wasn't it? A very long time. He must have had some vital purpose in mind."

"I suppose. I'm just a Walker. It's not for me to judge–"

The torch again. Searing agony.

"How long?" Orzili roared. "How many years did he take from you? How many have you taken from us?"

"Taken from... Truly I don't understand."

Flame raked at his chest. He bucked and screamed, until

finally he could take no more. "Fourteen years!" he bellowed. "That's how long!"

The assassin stared at him, mouth open, and let the torch fall to his side. "Fourteen," he repeated, the word coming out like the whisper of steel clearing leather. "Fourteen years." He raised the torch, holding it just below Tobias's chin.

Tobias tried in vain to twist away. He would have done nearly anything to make it stop, but the man hadn't asked anything more. He held the flame there as if it were a punishment, for what Tobias wasn't certain.

By the time he lowered it, Tobias was weeping.

"Why did he send you?" the man asked. "I want an answer. And if fire and chains aren't enough to draw one from you, I'll find other means."

It was, Tobias realized, a secret robbed of import. That future was lost, and if he was to make it whole again, he would first have to destroy this man. In either case, what he said now was of little consequence.

"I came back to stop a war. Mearlan was about to commit to a prolonged campaign against the autarchy, one Daerjen was destined to lose. The Mearlan I served, the one fourteen years in the future, came to recognize his error. He sent me to prevent it."

"Do you hate him?"

Tobias blinked, his vision blurred by tears. "Why would I?"

"Why wouldn't you? Fourteen years he cost you. That's time enough to create a life for yourself. To live and love–" His voice caught, but then he went on. "And work and build something that could last into your dotage." He narrowed his glance. "I would guess fourteen years represents half your life. Or rather half your age as you appear now. You couldn't have been much more than fourteen when you Walked. Isn't that right?"

He answered with a tentative nod.

"So why don't you hate him?"

Tobias glanced at the other man, the one who could hurt him with a turn of that iron handle.

"I ask out of curiosity," the assassin said, pulling his gaze back. "This once, if you don't wish to tell me, you don't have to. But I truly would like to know."

He would have shrugged if he could. "He didn't make me Walk. He couldn't. There are contracts. Any Walk of over a year is proscribed. I chose to do this for him. He explained what he wanted and why, and I agreed to help him."

"And look where it landed you. A boy in a man's body, held for torture in Mearlan's own dungeon. There's a bit of justice there, don't you think?"

Tobias refused to respond, even knowing it might result in another turn.

It didn't.

"Very well," the assassin said. "There remains the matter of the princess. Where is she?"

Even having prepared for this, he couldn't keep himself from going cold at the question. The assassin must have sensed his panic. His grin put Tobias in mind of a jackal.

"You mean the sovereign princess? Mearlan's–"

The man lifted the torch and held it at the base of Tobias's neck. The heat of the flame scorched his chin and cheeks.

He gritted his teeth, willing himself not to scream.

"You know damn well who I mean," the assassin said, lowering the torch, though, Tobias knew, not for long. "Where is she?"

"Isn't she dead?"

The man thrust the torch so hard that it hit Tobias's skin, again at the hollow of his neck. He couldn't help but wail, and the assassin held it there for so long that Tobias was certain his flesh must have blackened and peeled back.

When the man finally pulled the flame away, Tobias sagged, the strain on his shoulder making him whimper. His throat was raw and his heart labored. He didn't know how much of this he could endure. He hoped not a lot. Death would be a welcome escape. Better that than betrayal of Sofya, Jivv, and Elinor.

"You're not fooling me. And you're not saving her, not really. Eventually you'll break. Everyone does. At which point, I will know what I want to know, and you will have surrendered, and all that you endure here will be for nothing. Spare yourself. Answer my questions, and I'll lower you from those chains. I'll put this torch back where it belongs. Your suffering will end."

Tobias forced his eyes open to stare down at the man. And he made himself smile. "What was the question again?" he asked, managing no more than a hoarse whisper.

Flame and agony and screams torn from his gut.

"You are a fool," the assassin said. "You're not brave, and you're not winning." He handed the torch to the man standing at the winch.

"Do what you like. Just don't kill him. When I come back, I want him so eager to speak he can't contain himself."

The man wearing black nodded, exchanged glances with the other two dressed like him, and said something to the assassin in Oaqamaran. They didn't smile or leer at him or give any indication that they relished the thought of torture. Their stoicism only served to chill Tobias more. He didn't doubt that they would prove all too adept at their task.

The assassin left the chamber without so much as a glance at Tobias. The echo of his tread on the stairway faded until it vanished.

The three men clustered near the winch, speaking in low tones. Tobias heard little of what they said, and could decipher even less. Not that he needed to in order to get the gist.

They took their time gathering tools. Blades, additional torches, pikes, ball hammers, chains. Tobias tried to fix his eyes on the wall in front of him, but he couldn't help but glance down with each clatter of a new implement. Anticipation of what was to come left him shuddering with every drawn breath, his throat so thick he could hardly swallow without choking. No matter what they did to him, he thought, it couldn't be as bad as what he imagined in those endless moments of dread.

He had never been more wrong.

They started with blades. Honed to a razor's edge and heated over torches, they bit and burned with every touch. In short order, they had sliced him open in so many places that blood pooled on the floor beneath him. Yet only when they began to rub lye in the wounds did he surrender to tears and howls. Again he writhed against his restraints, further abusing his shoulder, but unable to stop himself.

After that, they took up the ball hammers, and the true horror began. Blows to his knees and elbows, his aching shoulders and ribs, the bones just below his thumb and at his wrist.

At some point, mercifully, he lost consciousness.

When next he was aware, he lay on the stone floor, manacles still holding his feet, but his arms free. Not that he could do anything with them.

"Drink this."

He forced his eyes open. The assassin knelt beside him holding a metal cup. Tobias flinched away. The man's breath stank of wine.

"It's just water. You have my word. I'm not yet ready to kill you."

Odd that this should reassure him, but it did. He allowed the man to raise the cup to his mouth and he sipped the water, which was cool and sweet, though it stung his cracked lips.

He lay back on the floor, not caring that his head rested on stone.

"My men will return before long. Tonight maybe, or tomorrow. And they'll resume their... their work."

Tobias's lips quivered and tears leaked from his eyes. Perhaps he should have shown more courage in the face of the torture. Maybe he would have had he been as old as he appeared, but he was a boy still, on the inside. He had never endured anything remotely like this. The one gap in his Windhome training.

"Or," the man went on, his voice as gentle as a spring rain, "you can tell me what I wish to know, and all this will be over."

"Is that what you would do?" Tobias asked. The words came out as mangled as his body, but the assassin seemed to understand.

"To escape torture? Of course."

Tobias eyed him. Even on his knees in the filthy dungeon, the man appeared elegant, impressive.

"I don't believe you."

The assassin regarded him in turn, his expression thoughtful.

"What I would do is irrelevant," he said. "This is your decision. And you've all but admitted now that you know where she is."

Maybe he should have been dismayed by this. He hadn't thought through the question when he asked it. The miasma of pain had robbed him of his judgment. But it didn't matter. The assassin assumed he knew, and nothing Tobias told him would have convinced him otherwise.

"You'll kill her," Tobias said.

"Yes. She's dangerous. Mearlan's lone heir. Already there's unrest in the city. If these people were to learn that she lives, they'd rally around her. She'd become a symbol of hope. We can't allow that."

"Can't stop it. Whoever has her has eluded you so far."

"Days." He said it so dismissively, Tobias wanted to hit him. "Anyone could do that."

"Who do you work for? Don't tell me Sheraigh. I know better. Who really?"

The assassin shook his head. "I have secrets, too. The difference is, yours are poorly hidden."

He allowed Tobias to drink more water. Again Tobias smelled the wine on him.

"Your name?" Tobias asked, croaking the words.

"You wish to know my name? Why?"

"Want to know who is killing me."

"You're killing yourself." A pause and then. "I believe to you I'm 'minister.'"

No, you're the assassin. Tobias didn't say this. He didn't say anything. He waited.

Eventually a dry huff of a laugh escaped him. "All right. I'm Quinnel Orzili. I come from the Sisters, as you do, from a tiny fishing village on Safsi. I was taken to Windhome as a boy. I was trained and tutored there." His gaze strayed over Tobias's form, taking in the damage his men had done. "We're not all that different, you and I. That's a cliché, of course, something that men in my position say to men in yours in an attempt to win their favor. In this case, however, there's more than a little truth to it. The fact is," he went on after a fivecount, "I could use a Walker. Another one."

"Offering me a job?" Tobias asked, exhaling the words.

"Hardly. I'm lamenting the waste."

Tobias thought of the lad he'd killed, and of a similar remark the Tirribin had made. It seemed like days ago.

"You're not the first."

Orzili frowned. "Meaning?"

"Doesn't matter."

"No, I don't suppose it does." He allowed Tobias to drink a bit more. Then he climbed unsteadily to his feet, looming over him. "Where is she, Tobias? Where is the princess?"

"I don't know."

Orzili shook his head and dashed the contents of the water cup onto Tobias's torso. It splashed onto several lye-burned gashes. Tobias cried out, a spasm of anguish contorting his body.

"As I said before, you're a fool."

He kicked Tobias in the knee, and another wave of agony pulsed through him. His stomach heaved and he vomited the water he'd just swallowed.

"I'm trying to keep you alive, but you're making this very difficult."

Orzili left him, climbed the stairs, and let himself out of the dungeon. Tobias lay still, too sore to move, too frightened and dispirited to consider how he might escape this place.

But pride, it seemed, could be a balm, and as Chancellor Shaan had observed long ago, in a future destroyed by all that had happened since Tobias's Walk back through the years, arrogance had long been the most obvious of his flaws. He made himself sit up, this most simple of motions bringing waves of torment.

His breeches were in tatters, stained and rigid with blood. His discarded shirt lay beyond reach.

The iron cuffs clamped around his ankles had no locks on them. Under other circumstances, it would have been but a small matter to unfasten them, but his hands were swollen and stiff. He could barely bend his fingers, much less use them for anything so intricate and difficult.

He didn't bother trying to stand. The pain in his knees was unbearable. Putting weight on them was out of the question. He scanned the chamber in which they'd left him, searching for a way out. If he could remove the manacles. If he could walk, or even crawl.

His torturers had left their blades and other tools on a table near the entrance to the chamber. Apparently they didn't believe him capable of freeing himself.

Which made him want to try. Pride again. A balm and a spur both.

He fumbled with the clasps at his ankles. An iron pin, with an eye and hook at one end, had been pushed through a set of alternating curls. If he could remove the hook, and push out the pin, the cuff would fall open.

And if he could grow wings, he might fly like a Belvora.

He was still trying when Orzili's men returned.

Try as he might, Tobias couldn't stop himself from cowering at their approach. When they reached once more for the blades and lye, he started to sob.

CHAPTER 26

24th Day of Sipar's Settling, Year 633

Sleep eluded her. Elinor remained suspicious of the dark-skinned man the God had brought into their lives. She thought it likely that he would bring the wrath of Hayncalde's new masters down on their small household. Perhaps tonight.

That, she told herself, was why she feared for him. She dreaded the mischief he'd get into, and the consequences for Jivv and her. And for the wee one the lad had carried with him. The babe – the sovereign princess – who had stolen into their lives, and into Elinor's heart.

The man was trouble. For all she knew, his tale of what happened the night of Mearlan IV's assassination was some elaborate fabrication he'd dreamed up for reasons Sipar himself couldn't fathom. Maybe he'd stolen the child.

At a cost.

There could be no disputing the seriousness of his injuries. He had come through a fight. At least one. Jivv remained worried about that wound on his back. Clearly it still pained the man. Yet he'd gone out into the night. Far from finding excuses to remain with them and live off their charity, like vermin on a dog, he seemed determined to leave, to unburden them and spirit the girl away. Maybe, just maybe, he was what he claimed.

In truth, Elinor desperately hoped this was so, and she worried for him with a fervor she usually reserved for her own sons.

The wee one cried out in her sleep and began to fuss. Jivv stirred.

"I'll get her," Elinor said, throwing off her blanket. "I'm awake anyway."

"So am I."

She glanced at him, found him staring back at her, eyes clear in the faint glow of moonlight seeping in at the corners of the shuttered windows. A moment's shared look. After all their years together, that was all she needed to know he was concerned as well, wondering, like her, what they would do with the princess if Tobias didn't return.

Elinor crossed to the cradle, where the wee one cried and beat her tiny legs. Her swaddling smelled.

"All right," Elinor whispered, lifting her from the blankets. "Let's get you dry and maybe see if you're hungry. How does that sound?"

The princess quieted, but continued to snuffle.

"He should have been back long ago," Jivv said, eyeing the door.

Elinor retrieved fresh swaddling from a pile by the cradle, and untied the corner knots on the damp cloth the wee one wore.

"It will have taken him some time to get there and back," she answered. "Avoiding patrols and all. And who knows what questions the priests and priestesses might have for him? Besides, I have the sense he can take care of himself."

"Do you now? Is that why you've been lying awake for the better part of two bells?"

She cast another glance his way.

"He's odd," she said, turning her attention back to the wee one. "He's strong one moment and utterly lost the next. I don't know what to make of him."

"Nor do I. But I trust he cares about her, and I've been trying to tell myself that if he managed to escape Mearlan's assassins, he should be able to find his way past Sheraigh blue."

She wanted to believe this.

Once changed, the princess was wide awake. Elinor carried her to the kitchen, retrieved some bread and goat's milk, and sat. As she soaked morsels of bread for the babe, she watched the door, aware that Jivv watched her. Crow padded over, hoping for a bite of his own, but she shooed him away.

Eventually Jivv returned to their bed, wordless, his steps light. Crow settled near the hearth, chin on his paws, eyes on Elinor. The princess lost interest in food and her eyes drooped. Soon she was asleep, but still Elinor held her, watching the door, her ears tuned to the lane. At one point she thought she heard furtive steps on the cobblestone, and relief flooded her heart. The sound drifted off, and the door never opened. Her fears returned, redoubled.

She kept herself up for another two bells before setting the wee one in the cradle and slipping into bed.

"I'll search for him come morning," Jivv said, sounding very much awake.

"How?"

"Quietly, carefully. If he can be found, I'll find him."

He'd been like this since the day she met him. Never boastful, but reassuring, competent, confident. She harried him at times, and teased him every day, but she wouldn't have known how to live without him. She laid a hand on his shoulder and gave it a gentle squeeze.

She did slumber, but only in fits and starts. Each time she woke, she raised her head to peer at Tobias's blankets. They remained as they had been, empty and undisturbed.

In the morning, as Elinor fed the babe again, Jivv donned an overshirt and called Crow to his side. But during the course of the night, she had come to a decision.

"Don't go to the temple," she said.

He scowled. "Why not?"

"Because I should go."

"This is not–"

"When was the last time you darkened the sanctuary gate?"

His scowl deepened, but he didn't answer.

"You and that mutt are liable to draw the attention of every soldier in Hayncalde if you go within three lanes of those spires. Best I go. The temple guards know my face. If he's not with the priests, they won't think twice of having me come and go. And if he is, they'll know me well enough to trust me."

Jivv shook his head. "I don't like this."

"Of course not. You never liked being left alone with the wee ones."

"That's not… I did fine by our boys."

She nodded. "Yes, you did. And you'll do fine by this lovely lass."

The first hint of panic widened his eyes.

"I've never cared for a girl," he said, his voice dropping nearly to a whisper.

"Now you sound like Tobias. It's not all that different, and a man your age ought to be familiar enough with the differences there are."

His cheeks reddened, which usually would have made her laugh. At her mention of the lad's name, though, both of them had sobered.

"Aye, all right," he said. He pulled off his overshirt and took the princess from her. "Have a care," he said, his brown eyes locked on hers.

"I will."

He bent and kissed her on the lips, something he hadn't done in some time. She caressed his cheek. Then she pivoted, stepped to the door, and left the house.

Her hands shook, and she couldn't help but pause on the footpath to scan the lane, like a thief scenting trouble.

That wouldn't do. She took a steadying breath, let the

tension drain from her shoulders. Setting out at a pace she hoped would appear unhurried, she made her way toward the sanctuary. At the first sign of a Sheraigh patrol, she faltered and barely curbed an impulse to turn off the lane.

You're not doing anything wrong. You're a supplicant headed to the God's temple.

She walked on.

Twice more she encountered soldiers, and each time she kept her gaze lowered and her stride steady. They would expect her to be timid. The trick was not to look guilty.

Upon reaching the temple gate and its formidable guards, she hesitated again.

"You may pass," one of the women said.

Elinor nodded, but lingered. "I– I need to speak with… with someone."

"There is a priestess in the sanctuary. She'll hear your supplication."

"No, it's…" She looked over her shoulder as a trio of soldiers turned onto the lane and started in their direction. "Of course, thank you."

She followed the winding stone path to the shrine. Other supplicants trod the walkway as well, some making their way to the temple, a few already leaving it. Too many people. She needed time alone with a priest or priestess.

Usually she kept to the rear of the great sanctuary, but today she walked to the very front and sat in the first wooden pew, in the center, directly in front of the priestess who blessed supplicants. She thanked Sipar for her good fortune: Nuala, the high priestess herself, was greeting worshippers this day.

She wore a flowing white robe, and her hair, also white, hung loose past her shoulders, so that she looked ethereal, like some creature of wind and flame. Her skin was smooth, her pale eyes youthful. Elinor had listened to her lead rites in this building for years, but she wouldn't have dared hazard a guess as to the woman's age.

She breathed a prayer, staring at the priestess the entire time. Finally, she rose and joined the line of those awaiting benison.

As she waited, she stared past the altar and through the apse at the stunning colored glass window at the far end of the temple. The sanctuary was filled with statues and images of the God, including a dramatic one on the soaring ceiling of the shrine. The window had been her favorite since childhood. When she thought of Sipar, she pictured him as he appeared here, one arm hanging at his side, the other reaching toward those within the temple, his chin raised, his eyes blazing with golden light, his robe glimmering with every hue of the rainbow. In the image, flocks of worshippers stood behind him; men, women, and children gazed up at him, rapt, awestruck. That was how she felt when she stood in the light of this window. Even today. Especially today.

"You're next." A whispered voice behind her.

She muttered an apology and stepped forward to kneel in obeisance before Nuala.

"Welcome, friend," the priestess said, placing her hands on Elinor's bowed head. "May Sipar bless you and your loved ones in all you do, and may His glory be in your life as shelter, as sustenance, as enlightenment, and as love."

A ritual prayer, to which Elinor was to respond, "My thanks to you, Mother Priestess. May I prove myself worthy of His bounty."

Instead, she whispered, "I require a word, Mother Priestess. In private. Please."

Nuala's pause would have been too subtle for most to notice. "I'm sorry. As you can see, many await my blessing. Perhaps another day–"

"No. It can't wait."

Her expression turned stony. One of the attendants near the

altar took a step in their direction, but the priestess waved him off.

"I'm not accustomed to having others dictate to me what I ought and when."

"I know. I beg your forgiveness, Mother Priestess. This is a matter of grave import. Lives hang in the balance."

"Lives. Your own?"

"Perhaps, yes. Others as well. Including–" She broke off, wet her lips with the tip of her tongue. Tobias might never forgive her, but she saw no other way to convince the woman. "Including one," she went on, dropping her voice so that the priestess had to bend closer, "who belongs to our city's greatest family."

Nuala's eyes widened. "That family is said to be lost," she whispered.

"Not all, and this last one is in danger. Please."

The priestess dipped her chin, straightened, and said in a voice that carried, "Of course, friend. You have my blessing, and the forgiveness of the God." Again she rested her hands on Elinor's head and bent lower. "Return to the pews." She breathed the words. "Sit, pray, contemplate. I will leave the temple shortly. After I do, you should do the same, through the main doors. Come around to the other side. I will meet you outside the window that distracted you so."

Elinor looked up at that. Nuala graced her with a smile.

"Thank you," Elinor whispered. She stood, and did as the priestess had instructed, this time choosing to sit farther back in the shrine. Her entire body shook, but at last she had some hope. As she took her place in the rear pew, she saw Nuala speak briefly with a younger priestess before returning to the altar to bless more supplicants.

Perhaps a quarter bell later, the young priestess approached Nuala and leaned close to say something. The high priestess nodded, indicated the ever growing line of worshippers, and left the temple through a small door at the entrance to the apse. The younger priestess greeted the next supplicant.

Elinor waited a few spirecounts before standing and leaving the temple.

Once outside, she trod a stone path around the sanctuary to the far end of the apse. There she found... no one.

Had the priestess forgotten her? Was this the wrong place? She was about to hurry back to the main doors when she heard a sound behind her. Another door opened on a small structure that stood a short distance from the temple, among fragrant spruce and pines. Nuala stood in the doorway, though back in shadow. The priestess beckoned to her with an open hand.

Checking to be sure she wasn't seen, Elinor walked to the door. Nuala stepped back to let her enter, and closed the door behind them. Only when Elinor was inside did she understand how Nuala had honored her. This was her private residence.

"Please sit," Nuala said, following her into a modest common room. "Can I offer you tea? Perhaps some bread and jam?"

"No, Mother Priestess, thank you."

"Sit," the priestess said again, indicating a wooden chair near the hearth.

Feeling awkward, frightened, beyond her depth, Elinor sat. Nuala did the same.

"Let's begin with your name."

"Elinor, Mother Priestess. Elinor Timmin."

"I'm glad to meet you, Elinor. I recognize you. You come here often, don't you?"

"Yes."

"You have information for me?"

"I have it, and I seek it."

The priestess frowned, the penetrating gaze of those pale eyes discomfiting. "You're speaking in riddles."

"Yes, I know. I'm... I'm not... I make jams!" she said, blurting the words. "I'm not used to playing at this sort of game." She took a fivecount to compose herself. "A man came to us the morning after Mearlan was killed. And... he had a child with him. He claims she's the sovereign princess, and we believe him."

"Who is he?"

Elinor shrugged. "He calls himself Tobias. He's young, a Northisler."

Nuala sat forward. "A Northisler, you say? Dark-skinned, tall, with the beginnings of a beard?"

"Yes! You've seen him."

She shook her head. "Sadly, no. My guards did, but before they granted him access to our grounds, he was taken into custody by men from the castle."

"Soldiers?"

"I don't believe so. Not as they were described. I'm afraid that may bode ill. I fear for him."

"Can you help him? Can you help the child?"

Nuala's cheeks drained of color. "We can't risk antagonizing the Sheraigh army. As I say, I'm afraid for him, but I have a larger responsibility to the people of this city. Making an enemy of the new sovereign for a single man–"

"It's not for a single man. It's for the princess as well. It's for Hayncalde, the house as well as the city. Surely that means something."

The high priestess studied her. "You said you make jams?"

"Yes, Mother Priestess."

"And do you talk the fruit into giving itself up?"

Elinor's cheeks warmed.

"There may be a way," Nuala said, her gaze drifting. "If this man is still alive, and if my suspicions of where they've taken him are correct, we may be able to help him. The danger is... considerable, but less than it would be if the Sheraighs knew the city better."

"I don't understand. Where do you think he is?"

She shook her head. "Leave that to me. Can you bring the child here?"

Elinor's mouth went dry. "I wouldn't know how. By day or by night?"

"Day would be better. If you're found at night, you'll be in violation of curfew, with the child. By day, at least, you can hide in a crowd."

"She doesn't look anything like me. They'll know she's not mine."

"I know. She's a perfect reflection of her mother. You'll have to cover her, keep her face hidden. If you can do that, you'll seem nothing more or less than a woman with her child."

"Her grandchild, I fear."

The priestess smiled. "Yes, I suppose."

"All right," Elinor said, sighing. "I'll try. He left things with us. Should I–"

"Yes, bring those as well. I'll have the guards watch for you. You'll speak only with me, hand her over only to me. Do you understand?"

"Yes."

Another smile softened her face. "Good. You should be on your way then. I have work to do. It seems I need to investigate some of our hidden history."

Time lost meaning for him. In a corner of his mind that remained relatively whole, despite the torture, the anguish, the waking nightmare of cruelty heaped upon him by these grim, silent men, he recognized the irony in this.

He couldn't have said whether it was night or morning, or whether his time in the dungeon could be counted in bells or in days.

They came for him and he screamed. The assassin – Orzili – followed, with water and kind words. Once he put some sort of salve on one of Tobias's cuts. The relief it brought was immediate and profound. But each time, inevitably, Orzili would ask about Sofya, and just as inevitably, Tobias would refuse to answer. Pride. Stubbornness. Devotion. Love.

All led to the same place. Pain.

Orzili would leave, his men would return and renew their meticulous assault, until Tobias passed out.

So when he woke to whispered words and the flame of several torches, he moaned, turned his face away, tried to curl into a ball, though every muscle screamed in protest.

"Tobias," someone whispered. A woman's voice. "That is your name, yes?"

He opened his eyes, his vision swimming. The woman kneeling beside him wore white. A dream then. Perhaps he was finally dying. He let his eyes flutter closed.

She touched his arm and he jerked away, bringing more pain.

"We've come to get you out of here."

"Impossible," he said, his voice like a blade scraped on stone.

"No, it's not. There are ways into this place. And out. They were known to the Hayncaldes, but not to the Sheraighs. Not yet."

"Not a dream?"

She smiled, shook her head. "No. We must go right now."

He started to cry again. He had cried more as an adult in this dungeon than he had during his entire childhood in Windhome. Another irony.

Someone grappled with the cuffs at his ankles. In moments they fell away. So simple, yet beyond him. Strong hands gripped his arms and hoisted him to his feet. Tobias swayed, but they held him upright, their touch burning his skin, his bones. He wailed, and they shushed him.

They dragged him deeper into the dungeon, away from the stairway, away from the torches and blades and hammers.

Shadows blurred, melded. He saw an opening in a wall, a

dim orange glow emanating from it.

"That's right," said one of the women supporting him. The same one who knelt next to him. "Through here. It's a long way, but we'll help you. You're safe now. You're with us."

He didn't resist. Wherever they were taking him, it had to be better than this place. But he wasn't foolish enough to believe he was safe.

CHAPTER 27

26th Day of Sipar's Settling, Year 633

He drifted through dim corridors of damp stone, following the inconstant glow of torches, held upright by shadowy figures who whispered encouragement and told him they hadn't far to go. It felt like they were walking leagues.

Everything hurt, every movement jarred his tender bones and abraded his ravaged skin. He could hardly remember a time when he hadn't been in pain.

He was almost certain that he hadn't told Orzili and his men anything important. Almost. He'd been in a daze of exhaustion, fear, agony. What if he'd said more than he remembered, more than he intended? What if he'd let slip enough to let them find Sofya? The thought nearly paralyzed him.

"Not yet, Tobias." A woman's voice. At his elbow. Apparently he'd tried to stop. "We've some distance yet to cover. Do you need to rest?"

He shook his head, not trusting his voice.

They passed through doorways. Each time, they paused while someone ahead of them unlocked an iron door. Each time, he heard the door close behind them after they crossed through.

Eventually the path they followed angled upward. The air warmed, grew drier. The smells of stale water and must receded like a spent wave. The incline made each step an ordeal, but he welcomed this respite from the chill.

One last door, and after a lengthy wait they stepped into the night.

"The streets are clear for now. But we need to hurry."

He nodded and let them steer him along.

Cobblestone brushed at the soles of his pained feet, blessed wind touched his face and neck. They had covered him with a soft blanket, but now he shrugged it off, sighed as the air caressed his burns and cuts.

"This way," the woman whispered.

A thin mist haunted the lanes. Faint stars shone overhead and a blood red crescent moon hung low in the east.

Outside the tunnels he saw what he had missed before. Eight guards surrounded him in a tight diamond formation. All wore the white robes of Sipar's sanctuary and carried curved blades. They walked in utter silence. His ragged breathing made more sound than their boots on the cobbles. If they were discovered before they reached the temple, it would be his fault.

He made no attempt to trace the turns. His knowledge of the city was too limited, his grip on consciousness too tenuous. They conducted him and he allowed it. If this turned out to be a ruse of Orzili's, an elaborate scheme intended to win his trust, he was lost. He had abandoned all to this single last hope.

When they turned one final corner and approached the sanctuary gate, tears sprang from his eyes once again.

"I didn't believe," he said, the words choked.

None of his escort said a word. They led him through the gate, past the grand spires of the temple itself, to a smaller structure. A corridor, a chamber, a bed and blankets and pillows. A lamp extinguished, and whispered voices at his door.

Sleep.

He was aware of others speaking to him or about him, touching him, prodding him, causing him additional pain, though nothing like what he had endured amid the stone and iron and flame of Orzili's dungeon.

He knew that was wrong. The dungeon belonged to Mearlan and his line. An odd thought, since Mearlan was dead. Yet in this dream state such things seemed to matter. It was Hayncalde Castle. Those were Hayncalde torches and, quite possibly, Hayncalde steel.

Right or wrong, though, forevermore in Tobias's mind that place would be Orzili's dungeon.

At times, as he lay in the softest, warmest bed he had ever known, he was aware of gentle hands on his knees, his wrists, his ankles, his elbows and ribs and shoulders. Warmth radiated from those hands, penetrating skin, muscle, and bone, bringing relief from pain that had become so constant, so much a part of his existence he had forgotten it.

The words he heard almost made sense to him, were nearly enough to pull him from his slumber. But as the pain diminished, the voices withdrew. Tobias slipped away again, content to feel nothing, to hold to no one thought, to wonder in passing if he was dead rather than asleep. Not that he cared. His pain was gone. The rest was of no consequence.

That was what he thought.

Yet one sound did reach him, drilling through his weariness, his desire to be left alone.

A cry, and then chatter.

Tobias forced his eyes open, blinked against the light of too many candles.

A woman he didn't know sat in a chair beside his bed, holding Sofya. Barely. The princess strained against the woman's grip trying to reach Tobias. Tears smeared the light and dampened his cheeks.

"She's happy to see you."

"I'm happy to see her." His voice was like a rasp on brittle wood.

The woman retrieved a cup from the table by his bed and

held it to his lips. It was naught but water, yet it burned his throat going down. Still, he drank deeply, emptying the cup.

"More?"

He shook his head, and surveyed the chamber, which was spare and simple. A fire burned in a small hearth. A sack that might have been his leaned against the wall by his bed.

"What is this place?"

The woman shifted Sofya, drawing another cry of protest from the girl. "You're in the sanctuary of Sipar, still in Hayncalde."

She was white-haired, but otherwise youthful, with soft gray eyes and a kind smile. She wore robes of white, clasped at her neck with a small golden medallion.

"And you are?"

"I am Nuala, high priestess of this temple."

Perhaps he should have been awed, honored that so lofty a personage should show such interest in him, but just then he had more questions than manners.

"How did you get me out of there?"

"Through His Glory," she said. A smile tugged at her lips. "And by way of tunnels built beneath the city some centuries ago. Tunnels of which the Sheraighs had been ignorant."

"Had been?"

She lifted a shoulder. "You're gone. They'll have found the doorway by now. And the first short span that leads from there."

The muscles in his chest clenched. "Won't that lead them here?"

"No. There are iron doors throughout what is essentially a labyrinth. Each door opens with a different key. It would take them turns and turns to trace our path." Her brow creased. "Which is not to say that you'll be safe here for long."

Sofya reached for him again.

"I can take her," he said.

"No, you can't. Not yet. Our healer was quite insistent in this regard. You're to do nothing for another day or two. Not even feed yourself. The men who held you were all too thorough with their torture."

Something in her tone chilled him.

"Tell me," he said. "Please."

She winced, canted her head. "The bones should mend with a bit more of the healer's magick. He's quite hopeful about them. One knee was shattered almost beyond his capacity to heal it, but in time even that should be all right. And the burns have responded well. But the gashes." She shook her head. "They were so deep, and the lye so damaging... I'm sorry, but he says the scarring will never go away."

Tobias closed his eyes, relieved. It could have been far worse. He raised a bandaged hand to his face, felt his cheek with numb, swollen fingers. A jagged ridge ran from his left ear to his jawline. On the other side, another started at his ear and dropped to his collarbone.

"Yes, those two. There's also one on your brow. And, of course–"

"All over my body."

She nodded. "Yes."

He shifted his gaze from her eyes to Sofya's face. She grinned, gave a small shriek of delight.

Tears again, more than he could contain. What were a few scars balanced against her life?

He wanted to ask about Elinor and Jivv, but feared doing so might endanger their lives in some way. Then again, Sofya was here, and so was his carry sack.

"There was a couple. Older. They sheltered us."

"Elinor and Jivv Timmin."

Shame heated his face. He had never learned their family name.

"Yes," he said. "Elinor and Jivv. Are they all right?"

"They are, with none in the castle any the wiser. If it wasn't for them, for Elinor in particular, and also for the guards you met the night you were taken, you'd still be in that dungeon."

Tobias shuddered, which brought a dull throbbing to all of his joints.

Concern creased Nuala's forehead. "I should leave you to rest. Or I can send someone to feed you. Are you hungry?"

At the question, he realized that he was famished.

"Yes, please."

"Very well."

She stood, drawing a complaint from Sofya. After a moment's hesitation, she held the babe to Tobias, allowing him to kiss Sofya's brow. The princess grinned at him, and traced a chubby hand along the scar on his cheek.

"She doesn't seem to mind," he said.

Nuala smiled. "No, she doesn't."

Once they were gone, Tobias closed his eyes, wearied by the simple task of carrying on a conversation. As sleep came over him, however, so did visions of the dungeon. Blood. Fire. The sound of his own screams. He forced his eyes open, his breathing coming in gasps, sweat tickling his brow.

He was still trying to slow his heartbeat when a knock on his door made him start.

"Enter," he managed.

A young man let himself into the room, a priest Tobias gathered from the simple white robe he wore. He bore a platter of food: bread, cheese, dried barrowfruit. Tobias's appetite had faded with his memories of the dungeon, but he allowed the man to help him sit up. The priest fed him, which might have been uncomfortable had he not also spoken ceaselessly about trifles – the weather, the sanctuary garden, his childhood in the Daerjen hinterlands. Tobias listened, chewed, swallowed. His hunger returned with the taste of food.

He grew weary before he had eaten his fill, and the priest left him. Alone once more, Tobias lay back down. Sleep pulled at him, and in that netherworld between wakefulness and slumber came again images of his prison, the weight of iron on his wrists and ankles, the burning agony of lye scalding his wounds.

He fought to remain awake, but he was so very tired. His dreams, when they came, were torment. He tried to rouse himself, but couldn't. Sleep held him fast, like manacles. Orzili was there, hurting him again, dousing him with water that seared his skin wherever it touched. He had someone with him. A boy. The lad Tobias killed in the lanes. Blood still pumped from the wound in his chest, but he held a sword in one hand and a torch in the other. And he leered at Tobias as he burned and carved his flesh.

Tobias finally woke to a room crowded with people. Nuala was present, with two priests, a pair of guards, and a grizzled man who had to be the healer. The faint white glow of magick haloed his head and clung to his slender hands, which rested on Tobias's knees.

"You're flailing," he said, an accusation. "You must lie still."

Nuala eyed the man. "I believe he would if he could, healer."

The healer scowled but nodded. "I'd like to give you a sleeping draught. You won't be of much use to anyone for a few days, but you'll sleep, and you'll heal."

"Sleeping isn't the problem," Tobias said, his throat raw again. He must have been screaming. That was why all these people had come. A part of him was embarrassed; another didn't care. "The problem is my dreams." *My memories.*

The healer answered with a curt nod, and a look that conveyed unexpected sympathy. "I understand. The draught should help with those as well." He raised his eyebrows, questioning.

"Yes, all right."

The man released Tobias's knees, the glow around his hands and head melting away. "Good. I'll be back shortly."

"The rest of you can go," Nuala said, adding to the guards, "I think we're quite safe."

The guards and priests left, and Nuala closed the door before sitting beside Tobias on his bed.

"I'm sorry to disturb your temple," he said. "Is it very late?"

"Not very, no. You were dreaming of the dungeon?"

He turned away, nodded. He couldn't bring himself to mention the boy.

"There's no healing those scars. At least not quickly. It will take time."

"I have no time. The princess and I have to get away from here."

He hoped she would dispute this. She didn't.

"We can keep you safe for a while, but not indefinitely. The temples enjoy some autonomy from the royal houses, but we're still subject to the laws of the land. And because the people of Sheraigh worship Kheraya, they're likely to give us less consideration. If they demand to search the grounds… when they do – I can't deny them entry."

"I understand."

They lapsed into a silence that lasted until the healer returned with his elixir.

"Drink it all," the man said.

He gave the cup to the high priestess, who held it to Tobias's lips. The smell reminded Tobias of rotting vegetables and sour milk. He cringed and turned his head away.

"All of it," the healer said again.

"For the girl," Nuala added. "You can't save her if you don't heal."

He knew she was right, but drinking the stuff seemed only moderately easier than surviving Orzili's abuse.

It tasted as foul as it smelled. Twice he gagged as he tried to choke it down. But it worked as promised. Within a spirecount or two of downing the last of it, Tobias drifted into a deep slumber.

This time he woke to an empty room. A single candle burned on the table beside him, the flame dully reflecting off the rounded edge of a metal cup. No light showed around the shuttered window. Night.

A sound reached him, faint but as familiar as the whisper of his own breathing. Somewhere nearby, Sofya was crying.

Without a thought, he threw off the blankets covering him and swung himself off the bed. Only with his first lurching step did he remember his wounds. He froze, took stock. His knees, shoulders, elbows – every part of him, really – felt stiff. There was no real pain, though. He took a step toward the door. Maybe a twinge in his right knee, and in his shoulder on the same side. That was all. The healer had done well.

He opened the door to his room and staggered out into the corridor. Sofya's cries were more distinct here. Tobias followed them to a door on the other side of the hallway. Pushing the door open, he found a chamber much like his own, also lit by a candle.

Sofya lay in a cradle, tears on her face, her swaddling smelling.

At the sight of him, she stopped squalling, smiled, and began to chatter, as if catching up an old friend on the day's tidings.

"I'm glad to see you, too."

He lifted her out of the cradle, wincing at the soreness in his shoulder. A pile of clean swaddling lay on the floor beside a table. He retrieved a cloth and changed her as Elinor had taught him.

"What are you–"

Tobias turned. Nuala stood in the doorway, a second candle in her hand.

"You're up," she said, the alarm on her smooth features giving way to surprise and pleasure.

"I heard her crying, and it didn't hurt too much to walk here."

"The healer will be pleased."

"How long have I been sleeping?" he asked, turning back to Sofya, and finishing with her swaddling.

Nuala joined him by the table. "You do that well."

"No, I really don't," he said, thinking of Elinor's deft touch.

"You do it as well as I would. More, you do it well enough to convince a stranger that you're her father." She faced him. "You drank that sleeping draught yesterday morning. You've been asleep for a day and a half."

Tobias blew out a breath. *Too long.*

"I suppose that's why I'm so hungry," he said, trying to smile.

"I can have food brought to you."

He lifted Sofya into his arms. She balled her fist into the shirt he wore – a shirt he didn't recognize – and put her other thumb in her mouth. For her at least, it seemed no time had passed.

"No, thank you. I've been in that room, and that bed, for long enough. I'd like to walk, and then eat."

She considered him, then nodded. "All right. Come along."

Tobias followed her out of the room, through the narrow corridor to a stone stairway, and down a single flight to an arched doorway. Opening it, Nuala led him out into the night. Clouds covered the sky, and a fine mist fell, but the air was warm for Sipar's Settling.

Torches burned throughout the grounds of the sanctuary, lighting the space as if it were day. The single stone path leading from the building in which he had slept soon split into several walkways that wound off in different directions.

The priestess led Tobias along one such path toward the enormous temple at the center of the domain. Sofya stared with bright wide eyes at every building, every torch, every bare tree in the dormant gardens. Occasionally she pointed and chattered.

Upon reaching the temple, Nuala climbed the broad marble stairway. Tobias halted at the base of the steps to admire the structure before him. Twin wooden doors at the top of the stairs had been polished to a glassy shine that reflected the nearest torches like mirrors. The wood itself had been inlaid so that when closed the doors formed an image of Sipar standing with his arms raised and his head lowered, silhouetted against a half-risen sun.

"It's even more impressive inside," the priestess said.

Tobias climbed the stairs. Above the door, figures had been carved into the stone façade. Farmers pushing plows, hunters drawing back bowstrings, warriors locked in battle, lovers tangled in passion, craftsmen and tradeswomen engaged in every sort of commerce. It had to have taken someone years to carve this one thin arc of stone. On top of that, columns reached upward, supporting elaborate archways, which supported more pillars and more arches. It seemed to go on forever, stretching ever higher into the night sky, ending in one of those astounding steeples.

Back in Windhome, it had been all too easy to take for granted the magnificence of the Travelers' palace. Tobias had made every effort to appreciate the ancient grace and power of its towers and crenellations. But he had never seen anything to rival this place.

Nuala pulled open one of the great doors and gestured for Tobias to enter. He stepped forward but paused on the threshold.

"Where I come from," he said, "the Two are worshipped together. There aren't Temples of Sipar or Temples of Kheraya. All the sanctuaries are devoted to them both."

"I understand. You're welcome here."

He entered the structure.

In the antechamber, he set Sofya on the shining stone floor and removed his leather shoes, as he had been taught since the earliest days of his childhood. Then he scooped the girl into his arms once more and entered the nave.

Only to halt once more, his body swaying, his breath trapped in his chest. The sanctuary appeared endless. Arches and columns lined both sides of the central space, the intervals of stone and open air drawing the eye toward the altar and past it to the apse at the distant end. The apex of every arch had to be at least fifty hands above the marble floor. Yet pairs of white candles burned in golden sconces over each one. The vaulted ceiling, also made of stone, soared impossibly high – Tobias couldn't guess at the height – but the vaults themselves looked as delicate as vine tendrils.

The ceiling was a mosaic, depicting the God in his naked glory. Once more, he stood with his arms raised, his head lowered, the sun at his back. Rather than being rendered in silhouette, here his face and body were clear to see, his expression as changeable as a summer sky. At first view he looked gentle, kind. As Tobias walked farther into the sanctuary, passing between rows of wooden pews, Sipar's face shifted, his expression at turns wrathful or bereft, contemplative or exultant.

Two-thirds of the way down the central aisle of the nave, Tobias came to the altar, a massive block of ancient rough stone, crudely carved with more depictions of the God, many of them so worn that he couldn't tell what they were supposed to show Sipar doing. Atop the altar stood a smaller, far more refined carving of the God in his classic pose – arms raised, head down. Beside this rested a smooth stone bowl and a matching knife with a wicked blade.

"Do I need to shed blood?" Tobias asked.

"I believe you have already," Nuala said from behind him. "Too much."

Tobias nodded at this and stepped around the altar, continuing into the apse. The benches here were as ancient as the altar, carved from stone rather than the polished dark wood of the pews. The ceiling was lower, vaulted as well, but with no tiles to cover the raw gray stone. After the openness of the nave, this part of the temple felt far more intimate. It was also more plain, save for the brilliant glass image of the God in the great window. Lit only by the torches outside, the colors had to be far more muted than they were during the day. Yet they stole his breath.

Sofya made not a sound as they walked through the sanctuary, but now she let out a small delighted shriek, her tiny fist raised toward Sipar, as if she sought to take hold of his extended hand.

"She likes what she sees."

Tobias didn't answer right away. "Thank you for all you've done for us. I'm grateful."

"I'd do anything for this child."

He turned. "Even at the risk of your temple?"

The priestess smiled. "I attended her birth, prayed over her with her mother and father, and just over two turns ago, I initiated her into the temple as a daughter of the God. If it was my temple to risk, yes, I would risk it. But you know it's not. I serve the God and I serve this city. My responsibilities can't end with her."

"We have to leave," he said, confirming what they both knew. "Soon."

"Are you well enough?"

"That doesn't matter."

She raised an eyebrow. "The healer might beg to differ."

"If he can promise me that Orzili and his men won't show up at your gates in the morning demanding to search the grounds, I'll gladly rest another day."

"Orzili?"

"The man who tortured me. The man who killed Mearlan and Keeda, and too many others to count."

Nuala's mouth twitched. "He can't, of course. The healer I mean. You're right about that. Still, you shouldn't leave tonight."

"I–"

She held up a hand, silencing him. "Give me a day and I can arrange passage aboard a ship."

"Aren't the wharves closed?"

"The temples are accorded certain privileges," she said with an inscrutable smile, "even in an occupied city, and even when we worship the God and our enemies the Goddess. We have many mouths to feed, and at night, when the docks are quiet, the Sheraigh authorities allow our ships to tie in. Give me a day, and I'll secure passage for you both aboard a ship leaving these shores."

It was more by far than he might accomplish on his own, and the best chance he and Sofya would have of getting away from Orzili and the Sheraighs. Nevertheless, he couldn't help but wonder where they should go. Where would they be safe? Where would he be able to build a life for them?

"Yes, all right. Again, thank you."

Nuala studied him, her expression cool, but curious. "How did you come to be here? In Hayncalde, I mean."

"I was summoned to serve in Mearlan's court," he said, avoiding her gaze. *Fourteen years from now.*

"As a Traveler?"

He nodded. "It's obvious."

"You do have the look of one."

"Of a Northisler, you mean."

She conceded the point with a lift of one shoulder. "Your color serves you well. Most would think you and the princess belong together."

A faint smile crossed his lips. Not long ago by his reckoning, though in his own time, he would have been flattered.

"How did you get her out of the castle?"

"Luck, and desperation. I was there when Mearlan and the others died. I was hurt, and so was the princess. I heard her crying, and I... I fought our way free before Mearlan's killers found her."

"Did you have to kill?" she asked, her tone gentle.

He nodded again.

"The Two will understand, and forgive. You were saving her life, and your own."

What about when I killed that boy? Will they understand that, too? He kept this to himself.

Perhaps she sensed his unease. She started toward a small door along the side of the apse, motioning for him to follow. "Do you have any coin?" she asked as they walked, their footsteps echoing. "Weapons?"

"Weapons. In the sack Jivv and Elinor brought. I also have some items I can trade, but no coin."

"Good. Coin we can provide. Weapons would have been more difficult." They stepped back into the mist. "What kind of Traveler are you?"

"It doesn't matter. I can't take her with me using those powers."

She watched him, silent.

"I'm a Walker."

"So you came back in time?"

"Yes. Mearlan asked me... He needed a Walker, and he got me."

Nuala halted. So did Tobias.

"How far back did you come?"

"Please don't make me tell you more."

The look she gave him conveyed such sympathy that his eyes brimmed. He muttered a curse. Grown men weren't supposed to cry so much.

Nuala walked on, and he fell in step beside her. For her part, Sofya chattered and pointed at the torches, happily unmindful of the dangers lurking beyond the sanctuary walls.

"Let's find you some food," the priestess said. "Then I want you to rest a bit more, even if it means more of the healer's draught. If you're to leave us so soon, I want you as mended as possible."

"Yes, Mother Priestess," he said, content for the moment to be treated like a child.

CHAPTER 28

26th Day of Sipar's Settling, Year 633

Orzili couldn't blame his men, not without shouldering a considerable amount of blame himself. It had never occurred to him that there might be another way into – or out of – Hayncalde's dungeon. A miscalculation. Passageways and tunnels ran beneath many of these old cities. He should have thought to search.

Though even if he had, they might not have found it. The entry was nearly impossible to spot. Three times he and his men scoured this foul place before they did so. Even now, staring at the stone wall in the bright flicker of half a dozen torches, he could barely make out the contours of the doorway.

They had tried to follow the twists and turns of the tunnels. After a distance of perhaps a thousand hands, they were blocked by an iron door. Locked, naturally. Probably there were ten more between here and wherever they had taken the Walker. The old Hayncaldes had been clever.

He would have wagered every round he had that Tobias was in the sanctuary. No one else in the city had the wherewithal to rescue and protect him.

He thought he could convince Noak Sheraigh to let him enter the sanctuary grounds and take the Walker. If he was right, the clerics had violated Sheraigh law, an act of defiance that might justify any number of reprisals. The new sovereign, he knew, had no affection for Siparites.

If he wanted Noak's permission, though, he would have to Span to Sheraigh, and he had no desire to submit to the fool if he didn't have to. The priestess wouldn't allow Tobias to remain there forever, and when he left the temple grounds he would be at the mercy of the lanes and Sheraigh's soldiers.

In the meantime, Orzili would double, or perhaps triple, the bounty on Tobias's head. The Walker wouldn't remain free for long.

His men watched him, silent, waiting for an explosion of temper.

"There's nothing more we can do," he said, his tone level. "We'll find him. I promise. For now, leave everything down here. When he's ours again, we'll continue where we left off."

"Yes, my lord," said one of them, speaking for the others.

"In the meantime..." He shrugged. "Find yourselves a tavern, and enjoy a night off."

They exchanged glances, surprised by this.

"Thank you, my lord."

Orzili spun away and climbed the stairs out of the dungeon, glad to be free of the place for a short while.

He returned to his chamber in the castle, but then bypassed his own door and approached Lenna's.

Separate chambers had been her idea. Starting their first night away from Kantaad, she had insisted that they keep their distance from each other.

"The man I love waits for me in my own time," she said. "And the woman who loves you is back in Fanquir."

That night he had tried to convince himself that he didn't mind. His Lenna was younger, more beautiful, more alluring.

As their time together went on, though, his attraction for this Lenna grew, deepened, until it weighed on his every thought. She was still beautiful, less perfect perhaps, but more compelling and exotic. She was older, wiser, with qualities the younger one lacked. Her mind was more agile, her thinking more nuanced, her humor both gentler and more incisive. The years had both softened and strengthened her. He loved her more than ever.

Upon arriving in Daerjen, he tried repeatedly to seduce her. Always she refused him. Resentment crept into their interactions, his from being spurned, hers from being hounded.

After a qua'turn of this, she threatened to Walk back to her own time.

"Why do you refuse me?" he demanded of her. "We've been together for most of our lives."

"Not like this. It would be a betrayal of the younger me, and the older you. I won't do it. Ask me again, and I swear to you I'll leave."

"You can't. I need you here. Until the Walker is dead, I need to know that we can pursue him through time."

"Then don't pursue me anymore."

He gave his word, reluctantly. Since that time they had fought less. He had been busy with Mearlan and his Walker. The assassination, the search for Tobias, the torture. These had consumed his days and nights, which was probably just as well.

On this day, though, he knocked on her door. She needed to know of Tobias's escape. That was what he told himself.

At her response from within, he opened the door and entered.

Lenna sat by the hearth, elegant in an aqua gown, a book in her hands. She set the volume aside, gestured at the chair beside hers.

"Word is he escaped," she said as he sat.

He scowled. "This castle has ears. And too many wagging tongues."

She watched him, expectant.

"Yes, he escaped. Someone spirited him from the dungeon through tunnels that run under the city."

"Remnants of Mearlan's court?"

"Maybe. Or servants of the God."

"Either way, you should send me back. I can warn you, prevent the escape."

"No." He spoke without thought, his reaction to her suggestion visceral.

She knew him well. "It's a day, two at the most. It hardly matters given how far I've come."

"It's not necessary." *I won't spend any more of your life.* "He won't escape the city. He can't get away from me."

"Conceit?"

"Confidence."

"Arrogance."

"Resolve."

She shrugged, surrender in the gesture. "I suppose he shouldn't be too hard to find. Especially if he has the princess."

"He does. I'm sure of it."

"So you've said."

He eyed her sidelong, an eyebrow raised. "You doubt me?"

"Never," she said, and smiled. His heart turned over.

"I do think, though," she went on, "that you should reconsider your tactics."

"Meaning?"

"Torturing the lad to within an inch of his life isn't going to make me any younger."

He scowled, braced his hands on the arms of his chair, intending to stand. She laid cool fingers on one hand, stopping him.

"My men should know better than to talk about what we do down there."

"Your men didn't say anything. They didn't have to. The boy's screams speak volumes."

He wouldn't look at her. "He has information I need."

"I know. And I expect you to extract it. But you should ask yourself: are you hurting him to get that information? Or are you punishing him because he came back so many years, and I had to follow?"

"Why do you care about him?"

Her laugh was as deep and rich as the finest Miejan red. "I don't, foolish man. I care about you." Her smile dissolved. "What you're doing to him will tear at your soul for the rest of your life."

How could he answer. He knew she was right, just as he knew that he couldn't help himself. Yes, he sought the princess. She had to die. But he couldn't deny that he also wanted the boy to suffer. Years had been stolen from them, by Mearlan, by Pemin, by this Walker. Mearlan was already dead, and the autarch would forever be beyond his reach. But he could strike back at the boy.

"I have wondered," she said, after a brief silence, "why he hasn't gone back to fix all of this. That's what I would have done that first night. As soon as Mearlan was killed and the girl orphaned, I would have gone back a bell or a day or a turn – whatever it took to set things right. Why hasn't he?"

It was a question he hadn't thought to ask himself. Or the Walker.

"He must have lost his chronofor," she went on. "Maybe it was broken, or maybe it was taken from him. That's the only explanation that makes any sense."

He couldn't question her logic. "In which case," he said, "he would be trapped in this time."

"Yes. And you would no longer need me here."

Their eyes met, locked. Her expression remained maddeningly placid. He thrust himself out of his chair.

"We know nothing for certain."

"That's true."

"Until we do, we shouldn't make any rash decisions."

"I want to go back."

He flinched at the words. In all their exchanges, even the

least pleasant, she hadn't said this so baldly.

"I miss you. The you I left in the future. The one I love. The fact that you love me here and now, gives me hope that this other you will love me when I return. So I'm asking you: please, let me go."

"You don't need my permission."

"No, I don't. But I won't leave without it. We have a task to complete, and I intend to see it through. You know better than I what needs doing, and how you might use me to capture the Walker and the princess. So I'm relying on you to be honest with me. I won't leave until you say I can, but I beg you, when I can go, tell me as much."

He didn't answer right away.

"I'm waiting for you in Kantaad," she said. "The young, pretty me I saw leave our home that first morning. That Lenna needs you, and you need her."

"Yes, all right. I'll... I'll let you know as soon as you can Walk back. You have my word."

He didn't quite meet her gaze, and he left before she could say more.

CHAPTER 29

28th Day of Sipar's Settling, Year 633

Even without another cup of the healer's foul elixir, Tobias was ready to return to his bed the moment he finished his meal. He changed Sofya's swaddling again, placed her in her cradle, and plodded back to his chamber.

He slept well into the following day, roused by the sound of tolling bells. He swung himself out of bed and walked down the corridor to check on the princess.

Her cradle was empty.

Panic seized him. Ignoring the dull discomfort in his knees, he sprinted from the chamber, down the stairs, and out into the courtyard. Seeing no one, he faltered. He was unfamiliar with the layout of the sanctuary, and didn't know how someone might bear the princess past the sanctuary guards.

He ran toward the spires looming above the other structures. As he came around a bend in the path, he heard a child's laugh.

Turning, he spotted Sofya in the arms of a young woman he didn't know. He strode in their direction, fists clenched, pain forgotten.

The woman smiled at his approach, but then quailed at his expression.

"Who are you?" he demanded, halting directly in front of her. "What are you doing with her?"

She wore gray robes – an initiate perhaps. She had blue eyes and a smattering of freckles across the bridge of her nose. She couldn't have been more than fifteen or sixteen.

Mara's age.

"I– I heard her crying, and no one else was nearby. I just brought her outside to stop her tears. And I changed her swaddling. That's all."

Sofya appeared to be fine. More than fine. She grinned and reached for him, opening and closing her tiny hands.

Tobias took a long breath, looked away. After a moment, he closed his eyes and ran a hand through the tangle of his hair. He needed to bathe, to change his clothes. But first...

"Forgive me," he said, meeting the girl's troubled gaze. "I– I found her room empty, and I was afraid. I shouldn't have... You did nothing wrong."

"I didn't mean to frighten you."

She held Sofya out to him, and after the briefest of hesitations, he took her.

"Thank you. Again, I'm sorry."

Her smile was strained. "She's quite beautiful. How old is she?"

Tobias opened his mouth, closed it again. He should have had an answer at the ready. He was supposed to be her father.

"Nearly a year," he said, hoping his uncertainty wasn't too obvious. "The time goes by quickly."

"I'm sure."

Footfalls on the path made both of them turn. Nuala walked toward them, her brow creased.

"What's happened?"

The initiate sent a quick look Tobias's way.

"Nothing at all," he said. "This young woman was kind enough to take care of my daughter as I slept the morning away."

Nuala frowned, but dipped her chin. "Thank you, Inva. You may go."

The girl bowed to Tobias and then to Nuala before withdrawing.

When she was gone, Nuala quirked an eyebrow.

"She did nothing wrong," Tobias said softly. "When Sofya wasn't in her room, I panicked. She probably thought it odd. Too odd."

"I'll speak with her. She's smart and discreet. It will be all right."

"Thank you."

They began to walk. The skies remained cloudy, the air heavy with mist and the scent of brine.

"I've sent someone to make inquiries at the wharf," the priestess said. "I hope to secure passage for you aboard a ship before the end of the day."

Uncertainty flooded his mind again. "Passage to where?"

"Away from here. Where doesn't matter. Not now. You can choose later where you wish to settle. My only concern is getting you both out of Hayncalde, unharmed and undetected."

"The items I have to trade might not be enough for transit–"

"We have gold. Enough for you, and enough to pay your passage."

"Thank you," Tobias said, subdued.

"Your gratitude is premature. You aren't out of Hayncalde yet." Seeing his frown, she added, "The wharves are guarded by Sheraigh men. Getting you on a ship won't be easy, but we'll manage it. You have my word."

"Again, my thanks."

She made a small motion with her hand. Acknowledgment, dismissal. "I have duties that will occupy much of my day. You and the princess should return to your chamber. I trust all who dwell here, but the less that's known about you, the better for all."

"I understand."

"Good. I'll bring word as soon as I hear something from the waterfront. In the meantime, I'll have food sent to you."

She started away.

"Does whoever you sent to the wharves know who we are?"

"Yes," she said. "I trust her more than I do anyone else in this city. She wouldn't betray us."

"Very well."

She spoke with confidence, but as she walked on, her brow furrowed again.

Tobias carried Sofya back to his chamber. Soon, a servant brought food. Tobias ate a bit; the princess gorged herself. He didn't know when she'd eaten last. Something else for him to learn and remember. He could eat as opportunity allowed; she needed to eat regularly.

I can't do this.

He heard Elinor's voice in his mind answer, *What choice do you have?*

"I'll get you back here eventually," Tobias whispered to the princess. "You have my word on that. This is your land. Someday you'll rule Daerjen, just as you were meant to."

Sofya grabbed a fistful of his shirt and sucked her thumb.

They spent the rest of the morning, and another bell or two past midday, alone in Tobias's room. They napped, and for a time they played, Tobias hiding from Sofya and popping into view, until the princess's body shook with belly laughs.

He kept the window open, replacing the stale air in his chamber with cool breezes and that silvering, misting rain.

Eventually, a knock on his door interrupted their play. At his word, the door opened and the high priestess entered the chamber. She closed the door behind her.

"You sail tonight," she said, speaking quietly, eyes on the open window. "There's a merchant ship – a Kant – that sails under the flag of Rencyr. She's headed to Herjes, and her captain has agreed to grant you passage."

"Does he know who we are?"

"He believes you to be a Northisle mercenary who refuses to serve Sheraigh's new sovereign. You and your daughter are eager to escape the city."

"And the girl's mother?"

"Dead."

"All right."

"The ship is the *Crystal Wing*, out of Rooktown. One of my guards will accompany you to the wharf at dusk."

It sounded too easy. After all Tobias had been through in recent days, he could hardly believe that in only a few bells he and Sofya would be sailing from Hayncalde to the relative safety of another isle.

"Something troubles you."

"No." He shook his head and forced a smile. "I'm grateful to you."

"There's more."

How did he give voice to the thoughts flooding his mind? He had vowed to keep Sofya safe, and by sailing from Daerjen this evening, he would be doing that. But he felt like a general in retreat, ceding a besieged city to his enemy. This was Sofya's home. To the extent that he could call any place home, it was his as well. He wondered if he was giving it up too easily.

He saw little point, however, in sharing his doubts with Nuala.

"It's nothing, Mother Priestess. Thank you for arranging this."

She eyed him with concern. "What else do you need?"

"I need a change of clothes and a chance to bathe. And..." He faltered.

"I've arranged for coin. You'll have it before you leave. I'll see to the clothes and bath as well."

"I can't thank you enough."

"Keep her safe. That will do."

He nodded, doubts crowding his thoughts once more.

Her frown returned. "You're frightened."

She read him too easily. So had Orzili. He would have to

learn to mask his emotions. Another lesson denied him because of the years he had lost.

"A little," he said. "Wouldn't you be?"

"How old are you, Tobias?"

He picked up the princess and gave her a piece of bread from the platter brought to them bells before. "How old do I look?"

"I know enough about Walkers to understand that your apparent age and your true years might not be the same."

"In my case they're not all that different."

"I'm not sure I believe you. Why were you sent back?"

The questions followed him everywhere. How far back had he come? Why had Mearlan sent him? He tried to act like a grown man, and his deception fooled some. Not all though. If he spent too long with certain people, they saw through his subterfuge.

"It doesn't matter." He met her gaze. "Neither does my age. I'm here now. Mearlan is dead. And I've vowed to keep his daughter safe."

Nuala regarded him, solemn and silent.

"Maybe we should go north," Tobias said, giving Sofya a crumble of cheese. "Everyone here knows me for a Northisler, and many assume I must be a Traveler. In the Labyrinth, or on one of the Sisters, we'd fit in. No one would notice us."

"You may be right. The temple can give you as much gold as you think you'll need to make the journey."

"Thank you." He broke off a piece of bread for himself.

"I'll leave you," Nuala said. "And I'll see to your requests."

"You've been kind to us," he said as she reached for the door. "So were Jivv and Elinor." He worried that others wouldn't be so charitable. How would he fare without such aid. *I'm fifteen.*

"I can't speak for Elinor and her husband," she said, after a pause. "But the God brought you to our gates. Of course we helped you." One would have thought he had thanked her for the smallest of considerations.

"What if I had been wearing Sheraigh blue?"

A small smile tugged at the corners of her mouth. "Fortunately, you weren't."

She left them. A short time later servants arrived bearing clothes, a large vat of heated water, and cloths, soaps, and oils for washing. When they were gone, Tobias stripped off his stale shirt.

Looking down at his body, he let out an involuntary gasp. This was the first time he had seen himself since the dungeon, and his stomach turned over at the sight of what Orzili's men had done to him.

A lattice of raised, angry scars covered his torso, his arms. He reached around to his back, straining his shoulders, and felt a network of scars there as well.

"Demons and blood," he whispered, tears streaking his cheeks again. He couldn't say why he was crying. Thanks to the healer, he wasn't in pain anymore. Nevertheless, he grieved for what had been done to him. This body, which still didn't feel like his own, had been ill-treated nearly beyond comprehension. He longed to be fifteen again. Truly fifteen. Unmarked, with a lifetime ahead of him.

He winced at the first touch of the dampened cloth anticipating pain, but it didn't hurt. He was healed, as healed as he would be. Somehow, that made it worse.

When he had cleaned himself and dressed in fresh clothes, he bathed Sofya as well. She chattered and laughed the whole time.

After, he rocked her to sleep and tried to sleep himself. He couldn't.

He prowled the room, stood at the window, watched the rain, chewed more bread, waited anxiously for dusk. He dreaded their journey through the lanes to the wharves, even as he begrudged the time until their departure. He had never been patient.

At last, when the gray sky started to darken and the twilight bells echoed across the temple grounds, Nuala came to the room bearing a leather purse that rang with coins. Tobias strapped a blade and pistol to his belt and shouldered his sack, which still held another pistol, his powder bag, and the apertures he had taken from the castle. It also contained swaddling and food from the temple kitchens: bread, cheese, a skin of goat's milk for the princess.

Led by Nuala, he carried Sofya across the grounds to another building. There he said his goodbyes to the high priestess, and followed a cloaked woman, whom the high priestess named as Della, back into the tunnels. They remained in them only briefly before returning to the streets.

"The passages in this part of the city have been neglected," Della explained as they walked. "Sections of them aren't safe. We have no choice but to make our way above ground."

Tobias nodded and followed.

As they walked, Sofya looked up at the sky and at the houses they passed, smiling around the thumb she held in her mouth. To her, this was all a great adventure. Tobias envied her.

For some time their guide said not a word. She walked swiftly, and Tobias kept pace. They stuck to alleyways and narrow lanes, their route circuitous, but always angling eastward. The smells of fish, salt water, and ship's tar grew ever stronger. At one point, as the terrain began to slope more steeply toward the water, their guide reached a corner ahead of them, peered out into the lane, and jumped back. She flattened herself against the side of a house and motioned for Tobias to do the same.

A patrol marched past, their footsteps and voices loud enough to drown out the noises Sofya made upon seeing them.

Even after they had walked on, Della remained in the alley, her head canted as she listened for the soldiers. In time, she peeked out again into the crossing lane and waved Tobias forward.

They encountered no more guards and soon spied the city gate, and beyond it the waterfront.

"How do we get through?" Tobias whispered.

Mischief glinted in Della's eyes. "We don't."

She stepped off the lane at the next narrow alley, and followed the byway to a small open area surrounding an ancient stone house. Candlelight showed around a single shuttered window, and smoke rose from the chimney. Della knocked three times on the small wooden door, and then twice more.

The door opened, revealing a woman who appeared as old as the house itself. She was bent and frail. Wisps of white hair poked out from beneath a plain wimple, and one gnarled hand grasped a walking stick. Upon seeing Della, Tobias, and Sofya, she bobbed her head and grinned, exposing empty gums.

The three of them entered the house and the crone pushed the door closed. The building was cramped and sparsely furnished, but warm from the bright fire.

"There's a candle below," the old woman said, her voice surprisingly strong. "There's been no one on the other side."

Tobias didn't understand, but Della seemed to.

"Very good," she said. "Our thanks."

She stepped around the woman – difficult in the narrow structure – and gestured for Tobias to follow. He nodded to the crone as he passed her. She grinned again at Sofya, but the princess recoiled and clung to Tobias.

Della led him down a steep, dark stairway of uneven stone, which seemed to go on and on, into the very heart of Islevale. Long before they reached the bottom, Tobias's knees began to ache. Already his shoulders and arms hurt from carrying Sofya so far. Eventually, mercifully, the stairway ended. At the base they found a simple table on which rested a candle in a pewter holder. Della picked it up and continued across the small chamber into a dank corridor.

"What is this place?" Tobias asked.

"The house belongs to the temple," Della said, leading him into the curving passageway. "It conceals a tunnel that bypasses the gate. There have been times in our past when we didn't wish for the court to know of all our comings and goings."

He was sure this tunnel connected to those through which he had been rescued. He didn't remember much from that night, but the few images he could recall reminded him of this passage.

"The guards still don't know of it?"

She glanced over her shoulder. "Not yet."

They walked for a long time, the tunnel smelling of dirt and stone and water. Their steps echoed. Sofya let out little squeals, testing the echo herself.

Tobias tried to shush her, but this only encouraged her to make more noise.

"She's all right," Della said. "No one can hear us down here."

The path began to angle upward, and soon after they came to another stairway, as tight and uneven as the first. Sofya quieted as they climbed, earning a smile from Della.

"Smart child. She knows when to play and when to be wary."

The stairway ended abruptly at a heavy stone door with a large, blackened iron ring in its center. Della blew out the candle and set it on the floor. Then she pulled the door open and peered out at the night.

She waved Tobias through the doorway and into salty air and tall grasses, closing the door behind them. He turned a full circle to get his bearings. They had emerged from the city wall itself. Even having come through the doorway, he could barely see its outline in the weathered stone.

"Remarkable," he whispered.

"Indeed."

She led him at an oblique angle away from the wall and back toward the road, which they regained at some distance from the gate. The guards there didn't see them. The waterfront loomed before them.

Torches burned on the three main wharves, and on the small quays that jutted into the gulf alongside them. Several vessels were moored to each wharf, shifting with the swells that rolled to the shoreline, their lines creaking against the iron bollards.

Sheraigh warships still surrounded the wharves, and dozens of ships lay anchored beyond them, bobbing on the waters.

As they neared the water, the lane broadened to accommodate the hulking wooden warehouses that loomed on either side. Despite the blockade and the dark of night, a few wharfmen and sailors still prowled the quays. Some carried crates and barrels, perhaps to the temple's ship.

"Your vessel is on the south wharf," Della said, glancing back at they walked. "Your captain–"

The words caught in her throat, and she stood dumb, her mouth open, her eyes going wide. Her body swayed and she lifted a hand toward her face, then stopped.

"My captain?"

The woman twisted, fell to the cobblestones. Only then did Tobias see the crossbow bolt that jutted from the base of her skull.

CHAPTER 30

28th Day of Sipar's Settling, Year 633

For a single breath that might as well have been an entire turn, Tobias could do no more than stare. He had time to think that there was remarkably little blood for a wound that must have proved fatal the instant it struck.

Sofya pointed at the woman's corpse and gave a small cry, which jolted Tobias into motion. The bolt had come from ahead of them. He lurched off the north side of the lane and ran, seeking cover. He clutched the princess to his chest, hunching his shoulders, expecting at any instant to be killed.

He spotted a narrow gap between two warehouses and veered toward that. As he reached the buildings another bolt thudded into the wood less than a hand from his head.

"Blood and bone!"

Breathless, blood pounding in his ears, he leaned against one of the buildings. He sat Sofya on the ground and stepped back in the direction of the gap's opening, pulling his pistol free as he did. He paused to load the weapon and eased to the building's edge. He checked rooftops first, seeking the outline of a bowman against the overcast sky.

Seeing nothing, he scanned the road, the buildings ahead of him, the wharves themselves. Della's killer could have been anywhere. He glanced up at the bolt embedded in the wood, and tried to gauge where it might have come from. He shifted and rested his back against the other warehouse, peering out once more.

Still unsure of where his attacker hid, he reached up, grasped the bolt, and yanked it from the building's façade.

He ducked back into the gap, and none too soon. Another bolt struck two hands below where the first had hit, with a *thwack* that made Tobias jump.

He retreated into the shadows, and knelt by Sofya, who jabbered in a sing-song as if all was right with the world.

Tobias lifted her again and trod toward the back of the buildings, placing his feet with care, unable to see anything but the dim glow of torches touching the heavy clouds above. Rainwater dripped on them and tapped the ground in uncertain rhythm.

As they neared the back end of the warehouses, Tobias saw that the terrain beyond the gap was open.

A few paces short of freedom, he heard the rustle of grasses. Had there been wind this night? He hadn't noticed. He froze, waited, listened.

Hearing it again, his blood turned icy. Not a rustle. Footsteps. He backed away from the opening, raising the pistol as he did.

Fool! He had trapped himself. It wouldn't be long before the bowman planted himself at the front end of the gap, and then he and his friends would have them. Tobias could fire off one shot, but in the time it took him to reload, their pursuers would kill them both.

He continued his retreat, sliding along the wall. It was darkest near the middle of the gap. That was the extent of his strategic thinking.

The scrape of a boot behind them made him wheel. A shadow at the mouth of the narrow passageway blocked the torchlight. The bowman.

Tobias shifted again, placing his feet without a sound, readying himself to fire his pistol. If he could kill the bowman, he might escape the others.

Realization flashed in his mind with the power of epiphany. His foe might have been thinking the same thing. Tobias dropped to his knees.

As he hit the ground, a crossbow twanged. A bolt hissed over his head.

He set Sofya down with haste, drawing a cry. Aiming once more, he fired at the shadow.

Flame erupted in the darkness, and the report of the shot echoed violently in the confined space. Sofya began to wail. Through the haze of smoke, Tobias saw the shadow stagger and drop.

Despite the ringing in his ears, he heard shouts from the rear of the buildings. The other men would be coming for them. He picked up the screaming princess and hurried toward the man he'd shot. As he strode through the passage, he tried to reload. Sofya struggled to break free of his grip, hampering his efforts. He dropped one bullet, and knew better than to stop. He'd never find it in this darkness.

A pistol went off behind him, illuminating the passage for the blink of an eye and booming like thunder. Sofya shrieked again. Something struck Tobias's face, and for an instant he thought he'd been shot. But there was little pain. He rubbed the spot with the back of his pistol hand and realized he'd been hit by wood fragments. The shooter had missed. Tobias strode on. His enemy would need time to reload, too.

Just before reaching the front of the gap, Tobias managed to get the weapon loaded again. He cocked it and adjusted his hold on the princess.

"Another step... and I'll kill you."

He slowed. The bowman knelt in front of the building, a short sword in his hand. Blood glistened on his shirt front. The crossbow lay at his side, without a bolt in the catch. Tobias didn't believe the man posed a threat; he looked to be at death's door, and he sounded no better. Still, Tobias couldn't leave the gap without stepping over him.

He aimed the pistol at the man's head. "You'll let us pass, or I'll fire."

"I'm dead... already," he said, his breath coming in wet gasps. "You don't scare me. And my friends... are coming."

"If you're dead, and I can't get away, you won't mind telling me who sent you."

The man smiled weakly, resembling a ghoul in the faint light. He didn't answer.

Tobias took a step toward him, and then another. The bowman slashed at him with the sword, but Tobias remained beyond his reach. Footsteps slapped the ground behind him within the narrow alley. The man with the pistol. They were running out of time, and Tobias could only get off one shot.

A third man stepped into view at the corner of the building, a pistol in hand. Tobias ducked into the shadows.

"He's here," the bowman wheezed.

Demon's blood!

An idea came to him. Desperate, bordering on mad and risky beyond words. What other choice did he have, though? He could only hope he was near enough to the wharves.

"Teelo!" he called as loudly as he could. "Maeli! I need you!"

"You're not... you're not fooling us," the bowman said, his voice weakening. "You were... alone. Except for the girl."

"Teelo!" he cried again, listening for the footsteps at his back. "Maeli!"

"You needn't shout." The girl's voice was nearly lost in the cool wind, the distant lapping of waves, and the whisper of the grasses.

It took Tobias a moment to spot them. They appeared even smaller here in the open, away from houses and cobbled lanes. Their black hair and plain clothes blended with the darkness.

The bowman turned his head.

The man approaching from the corner of the building said,

"Who's that? Who's he talking to?"

"Dunno."

The time demons ignored them. Their ghostly eyes remained fixed on Tobias, gleaming with light for which he could find no source.

"You summoned us," Teelo said, as grave as Tobias remembered from the street. "It's no small thing to summon one Tirribin, much less two."

"He called for children? What's he thinking?"

"I know," Tobias said to the demon. "I'm sorry. I didn't think one of you would come without the other."

"He's right about that," Maeli said to her brother.

"Maybe."

She frowned, faced Tobias again. "We demand payment."

She had spoken of payment the last time they met. *A few years.* He shrank from what he was about to do. "Take the years from them," he said, his voice quavering. "I don't care."

Teeth flashed in a wicked grin.

"What's he talking about?"

The men hadn't time to say more. The demons winked out of sight. Something rushed past him, frigid air in its wake carrying a hint of decay. A scream behind him made him flinch. Another cry from in front of the warehouse roiled his stomach.

They ignored the bowman, whose eyes had gone wide. He dropped the blade, grabbed his crossbow, and fumbled with a bolt. Tobias strode forward and kicked the bow out of his hands. The man reached for his blade, but Tobias toed that beyond his grasp as well.

"What is it? What's… happening? What were those things you called?"

The man who had been stalking Tobias from the front of the warehouses lay on the lane, arms splayed. Teelo hovered over him, not quite kneeling, but not standing either. He resembled a timbercat or a wolf: stooped, but lithe and graceful. Tobias couldn't tell what he was doing to the man, but a faint glow surrounded them both.

He tore his eyes from Teelo to stare into the gap. Maeli loomed over the second man, her back to Tobias. That same nimbus of light surrounded her form, clearer in the deeper shadows. He had thought the demon glow silvery, like starlight. Now he realized that it consisted of many hues. Color eddied around her, like grease sliding across the surface of a puddle.

"Sipar have mercy," the bowman said, fear strengthening his voice.

Maybe Tobias should have whispered a prayer of his own to the Two. But he had summoned the Tirribin and loosed them on his attackers. He had no right to seek protection from Sipar or Kheraya.

Before long, the glow surrounding the time demons and their victims dimmed and vanished. Teelo and Maeli walked back to where Tobias stood holding the princess.

Sofya had quieted. Her thumb was in her mouth again, and she held fast to Tobias's shirt. Her eyelids drooped; she might fall asleep if given the chance.

"Stay away." The bowman eyed the demons with manifest terror.

"You have no years to give," Maeli said, cold dismissal in her tone. "And so nothing to fear from us."

Tobias noticed that the demon eyed Sofya hungrily.

"She's not for you," he said.

Maeli thrust out her lower lip, like a child denied a sweet. "She has so many to give."

"She doesn't belong here," Teelo told her. "No more than he does. Her years aren't for us."

"But babies are..." She sighed. "So many years. All of them so ripe and rich."

"I've heard of your kind," the bowman whispered, gaping at them, his face as white as the moon.

Questions swarmed in Tobias's mind. He didn't know where to begin, though Maeli had given him a hint. *You have no years to give.* If he wanted answers from the bowman, he had to ask them now, while the man still lived.

"Tell me who sent you," he said, raising his pistol again.

"I won't."

"Tell me," he said, glancing at the demons, "or they'll take from you what little time you have left."

"Did you kill them?" the man asked Teelo and Maeli. "Is that what you did to my men?"

Maeli sauntered closer, her bearing too provocative for a child's form. "We took their years."

"So they're… they're dead?"

"They're empty, yes." She halted beside the man. "He's got nothing left – barely worth the effort."

Tobias watched her. "Still, it would be something, a morsel."

She shrugged, indifferent. "One from the child would be worth far more. Just one."

"No."

"He's not very nice," she said to Teelo.

Teelo ignored her, eyeing the bowman. "If she won't, I will," he said. "Tell him what you know."

The bowman licked his lips.

"Give me a name."

"I have none to give," the man said, an admission of a sort. "Word came… from the castle. A reward, thrice what it had been. More even. Payment in gold."

"You're a bounty hawk."

The man showed his teeth in what could have been a grin, or a rictus of pain. "One of many," he said. "You're a dead man, no matter what happens to me."

"How much gold, and what else did they tell you?"

"Fifteen rounds. We were to hunt down a man coming here… to meet a ship. Maybe from the temple." He nodded toward the princess. "A Northisler... carrying a babe."

"How were you to collect your reward?"

The man didn't answer.

Tobias glanced at Teelo, who nodded, bent closer to the bowman.

He flinched away again. Something in his hand flashed with torch fire. Tobias cried out a warning, thinking the bowman meant to attack Teelo. Instead, the man drove the blade into his own chest. A grunt escaped him and his eyes went wide. He teetered, then toppled onto his side and moved no more.

"Well, that wasn't very nice," Maeli said, pouting again.

Tobias's shoulders slumped. "The Two have mercy." He should have been horrified, but after all he had seen in recent days, he couldn't dredge up much pity for this man who had tried to kill him. Wondering at his own audacity, he rifled through the man's pockets. They were empty. Tobias considered taking his blade and bow, but the former was bloodied, and he was better with a pistol than a crossbow.

"You summoned us," Teelo said again. Tobias heard a challenge in the words.

He straightened, stared down at the demon. "Yes. I needed your help. Forgive me if–"

"Do you count us allies?"

Tobias hesitated, wondering if the question carried more weight than the words might suggest. "I don't know. What would that mean?"

"He's clever," Maeli said. "I like that." She scrutinized his face. "But he's not as pretty as he used to be."

Tobias ran the fingers of his free hand over the scar on his cheek.

"They hurt you," Teelo said. He raised his chin in Sofya's direction. "For her?"

"Yes. They tortured me."

"And you didn't tell."

"No."

Teelo nodded with something akin to approval. "Why did you call for us?"

"I told you–"

"Why did you think we would help you?"

"Because you said as much the night… the night I killed that boy. You said I could find you near the wharves, and Maeli offered to help me get back to my time."

"For a few years," she said, canting her head to stare up at him. "Not yours, though. Your years aren't as desirable as others."

"Yes, Teelo said so that night. Why is that?"

Teelo lifted a shoulder. His gestures and manner struck Tobias as more childlike than those of his sister. If not for his teeth and pale eyes, he could have been a normal boy.

"You're a Walker," he said. "Your years are… altered, marred. They're not as pure."

Tobias didn't like the sound of that. "What was it you said about Sofya? She doesn't belong here. Not any more than I do. What does that mean?"

"Her time is altered, too."

"No, it's not. This is her time – I haven't taken her back. I can't."

"Your arrival, and the arrival of others, changed her life. This is not how her life is supposed to be."

"You could say that about every person in Hayncalde."

"That's true," Maeli said. "And these two tasted perfectly fine. At least mine did." She swung her gaze to her brother, her eyes narrowing to slits. "You just said that to keep me from taking her years."

"No one in Hayncalde has had their years changed more than she. We don't know what that might do to her."

"We can find out."

"No," Tobias said.

"You summoned us." Maeli's voice dripped with venom. Tobias resisted the impulse to back away.

"I paid you with the lives of those men."

"Payment you were more than happy to make. They would have killed you."

"Nevertheless." He held the demon's gaze, emboldened by the knowledge that she didn't want his years, and determined to keep Sofya beyond her reach.

"He's right, Maeli. It doesn't matter if he wanted the men dead. He gave us their years. The debt is paid."

She glared at them both. "I don't think I like either one of you."

She blurred away, as silent in leaving as she had been in arriving.

Teelo shrugged again, but he didn't follow her. Tobias walked to where the third man lay. He expected to see blood, teethmarks. There were none. He lay as if sleeping, but he looked nothing like he should have. His face and hands were withered, his eyes had sunk into his skull. One might have thought he'd died days or even weeks ago.

The Tirribin joined him, the air around the boy carrying the faintest hint of rot.

"Do you know that you glow when you kill?"

"Yes," Teelo said. "Whenever we eat."

"Isn't it the same thing?"

Teelo gave a somber shake of his head. "Maeli spoke true. We can take a single year, and we can take all. We don't always kill."

"What would I have had to give up had I named you an ally?"

"We would barter, settle on an arrangement. But it's too late for that now. Maeli's gone and you summoned both of us." He met Tobias's gaze again. "That was a mistake. Next time you should call only for me. Negotiations are more difficult with Maeli."

A chill ran through Tobias's body. He didn't ask the demon to explain.

"I need to get to the wharf," he said instead. He returned his pistol to his belt and adjusted his sack. Sofya had fallen asleep, raindrops on her smooth brow.

He and the time demon walked toward the waterfront. Pain, dull but insistent, pulsed in his shoulders, knees, and back: the price he paid for exerting himself so in his fight with the men.

"I haven't met many Walkers who have gone as far as you have," Teelo said.

"Have you known a lot of Walkers?"

"Of course. Hundreds. Maybe thousands."

"Thousands?"

Teelo shrugged again. "I meet one or two each year."

Tobias stumbled, jarring the princess. She stirred, but then settled back against his chest.

"How old are you?"

"We don't measure age as you do. For us, aging is a balance, years spent against years taken. But by your reckoning, I believe I've been alive for fourteen centuries."

Tobias halted. "Fourteen?"

Teelo continued walking. "That's an approximation," he said over his shoulder.

Tobias caught up with him. "And your sister?"

"She's older, though not by a lot. A century maybe?"

Tobias couldn't decide which was more ridiculous: that these children could be more than a thousand years old, or that Teelo should consider one hundred years' difference in age insignificant.

"How old do you feel?" Teelo asked.

"What?"

"Well, your body is – what? – twenty-five years?"

"Twenty-nine."

"And your mind?"

Tobias's mouth twitched. "Fifteen."

"So which do you feel?"

"I don't know. Both. Neither. Something in between, I suppose. I'm not fifteen anymore, but I'm not ready to be twenty-nine."

He stared ahead at the wharves. The torches still burned despite the rain, but fewer people walked the docks. And fewer ships were moored.

"Oh, no," he whispered.

The Tirribin said nothing. Tobias lengthened his stride, not caring if Teelo kept pace. Upon reaching the south wharf, he stopped the first worker he found.

"Can you point me to the *Crystal Wing*?" he asked.

The man frowned. "*Crystal Wing*?"

"She's out of Rooktown. I'm supposed to be aboard. She sails tonight."

The man regarded him with suspicion. "Wharf's closed."

"It's a temple ship."

"Still, it's late for a ship to be settin' sail."

"Right, of course. Thank you."

Tobias hurried on, searching for someone else to ask, checking the escutcheon of every vessel. The high priestess said the ship was a Kant. He saw none. Could she have been mistaken about the quay at which the ship was moored?

He found another dock worker and asked about the ship.

"Sure, she was here," he said. He pointed out over the water. "That's her there. She sailed half a bell ago, at least."

Tobias stared in the direction the man indicated, light-headed, his knees weak. A pair of dim lights bobbed on the swells between two Sheraigh warships. He thanked the man, though he thought he might be ill.

"There are other ships," Teelo said, watching the stranger walk away.

"The high priestess arranged passage on that one. The temple paid our way, and Della told the captain a tale about Sofya and me. It was perfect. There would have been no questions, and we would have reached Rooktown with enough gold to book passage farther north. Now..." He trailed off, still queasy. They had the coins from Nuala, but with no way off Daerjen, even twice as much wouldn't save their lives.

"I'm afraid we can't help you."

Tobias shook his head, weary as he could remember. "You already did, and I'm grateful."

"What will you do?"

Tobias had no answer. The bounty hawk had known they were coming from the temple; he couldn't risk returning there. Nor would he endanger Elinor and Jivv again. No place in the city was safe. If the bowman was right, others were hunting for them, lured by the promise of Orzili's reward.

It occurred to him that Orzili might have known enough to have the ship watched. When they failed to board, the watcher might have assumed that the bounty hawks succeeded.

"They might think we're dead."

Teelo considered him.

Tobias knew that Orzili would demand irrefutable evidence of their deaths before he gave up his pursuit, but in the meantime, the failed attempt on their lives might provide them with an opportunity to get away. "If they even suspect that the killers succeeded, we can go anywhere. By ship, on foot, on horse if I can find one. The only thing we *can't* do is remain in Hayncalde."

With the blockade still in place, they wouldn't be leaving the city by ship any time soon. He didn't know when another temple vessel would come. And he wouldn't find a horse or chance venturing beyond the city walls this night. He needed a place to sleep. Tomorrow he would work out the rest.

"You're still with him?"

Tobias turned. Maeli stood behind them, fists on her hips.

"What do you want?" her brother asked.

"I don't know. I'm bored."

"Surely you're not hungry again already."

"No, that's the problem." A smile exposed serrated teeth. "If I was hungry, we could hunt. But I'm not. I have nothing to do. I don't like it when you're away."

"He needs a place to sleep tonight," Teelo said.

A sly look flashed in Maeli's pale eyes, and her gaze darted to Sofya, asleep in his arms. "We can help him with that," she said, her voice like velvet.

Without a backward glance or a word of invitation, she started back toward the lanes. Teelo followed. After a few steps, he halted and beckoned to Tobias.

Reluctantly, he followed as well.

CHAPTER 31

28th Day of Sipar's Settling, Year 633

The Tirribin led him to the street that fronted the coastline, but turned southward, so that they walked parallel to the outer city walls and followed the waterfront. Cobblestones gave way to dirt, dirt to sand, sand to rough rock and strewn boulders. As the terrain grew more difficult, Tobias struggled to keep up. The demons scrambled over the stone like mountain sheep, fearless and agile, born to the coastline.

Tobias took his time, sore still, wearying quickly, and afraid he might fall and hurt the princess. Before long, he lost sight of them, and panic set in. Was this what Maeli had in mind? Had she lured him away from other people in order to attack him and steal Sofya? He climbed over yet another stone, expecting to find himself alone in the darkness. Instead, he spotted the demons some fifty paces ahead, standing atop a giant boulder, waving to him like children.

"You're too slow," Maeli called, a thread of laughter in her voice. "Too bad you're not younger."

Teelo laughed and waved Tobias on. He and his sister clambered down out of sight. Tobias paused where he was, sweating and out of breath. Scanning the coastline, he spotted a cluster of flames that burned in a narrow cleft of stone. Some were torches. At least one appeared to be a bonfire. Their destination?

He lowered himself off his stone perch and continued to chase the Tirribin.

After another half bell of this, Tobias no longer doubted that the demons were leading him toward the crevice of light in the rocky coast. Others milled in the glow of the torches: men, women, even some children. From this distance, he couldn't tell if they were demons or a mix of demons and people, but as his curiosity grew, so did his trepidation.

Teelo and Maeli awaited him at the base of a jagged rock face below the cleft. He halted in front of them, breathing hard. Sofya still slept, unmindful of their journey and the possible danger.

From above, Tobias heard laughter, voices, strains of music. He smelled smoke and some kind of roasting meat. His mouth watered and his stomach gave a loud rumble.

"Where are you leading me?"

"Didn't you see?" Maeli asked.

"I saw. What is this place?"

"It's called the Notch."

"That's a name. It doesn't tell me what this is."

"It's a gathering place," Teelo said, grave as always.

"For Tirribin?"

"For those who don't belong in the city."

Tobias looked up, but could only see light spilling out over the stone and shining on the shifting waters of the gulf. He turned a circle, taking in their surroundings. The Tirribin had led him into a tight, small cove that would have been hard to see from the shipping lanes of the gulf, and impossible to find from the wharves. The Notch was as good a name as any.

"Is it safe for us up there?"

"As safe as it is for you anywhere," Maeli said. "You know the perils of the city." She pointed out at the water. "Do you believe you would have been safe on that ship? Children are sold as slaves every day. There is no 'safe.' 'Safe' is an illusion."

"Some places are riskier than others," Tobias said, desperate to believe it true.

The demon shrugged with maddening calm. "I suppose. The greatest danger awaiting you in this place is probably me."

Teelo shook his head. "That's not nice, Maeli."

"I don't care. It's true."

"She's right about it being as safe as anywhere else," Teelo said. "And you don't have to worry about her. She won't do anything to you or to the child."

Maeli stared at Tobias, neither affirming nor denying what her brother said.

The rain had intensified again. Tobias was soaked, and he was having trouble keeping Sofya dry. "All right. Lead the way."

The Tirribin turned as one and started up a stairway that had been hacked into the stone. Tobias hadn't noticed it.

The steps were uneven and slick, and again he feared he might fall and injure the princess. It was a steep climb. Before they had covered half the distance, his legs were quivering with fatigue. At last, though, he staggered off the last step and onto a broad, flat stone shelf. Heat from the bonfire greeted him, as welcome after the cold rain as a blanket and bed.

Torches burned at intervals along the stone walls surrounding the tableland, revealing what had been hidden from below. This was more than a single depression in the stone face of the coastline. It was a series of shallow caverns stretching back through a fissure in the escarpment. Crude shelters had been built in each hollow, and smaller fires crackled in many of them. The aroma of cooking meat was stronger here than it had been on the strand.

Tobias saw men and women, some single, some in pairs, many in larger groups of five or ten. They talked and laughed. Some couples were locked in passionate embraces, seemingly unconcerned with those around them. A few took note of him and the Tirribin; most did not.

"Aren't they afraid of you?" he asked.

Teelo surveyed the shelf. "Some are. Most know that we wouldn't bother them. When we're hungry, we go to the city. We like it here; we don't want them to send us away."

He and Maeli led Tobias deeper into the crevice.

More scents reached them: spices Tobias didn't recognize, roasted tearroot, fresh bread, something that smelled like burning sugar. Sofya stirred, woke, looked around with puffy eyes. She made a small sound – something between a cry and a laugh. Tobias wasn't sure what it meant, but he guessed she was as hungry as he.

As they passed another cluster of people, a different smell tanged the air. Sour, but also cloyingly sweet, with an underlying bitterness that made his eyes tear. It reminded him of... something.

"What's that smell?" he whispered, staring at the people.

They ignored him, continuing their conversation in low voices. Several clutched dirty cloths in their hands. A few held the rags to their faces for a breath or two.

"Tincture," Teelo said.

"Like the Seers use?"

That explained the familiarity of the odor. But he didn't recall the cloud of Tincture surrounding Osten Cavensol having such a sour quality.

Teelo nodded. "Like that, but not quite the same."

"I don't understand."

"Magi aren't only in the courts," Maeli said, walking backward so she could face him. "Some who have the talent never draw the attention of nobles. They need Tincture as well, but they can't get the pure kind that your sovereign supplied to his Seer. They use this instead."

She turned again, and they continued on. Tobias glanced back several times.

The Tirribin took him deeper into the Notch, passing several caverns, all crowded with shelters. At one point, they walked through a broad area set up with rough booths constructed from scraps of wood. It had the look of a marketplace, though all the spaces were currently empty.

Soon after crossing through this open area, Teelo and Maeli halted and pointed to one particular shelter a few paces ahead. Little distinguished it from the others Tobias had seen, but the demons appeared quite certain.

"You'll find shelter there," Teelo said. "That's Kaarti's. She lets rooms to people like you."

"I'm not sure she's ever met anyone like him," Maeli said, mischief in the tone.

Teelo frowned at his sister. "People needing a place to stay, I mean."

"I understand."

"I'm bored," Maeli said, surveying the caverns. "I want to go back to the city."

Teelo stepped closer to Tobias. "We have to leave now. We'll see you again."

"I'm grateful to you. For everything you've done."

The Tirribin eyed the shelters around them. "Have a care," he said, dropping his voice. "You're safer here than you would be elsewhere – and you can trust Kaarti – but don't abandon all caution."

Tobias hardly needed the reminder. He watched as the demons walked away from the shelter. Their gait appeared as unhurried as ever, but they covered the distance back toward the outer shelf in a fraction of the time it would have taken him. Tobias wondered if they would hunt again tonight. He shuddered at the memory of what he had seen them do – of what they had done for him.

When they were gone, he approached the flap of canvas that covered the entrance to Kaarti's shelter.

"Good evening," he called. "Is anyone here?"

He heard footsteps scratch on stone. An instant later the

canvas was thrust aside, revealing a diminutive woman with fierce green eyes, a hooked nose, and vivid red hair.

Tobias fell back a stride and Sofya began to cry.

The woman frowned, sighed. "Didn't mean to do that."

She approached them, her attention on the babe. "I'm sorry, beautiful. Easy now. Easy. Shhhh."

Sofya shied from her.

"Well, I've made a mess of it, haven't I?"

"She'll be all right."

"Who are you?" she asked.

"I was told you might have a place where we can stay."

"That's why yous are here, isn't it? It's not who you is."

"My name is Tobias. This is my daughter, Nava."

The woman narrowed her eyes, scrutinized his face and clothes, her gaze lingering on his scars. "Not sure that's who you is, either."

He went cold, and he took another step back. "I think maybe we should go."

"No need for that. I'm not looking to trouble you. But yous stick out here like priests in a brothel. Wrong color, wrong clothes, babe in your arms."

"Thank you for your time," Tobias said. "I can find–"

"A trey per night for shelter and food. If'n yous intend to stay a full turn it's twenty treys for the total, but I don't get the sense yous will be here that long. Either way, yous pay in advance. If'n yous decide to stay longer, but leave before the turn is up, yous lose the rent. No dealing, no exceptions. Just the way it is. I can give you back a trey or two for the food. Most times I charge for food by the mouth, but I don't guess the wee one eats much. If I'm wrong about that, we'll work something out."

"I have food for her."

Kaarti dismissed this with a wave of her hand. "Nonsense. Nothing yous have will be hot." She stared, waiting.

Tobias wasn't certain what to do. The woman scared him nearly as much as she did Sofya. Maybe he'd been too quick to believe that the Notch would be safe for them. Then again, Teelo had brought them to this woman, and Tobias didn't think the road would be any safer. The truth was, he didn't know where to go or who to trust.

Kaarti watched him for another moment, then shuffled back into the shelter. "When yous have made up your mind, let me know." She left the canvas flap open.

Tobias stood in the rain, weighing his options. He had few. "What do you think we should do?" he asked the princess in a whisper. Tears clung to her cheeks, but she chattered again, her fright forgotten.

At last he carried her inside. The interior of the shelter far exceeded his expectations. It was spacious and well-lit with candles. He counted at least three separate chambers, set off from one another by canvas walls. Sound would travel among them, but they offered some privacy.

Kaarti stood at a cooking fire that vented through a hole in the cloth ceiling, stirring a pot filled with dark stew. It smelled incredibly good.

Swinging his sack off his shoulder, Tobias found the leather purse Nuala had given him and plucked out two silver treys. "We'll pay for two nights now," he said.

"Gods, do yous have a lot to learn," she said, her whisper a harsh rasp. "Pulling out a purse like that in a place like this?"

"I'm sorry, I–"

"What do you have in there? Five rounds? More? People come here – the Notch, I mean – for any number of reasons, none of them trifles. Theys down on their luck, or theys been driven from their homes. Maybe they never fit in with normal folk, and so they find a home here. Maybe they run afoul of the law. Or maybe theys trying to escape someone important – someone powerful. But they don't make a fuss, and they don't draw attention to themselves with foolishness." She closed the distance between them, her breath fouling the air. "I run away from a husband who beat me. It was either that or kill him, and I hadn't the guts. Yous are running from someone. That's the only way to match up the way you look with you being here. That's fine. I don't have no problem with that. But yous got to be smart. You bring trouble on yous, it get on me, too. You catch that?"

He nodded.

"Two nights you said."

"Yes. Please."

She took his coins and hid them in a pocket deep within her tattered gown.

"You'll be in that one," she said, tipping her head toward a chamber to the right of the fire. "I have a small pallet we can bring in for the wee one."

"That would be fine. Thank you."

"The wee one yours?" she asked, returning to the cooking pot.

"Yes. My daughter."

"Where's her mum?"

"She died, several turns ago."

Kaarti paused to look his way. "My condolences."

Tobias dipped his chin. Inside, he winced at the lie.

"That don't explain why yous winded up here."

"No, I don't suppose it does." Tobias said no more, but walked around the shelter, allowing Sofya to explore with her wide, dark eyes.

Kaarti chuckled. "That was better. It's not easy to tell an old woman to stay out of your business with nary a rude word. Yous might do all right after all."

She tasted the stew, nodded her satisfaction. "That's hot enough, I think." She waved Tobias over and indicated a battered chair and table. "Yous sit here. I'll bring out some bread."

Kaarti ladled stew into a bowl and placed it in front of Tobias, along with a cup of honey mead. She walked into what appeared to be a small larder between two of the sleeping chambers, and reemerged bearing a round of dark, flat bread, which she placed beside Tobias's bowl.

"It's a little stale, but the stew'll soften it up. I'll be making some fresh in the morning."

Tobias tasted the stew, hoping its flavor would match the promise of its aroma. It did, and more. It tasted of smoked nuts and roasted root, and it was flavored with baviseed and sweetpine. The bread was nutty and chewy – the perfect complement to the stew. He was so entranced that for a spirecount or two he fed only himself, forgetting about the princess. She finally grabbed for his spoon hand.

Kaarti laughed. "I think she's feelin' left out."

Tobias fed her a small piece of soaked bread. She chewed, gave a cry and a smile, and pointed at the bowl.

"Nice t'know she appreciates good food."

Together, Tobias and Sofya ate two bowls of the nut stew and two large pieces of bread. He helped Kaarti clean up, carried the princess to their small chamber, and settled her down to sleep before lying down on his pallet. The past few days had been more harrowing than he would have thought possible, and he should have been terrified by every sound.

For many reasons, though – their distance from the city, the assurances of the Tirribin, his belief that Orzili's men thought him dead – he felt safer here, surrounded by canvas rather than stone or wood, than he had anywhere else he'd been since Mearlan's death. He knew it couldn't last. A rocky strand and steep stairs wouldn't keep Orzili at bay for long. For tonight, however, he allowed himself to relax. In time, he fell into a deep slumber.

• • •

He and Sofya slept well into the morning, only waking when the aroma of their breakfast wafted past the cloth walls.

Tobias changed Sofya's swaddling and carried her out of the chamber. Kaarti was bent over the fire, frying minced meat, eggs, and butterbread.

"Thought this might wake yous," she said. "Should be ready soon."

Tobias thanked her and stepped outside, to the edge of the cavern. Dark clouds still hung over the coast and rain fell in windswept sheets of silver and gray. The air had turned colder. This might not be the day to begin their journey to another city.

People walked past Kaarti's establishment in both directions, some carrying sacks of food, others burdened with what could have been everything they owned. Most took no notice of Tobias and Sofya, and even those who glanced in their direction quickly looked away. Given what Kaarti had told him about the Notch the night before, he wasn't surprised.

Kaarti called them back for breakfast, which was as good as supper had been. The woman watched them, eating nothing from the full plate in front of her. Tobias fed the princess and himself, trying to ignore Kaarti's scrutiny.

"Yous come from the castle, don't you?" she said at length, keeping her voice low.

Tobias glanced toward the mouth of the cavern before answering.

"What makes you say that?"

"You look soft."

He bristled.

"Not weak," she said. "You have them scars, and you had to be strong to survive whatever they come from. But you look like you haven't never had to scrounge or beg."

Her remark rankled, but he couldn't deny it. After a fivecount he nodded.

"Some folks can spot things like that. I can. Others wouldn't know any of it. 'Round here, though, there's more like me, you catch? You be careful."

"I will."

"So did you?"

"Did I what?"

"Did yous come from the castle?"

He wasn't sure he liked the innkeeper, but for some reason he trusted her. "I did. I served in Mearlan's court."

"What you told me about the wee one's mother being dead. That true?"

There were limits to his trust. Fortunately her question was vague enough to allow him to tell the truth. "Yes, that was true." He considered her, feeding Sofya more bread. "What did folk here think of the overthrow of the Hayncalde Supremacy?"

"Most folks here don't care much one way or another."

Tobias allowed her words to hang between them.

"Some care," she whispered. "Folk don't come to the Notch if they have too much stake in what goes on in the city. But staying apart is one thing; seeing the Sheraighs come in and kill our sovereign is another."

"I thought as much. We're here because it wasn't safe for me in the city anymore. You say we don't belong, and you're probably right. But if we'd remained there, chances are I'd now be dead."

"And the wee one?"

"This is about me, not her."

"Yous are telling me this why?"

"Because I want you to know that I was loyal to Mearlan and to Hayncalde. I still am."

"All right," Kaarti said. "What will yous do today?"

"I don't know yet. We need to get away from here. Even the Notch won't be safe for us for long. I need to find some way to leave. And I need to know if the wharves are still closed."

"Outer Notch, then," Kaarti said, disapproval in her tone.

"If that's where I have to go, so be it. What's inland from here? Where does the Notch end?"

"More caverns. Good for hidin', but there's no way out."

"So we'll have to go back to the strand."

"I suppose. I don't think about it much. Folks in Inner Notch don't look to leave. They's here for good. Outer Notch? Folk there are like the tide. They come and they go. Though word is, since the Sheraighs come, they's stuck here."

"The blockade?"

"That's right. From here, there's few ways past the city on foot. It's all ships and dories."

He grimaced. He and Sofya might not have survived the previous night without help from the Tirribin. Yet the demons had trapped them here, inadvertently perhaps, but all too effectively.

"So, it comes back to the wharves. I need to know if they're open."

He glanced down at Sofya, who had lost interest in eating. She played with an old doll Kaarti said had been left behind by past renters, babbling at it and bouncing it on her lap.

"You can leave the wee one with me," Kaarti said.

Tobias looked away and rubbed a hand over his rough chin to hide his surprise. He hadn't expected such an offer.

"I– I wouldn't want to impose."

"Imposing ain't your worry. Yous don't trust me, just like I'm not sure I trust you." She raised her chin. "I wouldn't hurt her, and I'd never let anyone take her. She and I won't be anywheres but here." A smile transformed her face. "With that doll I gave her, she won't even know yous left until yous come back.

"I had two of my own. Long ago, now. It would–" She dropped her gaze. "It would be good to have a wee one here for a while."

He weighed the offer, eyeing her. "All right," he said. "Thank you. It would be easier to do this on my own."

"You have a care anyway," Kaarti said, gruff as ever. "This is only for a bell or two. I'm too old to start from scratch with a wee one."

"I'll keep that in mind."

Tobias set Sofya on the floor. She was so absorbed with her doll that she barely noticed. He retrieved her swaddling from his chamber so Kaarti would find it with ease. Then he shouldered his sack and crossed to the shelter's entrance.

"Yous remember what I said," she called after him. "Be smart. Don't bring us no trouble."

"I will. Be smart, I mean."

She frowned.

Tobias left her there and headed toward Outer Notch and the coastline. The rain had eased, but the air remained cold.

He soon understood why Kaarti spoke of the Outer Notch with such disdain. All in the caverns appeared ragged around the edges. There was no wealth here – everyone wore tatters, all the structures looked to be one strong wind away from collapse. The shelters of the Inner Notch, however, were kept neat; those who lived there had some purpose. As Tobias entered the Outer Notch, he saw more people lazing about, sitting along the path that fronted the caverns. It was barely midday and many were already – or still – far gone with drink. Others slept outside of shelters, singly and in pairs, blankets bundled around them.

Men and women engaged in hushed conversations, heads bent close together, coin changing hands. He averted his gaze lest they think him overly interested in their dealings. This part of the Notch, he realized, was to the caverns what the shady lanes west of the wharves were to the city itself. He spied one establishment that might have been a brothel, and passed several shelters that reeked of spirits and stale ale.

The rush and retreat of the surf reached him here, as did the smells of sea salt, fish, and seaweed.

"You lookin' for someone in particular, love?"

Tobias turned at the voice. A woman leaned against the stone edge of a shallow cavern, a diaphanous gown clinging to her form, dark curls spilling over her shoulders and down her back. She canted her head and smiled, revealing a gap between her front teeth.

"Two treys for the rest of the day. Four and I'm yours through the evening."

"Uh, no, thank you."

She laughed, reveling in his discomfort. "I won't hurt you. Unless you want me to."

"I'm fine," he said, backing away. "Really." He walked on apace, resisting the impulse to run.

Her laughter followed him along the stone path.

Tobias could still hear her, when a familiar odor stopped him in mid-stride. Sweet and also sour, with the powerful scent of spirit underlying the blend. Tincture. It emanated from the same shelter that had drawn his attention the night before. The tables and chairs out front stood empty, but the canvas entrance was tied open.

Tobias approached, glancing around to see if anyone watched him. He saw no one.

He entered the shelter and was assailed by the spirit smell. It made his eyes water and his throat constrict until he thought he might gag.

Three men sat at tables, all holding the stained cloths he had seen the previous night. One of the men pressed a cloth to his nose and mouth, his eyes half-closed. Another appeared to be asleep sitting up, his head lolling, his hands limp in his lap.

The third man faced the doorway. His eyelids drooped, and a vague smile rested comfortably on his thin lips.

"Welcome, young master." His voice was strong, but his

words came haltingly. "I have been expecting you."

The words shocked Tobias, but his surprise quickly gave way to mistrust. He thought it likely this was something the man said to all who wandered into the establishment.

The Seer regarded him with interest, but that could have been mere curiosity about the amount of silver Tobias carried in his purse. He was lean, small, nearly as dark-skinned as Tobias, with large, dark eyes and delicate hands, one of which held the Tincture-soaked cloth. He gestured at a fourth, empty chair.

"Please, sit," he said, in that same drawling, accented voice.

"Why?"

"I can divine your future. I am a Seer. And you are...?"

Tobias eyed the other two men. The one who remained awake resembled the man who had spoken. He breathed through his cloth, his eyes following Tobias's every move.

The first man said something in a tongue Tobias didn't know. The other replied in the same language, his voice higher. The words had grace, a lightness and flow that made the language of the courts sound ponderous and slow. Their speech sounded familiar, and after a moment he realized why. Servants in the Travelers' palace – those who came from the Labyrinth – spoke the same language.

The first Seer repeated himself, his tone more strident. The other man stood and left through the doorway Tobias had used. Their sleeping companion never stirred.

"Now, we may speak without fear of interruption," the first Seer said. He indicated the chair again. "Please, sit. Tell me who you are."

"I'm new to the Notch. I'm learning my way around."

"All the more reason to let me ply my trade."

Tobias shook his head and turned to go. "I don't think so."

"You are not alone."

He stopped.

"You came to this place with a companion. You are worried about her, afraid something will happen to her."

"That's too easy," Tobias said, his back to the man. His voice was steady despite his fear, his sweating palms. "I'm sure many come here with companions."

"Not like yours. She is... a child. A baby."

Tobias wheeled. He faltered, then crossed to the chair. He didn't sit, though, and he stared at the unconscious Seer.

"He will not wake for many bells. I promise you, he is insensate."

"You saw us together. Last night when we first arrived."

"I did not. But I understand your skepticism. I hear such things daily from people who do not understand divination." He sniffed at his cloth again. "She is not your child. You love her very much, and yet you have been with her for only a matter of days."

Tobias's chest tightened. "How much?"

"Pay you mean? You decide that. After I look at your future."

"I'm not sure I want you looking."

"Is it your future you fear to see, or hers?"

"That's not your concern."

"It is, though. Mention of her is what made you stay."

Again, he made to leave. "That was my mistake."

"A friend of mine died in the castle," the man said before Tobias reached the doorway.

Osten Cavensol? No. Why would the sovereign's Seer know a man who lived in the Notch and took Tincture from a filthy piece of cloth?

"Was he an addict as well?"

"*That* was rude."

Tobias exhaled, his shoulders slumping. "Yes, it was." He walked back to the table, swung the sack off his shoulders, and dropped into the chair. "I'm sorry."

The man flicked his fingers, dismissing the apology. His

expression remained stony.

"Did you really know I would come here, or is that just something you say to get people in the door?"

"Can it not be both?"

"Who did you know in the castle?"

"A woman. We had not spoken in many years, but she and I hailed from the same island. Xharef, in the Labyrinth."

"The sovereign queen," Tobias whispered. "You knew her?"

"As I say, it was long ago. We played together as children, before any of us knew she was fated for... for a life more grand than most. Those from my island took great pride in her rise to royal power." He held the cloth to his nose and mouth, and took a long breath. "And you, where are you from?"

"Redcove, in Onyi."

"I know the island. I have never been to your village."

"Few have," Tobias said.

"You are a Traveler."

Tobias stiffened.

"It's all right. I am no friend of Sheraigh, and no enemy of yours. I would guess that you are a Walker, and that you came here from another time."

Too many people knew about him. Elinor and Jivv, the Tirribin, now this man. And, of course, Orzili, the most dangerous of all.

"You were a member of Mearlan's court?"

"I thought you intended to glimpse my future, not question me about my past."

A thin smile touched the man's lips and vanished. "Quite so." He stared at Tobias, his face impassive, his eyes turning glassy. Tobias wondered if he was on the verge of passing out like his sleeping companion.

Then he shook his head once, and a second time.

"I don't see much, actually."

"Is that a reflection on your talents or my future?" He asked the question with bravado, but feared the answer.

"My talents are not in question. It could be that you have little time left. Or it could be that you have too many possible futures and none has come to the fore." His smile appeared genuine. "I hope the latter is the case."

Tobias shivered. He didn't want to die, but more than that, he feared what might happen to the princess if he was killed.

"Yes," the man said, staring at him still. "I sense that you are on a winding path, one with so many twists and turns, so many possible sources of opportunity and danger, that trying to read your life right now is as futile as trying to predict a swallow's flight. I am sorry. It seems I promised more than I could give."

"I think I'm just as glad." He reached into his pocket for coins.

"You owe me nothing," the man said. "Because that is what I told you: nothing."

Tobias hadn't expected that. "Thank you."

"We can try again another day. My name is Hanrid, and you are welcome here any time." He proffered a hand, which Tobias gripped.

He stood, shouldering his pack once more.

"The girl is in danger," Hanrid said. "You know this already, otherwise you would not be here. Her future is even more clouded than yours."

"I'll do my best to keep her safe."

"That may not be enough."

"What else can I–"

The Seer held up a hand. "You keep her safe now by running. A wise course thus far. But for her to survive, you will have to fight back. You can only run so far. Those who pursue you have resources that go far beyond yours."

"Then how do I fight them? What you're saying makes no sense."

"Of course it does. You have to find the means to make yourself their equals. Soon."

Tobias's stomach clenched, but he dug into his pocket, pulled out a silver trey, and tossed it to the man. "That was worth something."

Hanrid grinned.

"You know who she is, don't you?"

The Seer dropped his gaze. "I choose not to look there," he said. "For the sake of us all."

CHAPTER 32

29th Day of Sipar's Settling, Year 633

Tobias didn't need Hanrid to tell him of the danger to Sofya, but hearing the urgency in the Seer's final words made Tobias impatient to return to Kaarti's inn.

He had yet to determine, though, if the blockade remained in place. He continued to the edge of the stone shelf and the drop to the coastline, and looked out over the rocky beach to the gulf. The city waterfront was hidden from him, but vessels still crowded the waters, which were roiled and dotted with whitecaps. If the Sheraigh navy had opened the port, these ships would be at the wharves. Getting away from Hayncalde remained a challenge.

He surveyed the strand, the stairway below the shelf, the shelters nearest to the mouth of the Notch. The beach was deserted, the stairs empty. Few of those in the Outer Notch seemed inclined to leave the place, or do much of anything for that matter. It was as Kaarti had said. These people were stuck here, too.

Except Tobias and Sofya weren't stuck – they were cornered.

On this thought, he made his way back into the Notch, keeping an eye out for soldiers or people who looked out of place.

Sofya was awake when he entered the shelter. She sat on the floor of the common area holding her doll and sucking her thumb. Seeing Tobias, she let out a shriek, dropped the doll, and reached for him with both arms.

Tobias scooped her up, swung her high, eliciting another squeal, and planted a kiss on her nose. Only then did he turn to Kaarti, who stood over the cooking fire.

"Thank you," he said.

"What did you find?"

"There are too many ships anchored in the gulf. The wharves must still be closed."

She straightened and faced him. "Yous can stay here as long as you need. Same price, same terms. And you can pay when yous are ready to leave."

"Again, my thanks."

Kaarti narrowed her eyes. "Something's bothering you."

"No, it's just..." He reflected on his conversation with the Seer. "I'm grateful to you. But I'm afraid to stay much longer."

She turned back to her cooking. "That's for yous to decide, not me."

Not long after, Tobias carried Sofya to their room, laid her down for a nap, and stretched out on his own pallet.

He hadn't intended to sleep, but he remained exhausted from his ordeal in the dungeon. His body was still recovering. He dreamed he was in the streets again, chased by uniformed guards, all of them with bayonets. Of course, Orzili walked at the head of the company that pursued him. Tobias ran from them, but carrying Sofya slowed him, and every few steps he dropped something vital – her swaddling, the goat's milk skin, his blade, the apertures, her doll.

He woke soaked in sweat, his shirt and bedding damp, hair clinging to his forehead. The aroma of Kaarti's cooking reached him. Sofya sat in her cradle, gazing at him, her thumb in her mouth. He swung off the pallet and changed her swaddling. Stepping out into the common room, he found Kaarti much as he had left her. Candles burned in the shelter. Daylight had begun to fade.

"Yous both slept," she said.

He nodded, still groggy

"We'll eat soon."

"It smells good."

He carried Sofya outside into the cool evening air, and stood at the edge of the cavern. The sky was clearing and the first stars had emerged.

"Where do I take you?" he whispered to her. "Where can we be safe?"

She laughed and whispered gibberish back at him.

"I've told you, there is no safe."

Tobias whirled, and fell back a pace.

Maeli stood a few steps from him, her pallid features aglow with the twilight. She grinned at his discomfort, exposing those tiny sharp teeth.

"What are you doing here?"

"I came to see you. Brother and I were curious." She regarded the front of the boarding house. "You've done well enough so far."

"Why do you say that?" Tobias asked, his mind racing to catch up with their conversation. "'There is no safe.' Are we in danger right now?"

"Always. Don't you know that?"

He did, of course. "Where's Teelo?"

"Feeding. He'll be along."

"I don't have much time."

She canted her head, sniffed. The smell of cooking fish surrounded them. "Ah! You intend to feed, too."

"Yes. Is the danger imminent? Is someone coming for us?"

The demon weighed this, sniffing the air again. "I don't sense them now, no. But they will come."

Tobias shivered, hearing in this an echo of what the Seer had told him. "How do you know? Have you gleaned something of our futures?"

"We don't do that." Her smile was sly, coy. "But we know someone who does."

"The Seers. I spoke with one this morning."

"Not them. Someone else, with real power."

He couldn't mask his interest. Maeli laughed.

She was baiting him. She was a predator and she'd identified his greatest weakness, his deepest need. He was but one man, skilled with weapons to be sure, but powerless. Until his chronofor was repaired, he couldn't escape this time, or fix what Orzili and his friends had broken.

"Who do you mean?" he asked. "Can you introduce us?"

"For what sort of payment?" Her gaze darted down to Sofya.

"No," Tobias said, his tone as firm as he could make it.

The demon's expression flattened. "Then I don't believe I can help you."

Teelo blurred into view, like a flame conjured from the gloaming. Seeing Tobias's expression, he frowned and rounded on his sister.

"What did you do?"

She glared at him. A moment later she walked away at demon speed.

Teelo looked at Tobias again. "What was that?"

"She said she knew of someone who could help us, but she wanted payment, and she hinted that she wanted it from..." He stopped himself before using the princess's real name. "From this one."

The demon stared at the spot where his sister had stood. "I wonder who she was thinking of. Did she say anything more?"

"She said we weren't safe, but she wouldn't tell me why. Then she said she knew of someone who could help – someone, she said, with 'real power.'"

Teelo nodded. "Ujie."

"What?"

"She meant Ujie. I'm certain of it."

"Who is that?"

He looked past Tobias to the boarding house. "Not here. I'll tell you later. Meet us on the outer shelf, at the stairs."

"And my payment?"

Teelo went still, weighing the question. "I don't know. Don't bring the girl."

"I thought you said you'd keep your sister from hurting her."

"I did. But I didn't say anything about protecting her from Ujie."

A chill ran through Tobias's body. "I don't know when I can be there. If I'm not going to bring–"

"Come when you can. Call for us."

Teelo left them, giving Tobias no chance to say more.

The canvas behind him rustled.

"Time to eat," Kaarti said.

Tobias scanned the path and the cavern one last time, but saw no sign of the demons. He walked to the doorway, pausing when the old woman remained in his path.

"Who were you talking to?"

He bounced the princess in his arms. "This one, of course."

Kaarti appeared unconvinced, but she led him inside.

As the three of them ate – fresh bread, and a fish stew redolent of bay and tearroot – Tobias thought about the Tirribin and the Seer. He wondered who this Ujie might be. Kaarti regarded him throughout their meal, but nary a word passed between them. Not long after they had finished and cleared the table, Tobias bade Kaarti goodnight, and carried Sofya into their room to put her to bed.

He lay down as well, but he kept himself awake, listening to the innkeeper as she rattled about in the kitchen and larder, waiting for her to extinguish the candles in the common area and retire to her room.

Even after she did, he remained abed, giving her time to fall asleep. Sofya's breathing deepened into a steady slow rhythm.

Noise from beyond the canvas walls of the boarding house diminished.

When Tobias was convinced that Kaarti was sleeping, he rose, checked on Sofya, and stole from the shelter onto the cavern's stone shelf. He saw no one.

The night had grown cold, and he walked toward the shoreline with his hands in his pockets. Vapor from his breath billowed and vanished in the intermittent torchlight.

Once he crossed into the Outer Notch, he saw more people walking along the stone pathway, drinking in front of shelters, kissing in shadowed recesses. He kept his head down as he neared the brothel, ignoring the entreaties and laughter of the women he passed there. He slowed as he neared the Seers' shelter, but smelled no Tincture, and assumed that they slept.

Striding by the mouth of one last cavern, he came around a shallow bend and caught sight of the gulf, her waters sparkling with moonlight. Torches burned on the stone shelf and a few couples lay together on blankets, some clothed, some not.

Tobias walked to the farthest end of the shelf, beyond the last torch, and said, "Teelo, Maeli," in a low voice. He didn't think he would need to shout for them.

The Tirribin appeared before him on a narrow ledge along the rock face outside the shelf. Even if the couples had been looking, they wouldn't have seen the demons.

"What did you bring us?" Maeli asked, her voice as cold as starlight.

"Nothing."

"That wasn't smart. We don't offer help for nothing."

"You're not being nice."

She glared at Teelo. "We're Tirribin. We don't feed on nice. We don't feed on favors. We don't feed on charity. You forget that too often, brother."

A memory stirred in Tobias's mind – something Wansi had told him long ago.

"I don't have payment, but I have a riddle."

Teelo regarded him avidly. Even Maeli appeared intrigued, though she tried to mask her interest.

"We like riddles," she said. "But it had better be a good one. We don't like easy ones. A poor riddle is worse than no riddle at all."

"All right," Tobias said. "Listen carefully:

"Down I live, up I die,
In dark I thrive, in day turn dry;
Half of a whole, I mirror my twin,
But lack the glory, of her tresses and skin."

It was an old teaser, one that children puzzled over in the northern isles. He hoped the Tirribin didn't know it.

Sister and brother both blinked several times and then bent close to each other, whispering frantically.

"You promised me help," Tobias said.

Maeli frowned at the interruption, and annoyance flickered in Teelo's face as well. She turned toward the waters of the gulf and said, "Ujie."

Then they were whispering again. Tobias didn't dare disturb them a second time.

Barely a tencount passed before someone – something – stepped from the surf below, crossed the strand to the stone stairway and began to climb. Tobias watched the figure, fascination and fear warring within him. It looked to be a woman, naked, black hair flowing to the small of her back, wet skin the color of sea water and glistening with starlight and torch glow.

She moved with liquid grace, turning the simple act of ascending the stairs into a sort of dance. Tobias stood transfixed, unable to look away, embarrassed and aroused by the gentle swing of her breasts, the lithe beauty of her limbs.

When she finally reached the top of the stairway, she turned unerringly and walked to where Tobias stood with the Tirribin, her steps leaving damp footprints on the rock. Her face was as beautiful as her form, her cheekbones high, her jaw tapering softly to her chin, her lips full and sensuous, her eyes widely spaced. With her perfect features and gleaming black hair, she seemed a full grown version of the time demons. Only her eyes marked her as different. They were completely silver, without distinct irises. In place of round pupils, she had slitted ones like those of a serpent.

"She summoned me on your behalf?" the creature asked, her voice like waves crashing against stone.

Her scent reached him: brine, seaweed, rain, the sweet residue of lightning. It was intoxicating.

"Yes," he said, remembering that she had asked a question.

He could guess what she was, though he had never seen her kind before. The eyes, the sculpted, naked form, the long hair, and, of course, the fact that the creature had emerged from the water: these were all the hints he needed.

"You're an Arrokad demon."

"I am Arrokad, yes. Demon is a moniker your kind use to describe those of us who are strange to you. I am no more a demon than the Tirribin or Shonla."

Tobias had never encountered any Shonla, but he knew them as mist demons. Nevertheless, he didn't argue.

"Forgive me."

"You have paid the Tirribin?"

"In a way," Tobias said. "I refused to give them years, but distracted them with a riddle."

She gazed at Teelo and Maeli, her grin revealing teeth much like theirs.

"That was cleverly done. But you will have to pay me as well."

"I haven't asked you for anything. I don't even know what I

would ask if I could. Maeli summoned you without telling me what she was going to do."

"Yet, I was summoned. There is a price for that."

Of course. "What price?" he asked, his voice leeched of emotion.

In answer, the Arrokad brushed her gaze over the length of his body, at the same time tracing a finger lightly from the base of her throat, between her breasts, to her navel.

"A small price, really. One you might enjoy, if you can withstand it."

Tobias took an unsteady breath and looked off to the side. Somehow her scent grew stronger.

"The idea of lying with me makes you uncomfortable." Her voice had turned soothing: surf lapping at sandy shores. "Perhaps you would prefer one of my brothers?"

"It's not that," he said, his mouth dry.

She stepped closer. "Then what? You fear me? Perhaps you have heard that the act of love with my kind can be perilous? I promise to be as gentle as I can." She laughed and caressed his cheek with a crooked finger.

Her touch was as cold as ocean fog, and yet it set his pulse racing and lit a fire in his chest, his stomach, his loins. He took another ragged breath.

"You are not as you appear," Ujie said, withdrawing her hand, her smile slipping. Her eyes strayed again to the time demons, the slitted pupils widening slightly. "A Walker, then. More youthful than you appear. I should have known. What do you require of me?"

"I don't even know."

"Why did the Tirribin call for me?"

"I asked her if we were in danger, and—"

"We?"

He didn't falter for long. Arrokad were known to be as capricious as the sea, but from all that Tobias had heard and read of Ujie's kind, he didn't believe she would betray him. "I'm harboring the princess of Hayncalde, and have been since–"

She made an abrupt gesture, genuine disappointment manifest on her lovely face. "We do not involve ourselves in the squabblings of your courts."

"She's a child – she can't even walk yet, or speak – and men are trying to kill her."

"Which is why we want nothing to do with matters of this sort. Your kind are like animals. You are governed by your most base instincts. You know nothing of nuance, of compassion, of the subtler arts." Her laughter was the frothing of sea foam. "And you dare to call us demons."

"You save ships from storms. You grant wishes. You… you heal and give knowledge. All I ask is a bit of help to keep a child alive."

"And yourself?"

"Yes, and myself. I'm all she has. I'm responsible for her."

"Where is she now? Surely if you are responsible for her, you would not leave her alone, untended." She quirked an eyebrow. "Unguarded."

"She's safe," Tobias said, hoping it was true, and fighting the urge to run back to Kaarti's shelter. "For now, at least. But we need to leave this place. Can you help us?"

"I cannot," Ujie said. "I do not care to take a hand in your fight, and my powers do not allow me to transport you both. If you were alone, and willing to… to give yourself to me, I could carry you with me through the depths." She gestured toward the shoreline and the water beyond. Tobias shivered.

"But both of you?" she continued. "I have no help to offer you. As recompense for refusing you, though, I shall demand no payment for my summoning. I consider your debt to me paid in full."

She started away from him.

"No!"

The Arrokad stopped in mid-turn, a menacing gleam in her silver eyes.

"What other payment can I offer? There must be something I can give you."

"You refuse to lie with me, but would you offer a life?"

"What do you mean?"

"Another. Someone with whom I might... play, without having to concern myself with being gentle, or kind. It has been too long since I had such sport."

Tobias managed to keep from showing his distaste. "I'd rather not."

"I thought as much. For a barbaric species you are squeamish about the oddest things."

"There must be something else."

"I have no use of material things. I know more of this world than you ever will. What could you have that I want?" She leered. "Aside from the obvious."

"I have powers."

"I know this already." Her gaze narrowed. "Still, you would offer to Walk for me, to move through time?"

"That's right. I might be able to help you in return for whatever help you give me."

"You speak of a boon."

"Yes."

"Any boon, even one you have refused to give me tonight."

"All right."

Her lips curled, quickening his heart again. "And I could claim this boon at my whim?"

Tobias sensed that he had sailed into uncertain waters. It was said in the northern isles that only a fool bartered with demons. *A desperate fool.* "As long as it doesn't compromise in any way my ability to keep the princess safe."

Her eyes narrowed again. "To what end? I have already told you: I will not resort to violence on your behalf, and I cannot spirit you from this place. What else would you ask?"

What indeed? Despite his misgivings, he sensed that this was an opportunity he couldn't afford to squander. Even if the Arrokad couldn't help him now, eventually she might. "I'm not sure," he said, knowing better than to lie. "You have other abilities, and long after we leave this place, we'll still be in danger."

She appraised him anew. "You are foresighted for a human." After a fivecount, she lifted an aqua shoulder, the gesture strangely ordinary for such a creature. "Very well. An exchange of promises then. Boons to be determined in the future."

"Yes."

"That is fair." She made an odd, circular motion with her hand. "We have a bargain, you and I, freely entered and fairly sworn. Yes?"

He nodded, certain that he had made a terrible mistake, but unsure as to what it was exactly.

"Say it."

"We have a bargain. Freely entered, fairly sworn."

Her smile dazzled, made him forget his fear, if only for an instant. She reached out to touch him again. Tobias flinched and she hesitated. "I will not harm you."

He winced, an apology. "I know. Your touch is… unsettling."

"It can be much more." The look she gave him stole his breath. "Another time, perhaps. If I may…" Her eyes widened, a question in their depths.

Tobias dipped his chin once, held still as her fingertips pressed lightly on his brow. Again, the cold penetrated his skin, but then warmed as it spread through him.

"We are linked now," Ujie said. "You do not need the Tirribin to summon me. Simply speak my name, and I will come." She held up a finger. "Provided you are within a league of seawater. That is as far as my demesne goes. If you are too far from the shore, I cannot help you."

"I'll remember that."

She faced the time demons. "Cousins!"

Teelo and Maeli took only a single step, but in an instant they were standing directly in front of Tobias and Ujie. They paid the Arrokad little heed. Rather, they stared up at Tobias, wringing their hands, their bodies quivering.

"What is it?" Teelo asked, his voice higher than usual. "You have to tell us what it is."

Tobias had no idea what they meant.

"Your riddle," Ujie said.

"Oh, of course. Tree roots."

Both of them closed their eyes and sighed, as if they had just eaten the most satisfying of sweets.

"A good riddle," Maeli said, eyes still closed. "You must ask us another some time. That was better than feeding."

"I take my leave," Ujie said.

The Tirribin looked up at her.

"He's made payment?" Maeli asked.

"We have an arrangement. You need not concern yourself with the terms."

The girl frowned, but asked no more questions.

"Farewell, Walker," Ujie said. She crossed to the stairs, her hips swaying, torchlight shining on her shoulders.

Teelo sighed again, watching as she began her descent to the shore. "She's beautiful. Sometimes I wish–"

"Don't," Maeli said, a warning in her green eyes. "That's just disgusting."

After watching Ujie make her way into the gulf, Tobias bid goodnight to the Tirribin and hurried back through the Outer Notch. He had no trouble ignoring the invitations of the women outside the brothel. After speaking with Ujie… Well, he would need a good night's sleep to get the Arrokad out of his thoughts.

As he approached Kaarti's inn, he heard soft singing from

within. Shouldering the canvas aside, he found the woman sitting in the common room. A candle burned on the table beside her. Sofya lay in her lap, eyes closed, thumb in her mouth.

The matron glowered.

"What happened?"

She held a rigid finger to her lips.

He crossed to them and squatted before the chair. "What happened?" he asked again, this time in a whisper. "Is she all right?"

"She's fine. She woke, started crying. I thought for sure yous was gonna wake up, too, and take care of her. Feed her, and change her swaddling, or whatever it was that woke her. But no, she just kept up her squalling.

"Finally I gets up to see what the matter is, thinking yous might be dead or something. But it's worse than that. Yous was just gone. For all I know, yous ain't coming back."

"Of course I'd come back," he said, offended.

"How am I supposed to know that, eh? Yous was gone, without a word."

Tobias swallowed his first answer. "You're right. I'm sorry I left."

His apology seemed to sap her anger. She lifted Sofya into his arms and stood, stretching her back.

"Where were you anyway?"

"Outer Notch."

Her brow buckled in disapproval. "What were yous up to there?"

"I had a conversation. Nothing more."

"Folk don't usually go to the Outer Notch for conversation."

"It's the truth." He brushed a strand of hair from the princess's face. "I'm tired. I'll see you in the morning."

"This have anything to do with the voices I heard out front before supper?"

He tensed.

"I thought I heard yous talking to someone, and I thought I might have seen yous with a child. A boy. He was there and then in a blink he wasn't and I wasn't sure if I'd imagined it."

"There was no one," he said, but his denial lacked conviction.

"I've known demons in my time," she said. "Yous don't live this long by the sea without meeting one or two."

"I can't talk about this."

"Their kind aren't to be trusted. They talk in half-truths, they bargain in bad faith, and they don't give a fairy's fart about the likes of us."

He straightened, looked her in the eye. "I'll keep that in mind. And I won't bring trouble to your door."

"More trouble, you mean. I've already got my share, and I've an inkling yous carry some wherever yous go."

Tobias didn't answer.

"Very well. G'night to yous both." She shambled away.

"Thank you, Kaarti. Again, my apologies."

She stopped and favored him with a rare smile. "Truth is, it weren't so bad. Been a long time since I was up nights with a wee one."

CHAPTER 33

10th Day of Kheraya's Descent, Year 647

Despite her promise to Droë that she would commence her search for Tobias before long, Mara remained in her own time. Not that there was much to hold her here. After she refused Nat's invitation to join him in the upper courtyard, their friendship wilted. She and Hilta didn't speak. Delvin was still recovering from the wounds to his back. And she wanted little to do with any of the other trainees.

Trainees. Even thinking the word made her flinch.

It should be novitiates.

She had never felt more alone.

She attempted no more Walks in the damp and dark of pre-dawn. She had mastered the ability as much as she could hope, and refused to expend more of her days with the exercises.

She also avoided the courtyards at night, unwilling to risk another encounter with the Tirribin. At some point soon, she would make the journey. Until then, she didn't wish to answer questions about her intentions.

She kept her distance from Wansi, too. Each day, after working on her sextant, she stowed her tools with practiced care and fled the chamber with the rest of the trainees. She felt the Binder's gaze upon her as she walked out of the room, unable to explain the guilt that plagued her.

She attended her lessons, trained under Saffern's approving eye, slumbered and woke when the other trainees did. To all outward appearances, she existed as memory told her she always had.

All the while, her awareness of time's discontinuity deepened, further alienating her from the life she knew. Everything she did – even lessons and training – struck her as frivolous, as luxuries she couldn't afford.

Feidys's lessons on the current wars pounded at her like an assault. She absorbed every tidbit the mistress offered about the origins of the conflicts, but she could barely endure the discussions themselves. How could the others not see that all the mistress described for them should have been fiction? How could Feidys not understand this?

Unable to speak of this with anyone, she pondered what she learned in isolation, when walking from one lesson to the next, or awaiting her turn to shoot on the training grounds, or lying in bed at night. She was desperate to glean something that would explain how a Walker could trigger such events.

A Walker.

Tobias.

Her life had changed in this regard as well. She could picture him now; she had seen the two of them together. The image of their kiss remained with her, intruding upon her thoughts, her dreams, her purpose. She wanted to believe that if she Walked back so far, she would do so to change this future, to mend a rent in the fabric of history. But she would also be going back to find Tobias, to discover a friendship and, dare she hope, a love, that she should never have lost.

If she could gather the courage to Walk so many years.

Three nights after she Spanned across the courtyard with a chronofor in hand, she went to see Delvin in the infirmary.

A few days before, the palace healer had made clear, quietly, that he could have visitors. Hilta, Mara knew, had gone several times. Nat had visited twice. Mara hadn't intended to go at all, but his beating had forced her to practice Walking. Perhaps speaking with him would spur her to leave.

Guards stood outside his door. They marked her approach, saying nothing, gripping their muskets. Their bayonets gleamed with light from the open windows. She wanted to scream at them to go away, but she ignored them and let herself into the room.

He lay on his side with his back to the door. All the beds but his were empty. She closed the door and walked toward him.

"That you?" he asked, no doubt meaning Hilta.

"Wouldn't anyone answer yes?"

He craned his neck to look her way, his eyes wide.

"Mar! What are you… I wasn't expecting you."

"No, I don't suppose."

She walked to the far side of his bed and sat in a chair. He looked wan and thinner than usual. He wore no shirt. Thick bandages covered his back. She wished the Two would strike down the chancellor where he stood. An unworthy thought, the priestess would tell her. She didn't care.

"How are you feeling?" she asked, after a brief but deeply uncomfortable silence.

"Not too bad. The healer says I'll be out of here in another few days."

"Why has it taken so long?"

His gaze flitted away. "The chancellor wouldn't let her use magick. Said that would be too easy on me."

Their conversation flagged again.

"I'm sorry, Mar," he said after some time. "What I did wasn't… You didn't deserve that."

"Doesn't matter."

He grinned. The old grin she remembered so well, from a past that shouldn't have been real. "You could pretend it mattered a little."

Mara laughed.

"Did you ever figure out what was bothering you that day?"

"Yes," she said.

"What was it?"

"I'm not sure how to explain it. I was right in a way. I don't belong here, and I think I know what to do about that. I can't tell you more. I'm sorry."

He shook his head, eyes avoiding hers. "Don't apologize. Not for anything."

For a third time, they lapsed into silence. Whatever had driven her here, she needed to go.

"I'm not sure when I'll see you again," she said. It sounded strange, awkward, but she pressed on. "I wanted to say that… that I've missed you, and I hope the Two watch over you."

He looked at her as if she were mad. "I told you, I'm getting out in a few days."

"Right. I know. Anyway, I just wanted to come by and see how you were." She stood, but remained in place. "Don't steal any more food, all right?"

"Sure," he said, still frowning. "Whatever you say."

Mara left him, glancing his way once as she reached the door. He still lay on his side, his back to her. She let herself out of the room and hurried away from the soldiers.

The following day, as Mara and the other trainees put away their tools and filed out of Wansi's chamber, the Binder asked Mara to remain behind.

Nat regarded her, guarded curiosity in his expression.

Mara ignored him and detached herself from the group, letting the others step past her.

When they were gone, Wansi told her to shut the door, and motioned her back to the table. Mara sat on the bench, her pulse galloping.

"I'm sorry," the Binder said. "You've avoided me for several days, and I've tried to honor your desire to be left alone. I don't know what you've decided to do, but today I received word from the chancellor that a unit of Oaqamaran warriors will be arriving here this evening. They're to be piloted to Vleros in the morning. As one of our senior Spanners, you'll be expected to activate a tri-sextant on their behalf. I... I thought you should know."

She should have been terrified – and she was – but she felt relief as well. She couldn't delay any longer; events had moved beyond her control. "Then I'll have to leave tonight."

Wansi straightened. "So you've decided. I thought perhaps you were still struggling with your decision."

Mara stood and wandered to the open window. "I was. Now..." She left the thought unfinished.

"Have you practiced again?"

"No. I've learned that I can Span while holding a chronofor, and I assume I can Walk with a sextant as well. That's all I've done. I didn't want to spend any more days."

"Understandable."

Mara's laugh sounded bitter. "Is it? I'm contemplating a Walk of years. How can I worry about a day here and there?"

"Would you Walk first and then Span, or the other way around?"

She faced the Binder, irked that she would ask such a mundane question. "I hadn't given it much thought."

"You should. The Walk is by far the more dangerous journey. It might be better to do it somewhere safe. A place where you have a friend."

"Are you offering to help me?"

"I am. I've been in Windhome, with my workshop in this very chamber, for nearly twenty years: a longer time than you plan to Walk. We can't be certain of exactly when you'll arrive. It could be midnight. It could be in the middle of a lesson. But chances are I'll be here. And I believe I've long had the proper temperament to take your arrival in stride, no matter when it occurs."

When Mara didn't answer, the Binder's brow furrowed. "Unless you had some other location in mind."

"No, I haven't."

"But you aren't yet ready to make this choice."

She threw her arms wide. "When will I ever be ready? How am I supposed to prepare for something like this?"

"I don't know. Has the Tirribin been much help?"

"I've been avoiding her, too."

"I see."

She thought she heard disapproval in the Binder's tone. "You think I should go."

"I don't, actually."

Mara stared.

"Surprised you, didn't I?" At Mara's nod, she said, "Even as a young woman, I would never have done what you're considering. The sacrifice is too great, the chance of success too remote. I would have been frightened beyond words, and I would have hidden behind that fear. All along I've known that you're more likely to do this than not. I admire you."

"Even though I'm fated to fail?"

"I'm sorry?"

"You said my chance of success is remote."

"I meant that mine would be. Somehow, I think the odds are better for you."

Mara frowned. "You're confusing me. First you said you didn't think I should go. Now you're telling me the opposite."

"I'm saying what I always have: this is your decision to make."

Mara gazed out the window again and brushed her hair back off her shoulders. "I can't pilot those soldiers," she said, her voice low. "The war shouldn't be fought. Not like this. I don't want any part of it."

"The last time we spoke, I mentioned that Mearlan IV was assassinated some fourteen years ago, ending the Hayncalde

Supremacy in favor of Sheraigh's line. The wars as we know them began around that time, and large numbers of tri-devices came into use soon after. That assassination may well have been the event that triggered all of this."

"I've thought the same thing," Mara told her, "based on what we've learned from Feidys. But that makes no sense. Tobias was summoned to the court of Daerjen by their sovereign. We can't know who exactly, but none of the choices seems likely. If Noak Sheraigh was already sovereign, he wouldn't have needed to send him back to assassinate Mearlan. Certainly Mearlan wouldn't plot his own death, and I can't believe some other Hayncalde royal would destroy the family's supremacy."

"Maybe it was coincidence, and the Walker's actions had nothing to do with the assassination."

Mara rubbed her temples. "Thinking about this makes my head hurt."

Wansi smiled. "Indeed."

"Droë told me it was Tobias who changed history."

"Those were her words?"

"No, but that was the essence of what she said. He went back in time, and it all changed as a result."

"Which brings us back to where we were. You have a choice to make. Quickly, it would seem." She canted her head. "What matters to you more: this Walker, Tobias, and the discontinuity of time you've sensed, or the life you would leave behind were you to Walk so far?"

Mara opened her mouth, closed it again. An instant later, tears cascaded from her eyes and sobs choked off her breathing. Wansi blinked, appearing nonplussed by what her question had unleashed.

For some time, Mara couldn't speak. Wansi approached her and patted her shoulder in awkward solicitude. When Mara finally regained some measure of composure, she dabbed her eyes and cheeks with the fringe of her sleeve and forced a smile that couldn't have been convincing.

"You're all right?" Wansi asked.

"Yes. I'm sorry."

"I think I should be apologizing to you."

"No, it's not your fault, I just... Is it terrible to say that I don't care about my life here?"

"Not terrible," the Binder said, measuring her words. "I'm not sure I believe you, though."

"It's true."

"Your friends–"

"My friends are fools."

Wansi raised an eyebrow.

"All right, maybe that's not fair to them. But there's already this distance between all of them and me. No one knows what I'm feeling. None of them is even capable of understanding. I'm alone right now. And my family... I haven't seen any of them in years."

"Then why did what I said affect you so?"

More tears welled in her eyes. "Because I'm not ready yet to be an adult." Her voice cracked on the last word, and sobs shook her again.

"You don't have to do this."

"Yes, I do," she said through tears. "That's why I'm so afraid. Look at what they did to Delvin. I can't allow this to go on, and I can't pretend I don't know what's happened."

"Going back in time might not stop the chancellor from hurting Mister Ruhj."

"You don't understand. They're not supposed to be here. Not the chancellor. Not the soldiers. We're not supposed to be ruled by the Oaqamarans."

"You know this?"

Did she know it? Could she be sure about any of it? In the end, she decided she did, and could.

"Yes, I know it. That's why I *have* to go back. But I've never been more scared to do anything."

The Binder grimaced. "You know I'll help you in any way I can."

She bobbed her head, tears falling to the floor. "Thank you."

It took a qua'bell for Mara to stop crying. Wansi eyed her with sympathy, but held her tongue, which was probably for the best. Anything she said would probably have brought more tears.

When Mara had calmed herself, the Binder said, "Your friends will be wondering where you are. You should return here this evening, after the meal. We'll send you back then."

A shiver ran through Mara's body. "All right. I might take a little longer to get here. I want to speak with Droë first."

"I believe that's wise. You can bring her with you if you like. She might be able to help us."

Mara shook her head. "She won't come, but she'll speak to me alone." She crossed to the door. Her hands shook and her teeth chattered, though the chamber was warm. "Thank you, again," she said, looking back at the Binder.

"I'm not sure I deserve your thanks. I'm making it easier for you to do something that may prove an awful mistake."

Mara had no reply. She opened the door and slipped out into the dim corridor.

The girl's summons sang in Droë's mind like a plucked string on a harp. Even had she wanted to resist, she couldn't have. Compulsion drew her from the between, blunting sensation, muffling sound, slowing vision to a mind-numbing crawl. She felt herself take form, growing solid, heavy, slow, though not by human measures. Drawing breath, she tasted the wind: vegetation, stone, brine, the acrid smoke of cooking fires, and humans, ripe with so many years.

Moonlight rimed the grass in the courtyard and the palace stonework. Mara stood before her, out of sight of the soldiers on the ramparts. Her eyes were bright in her dark face and wind twisted her hair.

"Another summons," Droë said, testing her voice. It was always hard to speak at first. "You know there's a price."

"Not for me."

Confidence in the words, resolve. The girl was changed, though not from Walking. Droë sensed no more displacement in her years.

"You sound certain."

"I am. We're partners in this. You named me a friend and told me your true name."

Droë's mood soured further. She didn't like being reminded. Her love for Tobias, and her desperate need to find him, had colored her judgment.

"Even so. Nothing is free."

"I won't–" The girl clamped her mouth against whatever she'd intended to say.

I won't give you years. That was what she'd been thinking. She was learning. After the promises Droë had made – to Tobias and to her – such a declaration would have angered her.

Droë nodded. "Very good. You're getting smarter. Still, there are other forms of payment."

"You like riddles."

She dismissed the suggestion with a brush of her fingers. "I don't mean them, either."

"Then what?"

Droë approached the girl and began to circle, her hands held behind her back. "What's it like to kiss a boy?"

The girl's brow bunched. "What makes you think–"

"I've seen you and your friends up there." She pointed toward the upper reaches of the palace. "Boys and girls go there together. Sometimes girls are with girls and boys with boys, but always they kiss and touch each other. What's that like?"

Heat from the girl's cheeks could have kindled damp wood.

"The question embarrasses you. Why? Why do humans care so much about touching and kissing, but never want to talk about it?"

"It's… private. Kissing isn't just pressing lips together. It's emotional. It makes us feel exposed."

"I kissed Tobias once."

Surprise widened the girl's eyes.

"I made him kiss me, really. I don't think he wanted to. But I was curious. I'd seen him kiss you."

"Then you know."

Droë shook her head, solemn and a little sad. "No, I don't think I do. Does it feel nice when you kiss and touch?"

The girl's cheeks warmed again, and a self-conscious smile stole across her lips, but she didn't look away. "Yes, it does. It feels nice, and a bit exciting, and even comforting, all at the same time."

Droë pointed at the girl's breasts. "Do you let them touch those?"

Her smile vanished, and the heat rose to the top of her scalp. "I'm not going to talk about that."

She laughed and clapped her hands. "I thought so!"

The girl scowled and held a finger to her lips for quiet. Droë thought she might leave. Instead, she gathered herself and drew herself up to her full height. "I've decided to Walk back," she said, whispering, "to try to find Tobias. If you're still willing to help me, I'd be grateful."

"Help you how?" Droë asked, also in a whisper.

"I need to know how far I should go. What I know of history tells me that he might have gone back as much as fourteen years, but the palace Binder isn't certain that's even possible."

"It is. It would be very, very hard, but it can be done. Maybe not by you, though. You're a Walker now – you weren't before. You're still new to it, though. A Walk that far could kill you."

All the warmth left the girl's face in a rush. "Because there's no air in the between."

Droë nodded her approval. "Good."

"Do I have to do it all at once?"

Her eyebrows rose. "A clever question. No, you don't. If you go back in stages, though, you have to make certain that you don't bend the future along the way. Do you understand?"

"Yes, I can't interact with too many people."

"You shouldn't speak with anyone at all."

"I might need to, but only one."

Droë shook her head. "None would be better."

The girl took a long, shaky breath. "I'll see what I can do. Tell me how far. Is fourteen years right?"

Droë closed her eyes and sifted back through the folds, searching for the place where this misfuture began. She knew better than to think she could find it exactly, but her conversation with Tresz, and things the girl had said gave her some idea of where to look. She opened her eyes again. The girl watched her, eager, frightened.

"Fourteen years is close. Maybe half a year more. No farther than that. You shouldn't go back too far. You'll make matters worse."

"What if I don't go back far enough?"

She shrugged. "Fourteen years is where you'll start. This—" she gestured at the palace, the sky, the world, "—didn't happen at once. The new path began then, but it took... time to develop. If you're close, and you can change that path, it may be enough. Better too little than too much. Fourteen and four maybe."

"How should I do that? Change the path, I mean."

Droë opened her hands. "I don't know what you'll discover in that time, or where you'll have to go to find Tobias. By my nature, I can sense when time has been altered. What you're asking..." She shook her head. "That's more than I can know."

"I don't know what this future is supposed to be like. I sense that it's wrong, that certain things shouldn't be. But what's right?"

"I can't see it, either," Droë said. "That's why you need Tobias. He knows. He's lived the future that was lost. He knows what happened when he went back. You know how the world looks now. Together, the two of you know all you need to."

"Which means that finding Tobias has to be my first goal."

She said this in a voice like warm fire, a voice that sounded like kisses and touches. Envy flared in Droë's heart.

"Yes," she said. But she barely resisted the urge to take all the girl's years.

CHAPTER 34

Mara returned to Wansi's chamber along the covered paths, shielded from the Oaqamaran guards, her stomach as roiled as her thoughts. It felt odd to undertake such a journey with nothing in hand save her chronofor and sextant. She was going so far – she might never come back. Yet she could take nothing with her. No mementos of this life, no weapons to keep herself safe, not even a stitch of clothing. She would emerge into a different time as vulnerable as the day she was born.

Except she would be a grown woman.

She halted, tottered, nearly vomited.

You don't have to do this.

Wansi's words: true only in the most literal sense.

She continued around the courtyard. Footsteps ahead of her forced her to hide in shadows. Once the soldiers had passed, she went on, quickening her pace.

The Binder sat at her workbench, a loupe to her eye, a sextant before her. She spared Mara a glance as she let herself into the chamber, but said nothing and turned back to her task, as if this were any night, as if Mara's appearance there wasn't worthy of comment.

Anger bubbled up in Mara's chest.

Fortunately, before she could give voice to her irritation, the Binder removed the loupe and faced her.

"I want you to take this sextant," she said, holding up the

device on which she'd been working. "Yours is good, I'm sure. You do fine work. But you're going to be Spanning a long way, and I want to be certain that you arrive where you expect to."

Mara swallowed and walked to where the Binder sat. "Thank you," she said, taking the sextant.

She could hardly bring herself to look the Binder in the eye. If her instincts were so poor on a matter as simple as this, how could she trust herself to change the flow of history?

"You spoke with the Tirribin?"

Mara exhaled. "She said fourteen years and a few turns."

"The Two have mercy."

She ignored this. "She also said I don't have to go back all at once. I can go back some years and then go back more. I just have to take care not to interact with people along the way. And she told me not to go back too far. 'Better too little than too much,' she said."

Wansi frowned at this. "Do you know why?"

"If I go back too far, I risk affecting events leading up to whatever Tobias did."

"Thus compounding the problem."

"Yes."

The Binder stood, sighed. "Very well. Are you ready?"

No. "As ready as I'm likely to be."

"How far will you go?"

"I don't know. Fourteen years—"

"Is too much for you to risk right now. You're still an inexperienced Walker."

"Seven years then? And two turns?"

"Even that could be too far."

Mara couldn't argue. A day struck her as too far. This… this was impossible. But she couldn't go back a day at a time.

"Each time I show up in this chamber, I risk changing history. I can't go back in too many increments."

The Binder's expression sharpened, but she dipped her

chin. "You're right." She held out her hand. "Give me your chronofor. I want to adjust it."

"You adjusted it only a few days ago."

Wansi kept her hand extended, and raised an eyebrow. Mara pulled the device from her pocket and gave it to her.

Perching on her stool again, and setting the loupe in place, Wansi opened the back. "You know," she said as she worked, a glow of power surrounding her, "seven years is probably a good number. That long ago, you were too young to work in this chamber. Much less than seven years, and you risk meeting yourself here."

"You've spoken of that before. What happens if a Walker meets herself?"

Wansi paused to look her way. "Honestly, I don't know. Some say such interactions can cause insanity. Others claim they can upset the balance of a life forever, creating as much dissonance in one person's existence as you perceive in the world right now. And some are certain that nothing bad will happen at all. I've never met a Walker who had this sort of encounter, but it seems a terrible chance to take."

Mara murmured her agreement.

The Binder made another small adjustment in the chronofor and closed the back with an echoing click. Her glow receding, she handed the device back to Mara.

"All set," she said, with forced brightness.

Mara set the chronofor and her new sextant on the table beside her and removed her robe. As she took off the rest of her clothes, Wansi rose from her workbench and stepped to the window.

"Seven years, then," she said, staring out at the night.

"And two turns, I think."

"And two turns, of course."

Too soon Mara stood naked and shivering in the chamber, staring at the Binder's back. It occurred to her then to wonder how her actions in the next few moments might change the Binder's life. Wansi, of course, was too circumspect to say anything of this, and it seemed to Mara that she had come too far to reconsider. But that didn't stop her from doubting herself yet again.

"Droë told me her true name," she said, in a shaking voice, "so that she'd know to help me in the past. Do I need something similar for you?"

"I think not. You're here in this chamber, carrying a chronofor and a sextant of my own design, the latter a device I first constructed some eighteen years ago. That should be credential enough."

Mara eyed the sextant. It resembled others she had seen in the chamber. She wondered if the younger Wansi would recognize it.

"You know what to do?"

"Eighty-six clicks back," Mara said. "With the turns stem."

"Just so. Farewell, Miss Lijar. Our world depends on you."

"Thank you for all you've done."

The Binder pivoted slightly, just enough to reveal the smile on her lips. "It has been my distinct pleasure. Thank you for all you're about to do."

Mara pulled out the right-most stem and began to turn it, counting with care, her fear rising with each metallic click. Her fingers grew slick with sweat. Several times she paused to wipe her hand on the clothes piled before her. When at last she twisted the stem for the last time, she glanced at Wansi. The Binder stood like a statue, her back to Mara, her arms crossed.

Mara could think of nothing more to say. She filled her chest with a deep breath and pressed the center stem.

The tug in her gut felt no different, no more or less insistent for the distance she would Walk this time. It yanked her back into the between, irresistible and merciless.

Besieged by the inchoate clamor, the flare of countless

visions, the foul accretion of scents and flavors, the abrasion of her flesh, she could do nothing but wait and pray to the Two that seven years' of sensation would pass before her lungs failed her. She wanted to scream, to weep, to squeeze her eyes shut and cover her ears. She held the chronofor in one hand and the sextant in the other.

On it went. Her chest tightened. Her throat burned. She staggered; had there been anything here with her, she would have grabbed hold of it to keep from falling. The between held her upright, even as it slowly killed her.

Light. Sound. Smell. Taste. And no air. Unrelenting. Too far. She should have known better. She should have heeded Wansi's warnings. Who was Tobias that the lure of his affection should cost her so much?

She released the breath she held, tried to draw another. But, of course, that had been her last. Her vision swam. The sounds and smells retreated.

Still it didn't end. Yes, too far. Darkness took her.

Distant voices brought awareness: the din had gone. An ache in her throat; solid ground under her back. Cool air on her cheek, filling her. The beat of her own heart.

Those voices – they set off alarm bells in her mind. Voices were bad, dangerous. She'd arrived during a lesson. She heard no sounds from outside, but thought she could make out the low crackle of a fire burning in the hearth. One of the colder turns, then.

Mara opened her eyes, squinted against the glare. Faces peered down at her. Trainees her own age, and one person she recognized. The blanched skin and bright eyes. Wansi. Her hair was auburn, save for a few strands of white at the temples. Her face and forehead were smooth, but the spectacles remained: thick, distorting her eyes and the skin around them.

"Let's allow her to breathe, shall we?" she said, the lilt in her voice as welcoming as an embrace.

Mara couldn't move. She gripped the sextant and chronofor; cold metal bit at her cramped fingers. A blanket covered her, and cloth cushioned the back of her head. She had been here for some time, unconscious. The trainees backed away as Wansi instructed, but they continued to stare, clearly fascinated by her and what she might represent.

She shifted her gaze back to the Binder, hoping to convey in her glance that they needed to be alone. Wansi stared back and after a fivecount gave the slightest of nods.

"I doubt we're going to accomplish much more this morning," she said, encompassing her students in a sweeping gaze. "You should be on your way to the refectory. You can get a head start on the younger trainees. I hear there are fresh rounds of cheese from north Oaqamar, delivered just last night."

Mutterings of protest met her suggestion.

"I'd like time alone with our guest," the Binder said. "Please be on your way."

"You'll tell us what you learn about her?" asked one young man.

"Probably not. Still, I imagine there will be stories aplenty by the time night falls, all told with an improbable air of authority." She thinned a smile. "Now, go."

The young man frowned, as did his companions. They put away their tools and half-completed devices and exited the chamber. When they were gone, Wansi closed and locked the door.

She walked back to Mara and knelt beside her. "How are you feeling?"

"C- cold," Mara said. Her tongue felt thick and sluggish, and her voice sounded strange, a shade deeper than she remembered. "Tired, t- too."

"I don't doubt it. Can you tell me how far you've come?"

"What year, what day?"

The Binder gaped. "What year?" she whispered. "You poor thing. It's the fourth day of Kheraya's Waking. The year is... It's 640. How far?"

Mara couldn't help but be pleased. The chronofor had worked as it was supposed to. And she'd survived. "S- Seven years," she said.

Wansi rocked back on her heels, her eyes as wide as apertures. "Seven."

"And two t- turns."

"Indeed. You carry a sextant I made, one that is quite dear to me. And here you are in my chamber. So I trust that I sent you back. But why?"

Mara faltered. This was something she and the Binder hadn't discussed. How much could she tell Wansi herself? It wasn't a question of trust. How much could she confide without giving information that might twist the future?

"Not sent," she finally said. "H- Helped."

Wansi's brow furrowed. "I'm not certain I understand the difference."

"You d- didn't want me t- to go."

Her frown grew more pronounced. "I see. Still, that doesn't answer the question of why."

Mara held her gaze, but didn't reply.

Recognition flashed in the vivid blue eyes. "Ah, you have no intention of telling me, do you?"

"I'm sorry." Mara had begun to recuperate. She tried to sit up, but her arms weren't yet working well.

"You should lie still a bit longer, I think." She stood. "In the meantime, I can get you clothes."

"No."

She quirked an eyebrow. "I don't know how matters stand seven years from now, but in this time we tend to cover ourselves when walking around the palace."

Mara grinned briefly. "I'm sure. But I'm not staying long."

"What do you–" Wansi knelt again. "You mean to say you're going back farther?"

"Several years more."

The Binder pondered this, her face more ashen than usual. "You're right not to tell me how much more. It could have been a mistake to tell me as much as you did. I'm not certain." She squared her shoulders. "What do you need before you can Walk again? Food? Something to drink?"

"A bit of both, I think."

"All right. I'll return shortly. If anyone knocks on the door, don't make a sound."

Mara gave a shaky nod.

Wansi let herself out of the chamber, and Mara lay back, closing her eyes.

Next thing she knew, the door opened again and Wansi slipped into the room, hands full.

"You slept."

"Yes." She tried once more to sit up and managed it this time. She sensed subtle differences in her body. She was leaner, harder. She couldn't decide if she wanted to see herself in a mirror. She adjusted the blanket to keep herself covered and eyed the bundle Wansi held. Her stomach rumbled.

"Bread and cheese," the Binder said. She held up the carafe she carried in her other hand. "And watered Miejan red."

As Mara ate and sipped the wine, Wansi perched on a stool, regarding her.

"It would be best if you didn't arrive in the middle of another lesson when you Walk again."

"I know," Mara said around a mouthful of bread. "Traveling so far, I can't help it. I left at night, and, if I'm right, arrived near midday. Chronofors aren't exact over so much time."

"That's because they weren't meant to be used in this way. There's a reason they have stems for bells, days, and turns, but not years. You're Walking too far."

"I know."

Apparently Wansi had expected an argument. Mara's agreement deflated her.

"All right. I'll trust that you and the older me know what you're doing."

They lapsed into a lengthy silence, broken only by Mara's chewing and the tolling of bells in the palace courtyard. When she had eaten her fill and regained some strength, Mara climbed to her feet, the blanket draped around her.

"Thank you. I seem to say that to you a lot."

Wansi's smile was sad. "I wouldn't know. What's your name?"

"I don't think I should tell you."

"No, I suppose not. I'm curious about your age as well. Your true age. But knowing that could be equally… disruptive."

"Yes," Mara said, wondering what Wansi meant by her "true age." She chose not to dwell on the question.

Wansi crossed back to the door. "I think it best to let you do this in private."

"Yes, probably."

"Until we meet again."

Wansi left her.

Mara pulled out the turns stem and began counting. She dreaded her next journey through the between, but at least now she knew she could survive a Walk of this length. How many times, though, could she put herself through this in a single day?

She decided not to dwell on this either. With a deep breath, and a quick prayer to the Two, she let the blanket drop, clutched the sextant in her other hand, and pressed the center stem.

This time she woke to darkness, sprawled on the stone floor, naked, freezing cold, unable to move or speak. The windows of the chamber were shuttered and the faint silver of moon glow seeped in at the edges. Coals glowed and settled in the hearth, giving off little heat. She heard not a sound from outside.

This was another possibility that hadn't occurred to her, to them. Wansi spent much of her day in this room, but she slept elsewhere. Mara had no idea of the time. It could be bells before anyone found her, and in the meantime she could die of exposure. She lay there, shivering, teeth chattering, unable to lift a finger, much less a limb. She held the chronofor and sextant, but they did her little good.

She tried to sleep, hoping to doze off and wake again when she wasn't so helpless. But she was too cold, the floor too hard.

She wanted to shout for help, but even if she could have made a sound, she knew she couldn't afford to alert anyone other than Wansi to her presence. What if the Oaqamarans already controlled the palace?

In time, the courtyard bells pealed. Two past midnight. By then she had sat up and stretched her legs and arms. Her recuperation from this Walk took much longer than had her recovery from the first, something she should have expected.

She stood and tried to move. Though unsteady on her feet, she could get around. Maybe she didn't need to see Wansi at all, or anyone for that matter. If she could escape the palace without encountering any guards, she could limit the damage she might do to history. Droë would have thought this her best course of action.

As quickly as the idea came to her, she dismissed it. Exhausted, chilled, light-headed – she didn't like her chances of escaping notice. She searched the chamber for any sort of clothing and soon found a spare robe tucked away on a low shelf. It smelled of dust, and was stiff in spots, stained with some ancient liquid, but she didn't care. She bundled herself in the garment and placed a log on the embers. For a time it merely smoked, but she blew on the coals until the wood caught. Then she curled into a tight ball beside the hearth, and tried to sleep.

Slumber came grudgingly. Still cold, and impatient for Wansi's arrival, she woke with every toll of the palace bells. When the chamber began to brighten, she gave up. Standing and stretching again, she surveyed the room. It wasn't much changed from fourteen years in the future. Evidently, Wansi had long been tidy and intolerant of trainees who weren't. She retrieved her chronofor and sextant from beside the hearth and slipped the timepiece into a pocket. She considered doing the same with the sextant, but caught a glimpse of herself reflected off the polished metal.

Her breath caught. Of course she would have aged, but she hadn't stopped to wonder what she would look like at thirty years. Her face had grown lean, accentuating her cheekbones. Tiny lines textured her skin at the corners of her eyes and mouth, but her cheeks and brow were smooth. While her hair remained as she remembered it, seeing it swept back from that sculpted, unfamiliar face, she was forced to acknowledge something unexpected: she was beautiful. She felt vain even thinking it, though she might as well have been looking at a stranger, or a long-forgotten relative.

Mara set the sextant on a work table and walked away, only to orbit back to it so she could see herself again. The reflected visage fascinated her. She angled her chin this way and that, studying her features, memorizing them.

After a tencount, she put the sextant down again and deliberately moved away. Conceit had never been one of her faults, and she refused to let it become one now.

She resumed her search of the chamber, looking not for clothes, but for tri-devices. If she had come back far enough, she wouldn't find any. As she perused the shelves, she heard the click of the doorlock's tumblers.

Straightening, she looked to the door as it opened.

The Wansi who entered couldn't have been much older than the reflected face in the sextant. She appeared in the bloom of youth: her skin unblemished, her hair untouched by gray, her spectacles less cumbersome than those she would use later in life.

She entered the chamber, her arms laden with scrolls, and shouldered the door closed, all without taking note of Mara.

When the Binder turned again and saw her, she jumped and gave a sharp gasp. Several of the scrolls fell to the floor.

"Who are you?" she demanded, the familiar accent doing little to soften the question. "What are you doing in this chamber?"

"I'm a friend," Mara said, holding up both hands. She reached into her pocket and produced the chronofor. "And a Walker."

Wansi eyed the device and then her, marking the robe she wore. Notwithstanding her initial reaction, she seemed to take Mara's presence in the chamber in stride. "You arrived during the night?"

"Yes. I was tired and chose to wait for you. I didn't mean to frighten you."

Wansi set the scrolls on the nearest workbench and retrieved those she had dropped. "Can you tell me your name?"

"I don't think that would be wise."

The Binder considered her again. "How far back did you come?"

"I won't tell you that, either. But it would be helpful to me if you could tell me the date, and... and the year."

Wansi froze, a scroll in hand, the widening of her eyes making her look even younger. "You Walked years?" she asked, her tone hushed.

"Twice, actually. It was too great a time to cover in a single Walk."

"You're a child."

"Not quite. Not anymore."

A faint smile touched the Binder's lips. "No, I suppose not."

"The date?"

"This is the twenty-ninth day of Sipar's Settling. The year is 633."

Fourteen years. She'd made it.

"That's what you were hoping for."

"Yes."

"Does this mean our palace is destined for history-changing events?"

Mara smiled and lifted the sextant from the table. "I'll be leaving this place. I'm a Spanner as well."

Wansi's expression hardened. "Let me see that."

She held it out and the Binder grabbed it from her.

"You gave this to me before I left my time," Mara said. "You told me it was dear to you."

"It is," the Binder whispered. "I hope you've come a long way."

Mara frowned as Wansi gave her back the device.

"It was a gift to–" She shook her head. "I hadn't thought to see it again so soon."

"I'm sorry," Mara said. "I didn't know."

"Clearly, I did. A warning perhaps, a way of preparing myself for the loss." She forced another smile. "Not very discreet of me, was it?" She stepped around the workbench and past Mara to the hearth. "You must be cold. I assume you have nothing on beneath that old rag." She piled more wood on the ash and embers and soon had a bright fire burning.

Mara joined her by the blaze, standing as close to it as she dared.

"What do you need from me?" Wansi asked.

"Help getting out of the palace and to a place from which I can Span safely, without being seen."

"I won't ask where you're going, but I trust it's far."

"It is."

"Word has reached Trevynisle of events in the Inner Ring. Daerjen."

Mara held herself motionless, not trusting herself to look Wansi in the eye.

"I thought as much. I'll help you, of course. But if that's your destination, the between was just the beginning of the perils you're going to face."

CHAPTER 35

29th Day of Sipar's Settling, Year 633

Wansi brought her clothing and food. Mara wouldn't have thought that the skirt and tunic the Binder gave her would fit, but her face wasn't the only part of her that had grown lean.

It hadn't been long in bells since her last meal, but her Walks had left her famished. She ate nearly everything Wansi gave her and probably could have eaten more. She chose instead to take the rest with her.

As she chewed and washed down the salted meat and bread with watered wine, the Binder told her of events in Hayncalde. Word of Mearlan IV's assassination had reached Windhome by pigeon within the last day. Cryptic reports from the Inward Sea said that his entire family had been lost: the sovereign queen, Mearlan's son and namesake, and the sovereign princess, who was but a babe. Soldiers from Sheraigh controlled the city, and Noak was expected to name an interim authority until a duke could be chosen. Wansi said nothing about another Walker, and Mara didn't ask.

Upon leaving the chamber, the Binder made no effort to avoid being seen. "We're likely to fail, and being discovered will raise questions. Better we should appear unconcerned."

Mara agreed, but she remained tense as they walked to the lower gate. She saw, though, that the guards atop the palace walls wore uniforms of purple and black, rather than Oaqamaran brown. There were no Belvora. Her tension eased.

The Binder prattled on about the palace, speaking to Mara as she would a visitor from afar. Mara affected interest. Once they were beyond the palace walls and in the winding streets of Windhome, they headed northward away from the waterfront, which surprised her.

"Where are we going?"

"To a promontory overlooking the bay. If you were traveling by ship, I'd take you to the piers, but this is better for Spanners, and few know of it."

They crossed the city and followed a narrow, overgrown track that cut through brush and brambles and then a copse of cedar. Finches and jays scolded from above, and a timbercat eyed them before melting into the forest. The path, which wound on for more than a league, showed few signs of human traffic. By the time they emerged onto the headland, Mara was breathing hard and had sweated through her clothes.

Standing on the outcropping, staring over the water, Wansi said, "You should be quite safe here. In all the times I've come, I've never encountered a soul. Deer use the path. I'm sure people must, also, but I haven't seen them."

"Thank you. This is perfect."

"You say you're a Spanner as well as a Walker. But do you need help using the sextant?"

Mara shook her head. "I'm a Spanner first, actually. I'm more adept with the sextant than with the chronofor."

Wansi cast a glance her way. "Yet you Walked years. You must have been a very impressive young woman."

Mara blushed. "I have a friend – a Tirribin. I intend to speak with her before I Span. So I'm afraid I can't return your clothes right now. I'm sorry."

The Binder waved away her apology. "No matter. The clothes are old, and I'll be back soon enough. I love this place."

Mara could see why. Safsi Bay glittered below them in the hazy sunlight, ships on sweeps arrayed around the wharves, and others, their sails unfurled, carving through the water at the mouth of the inlet. Windhome was nestled against the cliff face, the white and gray walls and red slate roofs a mosaic in the midday light. A tawny falcon hovered on narrow wings just off the edge of the cliff, and sea eagles circled over the gulf.

"I should leave you."

Mara's eyes stung. She doubted she would see the Binder again.

"As far as you're concerned, we've only just met," she said. "But you've been a valued friend and–" She stopped herself before saying anything about Wansi's mentoring. "And I'm grateful."

"I don't know why you're doing this," the Binder said. "You've sacrificed a great deal to come so far. I believe we all owe you our gratitude." She proffered a hand, which Mara grasped. "Farewell. May the Two guide and protect you."

"And you."

Wansi left her, treading the path and soon disappearing from view amid the trees and shadows. Mara sat at the edge of the promontory and gathered the folds of the robe against the wind, thinking about Nat, Delvin, and the others. Even Hilta. Her fellow trainees would be with Saffern by now, or maybe in the refectory. She couldn't quite believe that life was lost to her. She knew she looked different, but she felt the same; it was easy to convince herself that if she returned to the palace, she could be a trainee again. A thirty year-old trainee. She didn't know whether to laugh at the thought or weep.

Over the next few bells, her thoughts careened in a hundred different directions. She shed tears for her mother and father, her brothers and friends. She wondered where Tobias was and, if she managed to find him, whether he would know how to stop the wars and steer history back toward the right trajectory. She wondered as well if she ought to go back a bit farther in time, to the days before the assassination of Daerjen's sovereign. Might that help Tobias? Or would it further tangle events? She knew so little about him, and why he had gone back. On this thought, she heard again Droë's ominous words. *Better too little than too much...* She remained in this time.

As the sun began its descent to the west, painting the high clouds over Safsi Bay in shades of yellow and orange and pink, she ate the last of her food. Then she pulled out her sextant and calibrated it for the journey she would make come nightfall.

She remained close enough to the palace to use the distances Wansi had made them commit to memory. The coordinates for Islevale's major isles and cities had been drilled into her for years. She knew them the way she did the date of her own birth. With the device ready for her Span, she set it aside and waited.

Mist gathered in the trees at her back and drifted over the headland, until torches in the streets below and on ships scattered across the bay appeared only as obscure points of light. A gibbous moon shone through the thin clouds and dancing fog, lighting the promontory and casting her pale shadow across the damp ground. The air chilled, making Mara wish she had asked the Binder for an extra overshirt. She didn't relish the idea of Spanning naked across the Aiyanthan and Inward Seas even this late in Sipar's Settling.

When she was satisfied that the western sky had darkened enough, she climbed to her feet and said, "Droë."

A tencount later, the Tirribin winked into view in disquieting proximity to where Mara stood. Mara fought the impulse to back away. The demon hadn't changed over fourteen years: the golden hair and perfect features, the wide eyes of lightest gray, the waiflike form.

"You summoned me," she said, icy menace in her tone. "Summoning Tirribin carries a price. Do you offer your years freely?"

"No," Mara said. "I name myself your friend, Droënalka."

Droë had crept closer, but she halted at this, genuine surprise in her gaze. "Who are you?" Before Mara could speak, she said, "Your years are wrong. You're a Walker."

"Yes. You and I know each other in the future. I've come back because of you."

The Tirribin's expression turned coy. "Still, there is a cost."

"Which I'm repaying by helping you. This was our agreement when I agreed to Walk back and you confided your true name."

Annoyance curled the demon's lip. "Yes, very well. What brings you back, Walker?"

"My name's Mara. And maybe you can answer your own question. What do you sense in the flow of time?"

Again, it seemed the Tirribin hadn't expected this. Droë eyed Mara with doubt, but approached the overlook and closed her eyes. She stood motionless, her face tipped to the moon, the rush of surf against the rocky shore below measuring out the spirecounts. Eventually, she turned back to Mara, her brow creased.

"I feel it," she said. "A beginning only, and still vague. All isn't as it's supposed to be. Another Walker?"

"Yes. His name is Tobias. I never knew him, at least not that I remember. You claim to care about him a great deal, and you tell me he and I were friends in a different future."

The Tirribin shook her head. "I know nothing of this, and I can't Walk through years as you do. What do you want of me?"

"I wanted you to confirm that I came back far enough. You've just done that. And..." She lifted a shoulder. "I wanted you to know that I'm here, that I'm doing something about it."

"Is he on Trevynisle?"

"No. He's in Daerjen, at least that's where he went after leaving the palace."

Droë glanced at the sextant on the ground at Mara's feet. "You're going there."

"Tonight."

"You'll be beyond my help when you do."

"Can't you travel?"

"Not as you do. I suppose I could voyage, if that's what you mean. Then again, what ship's captain would welcome a Tirribin aboard?"

"I don't know. I suppose I shouldn't have summoned you."

"You've made me aware of a growing misfuture. Your debt to me is paid."

Mara nodded once in acknowledgment.

"Do you love him, this Walker you're following?"

"I don't remember him. From what you've said, I gather that I did, when I knew him."

"Have you loved others?"

Mara couldn't quite suppress a smile.

The demon bristled. "Do you mock me?"

"No. But I know you to be curious about love, and I find it… interesting that you're like this now as well, even before you've met Tobias."

Her eyes widened. "Do *I* love him?"

The question caught Mara off guard. This hadn't occurred to her, though it should have. "I don't know."

She didn't say more, but pondering the matter she thought it possible that Droë did love him, which would make them rivals in the demon's thinking. Drawing attention to that struck her as perilous.

Droë stared at her own silvery shadow, looking pensive.

"I should be on my way," Mara said, retrieving the sextant.

The Tirribin raised her gaze to Mara's. "All right." She started away toward the wood. Reaching the first trees, she turned again. Mara thought she might say more, but the demon merely watched her for another moment before stepping into the shadows.

Relieved to be alone, Mara removed the robe and borrowed clothing, and folded them into a neat pile on the rock. Several times she glanced after Droë, half-expecting the demon to reappear. She didn't.

Shivering in the cold, daunted by the prospect of Spanning so much farther than she ever had before, Mara gripped both devices. She raised the sextant, aimed it, and thumbed the release.

The pull snapped her head back, nearly making her drop the chronofor. The gap of Spanning might have been gentle compared to the between of Walking, but perhaps because of the distance this Span felt more violent than any she'd experienced. Color, light, sound, and smell assailed her from all sides. A frigid, unrelenting gale battered her and she fought to breathe. Yes, there was air, but it rushed by with such fury she could barely gulp at it. It flayed her skin, as if the wind bore shards of glass. Tears streamed from her eyes and her hair lashed at her neck and shoulders, as cruel and sharp as a carriage master's whip.

Time dragged by, an irony she didn't care to consider. She thought she must be bleeding from a thousand gashes. Her head spun, her heart labored, every muscle in her body quivered with fatigue. Crossing the courtyard in the Travelers' palace had been almost instantaneous. These hundreds of leagues over ocean and isle seemed to take a full bell. More. Again, as in the between, she wondered if Travelers were meant to go so far.

The ending came without warning or dignity. One moment she was held upright by the gap, the next she was dropped onto a strand by dark waters. Her legs gave way and she collapsed to the sand, too weak and dizzy to move. She gasped for breath, salty air coating her tongue, the stink of fish in her nostrils. Her stomach heaved and she retched until her throat ached. Tears still ran down her face. She had been brutalized by her Travels over the past day. She wanted nothing more than to find a warm, soft bed and sleep for a qua'turn.

The between was just the beginning of the perils you're going to face. The memory of Wansi's words chased thoughts of comfort from her head.

When strength returned to her arms and legs, she crawled over the sand to the surf's edge, placed the sextant and chronofor on the beach, and rinsed the sick off her body, shivering in the cold air and colder water. Reclaiming the devices, she retreated onto dry sand, teeth clattering, shivers racking her. She knelt and scanned her surroundings. The sky was clear and the moon, lower to the west now, lit the shore. Not far away, small waves broke against the wood of several long piers. A few ships were tied in at the wharves, but most – a mix of warships and merchant vessels – floated on the body of water beyond.

Lanes led from the docks to a main avenue, which climbed to a formidable wall and a broad, arched gateway, well-lit by torches and guarded by at least four uniformed soldiers.

Until she could cover herself, Mara didn't dare approach the city. But where, other than in the city, would she find clothes? Travel by tri-sextant had its advantages.

"Is that what I think it is?" A man's voice.

Mara stiffened, then shoved her hands into the cool sand, concealing the sextant and chronofor.

"Gods, she's not wearing a stitch." A second voice, also a man's. The words were slurred.

Two shadows approached, bulky, one tall, the other of medium height. Both appeared unsteady on their feet. The moon was at their backs, allowing them to see her more clearly than she could see them. Not good.

"You waiting for us, darlin'?" They laughed.

Mara kept her hands buried, closing her fists around handfuls of sand.

"She must be cold. Not that I'm complaining." More laughter.

Her cheeks burned, but she didn't turn away or cover herself. Better to have them distracted. She stood, still clutching sand.

"I need help," she said, her voice steady. "I need to borrow some clothing from you."

"Why would we want to give it?" the first man asked. "We're enjoying the view."

The second man shared a grin with his companion. "We might give an item or two, if you was willing to share more than a look. You catch my meaning?"

I don't, she wanted to say. *You're being too subtle.* She kept the sarcasm to herself. "I'm not giving you anything. I'm asking for help, appealing to your honor as gentlemen."

They thought this hilarious. She'd expected as much.

"If you won't help me, someone else will." She took a step back.

The first man advanced on her. "Not so fast. It's cold, and I could use warming up."

Had she been stronger – had she not Walked across fourteen years, and Spanned hundreds of leagues – she would have tried to outrun him. As it was, she didn't trust herself to get away. She stood her ground, allowing him to draw near. When he had closed most of the distance, she took a quick step toward him and threw a handful of sand in his face. He halted with a bellow and clawed at his eyes.

Mara lowered her shoulder and pounded an elbow into his gut. He doubled over. She stepped back and kicked at his face, connecting with his nose. It gave with a sickening crunch and gushed blood. He pitched forward into the sand.

"What did you do?" the second man demanded.

Before she could answer, he lunged for her.

She wrenched herself to the side, and as he lurched past she threw the remaining sand at him.

His hands flew to his eyes. "You whore!"

Mara punched his throat, as Saffern had taught her. Once, twice. He dropped to his knees, and she kneed the side of his head. The man toppled over.

Glancing around to make certain the men's cries hadn't drawn more strangers, she knelt beside the second man, who was closer to her in size, and wrestled him out of his coat, shirt, and trousers. The clothes were filthy, and blood glistened on the shirt and coat, which gave her pause. She didn't need to draw any more attention to herself.

In the end, she took the second man's clothes, but the first man's overshirt. The shirt and trousers were itchy and made her skin crawl, but she was as unwilling to remove their undergarments as she was to wear them herself. These would have to do. She took the second man's shoes, but left his hose.

She took two small blades and a few bronze and silver coins from their pockets.

Mara returned to where she'd been when they found her, and dug through the sand for the chronofor and sextant. When at first she couldn't find them, she grew panicked. She scrabbled at the sand, flinging it away in every direction, her breath coming in ragged gasps.

She willed herself to calm down, and retraced her path from the water. Realizing she'd been digging in the wrong spot, she tried again. When her sand-coated fingers brushed cold metal, she sobbed her relief. She removed as much of the sand from the devices as she could, slipped the chronofor into her pocket, and concealed the sextant beneath the overshirt.

She trod the cobbled road to the city gate on stiff legs, uncomfortable in the stolen clothes. The spire of a sanctuary rose above the city rooftops, lit from within by torches or lamp fire. If she could reach it, she might pass the night in safety and search for Tobias come morning. First, though, she had to pass through the gate without drawing notice.

"Where do you think you're goin'?"

Mara halted and faced the guard. He was burly, older than her years, but younger than her appearance. His skin was bone white in the light of the torches. Even seeing Wansi every day, she remained accustomed to people as dark-skinned as she. Here in Daerjen she would stand out the way the Binder had in Trevynisle.

"I'm... I'm new to Hayncalde," she said. "I was just–"

"No one enters the city, or leaves for that matter." Narrowed eyes raked over her, taking in the begrimed, ill-fitting clothes, and lingering on her hair, her neck. "Where are you from? What are you doing skulkin' around the walls so late?"

She almost claimed to have arrived on a ship, but she considered how few vessels had been moored on the docks. *No one enters the city, or leaves...* A blockade to fortify the occupation?

"I came from our farm. My husband is sick. I need to buy medicine. Please, I've walked all day." She nearly winced at the inadvertent play on words.

The soldier glanced over his shoulder, then eyed her again, leering. "I suppose I could let you in. If you respond in kind."

Gods! Was every man in Daerjen in rut?

"My *husband* is sick," she said with all the indignity she could summon.

"That's all right. 'S not him I'm after."

"No!"

He glared. "I don't know how things go in the northern isles, but down here, nothin' is free."

"What's the trouble, Cobb?"

Two more soldiers stood at the far end of the gate, both with muskets held waist high.

The guard's gaze flicked to them before returning to Mara. "This shit-skinned whore thinks she's too good for us."

The aspersion stung like a slap. She knew that some in the lower isles looked down on northislers, but never had anyone spoken of her that way to her face. Tears blurred her sight. She could say nothing.

"Well, in your case she's right, isn't she?"

The two guards laughed. Cobb's expression didn't change,

but he hefted his weapon. One of the men walked to where Mara and Cobb stood.

"What does she want, anyway?"

"To enter the city," Mara said, her voice rough. "My husband needs medicine."

"Says she walked here from a farm. I'm not sure I believe her. Could be another one of those Hayncalde agitators."

"So you thought you'd give her a poke and that would make everything all right?"

Cobb's cheeks shaded to crimson.

The other soldier joined them. "Or did you think to get your poke and then turn her out anyway?"

"Doesn't matter," Cobb said. "She's not gettin' in either way."

"Neither are you, it seems."

The two men laughed again, only to fall silent as a fourth soldier entered the archway. She was older, stout and grim, with short hair and a dark scar on her chin.

"What's this?" she asked, her tone like a hammer.

The three guards snapped to attention. Cobb glowered at Mara, as if eager to run her through with his bayonet.

Mara told her story again, wishing she had tried to Span past the gate. Clothes and coin be damned.

"The city is occupied," the woman said. "No one is to enter or leave."

"I understand," Mara said, turning to leave, eager to be away.

The woman regarded the three men, disapproval in the glance. "So we won't speak of this to anyone, will we?"

"No, commander," said the guard who first questioned Cobb.

"Go on, then," the commander said, addressing Mara. "You won't find a healer tonight. Best you make your way to the temple. The servants of the God might shelter you."

The God. Sipar worshippers. "Yes, all right."

"You know the way?"

"I saw the spire from the road. I can find it."

"Best you do then."

Mara nodded, darted a glance at Cobb and the others, and hurried into the city. She made her way past squalid lanes and ramshackle buildings, following a direct path to the temple. That is, until she encountered a group of soldiers dressed in pale blue like the gate guards. She spied them before they noticed her, and ducked off the lane without being seen. After that, though, she proceeded with more caution and evaded two more patrols.

She was stopped at the temple gates by a pair of formidable women in white tunics and breaches. They carried swords instead of muskets, but in other respects they struck her as more than a match for Sheraigh's soldiers.

"How can we serve you, miss?" one asked.

"I seek shelter."

"This isn't an inn. If you need a place to rest, there are establishments throughout the city where you can let a room."

Mara teetered, feeling weak. Of all the trials she'd faced, she was least prepared for this one. Worse, she could think of no argument that might sway them. She did have coin. Not a lot, but probably enough for a room. She didn't need to take refuge here.

"I'm a Traveler, a Spanner." She spoke on instinct, uncertain as to why she bothered. "I've come far."

The warder studied her, her gaze critical but benign. "Your clothes?"

"We wear none when Traveling. I took these from two men who... who tried to force themselves on me after I reached Daerjen."

"I understand. But still–"

The other warder laid a hand her companion's arm. Leaning close, she whispered something. The first warder weighed her words. She dipped her chin, and the other woman strode into the sanctuary grounds. The remaining warder watched Mara, but said no more. Mara suffered her scrutiny in uncomfortable silence.

The warder soon returned with a white-haired woman in a flowing white robe. She appeared slight beside the guards, but carried herself with authority. A priestess, no doubt.

She looked Mara over, then turned, beckoning for her to follow. "She'll be with me," she said over her shoulder. "If any ask, even those who live and toil within these walls, you saw nothing."

They walked some distance without speaking, until they were beyond the hearing of the guards.

"You say you're a Traveler?" the priestess asked, regarding Mara sidelong.

"Yes. I only reached–"

"What kind?"

Mara sensed urgency in the question. "I have dual talents. I'm a Spanner and also a Walker."

"Did you Walk to come here?"

"I did both."

"How far? How many years?"

"I'm not sure I should–"

"Many, yes?"

She faltered. "Why do you want to know?"

"There was another here. A Walker. Only a day ago. He wouldn't tell me how far he'd come, but I sensed it was many years. I wonder if you knew him."

Abruptly she could hardly breathe. The priestess had to be speaking of Tobias. She'd seen the temple from the shore, and had been directed here by the Sheraigh commander. Perhaps the Gods were with her.

"You look like him," the priestess said. "More, you act like him. I sense youth in you, though you don't look particularly young."

Mara's breath caught at this as well, in an entirely different way. She would have to be more cautious with her speech and mannerisms.

The priestess eyed her again. "Can you tell me your name?"

"Mara Lijar."

"I'm Nuala. I'm high priestess of this sanctuary."

"I'm honored, Mother Priestess."

Mara followed the priestess along torchlit paths, a thousand questions vying to be given voice.

"You did know him, didn't you?" Nuala said.

"I know of him. I'm trying to find him."

The woman missed a step, then stopped. Belatedly, Mara recognized what she should have noticed earlier.

"You speak of him in the past tense. Why?"

Dismay shadowed Nuala's expression.

"Is he dead?"

"I don't know their fate. I sent him to the waterfront with a trusted servant of the temple. He was to board a merchant ship and sail from here. The woman who accompanied them was murdered. We found no sign of the Walker or his companion."

"His companion?"

"A child. A baby." She leaned closer. "Sofya," she whispered. "Sovereign princess of Daerjen."

"I was told the entire family had been killed."

"Sheraigh lies. They hunt for her still. And for her guardian. Their lives have been in the gravest danger."

"Could they have boarded the ship?"

"Possibly. They were clear of the gate when Della died. We found three others dead as well. Men. One was shot and stabbed; the others..." She shook her head. "Their deaths we don't understand."

"So they might have escaped."

"Yes. We've made enquiries, but as of yet, we've learned nothing."

"What sort of enquiries?"

The priestess answered with a brisk shake of her head. "I can't tell you that."

"I need to find Tobias – the Walker. I can help him, and he can help me. If you have sources who might know of his fate, I must speak with them."

Nuala regarded her for another breath, tight-lipped. When she walked on, Mara could only follow.

"You came seeking shelter," the priestess said. "We can provide that. The rest we'll discuss in the morning."

She led Mara to a small chamber with a simple pallet, a nightstand, and a narrow wardrobe. Mara wasn't convinced she would sleep; her mind hummed with thoughts of Tobias and questions about his fate. Almost as soon as she stretched out on the bed, however, exhaustion pulled her into a deep slumber.

Voices in the courtyard outside her shuttered window woke her. She had no idea how long she had slept, but she felt better, and her stomach rumbled with hunger. She opened the window to a high morning sun. She'd lost too much of the day.

A wash-basin and cloth had been left outside her door, along with a change of clothes: undergarments – the Two be praised – a linen tunic, soft woolen hose, a skirt, also made of wool, and a thick overshirt. She washed and dressed. After pocketing her chronofor and the stolen blades and coins, and placing the sextant in a large pocket within the overshirt, she left the room.

An initiate in gray robes waited for her outside the dormitory and led her to the refectory. Nuala was there, dining with several more initiates. She beckoned to Mara and indicated an empty space beside her on the bench.

Mara joined the woman, eyeing those around the table as she sat.

"This is Mara," Nuala said. "Please make her welcome."

The other women greeted her with smiles and bobs of their heads.

"Help yourself," the priestess said, indicating the platters spread across the table.

There were boiled eggs, fresh breads, sweet and savory, with clotted cream, stewed fruits, and fried ham. Mara tried to eat slowly, but she was ravenous and cleared her first dish in a rush, only to fill and empty it again in as little time.

Bells pealed from the spire, prompting the initiates to stand and file out of the refectory. Servants hurried to the table to clear their places, but Nuala waved them away. They retreated to the kitchen, leaving Mara and the priestess alone.

"You slept?"

"Very well, thank you."

"Good. I'd like to know whence you've come and who sent you."

"I came from Trevynisle, and no one sent me. Only one person knew of my Travels, and she's far from here, in leagues and years."

"Why did you come?"

"To help Tobias."

Nuala frowned. "Yes, so you've said."

"I can't tell you what you want to know. It's enough to say that the future I knew is not the right one. The world changed when Tobias came here. History changed. I seek to return it to a more proper path."

"Who's to say what's proper?"

Mara had asked the same of Droë, not so long ago, though it seemed another life.

"I am."

"That's not a satisfactory answer."

"I'm afraid it will have to be," Mara said, amazed at her own presumption.

Nuala stared, frost in the look. "Perhaps you're not as young as I first thought."

She thought it best not to respond.

"As I promised," the priestess cotinued, "I've been in contact with people who may be able to help you. When I told them you were a Traveler, they were most interested, and they suggested that they were near to discovering what happened to Tobias."

"Do they think he's alive?"

"They didn't say. But they want to meet you."

Mara couldn't believe her good fortune. "You trust these people?"

"I do. They have ties to the late sovereign, which is enough to convince me of their sincerity."

"All right. When can I meet them?"

"At dusk. They'll be waiting for you outside the city walls. You'll leave with the evening bells."

"Won't the gates be closed?"

Nuala smiled. "Leave that to us."

With nothing to do, Mara spent several bells walking the temple grounds. She was impatient to meet these people of whom the priestess spoke and, of course, to find Tobias. Yet once again, she had no choice but to wait, to wish away time she didn't have. When the sky began to darken, she returned to the refectory. There she was met by the priestess and a lone warder in white. Nuala gave her bread and cheese for her journey, and a purse that contained a few gold rounds and silver treys.

The warder led Mara through the city, keeping to narrow lanes and avoiding soldiers, until they came to a small stone house in a hidden courtyard. The structure concealed an entrance to a dank tunnel, which ran under Hayncalde's eastern lanes and ended at a hidden door in the city wall.

From there, the woman led Mara along the waterfront, across the road connecting the wharves to the city, and onto the same strand to which Mara Spanned the previous night. She watched for the men she'd fought, but didn't see them.

Eventually they halted at the mouth of a rocky cove beyond sight of the main gate.

"You're to wait here," the woman told her, the first words she had spoken since leaving the temple.

Mara looked around, expecting to see assailants converging on her.

The warder might have sensed her unease. "You'll be safe. I don't think you'll have to wait long. I can leave you my sword."

Mara pulled one of the knives from a pocket. "I'll be all right."

The woman nodded. "Sipar keep you safe."

Mara wasn't sure how to answer; she was used to blessings that invoked both God and Goddess. "And you," she said, after too long a pause.

The warder nodded again and started back toward the city.

Mara moved closer to one of the large boulders and surveyed the coast, shivering with apprehension more than the chill air. Vapor billowed each time she exhaled, and reflections of moonlight shifted like quicksilver on the surface of Daerjen's gulf.

Before long, footsteps approached from farther south, crunching on the rock and sand. Whoever it was seemed to care little for stealth, which put Mara at ease. She stepped away from the boulder and spotted the stranger. She hesitated, then raised a hand in greeting. The stranger waved back.

Mara thought it a man, but realized her error as the woman drew near. She had short dark hair, a handsome, square face, and pale eyes that might have been blue. The woman smiled and put out a hand, which Mara gripped.

"You're the Traveler."

"Yes. Mara Lijar. And you are?"

"Gillian Ainfor, formerly minister of protocol to the sovereign of Daerjen."

CHAPTER 36

30th Day of Sipar's Settling, Year 633

It was the second time in two days she had learned of survivors from an attack none were thought to have survived. This offered her a shred of hope that she could accomplish what she had come back to do.

"I was led to believe that all in the sovereign's court were lost."

The minister's expression sobered. "Not quite all."

Mara thought the woman intended to say more. When she didn't, Mara said, "The high priestess indicated that you might know about another Walker who came here."

"I do, but you'll have to forgive me: with all that's happened, I'm not yet sure I can trust you."

"I understand."

"You know this Walker's name?"

"Tobias."

"And his family name?"

"I don't know."

The woman frowned. "Can you tell me how far back you've come?"

Mara's hesitance deepened the minister's displeasure.

"If I'm to help you – if we're to help each other – you need to trust me. I know Tobias. I'm trying to find him, and I believe I'm close. But I want to be sure this isn't a Sheraigh ruse."

"Fourteen years," Mara said. "That's how far I Walked."

Gillian smiled again. "Tobias told us he came back just as far. Come along."

She led Mara along the coast, following the waterline through the cove and emerging from it onto another bouldered beach. They crossed this strand as well, climbing over huge rocks. Mara soon realized they were headed toward a rift in the coastal cliffs, which glowed with the warm light of fires.

"Is that where we're headed?" she asked, pointing.

"Yes. It's called the Notch. You'll be safe there."

On they walked, silent save for their footsteps and the rasp of their breathing as they clambered over the boulders. In time, they reached a stone stairway that had been carved out of a broad rock shelf.

"Just up here," the minister said, with a glance back and another smile.

The climb proved longer and more difficult than Mara had anticipated. Though low compared to the surrounding cliffs, the face of this outcropping had to be five hundred hands high. The stairs were uneven; several times, Mara nearly tripped. In time they reached the top. Or Gillian did. She held out a hand, signaling for Mara to stop, then put a finger to her lips.

She peeked over the edge of the cliff, only to duck back down and shake her head. They remained there for several spirecounts, allowing Mara to catch her breath. At last, Gillian checked again, nodded to Mara, and stepped on to the shelf. Mara followed.

She saw a few people on the expanse of stone: couples in intimate embraces, sprawled figures who might have been asleep or drunk, people curled up around a bright blaze burning in a round pit gouged out of the rock. She looked to the minister in alarm, but Gillian appeared unconcerned.

"It's all right. This way."

They walked into the rift, passing shelters made of canvas, some of them businesses, others apparently homes. Mara had never seen its like.

"What is this place?"

"I told you: it's the Notch."

"Yes, but–"

"It's a refuge for people who can't afford to live in the city proper, either for lack of coin or out of fear for their safety. They mind their own business, and they ask few questions."

Mara heard a warning in the words.

They didn't have to go far. They came to a curtain of cloth that defined the edge of a cavern. Mara couldn't tell how deep it was.

Gillian halted before the canvas, glanced in both directions, and pulled a section of the curtain aside.

"Quickly," she said, waving Mara inside.

Mara stepped through the opening into a spacious room shaped by still more hanging cloths. Additional chambers beyond this one? Several candles burned around the room, illuminating a table and two chairs, a small collection of pots and pans piled around a cooking fire, and an array of tools, familiar in design. A man sat with his back to the entrance, bent over something Mara couldn't see, haloed by a glow of binding magick.

Gillian cleared her throat, causing the man to start. He glanced in their direction and, as the glow receded, shoved something into a cloth sack at his feet.

But not before Mara caught a glimpse: shimmering gold in graceful arcs, a glass eyepiece.

"That's a tri-sextant," she said without thinking.

The man stared at her, then shifted his gaze to Gillian behind her.

"How inconvenient," the minister said, her tone dry.

Mara started to turn, intending to ask what she meant. Before she could, pain exploded at the back of her skull, and she fell into darkness.

· · ·

Consciousness brought throbbing pain, nausea, and, after a few heartbeats, the awareness of bindings on her wrists and ankles. Mara opened her eyes, and her world heaved and spun. She twisted her head to the side and vomited.

"You shouldn't have hit her." A man's voice. The Binder. The one who'd been working on the tri-sextant. She made herself focus on him, the world around her still shifting in a way that roiled her gut. He was tall, dark-haired, with a trim goatee and mustache.

"She was trained on Trevynisle." That was Gillian. "She knows how to fight. Were *you* going to subdue her?" Mara heard mockery in the question.

"Who are you?" Mara asked.

A smirk hardened the lines of the minister's face. "My answer hasn't changed." She tipped her head in the man's direction. "This is Bexler Filt, once Daerjen's Binder."

"Why have you done this to me?" She strained against the rope chafing her wrists. "I'm a friend. I came to help."

"Such a narrow view of the world. I expected more of a Traveler. Even the other Walker wasn't this dense."

Understanding crashed over her, as bracing as an ocean wave. The woman was right: it should have been clear.

"You're traitors."

"An ugly word." She didn't deny it, though.

"Sand isn't good for your chronofor," the Binder said. "Or for the sextant, for that matter."

With effort, Mara shifted her gaze in his direction. He was cleaning her time piece with a small brush. Wansi's sextant rested on the table beside him. She feared she might be sick again. Without the devices, she was lost.

"Are they yours?" the minister asked.

Mara opened her mouth to answer, only to realize the woman hadn't been speaking to her.

"No. Even in the future, I won't Bind like this. I'd guess they come from Windhome, probably from a Binder who hasn't assumed his duties yet. Or hers."

Gillian nodded and turned back to Mara. "Who sent you?"

Mara returned her stare, refusing to speak.

"Don't," the minister said. "You think you're being clever and brave. You're a child in a woman's body, and based on what I know of Trevynisle, I'd say you've been coddled much of your life. You study and you play with weapons. But you've never known a single day of true discomfort. I don't expect you'd hold up very well under torture."

Cold spread from Mara's chest through her stomach, her limbs, her neck and face.

A matching smile curved Gillian's lips. "As I thought. Now, who sent you?"

"I came here myself."

"That's not what I meant, and you know it."

"I know exactly what you meant. I'm telling you it was my idea."

The minister heaved a sigh and produced a small, curved blade from within her coat.

Mara shrank back. "It's true. I had help from a Tirribin, and the Binder gave me a chronofor, but the rest was me."

Gillian hesitated, glancing once more at Filt. "A Tirribin?"

"Yes. She sensed that our time was wrong. I sensed it, too. She knew of Tobias and knew that he'd gone back. She convinced me to go after him."

The minister walked to where Mara sat and loomed over her. "Let me understand. You don't know Tobias?"

"Not really. I know of him. I know he came back and that history changed when he did. The world as I know it doesn't include him."

"And you sensed the change in history? On your own?"

Gillian looked to the Binder again.

"Kill her now," he said. "It's too risky to let her live."

Mara drew her bound hands and knees to her chest, her body quaking violently. Tears slid down her cheeks. She couldn't bring herself to make a sound.

The minister shook her head. "Not yet. It may be our only choice before long, but not yet."

"She saw the tri–"

"That was unfortunate."

"It's more than that. She knows what it is. She might tell others. I'm not the only Binder who can make them, you know."

"I wouldn't have thought you were, brilliant though you are, my dear."

He frowned.

"She's not going anywhere. We can afford to keep her alive for a while longer. I was hoping she might know Tobias, but he's soft-hearted enough to care about her life, even if they haven't actually met."

"What if you're wrong?"

"That happens so seldom."

He lifted an eyebrow.

"If I'm wrong, we kill her and no one's the wiser. But I think she still has value."

Mara held her breath.

"Fine," he said. "We should tie something across her mouth to keep her quiet, and put her in the back room."

"An excellent idea. See to that, will you?"

He stood with a huffed breath and stalked to her, wrinkling his nose at the mess she'd made. "You going to clean that up?"

Gillian grimaced as well. "I suppose."

He pulled Mara to her feet and dragged her across the room to the back chamber. After flinging her onto a bare pallet, he retrieved a piece of cloth from a battered wardrobe and tied it across her mouth and around her head. He was none too gentle in doing so. He started to leave, but then checked the ties at her wrists and ankles. Satisfied that the knots remained tight, he left her without a word or a backward glance.

Mara didn't believe that Nuala would have betrayed her intentionally. The minister and Binder had the priestess fooled as well. She wondered how many others they had deceived. Clearly they intended to use Mara as a cudgel against Tobias, but she thought it likely they would first lure him here under the guise of friendship.

At least he was alive, though. She knew that for certain now. More, neither Gillian nor the Binder had mentioned the princess. Maybe they didn't know she had survived.

These were hardly enough to give her hope; her life hung by a thread, and Tobias was in more danger than he could know. But they were something at least. They were all she had.

It festered in Droë's mind like a wound. She didn't know him. She had only just met the woman. Still the thought remained: vivid, alluring, frightening, thrilling.

Do I love him?

What might that mean? Loving a human. It wasn't something most Tirribin would consider or want. Droë, though, had long felt uncomfortable among her kind. Most Tirribin traveled in pairs or groups. Not her. She didn't like to hunt in packs. She thought she preferred to be alone. That was what she'd told herself for so long. Alone was better. Alone, she was content.

What if she'd been wrong? What if she wished to be apart from her kind, but not alone after all?

He didn't exist in her mind. She couldn't imagine his face, or the taste of his years. But the woman – girl, really; Droë *had* tasted *her* years – had spoken true. Curiosity about love consumed her, had for centuries. She had seen humans in the act of love, had watched, fascinated, as encounters that appeared by turns tender and rough, joyful and unpleasant, passionate, animal, at times violent, brought such racking pleasure. How could that be? What would it be like to allow someone so close?

Not for us, other Tirribin would say. We aren't human or Arrokad. That isn't our way.

Perhaps they were right. It wasn't their way. Then again, neither was hunting alone.

She came back to the promontory to look down on the ships, to take comfort in solitude, to ponder. She hadn't intended to do more. And yet...

"Treszlish." The name crossed her lips before she gave thought to why, to what she wanted.

Below, on Safsi Bay, a cloud of mist twisted and danced across the gentle swells, ignoring her. A summons didn't work as well on Shonla.

Droë hummed. She had no song in mind, but she made up a melody, and sent it forth in a voice both thin and piercing. A needle in the darkness. The mist turned, gathered, rose toward the headland.

In moments it surrounded her, hiding the moon but aglow with its light. Droë shivered. A figure coalesced before her, tall, shadowed.

"I prefer songs with words," he said, in a voice like inky waters.

"I know. I'm sorry. Next time."

"The hunting is good tonight. What do you want?"

"I don't know."

He canted his head and eased closer, so that she could see the hairless form, the thin lips and gleaming eyes. "You summoned me without purpose?"

"I wanted to talk."

He bared his square teeth in what she took for a smile. "I am flattered."

She grinned in response.

"So," he said after a brief pause, "talk."

"Do your kind love?"

"Love?" he repeated, eyes widening. "Do you love me, Tirribin?"

She shook her head. "No. I love no one, but it seems I will in another time."

"That is beyond my knowing."

"I know. Answer me. Do your kind love?"

"We love after a fashion. I have lain with my kind. Do Tirribin not?"

"We don't need to do so to reproduce. We don't die, and so we have no need to make more. We simply are."

"Yet you say that you will love."

Droë's cheeks warmed. "Not a Tirribin. A human."

He tucked his chin. "That is... unexpected. Why speak to me of this?"

"I have no one else." As soon as she spoke the words, she realized this wasn't the reason. She hadn't summoned him without purpose after all.

"I'm sorry for that. But I know too little of your kind to be of help. And what I know of humans..." He opened his hands, the gesture bespeaking uncertainty. "I think you would tire of this creature before long. Then again, they don't live long, so that might not be a problem."

"Perhaps," she said, not because she agreed, but to keep him from saying more. "Can you help me leave this place?"

He stared, eyes wide once more. "Three times now you have surprised me, this last most of all."

"Can you?"

His face compressed into something resembling a scowl. "I don't know. Where would you go?"

She faltered. "Daerjen."

"That is a very long way."

"I know."

"Shonla travel alone. We don't suffer companions of any sort."

"I know that as well."

The scowl grew more pronounced.

"You're cold now. I see your skin is roughened. If I were to bear you it would be like this constantly, for a long time. I can travel swiftly, but I need to feed, and I don't journey in daylight."

"I don't like daylight either. You know that. And I can feed, when you do. I'll hunt on my own, away from your mists. I'll warm myself then."

Tresz glared. She sensed he had run out of arguments. So she offered one of her own.

"Time is wrong now. We're in the early days of a misfuture. This will affect you and your kind as well."

"What kind of misfuture? How is it wrong?"

Droë shrugged. "I can't say. Events have been altered, but I'm blind to what might have been."

He growled deep in his chest. "I find Tirribin confounding. I don't believe this is wise."

"I can sing for you. All night. I'll sing song after song."

The Shonla stilled, ever a creature of prey. "You know many songs?"

"I've lived for centuries, stalking sailors, merchants, humans in Windhome port. I've heard their songs, learned them."

He remained motionless, a dark mass in his shifting fog.

Droë rubbed her arms. It *was* cold. Journeying with the Shonla would be a trial. Yet the more she contemplated the idea, the more attractive it grew. She had been on this little island for too many centuries. She was desperate for him to agree.

"Very well," Tresz said after a time, rousing himself with a small shudder. "I will bear you, and listen to your songs, and together we will hunt and explore new waters. I've been too long in the north."

"I was thinking the same thing," Droë said.

The Shonla smiled. "Shall we hunt before we begin?"

Droë nodded, excitement buzzing in her chest like a swarm of bees. Tresz knelt and indicated with a turn of his blunt hand that she should climb onto his back. She approached him, wary, uncertain. Not that she feared him. Shonla had always looked... slimy, like a fish.

He wasn't at all. His skin was cool and dry and smooth, more like a snake than anything else. She wrapped her arms around his neck, her legs around his waist. She recalled seeing human children ride their parents in this way. As he straightened, she decided she liked it.

He walked to the promontory's edge, stepped off, and dropped with alarming speed, the cloud tightening around them. Before they hit the rocks and surf below, their path altered and they glided out across the bay toward a ship. Droë laughed aloud, drawing an amused rumble from the Shonla.

She was being rash, she knew. The girl had come back many years by her own reckoning to prevent a misfuture. By embarking on this journey together, by hunting along the way, she and Tresz would change the future themselves. Who knew what would come of their actions, their appetites?

Then again, to Tirribin and Shonla the concerns of humans were trifles, fleeting and insignificant. And she had a purpose that even Tresz couldn't know. *Do I love him?*

What might it mean to become more than what she was, to change from this girl-thing to someone older, someone who could love?

She couldn't do this on her own, but she believed there were others who could help her. They, too, could be found in the south.

CHAPTER 37

In the morning, after Tobias and Sofya broke their fast, Tobias again left the princess in Kaarti's care, this time to make his way to the marketplace through another misting rain. During the night, he had made up his mind to leave Kaarti's inn. They couldn't remain in one place for long, and he feared the apparent safety of the Notch would prove illusory. He would buy food, gather Sofya and his belongings, and move on.

In the market, he bought a sweet cake from one of the vendors to make himself less conspicuous. As he ate he walked a full circuit among the stalls, learning who sold what.

After finishing his cake, he brushed his fingers on his trousers, and started toward the food vendor whose prices seemed most reasonable.

"Good morning, Tobias," said a voice from behind.

He spun, reaching for his blade. He froze, blinked. Disbelief warred with joy. Gillian Ainfor stood before him, bobbed hair dampened by the rain, smile crinkling the lines around her blue eyes.

He wanted to throw his arms around her, but among so many he didn't dare.

"You're alive," he whispered. "I thought for certain–"

Her gaze traced his scars. "We managed to get away."

"We?"

She quirked an eyebrow, sly, elusive. "Come with me."

468

She set out toward Outer Notch, and he followed. They walked by homes and shops, she half a pace ahead, neither of them speaking a word, or sharing a glance. Tobias cast a wary eye at each shelter and every person they passed, but no one seemed interested in them. Gillian wore plain clothes in shades of dun. Only her lovely face would have drawn attention, and she kept her gaze fixed on the ground.

They walked nearly to the open shelf at the mouth of the Notch, halting at a shelter that wasn't far from the Seers' establishment. It was unmarked and unobtrusive. She pushed aside the canvas and entered, holding it open for Tobias. He stepped through and straightened as Bexler Filt turned to face him, a planing tool in his hand.

"Walker," the Binder said. "Gillian thought she had recognized you. I'm delighted to see she was right." His tone belied the words.

"Binder Filt, it's good to see you again." Tobias stepped to the center of the shelter, taking in his surroundings. Two chairs flanked a table. A small cage holding a pair of pigeons rested on the floor. Otherwise it was empty. "What is this place?"

The Binder looked past him to Gillian.

"It belonged to my father," she said, joining Tobias and hooking an arm through his. "He was a farrier in the city, and fell upon hard times. Even after he regained his business, he kept this. 'You never know when luck will run out,' he said. I suppose he saw it as a hedge against future troubles. When the Sheraighs came, this seemed the perfect place to hide."

"How did you escape?"

She lifted a shoulder. "Good fortune. We were on our way to dinner when we heard the explosions. We rescued a few devices from the Binder's workshop and fled."

"There was blood in the workshop that night. I saw it."

"What were you doing there?" Filt demanded.

"I went hoping to find a chronofor."

"What's the matter with yours?"

"It was shattered in the attack." His heart leapt, and he rounded on Filt. "I have the pieces with me! Can you can fix it?"

"Yes, maybe," he said, without enthusiasm.

The first tickle of a warning touched Tobias's mind. He thought he heard noise from the back of the shelter. The rain had intensified, though; he couldn't tell what was real and what he imagined. He chanced a look at Gillian, but she was watching Filt.

"I have only a few tools with me," the Binder said. "But I can have a look at it."

"That can wait." Gillian flashed that disarming smile. Tobias thought it strained. "Tell us how you got away."

He regarded them. "What about that blood?" He looked around again. "Where's your wife, Binder?"

"I fear she didn't make it out of the castle."

"I'm sorry," Tobias said. He had the distinct impression that his condolences were unnecessary.

"You were in the hall with the sovereign and his family?" the minister prompted.

"Yes. I... I pretended to be dead, and when the Sheraighs' attention was elsewhere, I snuck out through the back."

"What about the princess?"

He wanted to trust them. Half a bell before he would have, without hesitation. But that tickle had become a steady beat, like the pounding of war drums. Her question brought panic. He needed to get away, without revealing that Sofya still lived.

"I assume she was lost with the others."

The corners of her mouth turned down in reproach. "Come now, Walker. You can do better than that."

"What makes you think she's alive? Surely you've heard what I have: the entire family was killed."

Gillian and the Binder shared another glance. "Of course. We just–"

"We hoped for the best," Filt said.

"Yes, I'm sure."

"Those are nasty scars," the minister said. "Where did you get them?"

Tobias swallowed. "I was in the dungeon, a 'guest' of the man who killed the sovereign."

Gillian *tsked*. "Yet here you stand, free, healed. You've been fortunate."

He almost said, *I've had help*, but thought better of it. "Yes, I suppose I have."

"Where have you been hiding since your escape?" Gillian asked. "Clearly here in the Notch. A boarding house perhaps?"

Tobias tried to appear calm, but he felt as though Gillian had pressed cold steel against his throat.

"No, I hadn't any coin. Travelers can't carry any, and I haven't dared take a job. I've been depending on the kindness of strangers."

Her smile could have frozen Safsi Bay. "Well, you don't have to do that anymore, do you? You're welcome here."

"You're too kind."

"Hardly."

"I have a few items to retrieve from where I've been staying most recently."

Filt quirked an eyebrow. "I thought a Traveler couldn't carry anything."

"I took some items from the castle that night. A sword, two pistols, and two apertures from your workshop. Things I could barter if the need arose."

"How resourceful. Aren't those items in your carry sack?" He lifted his chin in the direction of the pack Tobias carried.

"Not all of them. I should be going."

"I don't think so," Gillian said. She had produced a pistol. Tobias wasn't sure from where. She aimed it at his chest, her hand steady.

"Let's begin again," Filt said. He crossed to Tobias and pulled the pack from his shoulder. "Where is the princess?"

"I have no idea."

"You're lying." The Binder opened the carry sack and peered inside. "He was telling the truth about the pistols and devices. Though not about where he had them hidden." He tossed the sack onto the floor, beyond Tobias's reach.

"You betrayed him, didn't you?" Tobias said. "You plotted with House Sheraigh against Mearlan."

Gillian laughed. "For an intelligent boy, you have a great deal to learn about court politics."

"Meaning what?"

"You'll have to suss that out for yourself. And you'll have time." Her gaze flicked to the Binder. "Take him in back. We'll tie him up."

Filt had drawn a pistol of his own and trained it on him as well. He tipped his head toward another curtain of canvas. "Back here."

He gave Tobias a wide berth, tracking him with the muzzle of his weapon. Tobias parted the curtain and stepped through. Again he halted, swaying. He *had* heard someone.

A woman sat on a low pallet, her back against the rock face of the cavern. She was dark-skinned, like him, with bronze hair that fell about her shoulders. Her wrists and ankles were bound, and a cloth across her mouth kept her from speaking. She stared up at him with bright hazel eyes that he knew.

As he approached, her eyes widened: recognition, acknowledgment, fear. She knew him as well.

How could this be? Mara was a Spanner, not a Walker, and this woman had to be in her late twenties or early thirties. *Just as you appear to be.*

"Mara?" he whispered.

"Good, you do know her."

Tobias turned again. Gillian stood by the opening in the

canvas, pistol in hand.

"She claimed to know of you, but she says you've never met."

He didn't gainsay her.

"Aren't we going to tie him up?" Filt asked.

"Wait." Gillian walked forward, halting just beyond Tobias's reach. "*She* said they'd never met. But that was because time had changed. You know her, don't you? She's aged fourteen years, and still you knew her on sight." She smiled. "I think we have a romance here, Bexler."

"So what?"

She stepped past Tobias, drawing a curved blade that glinted with light from the front room.

"So he might be interested in trading one life for another." She knelt beside Mara, setting the blade at the base of Mara's neck and gazing at Tobias. "The princess or the Traveler. Your choice."

"I've told you: I don't know where the princess is. I thought she was dead until–"

Gillian twitched her hand. No more. Mara gave a muffled cry. Blood dripped over the silver knife, staining her shirt.

A tear slipped from Mara's eye, but she stared back at Tobias. He perceived no plea in the look she gave him. Somehow she understood the stakes, and she was willing to die to protect the princess.

"Don't make me cut her again. There's an artery near here, and if I nick it…" Gillian shrugged. "Now, where is she?"

"I'm telling you, I don't know."

She pressed the knife into Mara's skin, drawing a moan and more blood.

"I can lie," Tobias said, allowing desperation to shade his tone. "I can tell you what I know you want to hear. But I don't know where she is!"

Filt looked from Tobias to Gillian. "Maybe he's telling the truth."

"And maybe you're a fool. He's lying."

"I'm not!"

"Orzili says you are."

Tobias held himself still, trying not to react.

Gillian smiled. "I believe him more than I believe you. Now, where is she?"

"Orzili's wrong."

Gillian jerked her hand, slashing Mara across the cheek. Blood poured from the wound, which cut dangerously close to Mara's eye. She was crying now, sobs shaking her body.

"I grow tired of this, Walker. I can just as easily kill her and hurt you instead. Is that what you want?"

"Yes! I mean, no, don't kill her. Let her go. You can torture me all you like and I'll still give you the same answer. The answer I gave Orzili again and again: I don't know anything about the princess." He pointed at Mara. "What I do know is that she has nothing to do with this. I don't even know why she's here."

"She seems to think she's here to save the future, or some such nonsense. And no, I won't release her."

"This is a waste of time," Filt said, his voice tight. "Are you going to kill her, or should we tie him up and call for Orzili?"

Gillian glared at Tobias for another moment. She gave Mara a needless shove and thrust herself off the pallet, pocketing her blade and aiming her pistol at Tobias again.

"Tie him," she said.

Mara righted herself, her eyes on Tobias. He returned her gaze, hoping to communicate what he needed her to do.

"Over here," Filt said, waving Tobias toward the cavern's back wall.

Tobias walked to the spot the Binder indicated. Gillian positioned herself in front of him, her pistol hand unwavering.

Filt stowed his weapon, produced a length of rope, and looped it around Tobias's wrists.

Before he could do more, Mara threw herself off the pallet with a violent contortion. Gillian turned. Filt's gaze snapped that way as well.

Tobias jerked his hands out of the Binder's grasp, and twisted his hands free of the rope. Filt grappled with him, trying to rip the rope away. When that failed, he reached for his weapon. Tobias pounded a fist into the Binder's side. Filt grunted, folding in on himself.

By the time Gillian recovered from her surprise, Tobias had the rope around Filt's neck, and the man's pistol in hand. He pressed the barrel against the Binder's temple. Filt struggled to get free, but he couldn't match Tobias's strength.

"Put down your weapon," Tobias said.

Gillian shook her head. "I don't think I will. Kill him, and I'll kill you."

Tobias tightened the loop of rope, eliciting a choked gasp from Filt. "I don't have to shoot him to kill him."

She shifted her aim to Mara. "Is this a trade you're willing to make?"

"I could ask the same of you. If I kill him with the rope, I can still shoot you. Now put your weapon on the floor and kick it away."

"By the Two, Gillian—"

"Shut up!"

The minister's brow furrowed. Perhaps she wasn't as devoted to the Binder as Tobias thought. She and Filt were going to have an interesting conversation when all of this was over. If they both survived.

At last, muttering a foul curse, she set her pistol on the floor and kicked it beyond her reach.

"And the knife."

She regarded the Binder with disgust. But she pulled out the bloodied blade and tossed it to the floor. Tobias pushed the Binder forward, intending to toe the knife beyond Gillian's reach. Filt struggled against him, slowing him.

Gillian spun and ran, darting through the narrow gap in the canvas. Spitting a curse of his own, Tobias hammered the side of his pistol into the back of Filt's skull. The first blow staggered the Binder; the second rendered him unconscious.

Tobias cast a glance at Mara, but followed Gillian, pausing at the opening in the cloth, in case the minister waited on the other side. He peered through the gap, searching for her. He saw nothing, and eased through, his weapon raised. She was gone. So was the cage holding the messenger pigeons.

He ran to the shelter's entrance and out onto the stone shelf. Seeing no sign of her, he cursed again and returned to the back room.

Filt hadn't moved. Blood oozed from an egg-sized lump on the back of his head. Mara had raised herself into a sitting position on the stone floor. Tobias hurried to her and untied the gag.

"Thank you," she said, her voice a rasp.

He worked to untie the knot in the rope binding her hands. The skin on her wrists was chafed raw.

"We have to hurry," he said. "The minister is gone, and she's taken the messenger pigeons. She's probably sent word to Orzili already."

"Who is that?"

"The man who killed Hayncalde's sovereign."

He finally untied her hands. While Mara worked her ankles free, he used the first piece of rope to truss the Binder's limp hands. Mara joined him and tied Filt's ankles. Tobias shoved the gag in the man's mouth.

He stood and helped her up. For a fivecount, they remained like that, gazing at each other. The cuts on her cheek and neck still bled, a dark match for his own scars.

"Those need to be cleaned and bandaged."

"Later. I'm all right."

Still he stared at her. Her face was leaner than he remembered, but the eyes, the hair, the lips...

"It's really you, isn't it?"

She nodded.

"I didn't know you could Walk."

"Neither did I. We should leave."

Her words jolted him into motion. He retrieved his pack from the front room while Mara went back for Filt's pistol. He took her hand and led her out of the shelter and back toward Kaarti's inn.

"Where are we going?"

"To get the rest of my things. And... a friend."

They walked quickly. The blood on Mara's face drew stares, but Tobias didn't dare stop. He wasn't sure how long it would take Orzili to get here, but he didn't think they had more than a bell to get away. Less if the assassin and his men Spanned.

"Did you notice if that woman took the tri-device?" Mara asked, half-running to keep up with him.

Tobias steered them among the people on the path, weaving in and out like a woodland hawk gliding among trees. "The what?"

"The tri-device. I think it was a tri-sextant."

He stopped to consider her. "A tri-sextant," he repeated, thinking of the golden object Filt tried to hide when first he entered the shelter, and of the odd devices he had seen in the hands of Orzili's men and with the assassins in his own time.

"Yes. It allows Spanners to bring others with them and–"

"And to carry objects, weapons. To remain clothed."

"That's right."

"They don't exist in our time."

"They do in mine."

"Yours? I don't understand."

"This is the first time I've met you, Tobias." A faint smile touched her lips as she spoke his name. "You weren't in my time, at least not the one I remember. The world has changed."

He nearly asked her in what ways it was different, but the question died on his lips. He didn't have to ask. His arrival in this time had coincided with upheavals that would have had ramifications through history. Daerjen was already in chaos, and he was certain Oaqamar was responsible. The Sheraighs owed their newfound power to the autarchy and would do their bidding. Oaqamar would soon be the dominant power between the oceans.

He had come back – Mearlan had sent him back – to change history. He'd succeeded all too well. They had been arrogant fools to believe they could shape a future to their liking.

"I didn't mean for any of this to happen," he said, knowing the words were empty.

"I know, and I came back to help you make it right again."

More arrogance, though he kept that thought to himself. "Do you know how? Because I wouldn't know where to begin."

"We'll figure that out. First we need to get away from here."

Right. He started forward again, reaching for her hand. Glancing her way, he stumbled. Beyond her, in the distance came several men in blue uniforms.

"Already?" he whispered.

She looked back. "The messenger pigeons. And the tri-sextants. It wouldn't take them long."

Tugging on her hand, Tobias broke into a run. She followed. Shouts and screams echoed behind them. Within a spirecount, the pathway was choked with men, women, and children fleeing their shelters. It seemed residents of the Notch lived their lives with one ear to the ground.

Tobias and Mara fought through the crowd, but progress came grudgingly, in fits and starts, until Tobias wanted to scream his frustration. The path widened at the marketplace, where peddlers were already packing up their goods. Tobias and Mara skirted the space, and ran to Kaarti's establishment.

Tobias shouldered the canvas door aside and entered. Kaarti stood in the center of the common room, a musket raised to her shoulder. She lowered it upon recognizing him. Sofya sat on the floor at her feet, playing with her doll and chattering happily.

"Who's this?" Kaarti demanded.

"A friend from home."

"I heard shouts, people yellin' about soldiers. Figured it was your fault." She grinned, softening the words.

Tobias lifted the princess into his arms. She stuck her thumb in her mouth, clutching the doll in her other hand. He grabbed the pile of swaddling and carried Sofya into his chamber to reclaim his few belongings.

When he reentered the common room, he found Kaarti watching the entrance and gripping her musket. Mara held herself still, as if waiting for the woman to turn the weapon on her. She had cleaned the blood from her face. The cut on her cheek was livid, the marks on her neck less so.

"You're all right?" he asked her.

"For now, yes."

Kaarti eyed them, but didn't lower her weapon.

"That's a fine way to get yourself shot," Tobias said.

"I won't allow Sheraigh blue to set foot in here."

"I understand. But…" He shook his head, knowing he would never convince the matron of anything. "I'd just hate to see you hurt."

"Yous are leaving," she said.

"Yes. We need to get away from here."

"Those soldiers really looking for yous?"

"I'm afraid so."

She appeared surprised by his candor. "I might be able to hide yous." She jerked her head at her sleeping chamber. "There's more to this place than one might think."

"I'm sure that's true, but we'll be safer far from Hayncalde."

"Why? Who are you?" She indicated the princess with a raised chin. "Who's she? Why are demons and soldiers so interested in yous?"

"It's best you don't know."

"Aye, probably. Where will yous go?"

"I don't know. Back to the wharves, I suppose."

"Most folk will be goin' the other way. To the caverns. Yous'll stand out."

"Going deeper into the Notch is too dangerous. Our one chance is to reach the wharves. Before we came here, the temple bought us passage on a ship. Maybe we can find another one tonight."

"Tonight," Kaarti repeated, breathless. "Of course. I should have remembered. Yous know what tonight is, right? Or what tomorrow is?"

"This isn't the time for riddles, Kaarti."

"I know that," she said, sounding more like her usual cross self. "This is the last day of Sipar's Settling. Tomorrow is–"

"Kheraya's Emergence," Mara said.

"That's right. Some of them ships on the gulf might be sending dories to land. Most go to the city, but a few always come here, especially ones that don't want attention from the royals. Go farther south from Outer Notch. You'll find them there."

Tobias blinked with surprise and hope. Perhaps they could get away after all. "We'll try that. Thank you."

Kaarti looked at the princess, her expression softening. "Such a beauty. She's almost..." Her cheeks went white, comprehension widening her eyes at long last. "I've been a fool, haven't I?" She shifted her gaze to Tobias. "Sipar bless you and keep you safe. All of you."

Tobias answered with a sad smile. Notwithstanding her abrupt manner, he liked the woman. "Goodbye, Kaarti. Again, my thanks." He crossed to the entrance and peered out, beckoning to Mara as he did. He saw no soldiers.

"If they ask me, I won't tell them yous were here. I won't tell them nothing. Sheraigh bastards."

He cast another smile over his shoulder and stepped out, Mara close behind. Pausing just outside the boarding house, he adjusted his pack and started toward Outer Notch, walking against the flood of people who crowded the walkway. He tried not to appear in too much haste, but if Mara's efforts to do the same were any indication, he probably failed. They hadn't gone more than a few paces when a soldier stepped into view in front of them, his musket at eye level.

They halted. Others continued past, eyeing the soldier, eyeing them, but content to walk on if it meant no trouble would come their way. Tobias couldn't blame them.

"If either of you so much as twitches a hand in the direction of your belt or your pack, I'll put a ball in your skull. Understand?"

Tobias held up one hand; with the other he cradled Sofya. Mara sidled closer to him, her hands raised.

The soldier's bayonet shone with sunlight, and a smug grin exposed crooked yellow teeth. "I was hoping I'd be the one to find yous. A shit-skinned Northisler and his shit-skinned baby. There's a bounty for you. Fifteen gold." He flicked a glance in Mara's direction. "I don't know what I'll get for you, but even if the money ain't good, I might get a bit of sport out of it." He grinned again.

"We have gold," Tobias said. "Let us go, and it's yours."

"Pretty sure it's mine anyway. Funny thing. No one ever told us if they wanted you alive or dead. I'm guessing it don't matter."

Tobias felt the blood drain from his cheeks.

The man chuckled. "Nothing to say, eh? Good. My colonel hinted there'd be an extra reward for the one what caught you. A bottle of somethin'. Looks like I'll be drinkin' to the two of yous tonight."

"Did yous get him?"

The soldier glanced toward the shelter, but kept the barrel of his weapon trained on Tobias. Kaarti stepped out of the boarding house. She had left her musket inside, and instead leaned on a crooked wooden cane.

"You know him?" the man asked.

"Do now. Showed up here a few nights ago. Strangers in the Notch are always curiosities, but this fella – and his woman – they was more curious than most. Acted odd, claimed to be on the run from a coin monger. I don't believe them, but what can I do? I'm lame and old and I don't want trouble. But I knew them for liars all along."

She hobbled closer to the man, watching Tobias and Mara, contempt on her wizened face.

"He's worse than a liar," the guard said. He sighted Tobias with his weapon. "He's a spy. Haven't decided yet whether to shoot him or let him hang."

"Ah, that's fine," Kaarti said. She stopped a pace or two short of the soldier. "That's just fine."

Tobias never would have believed an old woman could move with such speed. One moment she leaned on her walking stick. The next she straightened and swung the cane up in a tight arc, catching the man full in the groin. He grunted, doubled over, his eyes bulging, the musket dropping from his hands and clattering on the stone. Before he could fall, she swung the stick a second time, striking him at the base of the neck. A sickening crack echoed in the cavern. The guard dropped to the ground and moved no more.

People streamed past, gazes drawn by Kaarti's attack. They said nothing. A few grinned.

"I think I might have killed him," she said mildly, looking down at him.

Tobias stared at the soldier. His back rose and fell. "No, he's breathing."

"Well, I suppose that's good."

"There are more coming," Mara said, voice low.

Tobias saw them as well. The soldiers hadn't spotted them yet, but they would.

"Let me hide yous," Kaarti said. "It's the only way."

"What about him?" Tobias said, gesturing at the unconscious soldier.

The innkeeper grinned. "It's all right. They'll never think to look here. Who would beat a soldier senseless and then stay?"

"Aside from you, you mean?"

"Right. Aside from me." She shuffled back inside, gesturing for them to follow. Mara claimed the soldier's fallen musket and she, Tobias, and the princess retreated into the shelter.

CHAPTER 38

30th Day of Sipar's Settling, Year 633

Kaarti led them through a small bedchamber and into an alcove formed naturally by the cavern. At the back of this, they found a second alcove, also small, though spacious enough to accommodate all of them. A candle burned here, illuminating a cluster of water skins and several bundles that Mara assumed must hold food. The air was chill and stale, but it was as comfortable a haven as they could have hoped to find.

"There's enough here to keep us for days," Kaarti said in a whisper. "But we shouldn't have to wait that long."

The princess talked gibberish in a voice loud enough to make Mara cringe. Tobias walked her in a tight circle, bouncing her gently in his arms and singing to her in a low voice. She quieted, and soon slid her thumb into her mouth, her eyelids drooping.

Mara watched them, thinking they could easily be father and daughter.

"He's good with the wee one, isn't he?" Kaarti asked, breathing the words. Mara heard pride in the question.

"He is."

"How is it yous know each other?"

She hesitated, wondering how much Tobias had revealed. "We've been friends a long time."

"That's not quite what I asked." She held up a hand forestalling another response. "It's all right. It's not my business."

The princess fell asleep. Tobias continued to walk with her, setting his feet with care, making no sound. None of them spoke. They listened for noises in the common room or the other bedchambers. At one point Mara thought she heard someone. At the same time, Kaarti stiffened and cast a warning glance Tobias's way. He had already stopped, but when the princess stirred, he resumed his circling. Footsteps echoed outside the alcove – at least two pairs. Canvas rustled, plates and pots clattered. Kaarti picked up her musket, and Mara shouldered the one they'd taken from the soldier, drawing a nod of approval from the woman.

Tobias moved closer to Mara and pulled out a pistol with his free hand. He stared at the canvas that concealed them, a haunted look in his eyes.

Mara allowed her gaze to flick over his scars, though she took care not to let him see. From what she'd heard in the minister's shelter, she guessed that he'd been tortured. He wasn't as beautiful as he'd been in that vision Droë offered. He was older, marred. He carried burdens now that he hadn't before. She didn't care. She had Walked back for him, not because he was handsome, though he still was, but because he cared about her, and because he needed her help. None of that had changed.

He glanced at her, and she forced herself to look away. She rubbed the aching, red skin on her wrist. Both of them had been marked by their journeys back in time.

The noises from the common room continued. Something shattered. Wood cracked. But no one disturbed the cloth directly in front of them.

After a few more spirecounts of this, the footsteps retreated and silence gripped the shelter once again. They remained in the alcove, unwilling to risk revealing themselves. Mara sat, the musket resting across her thighs; Tobias circled with the princess. Time dragged by.

"There's voices outside," Kaarti said, eventually, not bothering to whisper. "Folks is coming back. I think the Sheraighs must be gone."

Tobias dragged a hand over his chin and glanced down at the sleeping princess.

He set her gently on the floor, and proceeded to change her swaddling, his hands deft and sure. Mara couldn't have done such a thing. By the time he was finished, the girl was awake and fussing. Kaarti unwrapped some hard cheese and bread, which Tobias fed to the child.

"Yous are still planning to leave?"

Tobias didn't look up from feeding the princess. "I think we have to."

"I can sell you a bit of food," the woman said. "Cheese, a loaf of my bread. Some milk."

"We'd be grateful."

She bundled some food for them, gave them a skin of milk. Tobias gave her several silver treys.

"You're a good lad," she said. "Take care of the wee one." She turned to Mara. "You see that he does."

Mara couldn't keep from smiling. "I will."

All of them left the alcove, crossed through the bedchamber, and entered the common room. The table and chairs had been smashed to pieces, as had several bowls and platters.

"Kaarti," Tobias said in a whisper.

"It's all right. There's more to be had in the market. And I can bake for coin. I'll be fine. Others had worse."

Faint daylight lit the edges of the canvas; Mara guessed that dusk wasn't more than a bell away. If they were to leave before nightfall, they had to go now. Kaarti seemed to have the same thought. She peered out into the Notch before pulling her head back in and closing the gap in the cloth.

"No soldiers. And the one I hit is gone. I'd say it's safe, but I's the feeling it's not." She grimaced. "At least not for yous."

"We'll be all right." Tobias checked his pistols.

Mara checked hers as well before returning it to her overshirt pocket and hefting the musket.

"That'll draw attention," Kaarti said.

Mara glanced at Tobias.

"She's probably right," he said. He handed her one of his pistols. "Chances are I won't get off two shots. Not with her in my arms. Anyway, you've always been as good a shot. If not better."

She frowned at this. Could it be that in his future she was changed from how she'd been in her own time, good at different things, interested in other subjects, even different in temperament? It felt odd to have him talk about her as someone he knew, had known. She didn't know how to respond.

Kaarti checked outside again and gestured that they could go.

Mara followed Tobias out onto the stone path, falling in step beside him.

The chasm looked like it had come through a cyclone. Many shelters had been torn down. Broken furniture, rent clothes, and shattered containers littered the stone. Everywhere Mara looked, men and women saw to the repair of their homes and shops. She and Tobias walked past them, saying nothing. She tried not to stare.

Most of those they encountered ignored them, but not all. Some stared hard at the three of them. Perhaps they saw nothing more than dark-skinned parents and their dark-skinned child, which would have been enough to mark them as different in this pale land. Mara sensed, though, that a few saw more. Though new to the Notch, she could tell that Tobias didn't belong here, and of course she didn't either. They wore their Windhome training like silken finery. It set them apart, made them conspicuous. She was certain some of the people glaring at them knew exactly who had drawn this destruction to their haven.

"Tobias—"

"I know," he said, his voice as low as hers. "Just keep walking."

They quickened their strides, which only made them more obvious. Even the princess seemed to understand the danger. She kept her thumb in her mouth, her eyes wide and watchful, one hand fisted in Tobias's overshirt.

As they neared the strand, and the stone shelf widened, Tobias slowed. "Blood and bone."

Mara saw them as well. Soldiers – only a pair, but she assumed there were others nearby.

Tobias veered, approaching a shelter that might have belonged to a peddler, but which appeared deserted, its canvas façade ripped in several places. From there, he backtracked until they reached another shelter that smelled of spirit and something cloying. Mara's eyes watered.

Tobias tapped on the shelter. After a brief wait, the canvas parted to reveal a man whose skin was only somewhat lighter than theirs. He was slight, and his eyes were glassy and bloodshot. He regarded the three of them for the span of a breath and then stood aside so they could enter.

More men sat on the floor inside, all of them Northislers. Two held small, soiled cloths to their faces. The man who had greeted them gripped such a cloth in a slender hand. A pile of shattered wood sat in the middle of the shelter; the remnants of tables and chairs. A fourth man sat against a wall. Mara couldn't tell whether he was wounded, passed out, or dead.

Tobias leaned closer to her. "They're—"

"Seers, I know."

"Your lives are in peril."

Tobias faced the man who had admitted them. "Yes. We're trying to get away."

"You avoided the caverns at the base of the escarpment. That was wise. But the threat remains. The snare is closing."

"Do you know how many soldiers guard this stairway?"

"Four."

Tobias muttered another curse. "Might we be better off hiding somewhere?"

"I believe not. Men will search here again, and again until they find you. Leaving now is the safer choice, though all is relative."

"He talks like a Seer," Mara muttered.

The man smirked. "We have not met. You are a Walker as well?"

"I'm a Traveler, yes."

The smirk lingered, but he turned back to Tobias. "You are running still."

"We've fought as well. And I'm convinced we'll have to fight our way through in order to leave."

"I believe you will, yes. The outcome is... uncertain."

"I assumed you'd say as much." Tobias's tone was dry.

"You think that a hedge. You may be correct."

One of the other men said something in a language Mara recognized from Windhome, but couldn't follow. His voice was sharp, the words strident.

"My colleague says you are a danger to us, and that you cannot remain here. I am afraid I must agree with him. Normally, I would argue on your behalf, but after today's show of force..."

"I understand," Tobias said. "We won't remain here for long."

The second man repeated whatever he had said, his voice rising.

The first Seer half-turned in his direction, before straightening. "We can brook no delay. You must leave us. Now."

"You'd let her die?" Tobias asked. "You know who's after her, and you know what they'll do when they find her. And still you'd send us away?"

Mara was afraid to inhale; the air felt brittle.

"You claimed to be a friend of her mother, Hanrid," Tobias went on. "Is this how you honor that friendship?"

The second Seer started to say more, but the one named Hanrid rounded on him and hissed a response, silencing the man, who flinched back a step.

"What would you have us do?" Hanrid asked. "If we are seen helping you, our lives are forfeit as well."

Tobias faltered, but Mara's heart jumped with the first inkling of a plan.

"The liquid soaked into those cloths–" She indicated Hanrid's square of fabric with a raised chin. "Tincture you call it, yes?"

The man gave a stiff nod.

"Is it as flammable as it smells?"

The Seer scowled. "An attack?"

"A diversion."

He studied her, his gaze honed.

"We'll pay you for what we use."

He flicked his fingers, a gesture bespeaking impatience, and perhaps umbrage. But he didn't dismiss the notion. "They will know we helped you."

"Not if we make it look like a theft," Tobias said.

"What would you burn?"

That brought Mara up short.

"There's a shelter near here where we were held against our will," Tobias said. "I have no compunction about burning them out."

The seer shook his head. "You will be noticed. Traced back to this shelter."

"I'll be careful," Tobias said.

"The fire you start might spread. The entire Notch could be lost."

"I'm hoping the soldiers will prevent that."

Hanrid's scowl deepened. He huddled with his colleagues, and even woke the fourth man, who, it seemed, had simply been sleeping. The man who had spoken earlier sounded wary of the idea, but the others agreed. Soon enough the second man acquiesced with a sullen shrug.

"Very well," Hanrid said. "Two treys will pay for the Tincture and cloth to ignite it. We have rope in back, if you would be so kind as to tie us up."

They soon had the Seers seated and bound in the middle of their common room. Tobias argued that he should be the one to burn Gillian Ainfor's shelter, but Mara disagreed.

"The Sheraighs are looking for you, and so is this Orzili you keep talking about. No one knows who I am. And besides, if..." She spared the Seers a glance. "If the child begins to fuss, I won't know what to do. She responds to you."

Tobias surrendered with a sigh. "All right. You know which shelter it is?"

"Of course." Mara gripped a bottle of Tincture in one hand, and a flint and metal in the other. Her pistol lay heavy in the pocket of her overshirt. She hid the bottle as well and slipped out of the shelter into the damp night air.

Even with soldiers positioned at the mouth of the Notch, the stone shelf wasn't empty. A few people darted from shelter to shelter, casting wary glances toward the uniformed men. Mara followed their example, watching the Sheraighs as she crept farther into the Notch. She didn't think they had seen her.

Despite her brave reply to Tobias, she wasn't certain she could find the shelter in which she had been imprisoned. She was exhausted and bewildered the night she arrived, and desperate to get away after she and Tobias subdued the Binder. Moreover, all these shelters looked much the same. She feared she might stride past it unawares.

To her surprise, though, she knew the shelter as soon as she spotted it. Her skin crawled with memories of the place. She paused in mid-stride and glanced around before approaching the entrance.

She put her ear to the canvas. Hearing nothing, she reached into her pocket, grasped her pistol, and stepped inside.

Nothing stirred within, but Mara noted that the minister's furniture had been spared. She crossed to the back room. The Binder was gone, as were his tools and devices. That suited her. Arson was one thing. Murder was another.

She shoved the chairs and table to the back of the common room so that they pressed up against the canvas separating the front space from the rear. Then she placed the bottle of Tincture at the base of the canvas as far from the furniture as possible. Finally, her hands trembling, she used the flint and metal to light the cloth that jutted from the bottle like a fuse from a bomb.

Hanrid had assured her that this would be enough to make the bottle explode, and she believed him.

Taking leave of the doomed shelter, she returned to the Seers' establishment, careful again not to be seen. The walk back felt much shorter than had her search for the minister's shelter.

"Did everything go all right?" Tobias asked as soon as she entered the cavern.

"I think so. We'll know soon enough."

Mara had listened for the explosion, but had heard nothing. Now, though, she smelled smoke. She and Tobias shared a look.

"Gag us," Hanrid said, "and watch for the soldiers. As soon as they pass this shelter, you must leave. Every moment you linger puts all our lives at risk."

Tobias did as the man said, but left Hanrid for last.

"Thank you," he said, his voice low. "I won't forget this." He pushed a lock of hair from the princess's brow. "I'll make sure she never does either."

The Seer nodded, grave as a cleric. "You honor us."

Tobias set the man's gag in place and joined Mara by the entrance. The smell of smoke strengthened. Peering out at the Notch, Mara thought she saw a flicker of firelight. But they kept out of sight, until at last she heard shouts as well. They didn't have to wait long after that. Three soldiers flashed past the Seers' shelter, brushing so close to the canvas that she could have reached out and touched them as they ran by.

"One left," Tobias whispered. He held his pistol in one hand, and had the babe cradled in his other arm. "That's probably the best we can hope for."

"I agree. Lead the way."

He didn't move. Instead, he turned his stunning green eyes on her. "I know as far as you're concerned we've never met. But I'm glad you're here."

Her cheeks heated. "Let's go," she said. "Standing here is making me nervous."

He spared the Seer one last look and pushed through the canvas. Mara followed.

As they neared the edge of the Notch, stepping out from under the overhanging cliffs into a cold, steady rain, the remaining soldier caught sight of them. He gave them the most cursory of glances. An instant later, though, his gaze snapped back and he fumbled with his musket.

"Don't," Tobias said, his voice carrying over the wind, the pelting raindrops, and the rush and retreat of the surf.

The man froze, eyes shifting from Tobias's pistol to the two Mara held. They strode to where he stood.

"Lay your musket on the ground."

"And if I don't?"

"You'll die," Mara said.

"I don't believe you. You won't shoot because you don't want to be heard."

They didn't have time for this.

The guard hadn't moved, but it wouldn't take much for him

to raise his weapon and fire.

"You're right," Tobias said. "I don't want to shoot. It would be much easier for me to summon a time demon."

The man gave a small shake of his head. "You're bluffin'."

"They'll have told you I'm a Walker. Our kind and the Tirribin share an affinity. They'll come at my summons, and they'll take your years. It's your choice. Put down your musket and live, or don't and die. It's not a pleasant death, by the way. I've seen it. We're in a hurry. So decide now."

The soldier's breathing had turned ragged.

"All right," Tobias said. He raised his gaze skyward and opened his mouth to speak.

"No!" The man set his weapon on the stone.

Tobias kicked it out of reach. "On your knees."

His eyes met Mara's. She nodded in response to what she saw in his look, and positioned herself behind the man. Tobias set the barrel of his pistol against the soldier's brow.

"How many men are on the strand?"

"None. There's just the four of us. But there's a fire and…" His mouth twisted and he muttered a curse.

Tobias raised his gaze, all the signal she needed.

Mara pounded the butt of one of her pistols into the back of the soldier's skull. He tipped onto his side and didn't move again.

Mara took the musket. At Tobias's look, she lifted a shoulder.

"I'm better with a long gun. And I don't think it matters anymore how conspicuous we are."

He didn't argue.

They descended the stone stairway toward the strand. The steps were slick with rain, and Tobias attempted to shelter the princess with his overshirt, which slowed them. Mara stared up repeatedly at the stone shelf, expecting to see the other guards coming for them. Their luck held, however, and as they neared the bottom of the stairway, the shadows deepened. With rain falling, and clouds blocking the moon and stars, she didn't think they could be seen from above. Mara's thighs burned and her knees ached. She didn't recall noticing such pains before her Walk back in time. The aging of her body had taken a toll.

They reached the strand at last and Tobias turned southward, away from the city proper, as Kaarti had instructed.

"What if there are no boats tonight?" she asked. "I know tomorrow is the Emergence, but this weather…"

"I'd thought of that. I don't know what else to do."

Mara didn't either, and so fell silent. Not for long, though. "What will we do when we're away from here? Do you have a plan? I know we have to keep Sofya alive. But beyond that…" She trailed off, overwhelmed by the responsibility he had shouldered, responsibility that she was now taking on as well.

For some time, Tobias didn't answer, and she feared she had angered him. But when at last he spoke, it was in a voice so low, she could barely hear him over the surf. "I don't know. It's not that I haven't given this thought; I have. I just… So far I've been consumed with keeping us alive. Eventually, I want to return her to the throne, but the truth is, I have no idea how to do that. Hanrid was right. I am still running. I have to run until I figure out what to do next." He glanced her way. "I suppose that sounds pretty foolish."

She stared back at him, her gaze again following the scars that traversed his face. "Keeping yourselves alive is no small thing. You'll work out the rest when you can."

His smile conveyed gratitude, and more. She blushed and faced forward again.

They soon lost sight of the Notch, and lost as well the meager glow spilling from the shelf. They picked their way along the shoreline, navigating rocks and driftwood by what little light seeped through the clouds. Progress came slowly, and Mara grew increasingly more frightened with each step. By now the Sheraigh had to know that the fire had been a ruse, and their colleague had been overpowered. Tobias maintained a stony silence that she couldn't interpret. Did he share her fears, or was he always so single-minded?

She kept her questions to herself.

They neared a bend in the strand. It curved around an outcropping of the escarpment, and Mara thought she discerned a faint glow of flame beyond it. Tobias might have seen it as well. He quickened his pace. The beach narrowed and, with the tide coming in, they had to wade around the cliff face. On the other side, the shore widened again revealing another cove, this one lit by a large fire and half a dozen torches. Dories bobbed on the waves, and people clustered on the beach around barrels, casks, crates, and burlap sacks. Musicians played, people danced and laughed.

Tobias cast a smile her way and led her toward the throng gathered there. Before they'd covered half the distance, he halted, astonishment lighting his damp face and widening his eyes.

"It can't be," he whispered.

"What?" When he didn't answer, she sidled closer to him. "Tobias, what is it?"

"A stroke of such incredible good fortune, I can't believe it." He raised his arm to point at something or someone.

He didn't get the chance to say more.

Four men appeared directly in front of them, as if dropped there by Sipar and Kheraya. Three of them, positioned to form a tight triangle, were clothed in black. The fourth, handsome and dark-skinned, stood at the center of the space these others defined. He wore ministerial robes fringed in Sheraigh blue, and held a sextant in one hand and a pistol in the other. The men around him carried tri-sextants, though Mara was sure they were armed as well.

She raised the musket to her shoulder and Tobias aimed his pistol at the minister. None of the other men moved.

Mara had only heard the name, and so could only guess at the man's identity.

"Good evening, Tobias," he said, a sharp smile exposing perfect teeth. "We've been looking for you."

It was all the confirmation she needed. This had to be Orzili.

CHAPTER 39

30th Day of Sipar's Settling, Year 633

They were so close to making their escape, closer even than Mara knew. They had only to secure passage and they would be free of Daerjen and the peril embodied in the man standing before them.

Which was why Tobias shouldn't have been surprised. It had been too easy. He should have known Orzili would find them.

The assassin looked just as Tobias remembered. A roguish smile on his lips, his bronze hair streaked with strands of gold that shone with torch fire, his eyes shrewd and cruel and intelligent. Tobias should have fired the instant he recognized him, but the assassin's appearance brought back a flood of dark memories. Flame, steel, anguish. He could barely breathe. He feared Sofya would die because of his hesitation.

"Put down your weapons, or I'll kill the princess," Orzili said, his gaze flicking to Mara. His pistol didn't waver.

"We won't." Tobias's voice remained level, despite the tripping of his heart. "Drop yours or we'll kill you where you stand."

The assassin shook his head. "I don't think so. You had the opportunity when we arrived. You didn't take it."

"That means nothing. We're leaving here tonight, and I won't let you stop us."

Orzili laughed. "Leaving? Why should I care if you leave? I can track you anywhere. Don't you understand that by now?

With these devices, I can go anywhere I wish, armed and accompanied by soldiers. You won't escape me again, Tobias." He spared Mara a glance and a grin. "He isn't as pretty as he once was. I'm sorry for that. Couldn't be helped. Shall I tell you how he wept at the mere thought of being subjected to more torture? Shall I tell you how he screamed and begged us for mercy?"

Mara kept her musket level, but she cast a glance at Tobias that bespoke pity and rage at what had been done to him.

"Give me the princess," Orzili said, eyes on Tobias once more. "Or die. Those are your choices."

Tobias didn't answer.

"I can spare your companion. She need not die. The two of you can go free. Just give me the child. Everything else is negotiable."

"No."

"What do you think to gain?" Orzili asked. "As I've already said, we can find you anywhere."

The report of Mara's musket was like a bomb going off by his ear. Tobias stumbled away from her. Sofya wailed. Even Orzili flinched.

But Mara's aim was true. Her shot had struck the golden device held by the nearest of Orzili's men, ripping it from the assassin's hand. It lay in the sand, glinting with torch fire, bent beyond repair. The man massaged his palm and fingers. All of them gaped at the ruined device. All, that is, except Mara, who dropped the musket and produced her pistols from her belt.

"You can't follow us anywhere now," she said.

The men and women on the beach had heard the shot and stared their way. Several strode in their direction.

"That was foolish!" Orzili said, aiming his pistol at Tobias again.

Tobias grinned. "Actually, I think it was bloody brilliant."

"Draw your weapons!"

At Orzili's command, his men reached for their pistols. Mara fired again. Tobias hesitated, torn between his impulse to protect Mara from the other assassins and his fear of Orzili. He shifted his gaze for an instant. Out of the corner of his eye, he saw Orzili's hand twitch.

With a cry, Tobias wrenched his body, tucking his shoulder and twisting away from the man. Shielding Sofya.

Flame belched from Orzili's pistol and the report boomed. White hot pain blazed in Tobias's arm. He sprawled to the sand, dropping his pistol, but landing on his elbows, above the squalling princess. The impact jolted agony through his wounded arm. Tears stung his eyes. Warm blood soaked his shirt. He held himself over the child, refusing to leave her unprotected. More shots echoed from where the others had been standing.

Mara shouted his name. Tobias looked up just as Orzili dove onto him, fist raised, a blade gleaming. He twisted again to meet this attack. Sofya continued to scream, vulnerable now.

The force of Orzili's weight jarred him, stole his breath. He grabbed hold of Orzili's wrist, just below the knife, but the man leaned into him, pressing the blade toward Tobias's face. Tobias fought, arms trembling. He knew he couldn't hold him off for long.

Orzili raised his other fist and pounded it into the bloody wound on Tobias's arm, once, then twice more. Tobias howled.

Somehow, he maintained his grip on the man's blade hand.

His wounded arm felt leaden, but he managed to move it. He snaked that hand under Orzili's gut, to his own belt. Groped for the blade he carried there.

Orzili hammered the bullet wound again, then lifted himself slightly and cracked Tobias across the jaw.

The blow made his vision swim, but it also gave him room to draw his knife. Before Orzili could strike him again, or harm the princess, Tobias buried the blade hilt deep in Orzili's thigh.

Orzili bellowed and threw himself off Tobias. Tobias kept hold of the knife, so that it ripped out of the assassin's leg, eliciting another cry. Blood poured from the gash he'd made.

With his good hand, Tobias grabbed for his pistol. Found it. Aimed.

Orzili stumbled to his feet before Tobias could fire. He fled, limping, but at speed. Tobias propped himself up, took aim again. His hand shook violently and his vision remained blurred. But he squeezed the trigger. The shot boomed, and the flintlock bucked in his hand. Orzili ran on, unhurt.

Voices reached Tobias. The others – the people on the beach. Nearer now, coming to help, he hoped. Tobias dragged himself to where his sack lay and pulled from it his other pistol.

Orzili retreated into the darkness, away from the torches, back toward the Notch. He shed clothes as he ran. His robe, his shirt. He paused to pull off his shoes and hose and to lurch out of his breeches. Then he was hobbling away again, naked, his sextant gleaming in one hand, one of the more elaborate sextants in the other.

Tobias forced himself up and raised his pistol once more, bracing it as best he could with the other hand. He fired. Orzili ducked, lurched, nearly tripped, but righted himself and ran on. A moment later, he vanished. The man was a Spanner, after all. Probably he would be back in Hayncalde Castle before... Well, he was probably there now.

"Tobias?" Mara knelt beside him. Concern knotted her brow and creased the lines around her mouth.

"I'm all right."

"You're not. There's a lot of blood."

He looked down at his arm. Blood glistened in the light and stained much of his sleeve. He shifted his gaze and shuddered, feeling faint.

"We can bind it," he said. "But we need to leave here. Now more than ever."

One of Orzili's assassins stood nearby, guarded by several men and women, all of them holding flintlocks. The other two killers lay on the sand, blood slicking their chests.

Sofya still screamed. Sand covered her clothes and dirtied her face, mingling with her tears. Tobias tried to lift her with one hand, but couldn't.

"I'll get her," Mara said. She lifted the princess and faced the crowd that had gathered around them. "My friend needs a healer. Can any of you help him?"

"I've sent for someone," said a young woman. "A surgeon. He'll be here soon."

Mara closed her eyes for a heartbeat. "Thank you."

"Who are you?" asked one of the others, a merchant by the look of him. "Who are these men? And who was that running away? The bare-assed one?"

His companions laughed.

Mara eyed Tobias.

"He's the assassin who killed Mearlan, sovereign of Hayncalde," Tobias said, his voice carrying. Sweat beaded on his forehead, chilling him. He didn't know how long he could remain upright, and he had arrangements to make. But he indicated the assassins with his good hand. "These are Sheraigh men."

"And you?"

"I was Mearlan's Walker. I was there the night he died."

Some nodded at this. Others regarded the princess, speculation in their glances. The surgeon arrived before they could ask more questions. He helped Tobias lie back on the sand and examined his bloodied arm. Tobias hissed a breath through clenched teeth, and closed his eyes.

"The God was kind," the man said after some time. "The ball missed bone and vein. It's still in there, though. I'm no healer; I have no powers. But I've some skill. If you wish to keep the arm, I should cut that bullet out tonight."

"All right. First, I need to speak with someone. A woman–"

"I'm right here," Mara said, stepping into his view.

Tobias shook his head. "Not you. There was a woman with the others. Tall, thin, with black hair and black eyes. She's from one of the ships. I saw her earlier."

"I know who he means." The man pointed. "She's over there. Have your conversation," he said, turning back to Tobias. "I'll gather what I need for the surgery."

He left Tobias and Mara. The others had bound the surviving assassin hand and foot. Tobias wondered what they would do with him.

"Do you want me to speak with the woman?" Mara shifted Sofya in her arms.

"Bring her to me," Tobias said. "This may be our best opportunity to get away, and I know her from… from before."

Mara nodded and strode away in the direction the surgeon had indicated. Tobias closed his eyes again, shivering with the tap of cold rain on his face. Sooner than he expected, Mara spoke his name. He hadn't heard her return.

She stood over him with the woman he had seen and recognized. He took a moment to look at the princess. She was calmer now, though streaks of sand still marked the path of her tears.

"You asked to speak with me," the tall woman said.

"Yes. You're Seris Larr, aren't you? Captain of the–" He stopped himself. "Of a merchant ship."

She narrowed her eyes. "Have we met?"

Tobias resisted the impulse to answer cryptically. He had been harboring secrets for too long. Right now he needed to be as candid as possible.

"We have, but not that you'd remember. I'm a Walker, and in another future I secured passage on your ship from Windhome Palace to Daerjen."

Her eyebrows went up.

"You don't believe me."

"It's an unusual claim."

"I can prove it. Your ship is called the *Gray Skate*."

She smirked, though again her eyebrows went up. "Actually, my ship is the *Sea Dove*. But I'll admit the *Gray Skate* is a name I've considered for the future."

This brought Tobias up short, but not for long. "In that other time, you offered to make me part of your crew. You thought having a Walker aboard your ship might prove profitable. You told me you would take me to lands I had never seen, never even dreamed of."

She shrugged. "Sounds like me. Apparently you refused my offer."

"I did. I had been promised to the sovereign. All that has changed, and we need to leave this place. If you seek Travelers for your crew, as you did then, you should consider the two of us. My friend here is a Spanner as well as a Walker."

"I'm..." Larr frowned. "You have me at a disadvantage. This isn't something I've even considered. It seems I'll be more forward-thinking in the future." She allowed herself a quick grin. "And I'm not sure you're in any condition to start a voyage. Not right now."

"We have no choice."

"I understand. But I don't care to take on passengers who are so likely to attract Sheraigh attention."

Tobias drew breath to argue, but the captain raised a hand and looked Mara's way. "Is this your child?"

Mara and Tobias exchanged another glance.

"No," Tobias said. "She's the sovereign princess of Hayncalde."

Larr exhaled, appearing to deflate. "Blood and bone."

"I have two apertures in my bag. They're yours to sell or barter as you see fit: additional payment, beyond our services, for passage aboard your ship."

She waved her hand, a vague dismissal of the offer. "That's

generous, but you're asking for far more than passage. You seek–"

"Refuge, yes."

"I'll need to consider this."

The surgeon approached, bearing a bottle and several instruments, including a blade that flickered with torchlight. Tobias looked away, swallowing against a wave of nausea.

"Please don't leave until the surgeon is done," he said through gritted teeth.

Larr hesitated, then nodded.

"Should I stay?" Mara asked.

"No. Find some food, for you and the babe. And make sure she's warm."

She considered him, as if to memorize his face. After another moment, she walked away. The surgeon dropped to his knees beside Tobias and uncorked the bottle. The smell of spirit reached him.

"Is that for the wound?"

"It's for you. I want you to drink a lot of it. This is going to hurt."

Tobias tried to smile, failed. "Aren't you supposed to tell me the opposite?"

The man held out the bottle. "Drink."

Tobias downed as much of the stuff as he could. Nevertheless, the first bite of the man's blade tore a scream from his throat. He passed out soon after.

He woke beside a fire, his arm still attached and throbbing. The rain had stopped, and a few stars peeked through gaps in the scudding clouds. A bandage, already stained with a circle of blood, covered his arm, elbow to shoulder.

Mara sat nearby, as did the surgeon.

Seeing that Tobias had opened his eyes, the man crawled closer. "How are you feeling?"

"It still hurts."

"I would think so. You'll keep the arm, and I expect you'll have full use of it eventually."

Tobias blew out a long breath. "Thank you."

Sofya gave a soft cry, her arms stretched toward him, her tiny hands opening and closing.

The surgeon smiled. "I'll leave you. Rest. That's the best thing you can do now."

"I'm in your debt."

The man shook his head as he climbed to his feet. "The enemy of my enemy and all that. You owe me nothing." He walked away.

Sofya fussed again.

"She wouldn't let me out of your sight," Mara said.

Tobias beckoned her closer with a waggle of the fingers on his good hand.

Mara scooted closer and set the princess on his stomach. The child clapped her hands and then laid her head on Tobias's chest, her thumb in her mouth.

"She might as well be yours," Mara said, her voice low.

"For the sake of us all, we might have to pretend she's ours."

Even in the dim light, he saw her cheeks flush. She held his gaze and said, "I can do that."

"Is the captain still here?"

"Yes. She's been avoiding me. She means to refuse us."

"She can't."

Mara didn't bother to argue. She didn't have to. Of course the captain could leave them here. He would have done the same.

"Help me up," he said.

"You're supposed to rest."

"I know. But if I can't stand, I certainly can't get on a ship, can I?"

Mara scowled, but she set the princess on the sand and helped him to his feet. A wave of dizziness crashed over him, and though he tried to keep his arm still, just getting up sent a jolt of agony through him, making him gasp again. Mara gripped his other shoulder, watching him with a keen eye.

"Maybe we can stay with Kaarti for a few days," she said.

"Orzili will find us again, and he'll come with greater numbers. We have to leave tonight, if not with Captain Larr, then with someone else."

Mara lifted the princess and handed her to Tobias. With Mara steadying him, they walked in the direction of the torches. Before they were halfway there, Larr strode to meet them.

"I thought I should do you the courtesy of waiting," she said, her tone crisp, her voice low. "I'm afraid I can't take you with me. The risks are too great."

"The risks to us are greater if you leave us here."

"I understand that, but in this case, I must act out of self-interest. I'm sorry."

"Self-interest," Tobias repeated, laughing the word even as another pulse of agony radiated from his arm. "If you were acting out of self-interest, you'd take us. Two Travelers, Windhome-trained? A pair of Bound apertures to trade as you wish? And, potentially, the gratitude of the lone surviving heir to Daerjen's richest house? Self-interest would have us on your ship already. You're acting out of fear."

"Tread carefully, Walker," the captain said, glowering and drawing herself up to her full height.

He remembered the expression from his time on the *Gray Skate*. It had cowed him then, but not now. He wasn't a boy anymore. He'd Walked too many years, endured too much pain, seen and spilled too much blood. More, she'd already stated her intention to leave them there, the worst thing she could do to them. He had nothing more to fear from her.

"No, I won't tread carefully. The Captain Larr I know from the future is canny, strong, fearless. Perhaps you haven't yet grown into your better, older self. I have. It's the advantage of being a Walker. And also the curse."

Her nostrils flared. He'd pushed her far, yet he wasn't through.

"We can help you, Mara and I. And you can help us. Such a partnership would be to the detriment of Sheraigh, and, I believe, Oaqamar as well. Surely that has some appeal."

"Appeal? You think I wish to be pursued by the navies of both Daerjen and the autarchy?"

"I think you're savvy enough to keep your ship out of danger. Do you already carry banners from the Axle and the Knot?"

The captain blinked. If she hadn't believed before that Tobias sailed with her in some lost future, she did now. "Aye," she said, speaking more softly. "I've been known to fly different colors at different times."

"That should help."

"No doubt. Still, why should I risk my life and the lives of my crew for the three of you?"

Tobias sighed, feeling more weary than he ever had. "I can't think of another reason beyond those I've given. In the future, you're hard, but fair-minded. I'm sure you possess similar qualities now. Taking us on carries risks. But if you leave us here, we'll be killed. I've no doubt of that." He indicated his wounded arm with a dip of his chin. "The proof is right here. So ask yourself: are whatever concerns you have so great that they can justify leaving us – leaving this child – to die at the hands of the man who shot me?"

Her glare remained, but she didn't stalk away, which he considered a small victory. After some tencounts, her expression turned speculative. "Do you have chronofors?"

Tobias frowned at the question, knowing it undermined his argument. She had every right to ask, though, and he wouldn't lie to her.

"Mara's was taken, and mine was broken the night of Mearlan's assassination. If I can find a Binder–" He thought of

Bexler Filt. "One I can trust, I can have it repaired."

Larr's shrug conveyed a lack of concern. "I know of an honest Binder on Aiyanth. I've also done business with a peddler who trades in Bound devices. She might have one."

He was afraid to trust what he heard in her words. "Are you saying... you've changed your mind?"

"No one has ever compared me unfavorably with my older self. I didn't like that. Nor did I appreciate having my courage questioned, especially since I gave you cause to question it." A crooked smile softened her features. "Besides, you raised an interesting point before: how often does a ship's captain have the opportunity to strike a blow against Sheraigh and the autarchy in the same evening?" She regarded the princess, the angles of her face sharpening again. "A ship is no place for a babe. I'll expect you to keep her out of the way. If she proves a distraction for me or my crew, I'll put you off at the nearest port. Understood?"

"Yes. Thank you, captain."

"Don't thank me yet. I fear I'll rue this decision." Another smile cushioned this. "Gather your things. If we're to get you away from here, we should return to the ship now and sail."

She walked away, leaving Tobias and Mara alone in the firelight.

"I revealed a lot to win her over," he said, looking down at the princess. Her eyelids had grown heavy.

"Do you trust her?"

"I trust the woman I met fourteen years from now. This one... Orzili and his allies would pay a lot of gold for Sofya. More than Larr can make selling those apertures."

"Then why tell her who this is?"

Tobias faced her. "Because if she'd thought Sofya was our child – that we were merely a family seeking passage – she would never have agreed to take us. You heard her: A ship is no place for a babe."

"She might have taken just you and Sofya."

He felt himself color. "That wasn't an option."

Mara's smile made him blush even more. "Thank you."

He was first to look away. "I should retrieve my sack. And your musket."

"I'll get them," she said, wheeling away. "You rest."

"Get Orzili's robe, too."

"I will. And the last tri-sextant."

Tobias stared after her, then called her name. "That was a good shot before."

She glanced back, eyes dancing. "I thought you said it was 'bloody brilliant.'"

"Heat of the moment. Saffern would have said you were too close."

Her smile reminded him of Windhome, of Wansi, of a youth lost only a turn or two ago. It warmed him and chilled him and left him wondering what awaited them on the Inward Sea and the waters beyond.

Sofya sighed, her eyes closed, her head nestled against his chest. At least one of them would sleep this night.

He thought of Jivv and Elinor, of Kaarti, of Hanrid, of Daria Belani who saved his life in the castle – good people all, and in their own way as committed as Tobias to keeping the Hayncalde sovereignty alive. Maybe they would be enough to preserve some shred of hope until Sofya came of age.

CHAPTER 40

Kheraya's Emergence, Year 634

Droë sang to him of ships and lost loves, the songs of sailors, which she had gathered in her memory over centuries. The unintended harvest of her hunting, now more valuable to Tresz than gold to a merchant captain.

Their progress came slower than she expected. The Shonla could move in swift bursts, but mostly he meandered, more mist than demon. He fed even more often than she.

Not that Droë minded too much. Free of Trevynisle, she was content to explore, to prey, to savor the novelty of constant change.

Somewhere to the south, the woman searched for Tobias, the man Droë might love. Jealousy twisted her insides. But so did fear, which she hadn't expected. Desperate as she was to find him and know him, she shied from the prospect of that first encounter.

"There are ships," Tresz said, interrupting her song. His mist parted and he pointed a spindly arm at the bay of a nearby island. Furled sails and torches pitched on shifting waters.

"You wish to feed again?" Droë asked, trying to conceal her impatience.

"Once more, before light."

"Where are we?"

"The southern fringe of the Labyrinth. I don't know what humans call this isle. My kind named it long ago."

The name he gave – a series of hisses and swishes and gurgles she couldn't interpret – sounded much like other names he had spoken in the tongue of the Shonla. She couldn't repeat the word, much less comprehend it. But knowing they were nearly clear of Sipar's Labyrinth pleased her.

In truth, she didn't mind feeding again, and she welcomed one last respite from the chill of his company before daylight.

"Very well," she said. "Leave me at the port."

He glided low over the swells, halting on a narrow strip of sand near a cluster of wharves. She climbed off his back and stretched her limbs.

"I will return shortly," he said. "And we will go as far as we can before first light. My word."

Droë stared after him as he closed in on a merchant ship. Then she sniffed the air. A small village, but ripe with prey. The shoreline alone might have fed her for years. She could leave the Shonla and his cloud of frigid vapor, and remain here. It was new, different. It might hold her interest for a time.

Not long ago, that would have been enough.

Do I love him? Can I love?

The questions burned in her chest like those torches on the distant ships. Fear and mist and cold might dampen the light, but they couldn't extinguish her curiosity. She had been driven from her home by the need to know, the desire to test the limits of what she might be, and might become. Finding a replacement for Trevynisle wouldn't content her. Neither would simply finding Tobias. At some point, over water and land, in darkness and damp, with a song on her lips, she had resolved to become something new. Not merely to seek change, but to become it. What began on the promontory of Trevynisle as a notion, had coalesced into purpose. She would do this, or spend her life in the pursuit.

First, tonight, she would hunt. What she had in mind would demand years, not in duration, but as a means of altering herself. She needed strength, which meant nourishment.

So she crept to the pier, her steps silent, her body conforming to shadow. Sniffing the air again, she caught a scent. Young, female, nearby. Once more, Tresz had said. Before light and leagues. Ever closer to what she hoped to become.

The *Sea Dove* was still on oars as the sun rose. In the eastern sky, dawn's light limned the clouds from the previous night's storm, like fire burning the edge of parchment. The sky overhead had cleared, and the surface of the Gulf of Daerjen reflected azure like a mirror.

Mara stood with Tobias and the princess at the bow, hands on the rail, a soft breeze stirring her hair. She hadn't spent much time at sea, and she feared that the pitch and roll of the ship would become unsettling once they cleared the gulf.

If they made it that far. For what might have been the hundredth time, she checked the water behind them. Tobias did the same. Larr's oarsmen had given them a substantial start, and the weak wind would keep Sheraigh's warships from pursuing them at speed. But how long would they remain safe?

Captain Larr said nothing to them after taking them aboard. The men and women of her crew watched them as they might looming storm clouds. For now at least, they eschewed the celebrations of the Goddess's Day, and there could be no doubt as to why. Those working the deck would blame them.

Tobias's concerns about the captain's motives, which Mara thought fanciful in the dark of night, became weightier as they settled on her mind.

At Tobias's insistence, Larr had introduced them to the men and women on the ship as a family, using Mara's surname: Lijar. Tobias admitted he had used the name with others, which both flattered and alarmed her. The princess would go by the name Nava.

Mara wasn't surprised to find herself a fugitive. Given what she had Walked back through the years to do, it seemed inevitable.

But she felt unmoored, adrift. No longer a girl, not even terribly young. A Walker now, as well as a Spanner, and more valued as the former. Far from Windhome, and the life she had known in the northern isles. Bound to a man she had sought of her volition, but didn't know at all. After the stability of her life in the Travelers' palace, change threatened to overwhelm her.

Yet the sense of wrongness that drove her to leave her old life had receded. Perhaps this was only because she had left that misfuture behind. Or maybe – a slim hope, but not beyond all bounds of possibility – whatever she had done, whatever Tobias and she had done together, was already changing the world back to what it ought to be.

"You're quiet."

Tobias's words roused her, as from a dream.

"I'm thinking of Windhome," she said

"Do you miss it?"

"Do you?"

His eyes followed a flock of cormorants, black against blue. His scars appeared less prominent in the soft light. "It's been so long. At least it seems that way. I miss feeling safe, and having the freedom of not being responsible for anyone. Mostly I don't think about it." He shifted the princess in his one good arm, and toed his pack, which held all their valuables. He hadn't let it out of their sight. "You didn't answer my question."

"I do miss it," she said. "It hasn't been so long for me, and these past few days have been… unnerving."

"I'm sorry."

"Don't be. I made the choice to come back. I know you're responsible for–" She stumbled on the name, something she couldn't afford to do. "For Nava. But you're not responsible for me or my decisions."

"Fair enough."

She gazed toward the mouth of the gulf, which loomed before them, framed by massive stone cliffs and twin mountain ranges to the north and south. Beyond the crags and the gap between them lay the Inward Sea and the Ring Isles.

"Where do you think we'll go from here?" Mara asked.

"I don't know. I suppose we'll get to Aiyanth eventually. The captain will want to see that Binder she mentioned. After that?" He lifted his good shoulder. "We have to keep moving. Orzili will be looking for us. Filt will Bind more tri-sextants for him soon enough. But we also have to find a place where we can be a family and raise Sofya. Living like a hunted animal is no way for a child to grow up. We have to find a home. I just hope the captain doesn't tire of us before then."

He said this with a smile, but fear tightened his voice.

She had no reassurances to offer, and she wasn't sure he would have believed them if she had. But she grasped his good arm and gave it a gentle squeeze. After a moment she leaned against his shoulder, and he rested his cheek against the top of her head.

Together, they waited for open water.

GLOSSARY OF TERMS

Aperture – A Bound device used by Crossers. An aperture is a golden circlet that expands and contracts according to the needs of the Crosser. When placed against a wooden or stone surface, it creates a portal that allows the Crosser to move through that surface.

Arrokad – Creatures of the sea, they are considered by humans to be demon-kind. They take human form and possess magicks that remain poorly understood. Capricious, sexual, powerful, dangerous, they can be reasoned with and bargained with, though their tolerance for human interaction is limited.

Bell – A measure of time equal to fifty spirecounts. There are twenty bells in a day.

Belvora – Also known as magick demons, they are winged predators, tall, muscular, lethal, but slow-witted. They are found mostly in Northern waters, near the Labyrinth and the Sisters, the isles from which Travelers and Seers hail.

Between, The – The space traversed by Walkers as they navigate from one time to another. A place of intense sensory stimulation, totally lacking in breathable air.

Binder – A crafter, usually employed in noble courts, who shapes and imbues with power the gold devices (apertures, chronofors, and sextants) used by Travelers.

Chronofor – A Bound, golden device used by Walkers. A chronofor resembles a chainwatch, but has three dials on its face, and three corresponding stems to set those dials, which represent turns, days, and bells. A fourth stem activates the device.

Crosser – A Traveler who can move through solid matter – stone or wood – with the use of an aperture. A Crosser who encounters metal or some other material created by humans during a Crossing risks injury or death.

Fivecount – A measure of time equal to counting to five.

Gap, The – The space traversed by Spanners as they navigate from one location to another. A place of significant sensory stimulation and stinging wind.

Ha'turn – A measure of time equal to fifteen days.

Kant – A small- to medium-sized merchant ship made in Kantaad.

Healers – Most similar in their magick to Binders, Healers can mend wounds and ease illness, though their powers are limited and they are not proof against death.

Kheraya – The Goddess, who represents birth, war, sexuality, water, the heat of summer.

Magi – Also known as Seers, they include those who can divine the future, perceive truth or falsehood in the words of others, and remember in perfect detail everything they see or hear. For their ability to manifest, they must constantly imbibe (through drink or vapor) Tincture, a highly addictive spirit.

Marauder – A large warship made in Oaqamar and used by Oaqamaran navy.

Press, The – The traverse experienced by Crossers as they move through matter, which can include painful compression of the body, blindness, and deafness.

Quad – A square brass coin, the least valuable piece of Islevale currency.

Qua'turn – A measure of time equal to approximately seven days.

Round – A round, gold coin equal in value to twenty silver treys.

Seer – Also known as Magi, they include those who can divine the future, perceive truth or falsehood in the words of others, and remember in perfect detail everything they see or hear. For their ability to manifest, they must constantly imbibe (through drink or vapor) Tincture, a highly addictive spirit.

Sextant – A Bound, golden device used by Spanners to cover great distances. A sextant includes an arc for plotting distance, an eyepiece for selecting a route, and a trigger for activation.

Shonla – Also known as mist demons, they only exist within clouds of vapor, though not all mists carry Shonla. They are vaguely human in form, smell of must, and bring cold. They are linked to one another and have knowledge of events occurring all through the world. They swallow sound and can be bribed with song. They disorient those at sea and even on land, feeding on screams. But they are not truly deadly.

Sipar – The God, who represents death, peace, love, land, the cold of winter.

Spanner – A Traveler who can cover great distance in a short period of time with the use of a sextant.

Spirecount – A measure of time equal to counting to one hundred. So named because all spires in all the sanctuaries of the Two have one hundred stairs. There are one hundred spirecounts in a bell.

Tencount – A measure of time equal to counting to ten.

Tincture – An addictive and narcotic spirit used by Seers (Magi) to enable their talents for divination, perception, and remembrance.

Tirribin – Also known as time demons, they appear as children, beautiful, but smelling faintly of rot and decay. They are deadly, preying on humans and consuming their years. They have an understanding of time that goes far beyond that of humans, even Walkers. But they can be distracted by riddles.

Traveler – Often a native of the Sisters or Sipar's Labyrinth, trained on Trevynisle, and assigned to a noble court, s/he can be a Crosser, Spanner, or Walker. A Traveler expresses his/her talent through the use of a Bound device (aperture for a Crosser, sextant for a Spanner, chronofor for a Walker). Travelers using these traditional devices must Travel unclothed and unburdened by any objects save the devices themselves.

Trey – A triangular silver coin equal in value to ten brass quads.

Tri-aperture – A Bound, golden device resembling an aperture, but constructed in three circlets that intersect to form a wedge. Three Crossers, standing in a triangular formation, can move themselves and any people standing in the space defined by their positions through matter, so long as one of the people within the triangle is also a Crosser bearing a traditional aperture. Crossers Traveling by tri-aperture can be clothed and can bear objects in addition to their bound devices.

Tri-devices – Bound, golden devices developed in the 630s and used by Travelers. They enable groups of Travelers to Span or Cross together, fully clothed and bearing objects, including weapons. There are tri-apertures and tri-sextants. There are, as of yet, no tri-chronofors.

Tri-sextant – A Bound, golden device resembling a sextant, but constructed with three arcs. Three Spanners, standing in a triangular formation, can transport themselves and any people standing in the space defined by their positions, so long as one of the people within the triangle is also a Spanner bearing a traditional sextant. Spanners Traveling by tri-sextant can be clothed and can bear objects in addition to their bound devices.

Turn – A measure of time equal to thirty days and corresponding to the cycle of the moon.

Two, The – Kheraya and Sipar, the Goddess and God, worshipped in some isles or cities in tandem, and in others individually.

Walker – A Traveler who can move through time with the use of a chronofor. For each day a Walker moves backward or forward through time, s/he ages a corresponding day.

The Year
Each season is equal to three turns; each turn is equal to thirty days.

SPRING
(*Kheraya's Emergence* – Equinox, Goddess's day, first day of the year. Powerful, sensual day and night.)

Kheraya's Stirring – Storms and wind, the first hint of life's return
Kheraya's Waking – Warm, rainy, peaceful, plantings begin in the northern isles
Kheraya's Ascent – Warmer, blooming, resplendent, plantings begin in the southern isles

SUMMER
(*Kheraya Ascendent* – Summer Solstice, a day of feasts, celebration, gift-giving)

Kheraya's Descent – Hot, dry, northern crops begin to come in
Kheraya's Fading – Hot, stormy, southern crops begin to come in
Kheraya's Settling – Hot, languid days

AUTUMN
(*Sipar's Emergence* – Equinox, God's day, the pivot of the year. Powerful, sensual day and night.)

Sipar's Stirring – Stormy, windy, harvest begins in the southern isles
Sipar's Waking – Cool, clear, harvest begins in the northern isles
Sipar's Ascent – End of harvest, leaves changing, resplendent

WINTER

(*Sipar Ascendent* – Winter Solstice, a day of fasting, contemplation)
Sipar's Descent – Cold, snows begin in southern isles
Sipar's Fading – Cold, storms and snow in northern isles
Sipar's Settling – Cold, quiet, shortest days.

ACKNOWLEDGMENTS

Writing this book challenged me, perhaps more than any other I've worked on. And so, predictably, I have many people to thank.

Faith Hunter endured many angst-filled phone conversations as I struggled with early drafts, and helped me brainstorm a key section during a memorable drive to ConCarolinas. Toni Weiskopf generously took time out of a Saturday at a convention to speak with me about the book and its broader themes. Misty Massey offered helpful feedback on the opening pages, and A J Hartley joined me for conversations over beers and dinners that contributed more to my work than he could ever know.

My dear friends in the original Rivendell Writer's Group – Laura Willis, Virginia Craighill, Megan Roberts, April Alvarez, and Patrick Dean – offered invaluable critiques on several chapters. Thanks as well to Carmen Toussaint, Director of the Rivendell Writers' Colony in Sewanee, Tennessee, for supporting our group and allowing us access to that magnificent venue. Thanks also to my sensitivity readers, Kia Goins and Kimberly Richardson, whose comments were extremely helpful.

Lucienne Diver, friend and agent extraordinaire, offered me a thorough and incisive critique of the first completed draft of this novel. She identified issues I had missed and pushed me to take chances from which I had shied away. Her input improved the book tremendously. Plus, you know, she sold it.

I am so grateful to the wonderful people at Angry Robot:

Marc Gascoigne, Phil Jourdan, Penny Reeve, Mike Underwood, and Nick Tyler. Their enthusiasm for the story and willingness to work with me on any number of issues have made this first venture together a pleasure.

Finally, and as always, my deepest gratitude goes to my wife, Nancy, and our daughters, Alex and Erin. This book is about magic and time travel, intrigue and suspense. But at root, when everything else is stripped away, it's about family. Much like real life for the fortunate among us. I am blessed to have these three brilliant, beautiful, loving women in my world.

WHAT COMES NEXT...

- THE ISLEVALE CYCLE -

D. B. JACKSON

"D. B. Jackson's
writing is amazing."
— KAT RICHARDSON

TIME'S DEMON

31192021587850